To the Duke, with Love

Amelia Grey

St. Martin's Paperbacks

This is a work of fiction. All of the characters, organizations, and events portrayed in this novel are either products of the author's imagination or are used fictitiously.

TO THE DUKE, WITH LOVE

Copyright © 2017 by Amelia Grey.

For information address St. Martin's Press, 175 Fifth Avenue, New York, NY 10010.

ISBN: 978-1-250-10251-5

Our books may be purchased in bulk for promotional, educational, or business use. Please contact your local bookseller or the Macmillan Corporate and Premium Sales Department at 1-800-221-7945, ext. 5442, or by e-mail at MacmillanSpecialMarkets@macmillan.com.

Printed in the United States of America

St. Martin's Paperbacks edition / December 2017

St. Martin's Paperbacks are published by St. Martin's Press, 175 Fifth Avenue, New York, NY 10010.

10 9 8 7 6 5 4 3 2 1

My Dear Readers:

Winter is waning and a new Season is approaching, but we find ourselves stirring the same old scandalbroth—only with a different rake. This year, with great expectation, we look forward to the Duke of Hawksthorn's sister, Lady Adele, making her debut. And while I haven't seen Lady Adele myself, I have it on good authority that she is a diamond of the first water and will be sought after by every eligible bachelor.

However, no one will have their ear closer to the murmurings and musings of the ton *this year than I, as London's elite Society unfolds its great wealth of speculation on how this Rake of St. James will do his best to see that his sister escapes being tainted by the duke's past wicked ways.*

MISS HONORA TRUTH'S WEEKLY SCANDAL SHEET

Chapter 1

There may be a rare occasion when a young lady is
wrong, but a gentleman must never resort to
pointing out that fact to her.

❧

*A Proper Gentleman's Guide to Wooing
the Perfect Lady*
Sir Vincent Tybalt Valentine

Through a hazy drizzle, the stately, two-story house
came into view. Sloane Knox, the Duke of Hawksthorn, stopped at the top of a rocky knoll. It was already
late in the day. On such a dreary afternoon it would have
been nice to see a welcoming light in one of the front windows, hear the warning bark of a dog—anything to keep
the massive stone structure from looking so forlorn. The
only visible sign of life was a barely discernible plume of
grayish-white smoke ascending from a chimney top and
quickly dissipating into the moist air.

Hawk had never been a patient man, and today had
stretched his limit further than he thought possible. That
his current situation was his own impulsive fault didn't
help his grumbling spirit. On this cold but bright Febru-
ary day, he'd thought to save time and make the journey

faster by leaving his carriage behind and leasing a horse from the inn where he'd lodged for the night. Now, several hours later, not only had the horse gone lame so that Hawk had to walk the poor creature, but the directions he'd been given to Mammoth House were severely wrong and he'd had to retrace his steps more than once. On top of that, a damned chilling rain had been falling on him for the last half hour.

However, if Mr. Quick accepted Hawk's offer and agreed to make a match with Adele, it would all be worth it. Hawk's search for the right man had not been impulsive. Quick was the nephew of an earl, more than average height, and even though Hawk considered him on the lean side, he assumed most young ladies would consider the man handsome enough. And the fellow seemed to always have a smile on his face and a bounce to his step.

What more could his sister want in a husband?

Still confident his plan for Adele was a good one, Hawk hunkered further down into his cloak and continued his slow trek toward the house, leading the limping horse behind him.

After all the trouble his friend Griffin had gone through with his sisters last year, Hawk wasn't going to take any chances with Adele's future. He wasn't one to stand around and wait for something to happen. He was taking matters into his own hands. And as he'd hoped, his sister had agreed.

The Season was still more than two months away and already *Miss Honora Truth's Scandal Sheet* was fueling gossipmongers all over London about Adele's debut in the spring. What the tittle-tattle writers didn't know was that Hawk intended to have his sister's betrothal already settled before the first dance of the Season began. That would fool them all, and there would be no opportunities for mischief from anyone who might be seeking to exact revenge on Hawk by pursuing his sister with less-than-honorable intentions.

A gust of icy wind whipped across Hawk's face as he tethered the animal to the hitching post and then strode up the three steps to the door. Knowing someone from inside the house could send a groom to take care of the mare, he rapped the iron knocker before peeling off his damp leather gloves and stuffing them into his pocket.

After a few moments, the door opened slowly. A round-cheeked woman's face appeared. "May I help you, sir?"

"I'm the Duke of Hawksthorn," he stated. "Mr. Quick is expecting me."

With dark, distrusting eyes, she looked him up and down as if she couldn't believe a duke was standing before her wearing a drenched cloak and a dripping hat. She then perused the landscape past him, no doubt wondering where his carriage and entourage were hiding.

"I am alone," he added, removing his hat and dusting off the excess rain.

"You'd best come warm yourself by the fire," she said.

That would be most welcome, he thought, swinging his cloak from his shoulders and giving it a good shake.

The woman opened the door and stepped back, giving the customary curtsy to Hawk as he passed the threshold and into the spacious, cavernous vestibule. It must have been a grand entrance at one time, but now it was hardly more than a large empty room. A worn settee was backed against one wall. Opposite the small sofa stood an ornately carved table with an unlit lamp sitting on one end and an unused candlestick on the other. He couldn't help but think the inside of the house looked as forsaken as the outside, but then he caught the aroma of bread baking in an oven and knew this was a lived-in home.

He handed off his cloak and hat to the short, rotund woman with a ruffle-edged mobcap covering her hair. She laid them on the table and said, "Follow me."

She preceded him down the wide corridor and into a drawing room that was furnished only a little better than the vestibule. Two floral-patterned settees faced each other in the center of the room, and a table barely large enough for a tea tray had been placed between the two. Matching armchairs upholstered in a brown-and-gold-striped fabric were arranged near the fireplace. Against the far wall by a window stood a highly polished secretary and chair. Little else filled the drafty room.

"Wait here," the woman said and left.

Hawk walked over to the fireplace. The flame was hardly more than a few sizzling embers, and while the heat immediately warmed him, it would do little to help dry out his boots or wet collar and neckcloth. Kneeling down, he grabbed the poker and stoked the fire before adding wood to the grate.

"Your Grace."

At the sound of the soft feminine voice, Hawk rose to his full height and turned. A tall, slender young lady was standing near the entrance to the room. She curtsied when their eyes met. She looked pure, sweet, and completely untouched by masculine hands. A sudden, deep rush of desire flamed through him, and the rhythm of his heartbeat changed.

She wore a modest dress of pale-blue wool, void of bows, lace, or any of the embellishments usually sewn on to enhance the common fabric. No jewelry hung around her neck or dangled from her ears. Her light-blond hair was pulled up on each side, but he couldn't see how far down her back it hung, or if there were satin ribbons or fancy combs to hold it in place. What struck him instantly about her was that he'd never seen such a beautiful young lady so unadorned by frivolous accessories meant to enhance her beauty.

"I am Loretta Quick, Your Grace. How can I help you?"

Mr. Quick's younger sister. It should have dawned on Hawk that he might see her, but quite frankly it hadn't. He'd been too caught up thinking only about his own sister. He knew Miss Quick's story, of course. Everyone in Society did. As he studied her lovely face, he was certain they'd never met. He would have remembered those dark-blue eyes that seemed so steady, yet wary. He would have remembered the strong surge of sensual awareness that seared through him at the sight of her.

"Miss Quick," he said with a nod. "I'm here to see your brother."

Her slightly arched brows furrowed with an uneasy expression, and she took a tentative step toward him. "Is something wrong?"

He thought that an odd question for her to ask but answered, "With what?"

"With my brother."

"Not that I'm aware of."

Her gaze continued to search his face as if surely he must be hiding something from her. "So he's not in any trouble?"

That comment gave him cause for concern. Perhaps there was something about the man Hawk didn't know. "Does he often get into trouble?"

"Often?" she asked, clearly dismayed by his question. "No, of course not. Not at all really. Why would you ask that?"

"Because you asked me if he were."

As if taking note of the slight accusation in his tone, her spine stiffened. "It was a logical question to ask."

"How so, if you say he never gets in trouble?"

"What else am I supposed to think?" she asked innocently.

"Perhaps that I wanted to talk to your brother, which I do."

She let out a deep audible breath and took another step farther into the drawing room. "So there are no problems?"

Hawk shook his head in exasperation. "I just said as much. You are frustrating me, Miss Quick."

"And you are the pot calling the kettle black, Your Grace," she said defensively.

Another prickle of awareness rushed through him. It was rare anyone had the nerve to speak their mind so quickly and candidly to a duke. It surprised him, but it also impressed him. "That's a rather rash statement."

He watched her softly rounded shoulders relax a little. "Nonetheless, true. You are the one making this conversation difficult."

"Me?" She was unbelievable. "Does your boldness have no boundaries, Miss Quick?"

"Not where my brother is concerned. But aside from that, what am I supposed to think other than something is wrong when a *duke* arrives unexpectedly to see my brother."

Unexpectedly? More reason for him to worry.

"We live a little too far from Hawksthorn for a social call, Your Grace," she added as if to give credence to her statement.

Hawk could easily attest to that fact. When he'd started this venture, he had no idea that Mammoth House was so far from the village of Grimsfield and still another half day's ride from London. He had doubts that even a hermit would embrace a place this far from civilization. Living out here took being alone to an extreme.

As the nephew of the Earl of Switchingham, Quick was a socially acceptable husband for Adele. Quick always wore a friendly smile and kept a cheerful attitude, which might become obnoxious to Hawk if he had to spend a good deal of time with the man, but he thought Adele would love it.

While Hawk had no idea what kind of allowance the earl had bestowed on Quick, it really didn't matter. Adele had a generous dowry and, once she married, she'd have access to a home in London as well. She wouldn't have to reside in Mammoth House if she preferred not to, which he was fairly certain would be the case.

With graceful movements, Miss Quick walked the rest of the way into the room to stand in front of him. He could see clearly the tempting shape of her inviting lips and her smooth, delicate-looking complexion, which enticed him to want to reach up and caress her cheek with the tips of his fingers. She had uncommonly long, dark lashes for someone with hair so satiny blond. Her eyes were so expressive he found it difficult to focus on the matter at hand.

Ah, yes. It would be easy to concentrate on the intriguing miss, if not for the important issue before him.

"I don't believe I'm unexpected."

"You must be," she answered without the least bit of hesitancy or caution that she might be wrong.

More impertinence.

"I have an appointment with him, Miss Quick."

"But Paxton isn't here."

Hawk's jaw tightened. He'd just walked for the better part of half a day on cold, rough, uneven ground, and was chilled to the bone for most of it. He was in no temperament to hear that her brother wasn't home. Perhaps Hawk had misjudged the man after all and should go on to one of the other gentlemen he'd considered for Adele's future.

"I know I'm late by a few hours because of unavoidable circumstances, but I would have assumed that he'd wait for my arrival before taking his leave."

Curiosity settled on her delicate features. "Your words puzzle me. I'm certain if Paxton had an arrangement with you he would be here. He's very reliable."

Apparently not.

The fire he'd stirred had caught hot and was warming the backs of his legs. The beautiful and outspoken Miss Quick was warming his temperament.

Hawk wasn't used to explaining himself, but felt compelled to say, "I sent him a post last week stating I'd be here today to discuss an important matter with him."

Her countenance went from inquisitive to affable. "Ah, therein lies the source of your problem."

"My problem?" She just wouldn't give up.

"Yes." She folded her arms across her chest in a comfortable pose and nodded. "Paxton has been gone almost three weeks. We only receive mail once a week, when Mr. Huddleston takes the carriage into the village for purchases. Paxton has had correspondence arrive but, of course, I don't open his private letters."

A few words that were not appropriate for Miss Quick's ears tumbled to the tip of Hawk's tongue, but he held them silent. What were the odds this would happen? He'd come all this way to the middle of nowhere and Quick was gone. That was damned inconvenient. Still, Hawk was a fair person. If Quick had never received his post, he supposed he couldn't fault the man for not being here to meet with him.

"Perhaps all is not lost," she said, lifting her chin and looking more solidly into his eyes. "Maybe I can help with whatever it is you wanted with Paxton."

"That would be unlikely, Miss Quick."

She dropped her arms by her side and assumed an air of authority. "I am quite capable of handling many things, Your Grace, and take care of most things here at Mammoth House."

He wasn't indifferent to her assertion. He believed her. She was strong and seductive, and he hadn't seen an ounce of fear in her. But neither her abilities nor her appeal had any bearing on his mission. He'd be damned before he'd let her admirable qualities let him stray from that.

"That I don't doubt in the least. Yet it is your brother I came to see. Where is he?"

Undaunted by his determination, she responded casually, "Paxton doesn't make me privy to all his goings and comings. He has several friends that he visits with from time to time. Besides, I'm not certain I would divulge Paxton's whereabouts even if I knew, when I don't know the reason you want to see him."

If she thought to discourage him, she was mistaken. If Hawk could arrange a betrothal for Adele before the Season began, her future would be settled. He wouldn't have to worry about her falling victim to a prankster or any bachelor hoping to get even with him for his past misdeeds.

It wasn't often he'd met an innocent who wasn't afraid to speak her mind. Perhaps he never had. And Miss Quick was a lively young lady to converse with, but they were not making much progress.

"Must you challenge me on every issue?"

She crossed her arms again. "When you aren't forthcoming about your reasons, yes. Dukes are very powerful. It's only natural for me to be concerned."

Hawk wondered what made her so wary. "It's not for nefarious purposes that I want to see him, I assure you. I have a proposition to make to him, and I'd rather do it sooner than later."

She tilted her chin upward again. "Oh. Then you won't mind if I ask what it is?"

Yes, actually, he did mind her asking. However, much to his chagrin, her imperious expression was more engaging than defiant. It took great courage to ask a duke what his business was with another man—even if she was asking about her own brother.

Hawk supposed there was no harm in telling her. If he did, it might speed up her telling him the whereabouts of her brother so he could get on with the matter of getting this business settled as quickly as possible. He wanted to find Adele a suitable husband and then get back to doing some of the things he wanted to do. Hawk was fairly certain Quick hadn't been in London the past week. He would have seen the blade at White's.

"Very well," he offered. "My sister will be making her debut this spring, and I'd very much like to arrange a betrothal between her and your brother before the Season starts."

Miss Quick went very still. "Surely you must know that arranged engagements don't end very well in this family."

There was no malice in her tone, just a statement of fact. Hawk summoned what he remembered about her and wondered how much of it was rumor and how much was true. The Earl of Switchingham had arranged for her to marry Viscount Denningcourt. Apparently, all the guests and the viscount had arrived at the church for the ceremony, but the bride never made an appearance.

Her uncle took a very harsh view of her rejecting his choice of husbands for her. If the rumors were true, she had vowed to never marry. The betrothal was broken and shortly thereafter the viscount married a different young lady. As far as Hawk knew, Miss Quick hadn't been seen in Society since.

"I heard," he said, "but I aim to change that. I've put a good deal of thought into this, Miss Quick, and your brother is the husband I want for Adele. I've never seen him too deep in his cups, and he never gambles more than a handful of dollars at the tables. I've never heard a harsh rumor about him at White's; nor have I heard Mr. Quick complain about anyone else. By all accounts he's a fine gentleman who prefers books over swords, poetry over carousing, and tea over brandy."

A soft, sweet smile came easily to her lips and she politely said, "In other words, he's nothing like the man you are."

She was even more incredibly daring than he first thought. To talk so freely and challengingly to a duke, and not be the least bit intimidated about how he might react, was astonishing. And to top off that, she managed to take him to task without being petulant about it. She had good reason to give him that satisfied smile.

Hawk grunted a laugh. "You go right for the throat, don't you, Miss Quick?"

"I'd rather think of it as going directly to the heart of the matter, Your Grace."

"Either way, you have unquestionable courage."

"And you have undoubtable arrogance to think you can come here and expect my brother to simply accept your bidding and take your sister to be his bride."

He met her confident stare. "In a word, yes."

She didn't waver. "You will not win me over on this issue, Your Grace. I will counsel him against such an alliance."

"Somehow that doesn't surprise me."

"And it doesn't surprise me that once again I have a peer standing before me who is trying to arrange a marriage between two people who don't know each other."

"Tell me, do you have something against my sister?"

"Of course not. I haven't met her."

"Maybe you are just against your brother marrying a young lady who is lovely, clever, and brings a generous dowry with her."

"Don't be ridiculous," she said, fending off his allegation without hesitation.

"Then perhaps you are simply against him marrying."

"You are wrong again," she said pragmatically. "I am for my brother making his own decision about who he will marry with no one else's interference. And quite frankly, Your Grace, I find all this talk of marriage beyond the pale. My brother has only just passed his twenty-fourth birthday."

"I am aware of his age, Miss Quick."

"Yet you seek him out to be a husband?" she argued. "What would you have said if someone had mentioned an arrangement of marriage to you at such a young age?"

When Hawk was twenty-four, he wasn't too far removed from the Rakes of St. James secret admirer scandal. "No one would have dared to suggest marriage to me, I assure you."

Raising her eyebrows as if sensing victory, she said, "Correct. And you should also know that Paxton probably hasn't given marriage a thought, either."

"That could very well be true, but there is nothing wrong with finding out if he might be tempted to at least meet Lady Adele. I would think that you would be pleased I thought highly enough of your brother to want him to marry my sister."

She shilly-shallied. At last he'd said something she

didn't have a saucy retort for. Maybe they were now making progress.

"Of course, that I'm happy you think so flatteringly of Paxton goes without saying," she finally admitted. "I have no doubt he would make your sister a fine husband."

"You are not helping your case, Miss Quick, only furthering mine."

"That is not my intention and you know it. I'm trying not to be completely disagreeable here. My brother does have much to recommend him, and I won't deny that. But since you are pressing the issue, I will say what I was trying to avoid and spare you the truth."

The muscles in Hawk's shoulders and back tightened. "I need no sparing from anyone, Miss Quick," he said through gritted teeth. "Especially from the truth."

"Good. Though I'm not in Society now, I have been. And I have met the daughters and sisters of dukes. I found them to be demanding, selfish, and terribly overindulged. I expect Paxton will marry someone who is sweet, thoughtful of others, and more suitable to his happy, gentle disposition. Perhaps a vicar's daughter."

Hawk's jaw hardened. Was she disparaging Adele? Now the bold miss had gone too far; for the first time, her tautly spoken words didn't sit well with Hawk.

"A vicar's daughter?" He repeated the phrase as though it were a curse. He took a menacing step toward Miss Quick. "Are you suggesting my sister isn't good enough for your brother?"

She stood her ground. "I'm not suggesting anything about your sister particularly, but overall about what I've heard, read, and observed the short time I was Society. And I only add the kind of lady I would like to see Paxton marry. Now do you still think I am furthering your cause, Your Grace?"

Her back was straight and her head tilted defiantly. She spoke her mind fearlessly better than most of the men he knew. If Hawk's sister were only half as strong-minded as Miss Quick, he wouldn't be seeking a husband for her; she'd be looking for one herself.

It hadn't been his choice for his sister to be his responsibility. His parents had been killed when a ship that was taking them to Portugal sank as it sailed into the harbor. He'd just come of age, so her guardianship had fallen to him. At the time, Hawk hadn't even learned how to take care of himself. Drinking, gambling, and women were his priorities. Not young girls. He'd solicited the help of his widowed cousin, Minerva Philbert, who'd moved into Hawksthorn to watch after Adele.

Hawk relaxed his stance and said, "No, Miss Quick, I'd say you've made your case very plainly."

"Good," she said, seeming pleased with herself.

He gave her a knowing smile. "But you must know that the more you tell me you don't want this to happen between our families, the more I intend to see that it does."

She moistened her lips and seemed to think on his comment before saying, "Your idea is rubbish. What does Lady Adele think of you trying to control her life by picking her husband? I don't know her but find it difficult to believe she's delighted with that idea."

"My sister agrees with me and knows I only want what's best for her. She knows I wouldn't force her to marry your brother or anyone else if she found him detestable."

Miss Quick huffed a soft breath. "No one could find Paxton detestable. And I would be pleased for my brother to marry whomever he wishes, whenever he wishes. What I don't want is him falling victim to a scoundrel duke like you waving money, position, and prestige in front of him for your own selfish reasons."

"You think I am doing this for me?" He took another step closer to Miss Quick. "My reasons are not for myself but for my sister. My only goal is to see to it she comes to no harm and makes a good match, and I make no excuses for putting her welfare above all else."

"Nor I my brother's."

"So then we understand each other."

"It appears we do. You will fight for Lady Adele and I will fight for Paxton. I didn't save myself from an arranged marriage only to watch my brother walk blindly into one."

"You don't think much of your brother's ability to take care of this himself, do you?"

"Nor you, your sister's."

Her defiance was commendable, but if she thought to frighten him away by her firm stand on this matter, she was mistaken. "Then the lines have been drawn and the battle has begun, Miss Quick."

"So it seems."

"Now, when do you expect your brother to return?"

"I really can't say for sure," she said with a slight lift to her chin. "Usually he's only gone a couple of weeks, but this time it's been longer. That's why when you first arrived I thought you might be bringing news of him. So yes, I expect he should return in a day or two."

"But you have no reason to think he won't be back by the end of next week."

Reluctantly, she answered, "No." Then she quickly added, "He'll be sorry to have missed you. Now, may I get you something to eat or drink? Or perhaps you'd just like to warm yourself by the fire a little longer before you take your leave."

Hawk's primal instinct rose. She was dismissing him. Treating him as if she had the rank of duke instead of him. And while it amazed him she had the audacity to do it, it also irritated the devil out of him. She had more mettle than any other lady he'd met. He couldn't let her pluck stand without redress. While she might be anxious to be rid of him, he wasn't in a hurry to depart from her.

"A glass of port, wine, or brandy would be welcomed." He looked around the sparsely furnished room. "If you have it."

A twitch of a smile played at the edges of her mouth, and Hawk found it downright enchanting. He hoped the faint amusement on her lips was because she knew he was delaying his departure just to irritate her. If so, good.

"Paxton always has a bottle of something available."

She turned away, and the tug of arousal tightened Hawk's lower body again. Waves of rich, shimmering blond hair that looked as if it could have been spun from moonlight cascaded down her back. For a moment, he envisioned her sitting astride him with all those glorious tresses falling delicately around her bare shoulders, and tickling his chest as she bent to kiss him.

Miss Quick glanced back at him and her gaze caught his, stare for stare. Hawk had little doubt Miss Quick suspected in her innocent way what he'd been thinking, but, more important, at that moment he saw that she was attracted to him, too.

"It's brandy," she said softly, opening one of the compartments on the secretary and pulling out a tray with glasses and a decanter on it.

"That's fine," he answered.

He watched her. Her movements were confident but refined as she took the top off the decanter and poured a generous splash into the glass.

Without taking her attention off him, she walked over and extended the drink to him. "There isn't much daylight left."

So this was to be a test of her courage and his resolve. She was still trying to get rid of him. It was admirable. And it was probably best if he did go soon, but . . . the rogue in him couldn't bend to her wishes.

He took the glass. "It's still raining."

She glanced out the window, too. "So it is. Please, do sit down and enjoy your drink and the fire for a while."

And your company.

"It will be my pleasure, Miss Quick, but first I must ask a favor. My horse stepped in a hole and can't be ridden. When I leave, I will have to ask to borrow one of yours to ride back to the village."

"Oh, my." Her fan-shaped brows lifted. "I'm afraid that's not going to be possible."

He smiled. She even had to take him to task over the use of one of her horses. "I'll see that it's returned, Miss Quick."

"I have no doubt of that, Your Grace." She glanced out the window again and worried her bottom lip for a few seconds. Concern was back in her expression when she faced him again.

"Is there a problem?"

"Yes. I would be more than happy to lend you a mount so that you can take your leave, if I had one. We have only four at Mammoth House. My brother and his valet are away on two of them and Mr. Huddleston and his helper have the other two. They left this morning for their weekly visit to Grimsfield for supplies. It's quite a distance, as you no doubt know, so they always stay overnight with Mr. Huddleston's brother. They aren't expected back until tomorrow."

"Only four horses on an estate this size?" That was unimaginable.

"There's no need for more, as we lead a simple life here at Mammoth House."

"That's a bit too simple as far as I'm concerned," he said irritably. "Does the earl know of this?"

"My uncle is very generous to allow my brother and me to live in such a grand home with servants to care for our needs."

So it was the Earl of Switchingham who had Miss Quick and her brother living in the middle of this vast valley with nothing surrounding it and few creature comforts. He should have guessed.

"So then, I'm to assume there is no one at the stable to care for my horse outside."

Her shoulders lifted. "I'm quite capable of doing that for you, Your Grace."

He grunted. What did she take him for? A pampered ninny? She was by far the most direct and unpretentious young lady he'd ever met.

"No, Miss Quick, you are not. I will not see the day I'll allow a female to care for my horse."

"As you wish." He watched as she swallowed hard, hesitating more than once before finally saying, "So then, unless you intend to walk back to the village, I'll have to offer you a bed for the night."

A slow roll of enticement started in Hawk's throat and rumbled down to his chest and into his lower stomach. Anticipation had his heartbeat thundering in his chest. Even though her words were soft, breathy, and oh so sensual to his ears, he knew she hadn't meant her invitation the way his body responded to it.

Her expression was apprehensive. Her dark-blue eyes questioned him. How would he answer?

She not only provoked every one of his senses, but also heated his desire and stimulated his mind. She was truly lovely, tempting, and undeniably innocent. Those things made for a powerful combination, and his body was let-

ting him know in no uncertain way that he wanted her with
an intensity that he hadn't felt in a very long time.

If ever.

He should offer to bed down in the stable. A true gentleman would and not leave the virtuous Miss Quick open
to any hint of scandal. But the cold, damp stable was as
appealing as a sickbed, and the last place Hawk wanted to
stay this night.

So should he do the right thing, be a gentleman and stay
in the stable, or—as he had so often done in the past—do
the wrong thing and continue to be a rake?

Chapter 2

A gentleman would never put a young lady's
reputation at risk. No matter how tempting the
thought of doing so might be.

～ఄం～

*A PROPER GENTLEMAN'S GUIDE TO WOOING
THE PERFECT LADY*
SIR VINCENT TYBALT VALENTINE

Loretta Quick was quite simply shaking in her slippers,
but the Duke of Hawksthorn would never know. Her
inner trembling wasn't from fear of him or even nervous-
ness that he was a duke. It was because the moment she
saw him, something changed inside her and she still wasn't
sure what to make of the new, startling, and unexplained
feelings that had swept over her at the sight of him. She
wasn't out of breath, yet she was breathless. She wasn't
dizzy, yet she felt light-headed. She wasn't hungry, yet looking at him caused a ravenous appetite to rise up within her.

The duke was as handsome a man as Loretta had ever
seen, with wide masculine lips, a narrow nose, and a
slightly square, clean-shaven chin. He was the most arrogant, too. He stood tall, broad-shouldered, and powerful-

looking dressed in buckskin-colored trousers that were
stuffed into over-the-knee boots. A well-fitted brown velvet coat with shiny brass buttons lined down the front and
on the sleeves did little to hide his muscular build. Rain
droplets clung to the ends of his thick light-brown hair and
had dampened the edges of his collar and neckcloth.

Standing before her so splendidly male, she could easily believe he was one of the notorious Rakes of St. James
she'd read so much about. The trio of titled gentlemen had
proved to a stunned Society that every young belle wanted
to be pursued by a secret admirer. Looking at him, Loretta could understand why, even after he'd demonstrated
his notably roguish ways, ladies all over London still
vied for the Duke of Hawksthorn's attention. From what
she'd read in the scandal sheets he and the other unwed
rakes were sought after by young misses, aging widows,
and beautiful heiresses.

The duke's eyes, such a deep shade of green, held steady
on hers. The seconds were ticking by and still he hadn't
responded to her offer of lodging for the night. Manners
had dictated she ask him. But what would he say?

The nerve-racking silence between them lengthened
until at last he said, "Thank you, Miss Quick, but out of
respect for your reputation, I'll stay in the stable."

So he was a gentleman after all. Loretta pushed her disturbing thoughts about the duke to the back of her mind
and forced herself to take control of her stirring emotions.

Her breath clogged her throat, but she managed to answer, "No, Your Grace. Just as you won't allow a lady to
care for your horse, I can't let a duke spend the night in an
earl's stable. This state of affairs in which we find ourselves is not something over which we have any control.
There's no need for you to be out in the cold on such a

stormy evening when there are so many rooms in this house."

"I'll accept," he said with a nod, "if you are sure it won't be a burden on you."

Mammoth House was an apt name for the stone building that was her home. It was massive. The rooms were large, the corridors wide, and the ceilings high. Though in truth, she wondered if it was big enough for the both of them to reside in for a night.

"Not in the least. Mrs. Huddleston, Bitsy, my maid, and two other servants are here with me. I am not alone." She paused and then added, "And I am not helpless."

A twitch of a grin lifted one corner of his mouth. "That I have already determined; however, I believe you are implying I should take your last comment as a warning?"

It didn't surprise her he was so astute.

"I would never presume that I should need to warn a duke about such established matters."

"But it was a warning just the same, wasn't it?"

His tone remained light. Loretta lifted her chin. She wanted to keep a straight, unaffected face, but in the end a smile quivered on her lips, too, as she said, "It was a statement of fact, Your Grace."

"Perhaps your forthright manner is why I'm so intrigued by you, Miss Quick."

Is he?

That thought had her feeling as if bees were swarming in her chest and butterflies fluttering in her stomach.

"It's not my desire to intrigue you."

"That's quite obvious, too. And I know you are as fascinated by me as I am by you."

Loretta frowned deeply. "You couldn't know that even if it were true. Which is isn't."

"I know," he insisted in a husky voice that sent a prickling of something wonderful skipping over her skin. "I see it in your eyes."

Loretta sucked in a deep and, she hoped, soundless breath. Could that possibly be true? Some people were more perceptive than others, but—did she dare to refute his claim again?

She hesitated, searching for the right words.

"While you contemplate your answer, Miss Quick," he continued in the same lighthearted tone that washed over her as soothingly as warm water, "I think you should know that, as outspoken as you are, I don't expect you to deny what I see so clearly."

Oh, he was a perceptive brute.

Of course she was attracted to him, and he was a miserable beast for realizing she wanted to disavow his assessment of her. But he was wrong if he thought to goad her into admitting anything.

She forced herself to relax. "I fear you mistake the reason for my interest in you."

His brows rose. "Really?"

"It's only natural that I should be a little awestruck, Your Grace."

"You? Awestruck? If so, you have an odd way of trying to get that point across."

"Nevertheless, as I mentioned, I've never had a duke visit Mammoth House. Surely you must know that your presence, or anyone's for that matter, is a rare occasion for the niece of an earl who has been all but banished from Society."

His eyes narrowed. "I don't know the complete story on that, Miss Quick. Perhaps we can discuss it later."

Loretta's proclamation to her uncle and its consequences

weren't things she wanted to talk about in any detail, and
the duke had to know that. She quirked her head and offered, "If that be the case, then I suppose you will also
want to discuss a certain *secret admirer letter* that was reportedly read around the world."

The Duke of Hawksthorn gave a hearty laugh. His eyes
sparkled invitingly. It lifted her spirits and made her feel
quite jolly to know that her comment had amused him so
much.

"Around the world? Your cleverness is refreshing."

She smiled. "As you said earlier, I don't know the complete story on that."

"While I have little doubt everyone in England heard
about my misguided participation in that youthful prank,
I have misgivings about the prospects of the entire world
knowing. However, in either case, I must wait for further
discussion on the matter." He extended the glass to her.
"And I'll wait to enjoy this until after I've put the mare in
the stable, rubbed her down, and fed her."

Loretta reached to take hold of the glass, and two of her
fingers landed on top of his. A tingling response rushed
up her arm and rippled across her breasts; a tightening
gripped her lower abdomen. The duke must have felt the
strange awareness at their unexpected contact, too. His
eyes blinked and narrowed. She was certain there was a
jump in his breathing as he slipped his fingers from beneath hers and let go of the glass.

Unlike her usually well-controlled self, she felt a blush
searing up her neck and quickly cleared her throat. It was
ridiculous for her to feel so tantalized at the slight touch
of his hand. That was something she'd have to consider at
a later date. This wasn't the time to think about what she'd
felt when her hand brushed the duke's.

She hurried to say, "Since you will be our guest for the

evening, what time would you like to have your dinner served?"

"I will dine at whatever time you do."

"Oh, but I don't stand on ceremony as far as dinner is concerned when Paxton is away. Mrs. Huddleston is an excellent cook and will consider it an honor to prepare something for you and to serve you in the dining room whenever you prefer."

He stepped in closer to her as he had earlier, and for an instant she had the wild thought that she should step closer to him, too.

"I welcome the opportunity to forgo ceremony," he said. "It matters not to me what we eat, where we dine, or the time. As a guest in your home, Miss Quick, I will have my evening meal with you."

At his nearness, a shivery feeling gently stole over her again, and all at once it felt as if her insides melted into a quivering heap at the bottom of her abdomen. "But that would be—" She stopped.

"Scandalous," he finished for her.

"Yes," she said, renewing her inner strength and refusing to back down or away from him. "More so than offering you lodging for the night. You know that is something that cannot be helped because of circumstances concerning your horse. No one, including my uncle, would expect a duke to sleep in a cold stable, but no one would expect that I would dine alone with him since my brother isn't here."

Without warning, his expression softened and he added, "If it makes my being here a little easier to bear, I would venture to say there isn't another person within an hour or two of this place, so unless you or your servants decide to tell of this unconventional evening, no one will be the wiser."

"My staff is very loyal," she defended.

"So it's settled. Tonight we shall share the same table and the same roof." He stepped back.

Sensing no further argument would sway the duke, Loretta knew she must now be the gracious hostess of Mammoth House. "We'll dine at eight. I'll see to it that a room is made up for you."

On the farthest end of the house.

He nodded. "Now I'll go take care of my horse." He pointed to her hand. She gripped the glass so hard her knuckles were white. "And then I'll return for that drink."

Loretta watched the duke stride from the room. Oh, it was devilishly frustrating that he was so stimulating. It was ridiculous that he was so handsome, his shoulders so wide and his hips so lean and narrow that she wanted to keep looking at him. It was downright maddening that her heartbeat was racing and her stomach had an extraordinary attack of the jitters.

She considered herself a strong, capable young lady. She had stood up to her uncle and refused to marry the viscount. She'd withstood the loneliness of Mammoth House when her brother often fell victim to the isolation and quietness and had to leave. But in a few short minutes, the duke had left her feeling very feminine and incredibly confused about all the emotions he'd stirred within her.

Yet he'd also had no problem living up to his reputation as a scoundrel. Insisting she dine alone with him in her home. What other gentleman would do such a thing? None, she dared to think. And why was the thought of dining alone with him so horrifying and thrilling at the same time?

It simply wasn't natural for her to be feeling the way she was about him. It was almost too much for her to comprehend. The duke was a rake of the highest order. Everyone in Society knew that. He'd proved years ago that he had little regard for young ladies' sensibilities, and by insisting on taking his evening meal with her, he'd made it clear he hadn't changed his wicked ways.

Loretta had read about what happened when the duke and two of his friends had outraged all of London by catching every young lady making her debut that year in an ill-conceived scheme that the rakes had yet to live down.

She'd never heard that there had been any apologies or even any excuses for what the Duke of Hawksthorn, the Duke of Griffin, and the Duke of Rathburne had done: sending secret admirer letters to twelve young ladies asking them to meet the anonymous sender in private. All of the young ladies had fallen for the scam. Not one had been prudent enough to refuse the invitation to meet her admirer in person.

And the truth of it was that Loretta probably would have done it, too, had it been the year of her debut. Once it was made known that the rakes had wagered to see which one of them would see the most ladies respond, the *ton* was in a state of panic, the Season all but lost, and the ladies and their parents devastated. The trio had been called the Rakes of St. James ever since, and the gossip columns had not let the story fade from the annals of Society.

So yes, she should be horrified that she would be dining alone with one of the rakes. She should be worried for her reputation. She should be fearful for her person.

But she wasn't.

God help her, she was looking forward to it.

And not just because the duke was a handsome man who had all her senses shooting to the stars and back. It had been such a long time since she'd dined with anyone other than her brother, occasionally with her uncle on his infrequent visits to Mammoth House, and her yearly visit to his estate on Christmas Day for the Yuletide dinner with a few of his elderly friends.

Loretta had never regretted not marrying the viscount her uncle had chosen for her, but she had missed the social life it could have afforded her. She wasn't one to dwell on what might have been. When she made her decision to defy her uncle, she knew there would be penalties, and knowing her uncle could be harsh, she should have assumed they would be severe.

The Earl of Switchingham had been honor-bound to take in his younger brother's two children, Paxton and Loretta, when their mother passed, his brother having died in a duel shortly after Loretta was born. Almost as soon as they arrived Paxton was sent to boarding school for his education. Loretta was kept at Switchingham under the care of governesses and tutors until she was ready for her debut. She seldom saw the earl, as he spent most of his time in London, but when he was home it was clear he expected to be obeyed without question. So yes, now that this rare opportunity had presented itself to her, she wanted to dine with the interesting Duke of Hawksthorn. She wanted to talk with him, and she even wanted to somehow once again feel the delicious sensations that had roused inside her when she looked at him, when their hands had touched. She didn't have to understand these things to enjoy them.

Besides, the duke was right. Wasn't he? Who would know that he'd overnighted under her roof and shared her table? She supposed that if, after all these years, her reputation was going to be ruined, she'd rather it be by a fine-looking gentleman who'd made her heart feel as if it were skipping a beat every time she looked at him.

"Is he a real duke?"

Loretta glanced over to see Mrs. Huddleston standing

in the doorway of the drawing room. "As real as they come."

"Is he leaving now?"

"No," Loretta answered, walking over to the secretary and placing the duke's drink on the tray. "He's going out to the stable to care for his horse."

"That's probably a first for a gentleman like him. Do you suppose he knows how to do it?"

"Now you are being unkind, Mrs. Huddleston," Loretta said with more good humor than reprimand in her tone. "I know even dukes are taught the proper care of their animals."

"If you say so." She pursed her lips a moment and then added, "Though I'd feel better if Mr. Huddleston or Arnold were here to take care of the horse for him."

"So would I, but they are not," Loretta said.

"I figure if a man can't tie his own neckcloth and needs a valet to do it for him, he probably can't stable his own horse."

Loretta cleared her throat to keep from laughing at that remark. "You have no idea whether or not he ties his own neckcloth. And I think you have more important things to worry about right now anyway."

"Me?"

"Yes. The duke will be staying for dinner. Do you have something you can prepare on short notice?"

Her eyes rounded and she picked up the tail of her apron and started wiping her hands as she often did when she was nervous or worried about something. "I don't know about that, miss. I've never cooked for a duke before."

Loretta gave her a comforting smile. "It will be like cooking for anyone else, Mrs. Huddleston. Don't worry. You'll do a superb job. You always do. And actually, he'll be staying the night. His horse is lame and he won't be able to leave until Mr. Huddleston returns tomorrow so he can borrow a mount. You'll need to see to it that a room is prepared for him. I suggest you prepare the earl's bed-chamber for him since it's on the farthest end of the house. Now, what can you cook tonight?"

"I suppose I could try making some of those fancy small courses I've heard about that go on at the earl's house. We have some pickled vegetables and roots. I could try to—"

"That's not necessary. I'm sure the duke wouldn't ex-pect anything as elaborate as what is served by his cook," Loretta interrupted her. "He knows we haven't the staff for a meal such as he would require in his home. Your usual fare will do just fine for him."

"I would think a gentleman such as the duke would want a bit more to sit down to than an egg on a piece of toast like you'd be eating if he wasn't here."

Mrs. Huddleston was right about that. "Whatever you prepare, just make it as nice for him as you can and don't try making anything you've never cooked before."

"I'll sizzle a slice of ham for him and make a honey sauce to go over it. Boil potatoes and eggs. I took bread out of the oven less than half an hour ago so we've plenty of that. Cheese, too. I'll make some fig tarts. Does that sound hearty enough for a man of his size?"

Loretta smiled. The duke was a big man. "That sounds delicious and perfect," she told the housekeeper.

Mrs. Huddleston beamed at her praise and dropped her apron. "I thought so, too. He won't walk away hungry or complaining from a table I've prepared for him."

"I'm sure of that."

"I'll get started in the kitchen and then take care of hav-ing a fire laid in the earl's room for him."

"Thank you. And perhaps you should lay out a night-shirt. The duke didn't expect to stay the night, and I don't know if he has a satchel with him."

"Yes, miss."

"One more thing, Mrs. Huddleston. You'll need to set up the dining room. For two."

The housekeeper pressed the palms of her hands down her hips in a worried manner. "Are you sure you want to be doing that, miss?"

"No, but the duke is. Apparently he has an aversion to eating alone and insists I join him. Put us at opposite ends of the table with plenty of candles between us."

Notwithstanding all that, Loretta would do all she could to make the duke's unexpected overnight stay at Mammoth House pleasant. The one thing she wouldn't do for him was agree to an arranged marriage between her brother and the duke's sister if it was in her power to keep it from happening. Though that could be harder than she allowed his grace to think. Contrary to everything she let the duke believe, she had very little control over her brother.

But she did have an opinion and she would state it. Whenever necessary. It was impossible for her to have that romantic, soul-capturing love she'd read about in poetry, but there was no reason Paxton couldn't find and woo the perfect lady to love.

"Not to worry, miss. I know what to do. I can keep my ear to the door."

Loretta laughed. "That won't be necessary. I assure you, I will not be in danger of being ravished by the duke to-night."

"Yes, miss. I'd best get started and you'd best get started changing for dinner, too."

Mrs. Huddleston hurried from the room, and Loretta

stared down at the simple day dress she wore. She may not
have been in Society for over two years, but she still knew
the rules. When dining with a duke, she must be properly
attired. Her hair should be up with a headpiece of jewels at
her crown and not unbound and swinging freely about her
shoulders as if she didn't know the proper way to present
herself. She needed to wear one of her best gowns.

And if she was honest with herself, she wanted the duke
to know that when not caught unaware, as she was this
afternoon by his unexpected arrival, she could be pre-
sentable. She'd put on some of her mother's jewelry, too. A
smile touched her lips as thoughts of her sweet, soft-spoken
mother, whom she'd lost far too soon, crossed her mind.
Loretta had lovely, expensive jewels that her uncle had allowed her to keep, maybe because they were her mother's
or perhaps because he knew she would seldom have a need
to wear any of them.

But tonight, as fate had declared, she did.

An odd feeling stole over her and she realized she was
actually excited about dressing for dinner. She still had
many of the gowns she'd had made for her debut. They
were no longer the latest fashion, she was sure, but all of
them were made from the finest of fabrics, ribbons, and
lace.

Loretta headed for the stairs. She didn't have much time
to turn herself from a simple country lady into a belle who
looked as if she were attending a Society ball. Her uncle
had spared no expense to prepare her for her first Season.
At the time, Loretta had no idea he never intended for her
to have one. He had already secretly arranged for her to
marry Viscount Denningcourt.

And she almost had.

After much scolding, berating, and guilt had been
heaped on her from her uncle for being an ungrateful lass

for all he'd done for her and her brother, she'd consented to the rushed wedding shortly after the Season had begun. But in the end, Loretta couldn't bring herself to go through with the ceremony, which was why she was now—more or less—a prisoner at Mammoth House.

Chapter 3

No gentleman should ever forget that he is one.

❧

A Proper Gentleman's Guide to Wooing
the Perfect Lady
Sir Vincent Tybalt Valentine

Hawk was damned glad Miss Quick had refused his gentlemanly offer and he wouldn't be sleeping in the stable. The slow drizzle of rain had turned to a sleety shower of ice that was setting up for a miserable night of freezing cold. It was unseasonably wintry for being less than a month from the first day of spring.

A little before eight in the evening Hawk strode down the long corridor that led to the dining room. After he'd done all he could for the mare, the housekeeper had shown him to a room where he took off his coat, shirt, collar, and neckcloth and let them dry by the fire before donning them again. He hadn't expected to stay the night at Mammoth House so he'd left his satchel at the inn where he'd left his carriage.

Hawk was looking forward to a hearty meal, a stout

wine, and an evening of interesting discussions with Miss Quick before he sought a warm bed.

He rounded the doorway and came to an abrupt halt when he saw Miss Quick standing in front of the fireplace. Flickering yellow and amber flames glowed behind her, giving her an almost ethereal appearance. His first thought was that she looked angelic.

His second was that he wanted to seduce her.

His third was that he'd best get his primal urges under control.

And fast.

She was the niece of an earl and not available for him to dally with no matter what desires his baser instincts were pressing upon him to engage in at the moment. He could enjoy her beauty, wit, and charm, but he couldn't touch her.

She wore a buttery-colored gown that looked as soft and velvety as her beautiful skin. Long, sheer sleeves were trimmed at the cuffs with white fur. The neckline swept low, revealing the enticing, gentle swell of her breasts. A brilliantly cut ruby hung from a delicate strand of pearls that circled her neck, and a matching strand had been fitted at the crown of her silky upswept hair.

Had she been his mistress he would have forgotten all about the growl of hunger in his stomach and fed the raging appetite in his loins. He wanted to scoop her up in his arms and take her straight to his bedchamber.

"Miss Quick," he said with a nod.

"Good evening, Your Grace," she answered with an abbreviated curtsy. "I hope the suite of rooms Mrs. Huddleston showed you are acceptable."

"Yes. Warm and comfortable."

"I'm glad to hear that," she answered and then walked over to stand by a chair.

Only then did Hawk notice the table. It was long. Very long and covered in a gleaming white cloth. An impressive six-pronged silver candlestand had been placed in the middle. Two single candlesticks flanked each side of the stand, adding their burning flames to the golden glow cast by the crackling fire and lighted wall sconces. There were ten chairs lining each side of the table. An attractive setting of china, silver, and crystal had been placed at each end.

If they were going to see each other, they would have to look around all the candles. And if they were to converse during dinner, apparently Miss Quick expected them to shout.

Hawk strode over to her and, pulling out the chair, said, "Allow me to assist you."

"Thank you," she answered, sounding quite pleased with herself as she took her seat.

The enticing scent of fresh-washed hair stirred the air beside him as she moved. It teased his senses. Watching her as she made herself comfortable, he had a great desire to reach down and kiss the back of her neck and let his lips skim along the crest of her bare shoulders. He wanted to snuggle his nose against the warm skin behind her ear and breathe in slowly. And though he knew it was futile thinking, he wanted to feel her tremble with passion in his arms.

Ah, he thought, *she is simply too tempting for words.*

He bent down close to the top of her head, but alas, not to indulge in his desired fantasy to kiss her but only to whisper, "You are lovely tonight, Miss Quick."

She remained staring straight ahead but murmured another, softer "Thank you."

Hawk pushed his thoughts away from his desires for

Miss Quick once again and headed to the opposite end of the table, counting the chairs between them as he passed. Eleven. He'd missed one when he'd glanced at them a few moments ago. There might as well be a gulf of fire between the two of them.

At the table where he was to sit, he grabbed the back of his chair to pull it out but stopped. He looked at Miss Quick sitting so lovely, so serene, and so far away. It was impossible to ignore the barriers she'd erected between them.

To be or not to be a gentleman was the question she'd silently put before him. And it really wasn't hard to answer. She obviously didn't know he wasn't one to back down from a challenge. What else could so many candles and silver be?

Hawk didn't mind accommodating a clever young lady, but, he could only go so far in doing so. After all, he was a man. The opportunity to dine alone with a beautiful, innocent lady of quality might never come his way again.

And that was all it took for the man inside him to win out over the gentleman. Why change his wicked ways tonight?

He let go of the chair, reached down and scooped up the silver on both sides of the plate in one hand. With the other he gathered the napkin and wineglass and marched to the chair that was on Miss Quick's right. She sat in stunned silence as he laid everything on the table in front of him, not as neatly as it had been, but it would do. He then went back and picked up the decanter of wine and the plate and carried them back to where he was preparing a place for himself.

After putting the items on the table, he noticed she had water in her goblet. "Do you drink wine, Miss Quick?"

"Sometimes. Usually only when Paxton is here."

"Ah. I've heard it's never a good idea to drink alone. Will you join me in a glass of wine tonight?"

"If you would like."

He picked up her water, carried it over to the fireplace, and poured it in the edge of the fire. It sizzled and hissed. He then placed the glass back in front of her and poured a serving of wine into it and then into his own glass before taking his seat.

"That's better," he said with a satisfied smile, loving the surprised expression on her face. "You did say you don't stand on ceremony when your brother isn't home, didn't you?"

Though he felt sure she hoped to hide it, he saw a measure of admiration in her eyes for his brashness. And that pleased him, too.

"Yes. And by all means, Your Grace, sit wherever you like."

Her voice was calm, her countenance relaxed. She was letting him know he might have won the skirmish, but she wasn't conceding the battle. Good. He was looking forward to more clashes between them before the evening was over.

He nodded once. "May I offer a toast?"

"Of course." She picked up her wine.

"To your brother and my sister and a long happy life for each of them." He waited until she had the glass to her lips and then added, "Together."

Miss Quick coughed as she swallowed. Her brows furrowed. "That wasn't fair of you," she said and put down her glass.

"We are in a war on opposite sides. It was strategic."

"It was underhanded."

"Perhaps it was sly."

"No matter the term you or I attach to it, I wouldn't toast to my brother and your sister *together* when they've never even met."

By the tone of her voice he knew she wasn't angry with him or even upset. She was simply taking him to task for doing something she didn't like, and that made her divinely appealing.

"You don't like to give an inch, do you, Miss Quick?"

She rearranged the napkin in her lap and then looked at him with her blue eyes and said, "I could easily say the same about you. Apparently you don't, either."

"Ah, but with me it is expected, is it not? I've always found that young ladies are usually more cooperative than men—yet you are tenacious to a fault."

Her gaze stayed on his. He saw that earlier, attractive strength return to her countenance. "Perhaps you didn't notice when we spoke this afternoon, Your Grace, but . . ." She paused, and her hint of a smile was confident. "I'm not known for being agreeable just to placate someone—not even an earl or a duke."

"Oh, I noticed, and you know I did, but thank you for attempting to give me the benefit of doubt. It was more than I deserved."

"And not for the first time," she murmured under her breath and then said more plainly, "Tell me, did you find everything you needed to care for your horse?"

"Yes. Including a blanket, which will be needed tonight. The stable is large and well stocked for only four horses."

"I know, it's a shame that much of it goes unused. There was a time many horses were stabled here. Years ago, when the house was built by the first Earl of Switchingham.

I'm told Mammoth House was a rather grand hunting lodge. The earl, along with family and friends, used to spend the winters here. They held grand house parties that are still talked about in the village."

Hawk settled against the back of his chair and sipped the wine again. He'd never made it back to the drawing room for the brandy she'd poured, and the wine was soothing. This is what he wanted from the night. A warm room, a glass of wine, and a strong, delightful, and intelligent lady to share it all with him.

"Does your uncle stay here and hunt?"

"No. I'm told there used to be a dense forest not too far north of here, but a great fire destroyed it close to twenty years ago. As unbelievable as it seems, there had been little rain for several weeks before the fire. Apparently the devastation was quite thorough, and regrowth has been slow."

The housekeeper entered the dining room and placed a plate of steaming food in front of him. The aroma of sweet honey mixed with smoked ham drifted up and made Hawk's mouth water. A mound of scrambled eggs and a serving of boiled potatoes were also on the plate. Miss Quick was served the same but with noticeably smaller portions.

"There are sporadic stands of scrub trees and brush," Miss Quick continued as Mrs. Huddleston left the dining room, "but unfortunately the forest hasn't returned to its former flourish yet. I'm assuming that's the reason the house is no longer used as a hunting lodge."

"And how long have you lived in Mammoth House?"

"Over two years," she answered, picking up her knife and fork.

"How often do you go to the village?"

"I don't." She motioned to his food. "Please enjoy your meal while it's hot."

Hawk put his glass down and picked up his silver. "What about London? Do you go there to visit family or friends?"

"No." She swallowed another bite and then said, "I am always invited to go to my uncle's house for Christmas dinner."

It was intriguing that she seldom traveled anywhere, and he wanted to know why. The real reason why.

The ham was salty, sweet, and delicious. He enjoyed his food for a few moments and thought on what she'd said before asking, "Yet your brother leaves Mammoth House often."

She quirked her head toward him as she lifted a forkful of eggs. "How do you know?"

"I see him in London."

"Oh, I'm sorry. Yes, of course, you would know." She laughed softly. "I should have assumed that. Paxton enjoys being with people. The solitude here doesn't agree with him as easily as it does me."

Hawk took a sip of the wine and watched her laugh at herself before returning to her food. He liked that her mistake hadn't flustered her. He liked seeing merriment sparkle in her eyes and light up her face.

"Does it agree with you or do you simply manage it better than your brother?"

"Either way, Your Grace," she said without looking up from her food. "This is where I live. I still have friends in London and we correspond regularly so I'm not completely cut off from the outside world."

There was such finality in her voice it gave him pause. He watched her cut a small piece of ham. She wasn't asking for sympathy or even understanding. Just stating the facts of her life.

"How frequently does the earl come for a visit?"

She swallowed. "Seldom."

"You are a master at giving short answers, Miss Quick."

"It is all your questions require."

He grinned at her cheeky answer, and so did she before continuing, "But I must admit that you have asked a lot of questions tonight."

"It's the best way to learn what you want to know."

"You must have an inquisitive mind." She put a piece of potato in her quite attractive mouth. Hawk wanted to reach over and kiss those pretty closed lips of hers, but knew the recklessness of that line of thinking and dug into the mound of eggs on his plate instead.

After eating a few more bites, he said, "I do. How often is seldom?"

"That my uncle visits?"

He nodded.

"Twice a year. Usually spring and fall. I assume he considers it his duty as my guardian to check on me from time to time. Maybe he simply wants to make sure I'm still here, or it could be that traveling is harder on him than it used to be. He doesn't get around as well as he did in his younger years. Stairs are particularly challenging for him. Even getting in and out of a carriage." She glanced at Hawk and added, "Is that answer long enough for you?"

There was a twinkle of mischief in her eyes, and Hawk chuckled. "Much better."

"Good."

"Why do you live here, Miss Quick?"

"It is my uncle's wish," she answered before laying her knife and fork aside and picking up her glass.

He smiled at her guileless answer. "Punishment?" he asked.

She lifted her gaze to his as she sipped the wine. He could see that she was contemplating her answer. Did she want to tell him the truth, a lie, or simply to mind his own business? He waited and gave her the time she needed to decide.

At last she said, "Perhaps some would think that."

"But you don't?"

"I have no use for self-pity, Your Grace. It festers and destroys. That said, I am resigned to the fact that I have no one to blame or to thank for the life I live other than myself."

Her face was somber, her words so honest, so quietly spoken that his heart lurched from the impact of their meaning. "Does your brother believe that?"

"I suppose you will have to ask Paxton when you tell him that you want him to marry your sister so she won't have to go out into Society and look for a husband herself among the rakes, scoundrels, and rapscallions. You know—" She gave him a rueful smile. "The kind of men who send gentle-bred young ladies anonymous letters and ask them to meet a secret admirer—that doesn't exist."

She was devilishly brave.

"I can't deny I once did that," he admitted. "Nor do I deny that I want to help my sister avoid men who can be as foolish as I was a few years ago."

"Was?" She lifted an arched brow as if in protest of his comment. "So you have mended your wicked ways?"

"To some extent." He laid his knife and fork on the empty plate. "I do try to behave myself around young ladies as much as possible, and I haven't written much of anything other than my signature since that note. I have my solicitor do it."

Miss Quick huffed a playful laugh. "Self-imposed punishment for yourself? I find that highly amusing."

"Maybe a measure of atonement as well, in order to spare others my regrettable ways. I suppose there would never be enough recompense for the writers of the scandal sheets."

"Nor perhaps the embarrassed belles who were left with only tainted reputations and the realization that no one was admiring them after all."

Hawk rubbed his thumb on the bottom of his wineglass. He'd come to expect that she wouldn't temper her words to spare him any ridicule or shame for what he'd already admitted was a mistake.

"It wasn't meant to be cruel to the young ladies. It wasn't even meant as a joke. It was a wager among friends that no one else was to ever know about. Our folly was that we were only thinking of ourselves and our own desire to win the wager."

"And now someone may want to endanger your sister's reputation in like kind in order to take revenge upon you for endangering the reputations of other young ladies."

"Though you might live far from the streets of London, I see you are up on the latest gossip."

"Mr. Huddleston always picks up copies of the all the latest newssheets when he's in Grimsfield each week. And I always read *Miss Honora Truth's Weekly Scandal Sheet*."

"You and the rest of the world," he grumbled.

"She's entertaining with her words. How much of the gossip she writes is true?" Miss Quick asked.

Probably far more than he was willing to admit.

"I don't know. That's the problem and why I make no apologies for what I'm doing to spare my sister. The same gossip that swirled around the Duke of Griffin's sisters last year is surfacing again now that Adele is making her debut. She could be in danger from someone wanting to ruin her chance at making a good match or simply playing her for a fool in the hope of breaking her heart just to get even with me for the secret admirer letters. As I told you, if she is already betrothed, no one will have reason to pursue her, and thereby I will keep her from being set upon by mischief-makers."

"And in order to keep this retaliation from happening, you want to completely alter my brother's life to save your sister because of something you did."

She wasn't teasing him when she said she liked to go straight to the heart of a matter. She knew how to put everything on the line. Hawk leaned forward, closer to her, but not in a threatening way, and said, "Because he would be a good match for Adele and she for him. Remember, I know them both."

Leaning back in her chair, she sipped her wine and then asked, "Why did you and your friends decide to wager on something as delicate as a young lady's heart?"

"You do like to thrust the knife in deep, Miss Quick."

"I am only stating the truth, am I not? I have nothing to lose by being honest with you. I am not seeking your favor or trying to impress you."

"Perhaps I wish you were. However, you can't make sense of what we did because you couldn't possibly understand the thoughts of a young man and his ego, especially one whose mind was befuddled by drink and arrogance and no fear whatsoever."

"That's probably true."

"We now know we shouldn't have done it—for a number of reasons, including the very real fact that not a one of us thought about our sisters and that they would grow up to be young ladies one day."

"That must have been sobering when you finally did."

Hawk grimaced. "It was never our intention to cause anyone harm. It was supposed to just be a simple wager among friends."

"So money was the reason you decided to send those letters to the young ladies?"

"Not the money. The winning. But there were several things that led to our downfall concerning that event."

"Share a few of them with me."

Share?

That wasn't a word he was used to hearing, and he certainly wasn't used to doing it. Furthermore, he'd never talked about that time almost ten years ago with anyone other than the other two men involved, Rath and Griffin, until Miss Quick. How had she managed to do so effortlessly what no one else had done?

Hawk took a sip of the wine and watched the candlelight play on her face. She looked even more beautiful than when he'd first entered the room. She looked comfortable, too, and that was probably the reason he was opening up to her and even discussing the wager.

Without further thought about why, he said, "The thing that started it all was a book that had just been published titled *A Proper Gentleman's Guide to Wooing the Perfect Lady.*"

Her brow creased. "I don't believe I've read it."

"There's no reason you should, and I wish I had never heard of it," he complained.

"How did such a book influence you?"

"For the worse, as you well know. Rath, Griffin, and I would enjoy reading a page or two of it and then have a good laugh at the useless and sometimes absurd things the man wrote, including *Never send a young lady a secret admirer letter.*"

"Oh."

"Yes," he answered dryly. "We were of an age and mind-set that, if we were told not to do something, that was the very first thing we wanted to do. And since we'd come to the bottom of a brandy bottle that particular evening, sending notes under the signature of *A Secret Admirer* seemed the suitable thing to do."

"How did you decide who should receive a letter?"

"That was easy. There were twelve young ladies making their debut that year. We decided those were the ones to receive our missive. We each took four different names and sent the letters asking them to meet us. At different locations, of course. We didn't know if any of them would come but agreed whoever had the most ladies show at the end of the evening would win the wager."

"But all three of you had all four of the ladies come for the secret meeting?"

"Yes."

"And you were found out one evening after you were overheard gloating about it."

He laughed at her rapid retort as he refilled his wineglass and added a splash to her glass as well. "Not gloating, Miss Quick, merely discussing it. But there were other reasons we made such an error. We were young, foolish, and had a great desire to win whatever bet we made." Hawk picked up his wine and leaned back in his chair. "Not a one of us laid a hand on any of the young ladies."

"But all of them were touched by the scandal of trying to meet an unknown man in secret."

"Yes." He lifted his glass to her in a toast. "I have already conceded it was improper for us to send the letters, to wager on them, and for the young ladies to respond to them. But it's egregious to me that Society would attempt to ruin a young lady's reputation over a secret admirer that never existed."

"Aside from the embarrassment it must have caused them, I can see where some fathers might think that if their daughter was willing to meet a secret admirer, she could be tempted to meet any gentleman in secret. A few could have even wondered if she'd actually done it before. It could have caused others to second-guess the young lady's virtue. I could go on with possibilities if you like?"

"No," he said dryly. "You mentioned enough. And all you said is probably true, but there seemed to be no lasting effects on any of them. When this rumor of possible revenge against us started last year, we checked on all the young ladies and from what we were able to find out, they are living quite happily now, despite their near ruination because of the letter."

"That's good to hear."

"It was for us, too," he said and enjoyed a sip of the wine. "Since we are on the subject of rumors and our past, is it true that you took a vow to never marry?"

She put her glass down. "Yes."

"Because you didn't want to marry Viscount Denningcourt."

It was slow in coming but she finally said, "Yes."

"But you didn't go into a convent. It seems I remember hearing you had."

Suddenly her eyes glowed with a genuine humor that he found so attractive, his lower body responded to the pull. Once again, he wanted to reach over and kiss her.

"That would have probably been fitting, Your Grace, but I wouldn't make a good nun and my uncle knew that. I am stubborn, not righteous. Even if I'd wanted to go to a nunnery and my uncle had agreed, I have no doubt the sisters would have sent me back to Switchingham before the end of the first day. I don't have the temperament to be submissive, and I believe that is a requirement for entering."

Hawk would agree to that. And that strength was one of the things that held his attention on her. He would much rather talk to a young lady with her honest approach to a conversation than the young ladies who were afraid to open their mouths and speak around him for fear they would say something to make him bored or, worse, angry.

Hawk studied her again as she picked up her glass and sipped her wine while staring at him. "So you made a vow to never marry. But did you make a vow of chastity as well?"

Though her gazed stayed intensely on his, he knew his question surprised her.

"Are they not one and the same, Your Grace?"

"I don't know, Miss Quick. It was your vow. You tell me."

Her hand remained steady and her eyes clear, yet he felt her tension increase. Her silence lengthened and he felt sure he knew why. She had not settled in her mind the answer to his question.

"Sorry to interrupt your dinner, Miss Quick."

The housekeeper stood at the doorway, worrying the hem of her apron in her hands. Hawk thought she must have been listening at the door and decided to step in and help her mistress.

"You're not, Mrs. Huddleston," Miss Quick said. "What do you need?"

"There's a young beggar at the back door looking for a piece of bread to eat."

"You know you don't have to ask me what to do if some-one is hungry. Give him more than he wants."

"Oh, yes, miss, I know. I told him to wait and I'd get him some, but I think you need to come see him, too. He doesn't look well to me, and I thought you'd want to know."

Hawk knew what the weather was like outside. "Well or not, no one should be out on a night like this."

"I agree," Miss Quick said. "We'll bring him inside, of course." She looked at the housekeeper. "Is he alone?"

"Appears to be. I asked him to step into the kitchen and warm himself, but he refused. Said he only wanted some bread and that he'd wait by the door for it. I came directly to tell you."

"I'm glad you did. Excuse me, Your Grace," she said, laying her napkin on the table. "I must attend to this."

"I'll come with you."

Hawk followed Miss Quick down the long, wide cor-ridor and into the kitchen. Three female servants he hadn't seen before were standing huddled near a table that held the remains from their supper. Mrs. Huddleston opened the back door and a blast of chilling air swept inside with a cold swoosh of wind. Hawk saw a boy of about twelve or thirteen looking pale as a ghost, shivering, and wet head-to-toe from the icy rain.

"Merciful heavens!" Miss Quick said earnestly and held out her hand to the lad. "Come inside at once."

But the beggar had already caught sight of Hawk, and for some reason that struck fear in him. He started to wob-ble on his feet. His eyes rounded and he jerked back as if he'd been struck. A split second later he turned and stag-gered away.

"No! Wait," Miss Quick called. "Don't go. We want to help you!"

Hawk knew the youngster would freeze to death if he tried to stay outside. He looked at Miss Quick. "I'll go find him and bring him back. You get him some dry clothes and something warm to drink and have it ready for when I return."

There was no time for Hawk to get his cloak. If he lost sight of the boy he might not locate him again with the night so dark. Hawk immediately rushed out in the direction the lad had vanished.

Icy sharp crystals slashed across Hawk's face and stung his eyes. Wet, blustery gusts of wind tore at his clothing, plastering it against his body as soon as he left the sanctuary of the roofed portico and started down the steps.

He lifted the collar of his coat against the frigid rain and trudged forward against the onslaught of sleet. Hawk's boots slid on the rapidly freezing ground, making it difficult for him to keep his balance. It was dark as Hades and Hawk almost lost sight of the rascal because of the stinging ice pellets hitting his eyes. He couldn't hear anything but the wind whipping around his ears.

"Damnation," he muttered to himself as his foot slipped on a frozen patch of earth again and he almost went down.

In the distance through the hazy air and stinging ice, he could barely see the movement of the boy. It looked as if he were half running and half stumbling.

Hawk picked up his pace, but it wasn't easy on the slippery ground. The youngster was fast, but Hawk was determined not to lose sight of him and let him get away. When Hawk was close enough, he reached out and grabbed the back of lad's coat. He grunted and kept pushing forward against the howling wind and ice. Suddenly all Hawk was holding was a coat. The imp had unbuttoned it so that it would be pulled off his arms.

Giving the coat a frustrated toss, Hawk exhaled sharply and kept running. This wasn't the first time the boy had bolted at the sight of a man. The imp was obviously used to being chased. He darted from side to side, trying to make it harder for Hawk to catch him. But Hawk wouldn't be fooled again. Waiting until he got closer the second time, Hawk grabbed the back of his shirt with one hand and clamped his other hand on the boy's shoulder and finally stopped him.

The boy swung around with both his fists flying in all directions. He grunted and hoarsely yelled, "Get away from me, ye cur! I didn't steal anything from ye fancy home."

"Stop fighting me," Hawk said to the lad, trying to catch his flailing arms and stop his panicked thrashing.

"Let me be, damn ye black soul! I didn't do anything to ye! Ye blackguard!"

From the boy's crude language, Hawk knew he wasn't a farmer's child who'd lost his way. But how could a street urchin find himself so far away from civilization?

"Calm down," Hawk grumbled while cold, hard crystals continued to hit his face. "I don't want to hurt you. I'm trying to save your life."

It must have taken the last of the ragamuffin's strength to strike out at Hawk. All of a sudden the youngster's body stilled. His eyes widened and rolled back in his head. He went limp and dropped like a sack of grain to the ground in a heap at Hawk's feet.

"Hellfire," Hawk muttered.

The sleet was brutal and unrelenting. He reached down and scooped the boy up in his arms. Over the whipping wind, a cracking noise sounded eerily in the quietness when he pulled the boy up to his chest. His clothing had already started to freeze, and no doubt his frail body had, too.

It crossed Hawk's mind that it might already be too late to save the lost lad.

Chapter 4

A proper gentleman should never tempt a lady to do
anything that might put a whisper of question to
her good name.

❧

*A PROPER GENTLEMAN'S GUIDE TO WOOING
THE PERFECT LADY*
SIR VINCENT TYBALT VALENTINE

Apprehension assailed her.

Loretta shivered and watched the gray darkness
swallow the duke. There had been a few times in her life
that she'd felt fear so raw and intense that had it collected
in her chest and throat, constricting her breathing.

And yet there was only one other time she could remember ever feeling such a sense of panic for someone's
life, and that was for her mother when she'd had pain in
her stomach and nothing she was given could make it go
away.

Loretta closed her eyes against the heartache of her
mother's suffering and loss of her life. It was long ago. Loretta was but a young girl of seven, yet she could remember it as if it had just been yesterday. She didn't like
recalling that time when she was so easily frightened by

the perils of life. There had been other times when she'd been fearful. When she'd defied her uncle's order to marry the viscount or take a vow that would forever change her life. But that had been a different kind of dread than what she felt now.

No one's safety had been in question.

Now there was.

Would the duke be able to keep up with the boy in the freezing storm? Did he have a family out there who needed help, too? Swirling around to the servants behind her, Loretta swept all that from her mind and said, "The duke is right. The boy can't stay in those wet clothes. Mrs. Huddleston, go to Paxton's room and bring a nightshirt and stockings. We'll find trousers to fit him later. Hazel, start a fire in Arnold's room. We'll put him in there to change. Nollie, prepare a warming pan to put at his feet. Bitsy, you go for extra blankets and start warming them so we can wrap him in them as soon as they return."

None of the four women moved. They all looked as shocked as she felt, or perhaps they just weren't as sure as she was that the duke would return with the boy in tow.

"Don't stand there staring at me," she said to the stricken women. "Go now."

Loretta whirled back to the open doorway. Watching the darkness was what she was going to do. She hugged her arms to her chest and stepped out. She thought the roof over the portico would keep her dry, but the howling wind immediately whipped at her hair and blew freezing rain into her face, causing her to shiver. The sheer sleeves of her velvet gown did nothing to help shield her from the weather, but she had to watch for them. It was the only thing she could do.

Her eyes searched the darkness, looking for any sign of the two. The only movement in the blustery storm was the barren branches of the surrounding trees. Seconds turned to minutes. Loretta's stomach started to quiver and her whole body shook, but she continued her watch.

If the duke didn't find the lad soon, they'd both catch a chill. The boy could already have one. He'd looked so deathly pale that it had frightened Loretta.

Where were they? Had the duke lost track of the youngster? Loretta's cold dress began to feel damp against her skin. Her nose, cheeks, and toes started to feel numb, but still she waited. She knew staying outside wasn't helping the duke find the boy, but she was determined that, if they could withstand the cold, so could she.

At last she saw movement. The duke walked out of the darkness toward her. He was carrying the lad. She stepped back inside and opened the door wider so they could enter without delay.

"What happened to him?" Loretta asked, closing the door behind them.

"He collapsed."

"Follow me," she said, leading the way out of the kitchen, down the wide corridor, and around a corner that led to Arnold's room. Hazel and Nollie were kneeling at the fireplace. Loretta flung back the covers on Arnold's bed and said, "Lay him down here. We must get his clothing off."

The duke laid him on the bed and turned to her. "Perhaps you should leave the room, Miss Quick. I can handle this."

Loretta stared down at the still, innocent-looking face. All color had drained from his lips and cheeks. His dark hair was wet and littered with fine crystals of ice. Her heart went out to the nameless boy.

She turned to the duke and said, "No. I want to help him."

"You are a lady."

"You are a duke," she countered.

"He will probably feel more comfortable when he wakes knowing that it was a man who undressed him and not a lady."

"Good heavens," she admonished, brushing aside his concern. "He's just a child. He won't care who undressed him. There's simply no need for you to worry about my sensibilities at a time like this. He needs help. I'll start with his shoes and you take off his other clothing, before it saturates the bedcovers."

With that she bent over the lad's feet and started untying his shoes. The wet, frozen laces had been knotted several times. She worked at the small, tight knots in the dim light, but they wouldn't budge. She tried just pulling the high-top boot off, but without undoing the laces, that wasn't going to work, either.

"Oh, gooseberries," she exclaimed under her breath and jerked her hands to her hips in frustration. "How could such a thin waif tie his strings so tight?"

The duke touched her shoulder, and she glanced up at him in surprise.

"Allow me to help you, Miss Quick." He reached down and pulled a small pearl-handled dagger from inside his boot and within seconds cut the laces all the way up the boot.

"Do you always have—"

"Yes," he answered before she finished her question.

"Thank you," she said and went back to her task.

Holes had been worn in the soles of the cheaply made boots, and as she tugged off the first one she realized that they were really too small for him. She wouldn't be surprised to find that his heels and toes had blisters on them. His stockings were in no better shape. Dirty, holey, and much too small. His trousers were worn at the knees, too short and frayed at the hem. Loretta had never been very good with a needle and she'd found out that her maid wasn't, either, but she would see to it that he had better clothing and coverings for his feet before he left her house.

Once the boots and stockings were removed, she lifted his cold feet and wrapped a blanket around them until the duke was ready to remove his trousers. When she looked back toward the lad, his shirt was off. His face was still. Not a twitch or flutter of his eyelids. His chest was rail-thin and a bluish white.

Loretta could have counted every rib if she'd had the courage to keep looking at him. Her throat closed and her heart went out to this youngster who'd been reduced to begging for food. It didn't seem right. Suddenly he didn't feel like a stranger, but a part of her household, and now her responsibility.

"I have some clothing," Mrs. Huddleston said, rushing up beside Loretta. "Oh, the poor dear," she whispered staring down on his frail body. "I'm here now. Out with the both of you," she said brushing her hands toward the duke. "I'll take care of him from here."

"We want to help him," Loretta said.

"I know," the housekeeper said. "You've already done more than you should. I've got the girls to help me. This isn't proper for either of you. Now go on, out with you. Go finish your dinner, your conversations, or what have you. Out."

Loretta looked at the duke, and he nodded. Perhaps it was time to let Mrs. Huddleston take over. She would know best what to do to warm him quickly.

"All right," Loretta said, looking at her housekeeper. "I'll check on him in a little while."

The duke looked down at Mrs. Huddleston, too, and said, "After you get him dressed and covered warmly, rouse him and give him something warm to drink. Do it often throughout the night."

"I will, Your Grace. I'll take good care of him."

"Thank you, Mrs. Huddleston."

The woman beamed a smile at him and turned to her task.

Loretta led the way out of Arnold's room and back the way they'd come and toward the dining room. She was chilled and shaken. And she desperately wanted the boy to be all right.

At the entrance to the dining room she stopped and asked, "Would you like to go back to the table? I don't believe dessert was served. I can do that."

The duke shook his head. "I think I have a brandy waiting for me in the drawing room, unless you'd like to go back to your dinner."

"No, I was finished." She turned and they walked back to the drawing room.

The corridor was wide in the old house, and the duke walked beside Loretta. She didn't turn to look at him but felt his presence. There was a calming sense of safety being so close to him. She entered the drawing room before the duke and walked over to the secretary where she'd left the glass of brandy she'd poured him earlier. The duke strode over the fireplace, picked up the poker, and stirred the embers before adding a piece of wood to the rekindling fire.

"I'm sorry we have so few servants here and you have to tend the fire yourself."

He turned back to her and, after a slight chuckle, said, "Though I seldom have the opportunity, I actually enjoy doing some things for myself." His gaze zeroed in on hers.

"Besides, there's something pleasing about stirring up warm, glowing embers."

Loretta had a suspicion he wasn't talking about the embers in the fireplace but the ones that had been simmering between the two of them all throughout the evening. She walked over and handed him the glass, holding it very close to the bottom so there would be no chance their fingers would touch. The sensations he'd stirred inside her last time were too confusing to repeat.

"Thank you," he said, and took a drink.

Loretta glanced toward the window. The storm hadn't abated. She could hear the sleet hitting the windowpanes and the howling wind whipping fiercely around the corners of the house. She breathed a sigh of relief that the duke had found the boy and that they were all safe inside. Shaking off the chill she felt, she rubbed her hands up and down her arms and moved closer to the fire. Her sleeves were damp from the short time she'd waited outside.

"I keep wondering what he was doing this far out. There are no other houses nearby, and it's almost half a day's ride to the village by carriage. We've had Gypsies once or twice stop and ask for food but not often. They don't usually travel this far out. Perhaps he could have been running away from someone and became disoriented and lost." She looked up at the duke and asked, "Did you have a chance to ask him anything?"

"No. He was already too weak to say much."

"Do you suppose he has a family who's out there lost somewhere in the cold, too? Should we go look for them?"

"No, Miss Quick. I can't say for sure, but I doubt anyone is with him. Judging from his worn clothing, he's probably been on his own for some time. He has the look of street urchins I've seen in London. Most likely he's been wandering around out here for days."

"Oh, no, Your Grace, I don't want to consider that possibility." She turned toward the fire and, without giving clear thought to exactly what she was going to say next, murmured, "It was just very disturbing seeing him looking so helpless. So cold. Thin."

The duke took hold of her arm and turned her to face him. "Here," he said and put the glass up to her lips. "Take a sip."

She shook her head and leaned away from him. "Oh, I couldn't possibly do that."

"Yes, you can. You're cold. It will warm you and help calm you."

"No, I'm all right. Really, it's just he appeared so lonely, neglected, and mistreated." The image of her mother lying in the bed, weak with pain so forceful she couldn't be still or quiet, flashed through Loretta's mind. "I don't want to see anyone suffering."

"Drink it," the duke commanded softly as the glass touched her lips again.

His expression was so comforting that Loretta opened her mouth and sipped. The thought of drinking from the duke's glass was so foreign to her, so intimate and unheard of, she hardly noticed the sting of the strong liquid on her tongue and at the back of her throat as she swallowed.

"Another," he said quietly.

There was something comforting about what he was doing and how softly he was speaking that she obeyed without further question.

He smiled at her. "I find it incredible that you are so strong you can not only hold your own with a duke, but give him a dressing-down, too, yet the sight of a poor derelict young beggar has you trembling."

"I'm not trembling," she argued defensively, but quickly

added, "Not exactly, anyway. But it's easy to worry about someone who is completely helpless. I won't apologize for that."

His eyes softened even more. "I wouldn't want you to. It doesn't astound me that you are a compassionate person. It pleases me."

"Anyone would be under the circumstances. He looked so lost and frightened when he saw you. And then when I saw how tattered his clothing was, I just wanted to help him."

He held the glass up to her lips for her to drink again. And she did.

"He's not suffering right now. I think it's best for you not to think about the boy at all until he wakes and we can talk to him and get answers."

"I suppose you're right," she answered, some of her unease about him fading, knowing he was safe and warm now at Mammoth House.

"That probably won't happen until tomorrow," the duke added. "I think we need to let him rest tonight."

She gazed up into the duke's green eyes. "It was kind of you to go out into the storm after him and then help undress him."

The duke finished off the brandy and placed the glass on the nearby table. "I may be a rake, Miss Quick, but I'm not heartless."

"Of course not. I would never think that you wouldn't help someone who was in such dire need of rescue."

"You helped him as well."

Loretta realized she was feeling calmer. Warmer. And for the first time in longer than she could remember, she felt softer. And still odder yet, she felt a strange closeness to the duke. It was as if both of them caring for the poor beggar had formed a bond between them, and she wondered if the duke felt it, too. Or perhaps what she was feeling was the direct effects of the brandy doing its job of relaxing her.

"Your hair is wet." She spoke quietly, letting her gaze stay on his eyes. "So is your coat. And for the second time today. You need to change out of your damp clothing."

"I am fine. But look at you. There are glistening droplets of water in your hair, too."

Feeling self-conscious, she lifted her hand to smooth her hair over her ear. First one side and then the other. "It was very windy outside."

"You shouldn't have stayed out on the portico watching for us."

"Everything was being handled inside. It was the only thing I could do to help."

"You missed a spot."

He reached up and brushed his fingertips through her hair along the crest of her ear. His touch startled her for an instant and she reached up to smooth her hair again. The duke caught her hand in his, and the warmth of his touch sizzled through her as he kissed the back of her hand. His kiss was so unexpected and gentle that Loretta's settled breathing became short, shallow gasps.

He continued to hold her hand in one of his while, with the other hand, he continued lightly threading his fingers through the side of her hair. A few strands tumbled from the chignon at her nape. The gentleness of his caress was soothing. Almost mesmerizing.

His fingers slipped farther down. Slowly, he outlined its shape before circling behind her ear to lightly caress the skin there and along the column of her neck.

The heat of his gentle touch seeped inside her soul. Her body soaked it up as if it were a dry cloth being submerged in a pan of cool water.

"Have you ever been kissed, Miss Quick?" He took her hand to his lips again. "On your lips."

His voice was husky and low, and the muted gleam in his eyes was seductive. She didn't want to be a victim caught under the sensual spell he was casting over her, but she had no will to fight what was happening between them. Loretta knew what their exchanged glances meant. Their mutual attraction was undeniable.

She stood there, barely breathing, and allowed him to titillate her with his compelling touch, provocative words, and anticipation of something more to come.

"Yes," she answered truthfully. "Viscount Denningcourt kissed me."

"Often?" he asked.

"Everyone has their own perception about things, about time. I don't know what you would consider often, Your Grace."

"Every time he saw you."

"No."

"More than once?"

She hesitated again and tried to pull her hand away, but his fingers tightened around hers. He wasn't letting go of her. His gaze remained firmly on her face, searching her eyes. His expression was so intense, her breaths became uncomfortably shallow.

"Yes," she admitted and looked down at the fire, needing to do something to distract from the tension that was building stronger between them with every second that passed. "But I only saw him a few times before the—" She stopped and looked back up at him again.

"The wedding?"

The *almost* wedding, she thought. Inhaling deeply, she turned back to the duke and stared into his searching eyes. "The planned wedding that never took place."

He nodded once. "I stand corrected. What did you think of the viscount's kisses?"

Another easy answer. "Nothing," she answered honestly.

A smile twitched the corners of the duke's handsome lips. "What did he say about them?"

Loretta lifted her chin and recalled the words. "That he was to be my husband and kisses were necessary."

The duke bent his head closer to hers. His gaze swept up and down her face, lingering on her lips for a few seconds before capturing her attention again. "Ah, Miss Quick, kisses shouldn't be necessary. They should be anticipated, desired, craved even, and most of all enjoyed. Tell me," he said, sliding his arms around her waist and catching her up against his chest. "Did he sweep you up in his arms with an urgent eagerness like this?"

She inhaled a sharp startled breath. A surprised "N-no" passed her lips. Not certain what he intended, her body stiffened in his strong embrace.

His sure hands slid up to the middle of her back and pressed her tightly against his chest, confining her with his warm, powerful body. "Did he hold you possessively like this and make you feel as if you were someone too precious to let go?"

"No," she whispered again on a raspy breath, trying to regain her composure before she completely lost herself in the wonderment of what he was doing and saying.

"Did his lips hover longingly just above yours as mine are now, just waiting for you to invite him to take a taste of you?"

"No," she said for the third time, but for some reason her tremulous voice made it sound more like a desperate moan.

His face came closer still, his mouth less than an inch

away from hers. His gaze was so penetrating, it was as if she were taking every breath he took. Excitement grew inside her. Her heart beat erratically and loudly in her chest, drowning out the sounds of the bits of ice hitting the windowpanes and the crackling of the fire behind them.

She wasn't a blushing eighteen-year-old as she had been the first time the viscount held her. She knew what she should do now. Push out of his arms. Run away. Scream, or at the very least try in some way to dislodge herself from his strong embrace that held her captive.

But reality was never quite as simple as it should be. The invitation he issued was far too seductive to rebuff. Against her better judgment and relying only on her feelings, she chose to stay in his arms.

The earl leaned his hard, muscular body closer into hers. She felt his strength, his heat, and though she'd never felt it before now, she understood the meaning of desire.

In a low and suggestive voice, he whispered, "Did he kiss you with such fervor your breath left your lungs and your knees turned so weak they wouldn't hold you? Did he make you feel like you were the only woman in the world who could satisfy his yearning for passion that churned like a raging storm in his soul?"

"No, of course not."

The duke's arms tightened around her even more and in a gruff whisper he said, "Then I'm going to do that for you, Miss Quick."

Chapter 5

It is never proper for a gentleman to even attempt
to kiss a proper young lady.

❧

A Proper Gentleman's Guide to Wooing
the Perfect Lady
Sir Vincent Tybalt Valentine

His voice was low. Persuasive.

A hasty puff of air forced past her lips, and it was
all she could do to not melt into a puddle of wanting. It
was too late to run or even deny what she was feeling. She
didn't know why or even how it had happened, but the
duke had her believing all he said. Stunned by the trail of
her own thoughts, she realized she wanted what the duke
had promised—a taste of unbridled passion.

Gazing into his summer-green eyes, she felt hot, excited. An uncommon eagerness to explore these new inner
desires had enveloped her. She didn't know exactly what
the duke was going to do, but she knew without a shadow
of doubt she wanted him to kiss her and to do it now.

His face descended closer, her eyes closed, and his lips
lightly brushed hers with warmth, sweetness, and the merest

amount of pressure. At first she didn't really know what to do. She remained still. But then her lips softened beneath his, her mouth softened and she joined the kiss. Slowly, curls of pleasure budded into life and opened inside her. The pressing of their lips together was tender, languid, and powerful. There was no other word to describe the feelings but *glorious*.

Instinct took over. She had never been kissed like this, but it didn't take long for her to learn how to follow the movements of his lips. Her body relaxed and, without conscious effort, she lifted her arms and let them slide slowly around his neck. She leaned her body into his, feeling as if she were melting into him. His lips moved seductively back and forth over hers, sending shimmers of sensations spiraling through her.

The touch of his lips to hers was delicate. Feathery. So enticing she couldn't deny herself these moments caught up so passionately in his embrace. Their kisses continued and her stomach quivered deliciously. She opened her mouth and willingly accepted his tongue with a sigh of magical discovery as he teased and played with the tip of her own. Her hands roamed over and around his wide shoulders and then slid down his strong, damp back.

Some kisses lingered, others were short, but all were abundantly delicious. She welcomed and savored each one. She responded to each by matching his movements and sighs. The endearments of passion stretched and melted them together in a sea of pleasure. His lips left hers and kissed across her cheek, over her chin, and down her neck to the strand of pearls she wore, and then back up to settle on her mouth again. Chills of thrilling desire rushed through her.

Loretta felt his breath on her ear before she heard his

whispered words, "Oh, yes. You feel as if you belong here in my arms."

Strangely, she felt that way, too, but instead of letting him know she agreed with his assessment, she said, "I didn't realize it would be so difficult to breathe while kissing."

"That is a good way to feel, is it not?" He smiled against her lips. "That is supposed to happen. You are meant to be breathless, weak-kneed, and eager when you are kissed."

"Yes, all of that and more," she answered, loving, craving that giddy and breathless feeling that she'd always expected would come with kisses from a man.

The duke's hand moved to the center of her back to press her tightly against him. The other slowly came around her rib cage to fully cup her breast in his large, gentle hand.

Loretta gasped, moaned, and then sighed contentedly. Through her clothing, he lifted and massaged her breast. His gentle fingers pressed into the soft swell of her flesh above her gown as his palm kneaded into the weight of it. Pleasure like she'd never known washed warmly over her and consumed her.

It was madness.

And it was wrong.

She shouldn't allow the duke such unrestrained freedom to be so intimate with her. Yet how could she deny herself these exquisite feelings that had taken control of her senses, her body, and her mind? They were pure luxury, and she was completely overwhelmed by all the new sensations swirling through her.

A tightening developed between her legs. The thrill of all that was happening to her and inside her body was overwhelming. She clung desperately to the duke because, as he'd promised, she didn't feel her legs were going to hold her up.

The duke let his lips hover above hers while his gaze seemed to devour hers and his hand slowly, gently massaged her breast.

"Are you anticipating my next kiss, Miss Quick?"

"Yes," she whispered on a ragged breath. She couldn't wait for his lips to touch hers again.

"Tell me what your thoughts are about kissing now?"

"That perhaps I misunderstood Viscount Denningcourt when he said they were necessary."

The corner of his mouth lifted in doubt. "How so?"

"Necessary in that you needed them and wouldn't want to live without them, and now—"

"And now what?"

"I know why someone might desire them, crave them."

"And you've never felt those yearnings for kissing before?"

"Not until now." Loretta lifted her head and placed her lips on his. She felt him smile and heard him chuckle before he joined her kiss.

The pressure of their lips became harder, deeper, and longer. His hands continued to caress her breasts, her waist, and over her bottom, cupping her to the hardness beneath his trousers. Loretta welcomed the urgent, demanding passion she sensed in him.

She didn't know how it had happened but she realized her hands were inside his coat, feeling the corded muscles in his shoulders and back beneath the fine fabric of his shirt. It was magical. Heavenly and exciting to explore the breadth and shape of his strong body. This unexpected opportunity might never come her way again. She wanted to go wherever this new discovery, this awakening of senses she didn't even know existed, was going to take her.

But then slowly, leaving short kiss after short kiss upon

her lips, the duke raised his head and looked down into her eyes. Her heart fluttered, her abdomen tightened again, and her womanhood clinched. He was questioning her with his expression, asking with his eyes if he should continue being the rake who was seducing her—caring not that she was an innocent, a lady—or if he should be a gentleman and step away.

They both knew the folly of continuing, and that was why he silently asked. If they carried through with this encounter and she invited him into her bedchamber, she would be forever changed. He would not. She would no longer be an innocent maiden. That she could accept, but what would she do if he left her with a child because of their union? Again, the duke's life would not change. He would go about his daily routine and Society wouldn't blink an eye should they find out. She, on the other hand, would have to tell her uncle she was with child.

He'd banished her to Mammoth for not marrying the man he wanted her to marry. That was already a burden that she had struggled to bear. She didn't want to think about what the earl would do to her, how he would treat her if she was expecting a babe. There was no way she could rely on her brother for help. He was completely supported by the earl, too. On her own, she would have no way to care for a child.

With that stark realization, Loretta knew what she must do.

It took all her courage and then some, but she gave the duke one long passionate kiss and then pushed out of his arms. Backing away from him on unsteady legs, she moistened her lips and managed to say, "I need to check with Mrs. Huddleston on how my second unexpected guest for the evening is doing." Loretta pulled on the waistline of her dress to resettle it over her bosom.

The duke held his questioning gaze steady, relentlessly on hers. "I'll go with you to check on the lad before I go up."

"Are you sure?"

"I want to tell your housekeeper to feel free to call on me during the night if she thinks I can be of help to her."

"That's very kind of you." Loretta took in a deep breath and held it for as long as she could before adding, "Before we go, you need to know that the answer to your question is yes."

A spark of surprise gleamed in the duke's eyes, and he took a step toward her. "I'm glad. Which room is yours?"

He was such a fearless rake. So clever. So enticing.

She was tempted to put all her earlier worries aside and go with her heart's desire.

Almost tempted beyond her strength to say no.

But thankfully her sanity and willpower hadn't completely left her. With an inner strength she would have sworn a few moments ago she no longer possessed, she smiled softly and said, "I think you must have forgotten what question you asked."

His brow wrinkled, and his head tilted just a fraction. "No, Miss Quick. I'm quite sure I left you with no doubt about what I was asking of you just now."

"Yes, but I was answering your earlier question about whether my vow to never marry was also a vow of chastity." Trying to leave all uncertainty out of her voice, she finished by saying, "And the answer is yes."

The corners of his eyes narrowed just enough to be perceptible, just enough to let her know he didn't like her answer. "I must admit I'd forgotten that question was even between us—anymore."

Once again Loretta had no one to blame or to thank but herself for the position she was in. And such a tumultuous position it was. This was her opportunity—maybe her only opportunity—to lie with a man. A man she greatly desired, but Loretta wasn't naive or simpleminded to the hazards. She had already thought about the realities of what was between them. Whether or not she ever saw him again, there could be a great cost for a night in his arms.

It wasn't a risk she was willing to take.

The silence between them stretched to an almost unbearable length until finally she found the courage to say, "I was wrong. I shouldn't have let you kiss me, but—"

The duke scowled and shook his head. "Please don't blame it on the brandy I gave you to drink, Miss Quick."

"No, I wouldn't," she argued. "It was something far more common than that and probably ages older as well. It was simply an urgent desire to be kissed by you."

She saw in his eyes that he appreciated her honesty, though he still wasn't happy she had, in effect, rebuffed his advances. It was a shame that he would never know how difficult that had been for her. For if she ever were to recant her vow, it would be tonight.

He looked away for a moment and then back to give her another intense stare. "Desire is a very strong emotion."

Now vividly aware of that, she expelled an exhausted breath and whispered, "So I found out."

"It's also difficult to control."

Oh, yes. She had discovered that as well. Once again she had to rely on her inner strength and answer him as truthfully as she could. "But it's not impossible, which is why at times it must be harnessed, as just now. I made the vow, and I will remain true to it."

"That is disappointing," he said.

She softened her expression, hoping to convey to him the sincerity she was feeling.

"For both of us," she answered and turned away.

Chapter 6

A gentleman should never leave a proper lady
questioning what his intentions are.

~•~

*A PROPER GENTLEMAN'S GUIDE TO WOOING
THE PERFECT LADY*
SIR VINCENT TYBALT VALENTINE

Hawk splashed cold water on his face and winced at
the chill it gave him. He picked up the small towel
and dried his face as he shoved back the drapery panel and
looked out the window. It was still snowing when he'd gone
to bed last night. Surprisingly, this morning the gray storm
clouds of yesterday were gone, and bright sun glistened
across the white, barren landscape.

That was a rare sight this time of year.

He quickly donned his trousers and boots, and then
combed his fingers through his hair. Rubbing his hand
across the day-old growth of beard on his cheeks and chin,
he looked into the small mirror on the chest. There was
nothing he could do about his stubble. The housekeeper
hadn't offered him a razor and soap.

It hadn't taken long for his thoughts to turn to Miss

Quick once he'd awakened. That she was lovely, engaging, and innocent was a powerful draw for him. He glanced back at the bed. He hadn't wanted to spend the night alone. Neither of them had tried to deny the attraction that had formed between them almost at first sight. He had little doubt that if he'd continued his seduction of her she would have willingly come to him, but he'd had to give her the opportunity to think about the consequences.

His honor demanded it.

And her honor prevailed.

Hawk pulled his shirt over his head and hurriedly stuffed it into his trousers. Next he grabbed his waistcoat and buttoned it before reaching for his wrinkled and limp neckcloth. How could he not think about Miss Quick after the way his body had responded to her? Not to mention the array of different emotions she'd caused him to experience over the course of his few hours with her. Especially since it'd never crossed his mind he might meet Quick's sister when he'd headed to Mammoth house yesterday morn.

First she'd irritated the hell out of him, when she as good as demanded he tell her what he wanted with her brother, and then had the nerve to take him to task for it when he did. She compounded his ire by suggesting his sister was selfish. He still couldn't believe she wouldn't want a very lucrative betrothal for her brother.

She'd made him laugh at her cleverness when she'd said the secret admirer letter had been read around the world, and she'd enchanted him with her honest, thoughtful conversation about her past. Hawk had felt admiration for her when she'd stood watch on the portico and insisted she help undress the boy. He'd bet anyone a handful of coins no other lady would have touched those cold muddy boots. Most, if not all, of the ladies he knew would have either

fainted or rushed from the room in tears at the pitiful condition of the lad. That included all the mistresses he'd
known over the years, too.

Not Miss Quick.

She rallied against his attempts to shield her from the
uglier realities of life. That the boy's stockings were soiled
and wet, and his laces knotted several times had been no
deterrent to her soft hands or delicate sensibilities. She had
immediately gone to work to remove them. And then . . .

Hawk smiled as the sensual feelings of desire he had
for her came to mind and washed over him like summer's
first breeze. She'd tempted him sorely to forgo his honor,
his vow to never take a young lady's innocence when he'd
held her in his arms, kissed her, and explored her shape.
She had him experiencing a depth of passion he hadn't felt
in a long time, if ever. He'd wanted nothing more than to
take her to his bedchamber and make her his.

The hell of it was that his passion for her hadn't ebbed
with the light of day. If the throb in his lower body at this
moment was any indication, it had increased. But now was
not the time to linger over thoughts of his desire for the
lovely miss. His long, cold ride back to Grimsfield would
be the perfect time to do that.

Grabbing his coat, Hawk pushed the tempting remembrances from his mind and headed out the door. The first
thing he wanted to do was check on the boy. He'd told
Mrs. Huddleston to come for him if things didn't go well
during the night. He hadn't heard from the woman and
hoped that meant the lad had made it through with no ill
effects. If so, Hawk intended to have a word or two with
him about his foul language before leaving Mammoth
House. He was certain Miss Quick wasn't used to a street
urchin's guttersnipe tongue.

Hawk made his way down the stairs then along the long

corridor past the drawing room, dining room, and kitchen, around the corner, and into the small room where they'd laid the youngster last night. Miss Quick sat on the edge of the bed with her back to the door. She rose and turned toward him when he entered the room. He hadn't expected to find her eyes filled with uncertainty.

Because of him?

The lad?

She wore a plain dress of light-blue wool banded with a satin sash at the high waist. A dark-green shawl fitted loosely across her slim shoulders. Her hair was unadorned and in a tidy chignon at the back of her head. He was struck once again by how beautiful she was even when wearing the simplest of clothing.

Hawk knew at once she was troubled. Concern etched the corners of her mouth and around her eyes. But for which reason? Was it for the condition of the boy who'd stolen his way into her life, or for the way she'd responded to their stolen kisses last night?

Their gazes held for a brief moment before she said, "Good morning, Your Grace."

"Miss Quick," he answered, stopping beside her and the pale-faced, sleeping child. He lay as still as a windless day, covered in blankets up to his chin. It didn't appear there was any change in his condition, but still Hawk asked, "How is he this morning?"

"He developed a fever during the night," she said, looking down at the poor lad.

Hawk blew out a short breath of concern. That wasn't good and it wasn't a surprise. He'd known last night that the youngster was ill.

"Any coughing?" he asked.

"No."

"That's a hopeful sign."

"Mrs. Huddleston is making a poultice right now for his chest that she thinks will help keep his lungs clear. She's preparing him something for the fever, too."

Hawk didn't like seeing the worry in her eyes. It made him want to take her in his arms and soothe her. Smooth the wrinkle from her troubled brow. He didn't want the boy to be sick, but it was good to know her concern wasn't because she regretted what had happened between them last night.

He asked, "Was she able to get him to take nourishment?"

"A few sips of broth from a spoon throughout the night," Miss Quick answered, rubbing her hands together as if they were cold. "Mrs. Huddleston said it wasn't easy, and she was sure it wasn't nearly enough. We'll continue throughout the day."

Doubts that the lad would make it crossed Hawk's mind. They had no way of knowing how long he'd been out in the freezing cold or how long since he'd had a proper meal. The only thing Hawk knew to do was to get him help before it was too late.

"He was ill when he came to your door. You know that, don't you?"

She glanced up at Hawk with anxious eyes. "It did appear he wasn't well, but I had hoped that wasn't the case."

"Content yourself with the fact you are doing all you can for him now. He's in a warm, soft bed. Safe. You will do all you can for him, so try not to worry about what will become of him in the days ahead."

She gave Hawk a twitch of a smile and wrapped her green woolen shawl tighter around her shoulders. "That's difficult to do since he is now under my roof and, thereby, under my care."

"I know he won't lack proper attention." And he hoped she wouldn't blame herself if the lad didn't make it.

Her gaze swept up and down his face as if she were searching for something. "What about you? I hope you aren't feeling any ill effects from being out in the storm last night."

Hawk's chest tightened for a second. He liked the fact that she asked after his welfare. "I'm fine. You?"

"Yes, of course. I wasn't out in the cold for very long, and I didn't get wet."

His brows drew together. "Are you sure about that? I seem to remember ice crystals in your hair and a dampness to your sleeves."

"All right, not very wet," she amended almost reluctantly. "And I trust your sleep was sound."

Oh, hell, he thought selfishly. Did she have to remind him of sleeping, which reminded him of the bed, which reminded him that he'd wanted her there with him last night?

"I slept well," he answered.

"Good. Mrs. Huddleston has tea, chocolate, and coffee set up in the breakfast room. Whichever you prefer. Toast, preserves, eggs, and cheese as well, if you'd like."

"I want to check on the mare first."

She nodded slightly. "Since the storm has passed, I expect Mr. Huddleston to arrive soon. I'm sure they were worried about us with the weather so grave, and no doubt he and Arnold were up and on their way at first light."

"I'll plan to leave for Grimsfield as soon as Mr. Huddleston arrives, so I may not see you again. When I get to the village, I'll send an apothecary, or physician, or whoever I can find to check on him." Hawk inclined his head toward the lad.

Hope flared in her eyes. "Thank you. That would be so kind of you. I wouldn't have asked it of you, but I'm glad you offered. I believe he does need more than we have here to provide."

"I knew you'd probably turn Mr. Huddleston around and send him back for one."

"I'm not sure I find it comforting that you know me so well after such a short time in my presence, but yes, I would have immediately sent him to fetch someone."

"I'll take care of it."

She nodded. "There is an apothecary there. I believe he will come if you ask him. Our medicinal supplies are meager here, and Mrs. Huddleston can only do so much."

"I'll see that your horse is returned today and I'll make arrangements for the mare to be returned to the innkeeper once she's sound, but that may take longer."

"There will be no hurry. Arnold will enjoy taking care of the horse until it can be returned."

"You'll tell your brother that I came to see him?"

A soft, short laugh parted her beautiful lips just enough to make him wish that he were kissing her again.

"Without delay, Your Grace. You may count on that. And the reason for your visit."

He saw that unbendable determination in her expression and humor in her eyes. Both traits drew him. She wouldn't waver from what she saw as her duty to counsel her brother on the ills of arranged marriages. That didn't bother Hawk. It satisfied him. He liked a good fight. And he always expected to win.

"I never considered that you wouldn't tell him," Hawk assured her. "Add that I'll be back next Thursday." He paused. "I'll expect him to be here waiting. And that you and he will keep everything about this visit and this proposal quiet and between only yourselves."

She lifted her shoulders just enough to make her appear defiant. "The last thing I want is for anyone, least of all Paxton's friends, to know of this proposition. They would be encouraging him to accept the offer posthaste. The lot of them would be thrilled to have a friend who was married to a duke's sister, hoping that it would in some way benefit them, if only to give them something to crow about. It is my hope that no one other than the three of us ever hears about this, Your Grace."

Hawk chuckled. When she was opposed to something, he wasn't sure anything could daunt her spirit.

"I would hope your brother will listen to all you have to say but that in the end, he will make up his own mind about what will be best for him and not let you decide for him."

She moistened her lips and swallowed. "Certainly. He will. He is his own man. However, there's really no need for you to return to Mammoth House. I'm sure Paxton won't mind traveling to London to see you. He seldom stays here for long stretches anyway."

A grin lifted one corner of Hawk's mouth. "If I didn't know better, Miss Quick, I would think that you don't want to see me again."

She moved farther away from the bed and pulled her shawl tighter again. "I'm only trying to keep you from making the long and unnecessary journey back here."

"No." He walked over to stand close to her again. "You are trying to keep me from coming back to see you."

He liked that she didn't cower from his nearness but looked him straight in the eyes and said, "I do think that would be best."

Her honesty gave Hawk another moment of conscience. Was she really the reason he wanted to return? Admittedly he was more than a little infatuated with her. And yes, he wanted to see her again, but to what end other than he desired her? He didn't know. And wanting to find the answer to that was going to bring him back.

"I'll want to check in and see how he's doing." Hawk quirked his head toward the boy again. "With the excellent care he is going to receive from you and Mrs. Huddleston, I expect he'll be ready to travel by the time I return. I'll see to it that he gets back to Grimsfield, or London, or wherever it is he came from."

"What if he doesn't want to go back where he came from?" Her expression turned worried once again. "I mean, whoever he was with didn't take proper care of him. He could have been with someone who mistreated him. Perhaps he ran away to save himself and that is why he's on his own."

She wasn't going to be easily placated concerning the boy, and Hawk knew that if it was already too late to save him, Miss Quick wouldn't take the news well.

"Then I'll take him wherever he wants to go."

That seemed to satisfy her a little better. Her shoulders relaxed and her breathing settled to a calm rhythm. Hawk should have left his words at that, but he seldom knew when to leave well enough alone.

Without much forethought, he bent his head closer to hers and added, "Besides, Miss Quick, I think you want to see me again."

She stiffened. "I believe you might be speaking for yourself and how you feel, Your Grace, but you are not speaking for me."

"I am speaking for both of us and, whether you will admit it or not, you know I speak the truth. We have a battle going on, you and I. And it won't surprise you to know that I never walk away from a fight. I don't think you do, either."

"Not if I believe it's winnable, and I believe this one is."

"So do I."

"You know I will counsel my brother against contemplating any kind of betrothal arrangement with you concerning your sister."

He nodded once. "I know, but that's not the battle I was talking about just now."

Her forehead furrowed and her eyes searched his face again. Her breathing became more labored. "What other battle could you possibly be referring to?"

Hawk knew she had no idea what he was talking about, because he'd had no inclination of it himself until that moment. But now he knew it as clearly as he knew his own name.

A second or two passed before he answered, "The battle for you, Miss Quick."

Chapter 7

A gentleman should never be talking to one
young lady and allow his thoughts to wander
to different young lady.

*A Proper Gentleman's Guide to Wooing
the Perfect Lady*
Sir Vincent Tybalt Valentine

Hawk was sure there were worse things than being the
guardian of a younger sister but at the moment he
didn't know what they were. He stood in the vestibule of
his London town house shaking his head. Adele was the
last person he expected to see upon his arrival back in
Town. He would have immediately assumed something
was seriously wrong at Hawksthorn if not for the sparkle of warmth and happiness showing in her light-green
eyes.

"What the devil are you doing here?" he asked, removing his hat and tossing it onto the side table.

"I came to see you, of course," she answered in her
usual perky manner.

"To see me?" Exasperated, Hawk dragged his cloak
from around his shoulders and glared at her. "Alone? In

the dead of winter? Whatever for? I saw you less than a month ago at Hawksthorn."

"First, I wasn't alone." She smiled, took the cloak from his hands, and laid it beside his hat. "I had Minerva, a footman, a driver, and, of course, my maid with me. The same group as when I travel to London with you. And how ridiculous of you to suggest it's the dead of winter with spring only weeks away. The roads weren't bad at all. And why are you looking so glum? I thought you'd be happy to see me."

"Did you really?" he asked, waving away the servant who'd walked into the vestibule to greet him.

"Yes, of course I did."

It irritated Hawk all the more that Adele didn't seem to have any idea how foolish she'd been to travel to London without him as her escort. She could have been in grave danger if the coach had been set upon by highwaymen. Armed footman or not.

He would speak to Minerva about allowing her to undertake this folly. Not that it would do any good. Adele had her older cousin wrapped tightly about her finger. Minerva would never object to anything Adele wanted. His sister had been allowed to have her way since the day she was born to his aging parents. When they died within weeks of each other from a relentless plague of dysentery, Minerva had come to live at Hawksthorn and had followed their lead concerning Adele.

"Don't be so cross with me, Hawk." She clasped her hands together in front of her skirt and looked positively joyous. "I have the most wonderful news that I knew you'd want to hear right away. Miss Wiggins is going to have puppies! Soon!"

By the devil! Hawk could have bit nails. "You came to London to tell me that?"

"I thought you'd be happy to hear. You know how much I love Miss Wiggins."

"I would have been happy to hear it when I returned to Hawksthorn. I don't like you traveling to London without me and especially when I don't even know you are coming."

He didn't like returning home from a grueling carriage ride over bumpy roads, cold, tired, and ready to settle in front of the fire with a glass of brandy and think about Miss Quick, only to find his sister standing in the doorway expecting him to be delighted with her presence.

Hawk loved his sister but she was work. She wanted to be taken care of—which was fine, but along with that she had an independent streak that was difficult to manage at times. Now that she was of marriageable age it was time someone other than Hawk took on the job.

"Your bluster is not going to diminish my enthusiasm," Adele declared confidently.

That he was certain. Not much did.

"I know you're weary from your journey and need to relax. Come into the drawing room and I'll pour you a glass of your favorite brandy."

With that she turned and headed down the corridor.

"I can pour my own drink," he muttered to himself and then breathed in deeply as he tossed his gloves on top of his cloak.

He couldn't wait to deliver her to a husband so *he* could worry about her. The years he'd been her guardian had been a struggle. Perhaps he could have pushed thoughts of her welfare aside, left her to the threat of possible mischief while she searched for a husband at the balls, parties, and teas, if she weren't so easy to love.

Spoiled though she may be, Adele didn't have a malicious word to say or think about anyone. She wasn't mean-spirited, or ill-tempered. She had a simple, engaging charm about her, and because she had no callousness or heartlessness in her soul she couldn't see it in other people. Which was why he didn't want her to attend the Season and be subjected to every bachelor who wanted to marry a duke's sister. If there was the slightest possibility of anyone wanting to embarrass her or sully her reputation because of what he did years ago, Hawk wanted to preempt it.

"You know Miss Wiggins isn't the only reason I'm here," Adele said as he walked into the drawing room behind her.

"No, I don't know," Hawk answered, making himself comfortable in one of the upholstered armchairs by stretching his legs out in front of the fireplace while she made herself busy with the decanter.

"Well, it would have been silly of me to come all this way just to tell you that."

Hawk grunted a laugh and brushed his hair away from his forehead. Did she really think he hadn't already thought of that?

She handed him the glass of brandy. Hawked smiled up at her and said, "Thank you."

Adele smiled, too, knelt down beside him, and said, "I couldn't wait until you decided to return to Hawksthorn to hear what Mr. Quick had to say about an arrangement between us."

"Why not?"

"Because I didn't know when you'd return. You stay away from Hawksthorn for weeks at a time."

There was no way Hawk was going to enlighten his innocent sister to the fact there were few things at the family estate to satisfy the appetites of a twenty-eight-year-old man. There were no friends to play cards, throw dice, or fence with. There were no fighting clubs to attend, no horse races to watch, no deep political discussions to argue. Most of all, there were no women to enjoy. In fact, his father's collection of fine brandy, which he stopped and took a sip of, was about the only thing he could indulge in when he was there.

"We've discussed this before, Adele. I am not your doting father. I am your brother and there are commitments that keep me here in London. I told you I would return to Hawthorn as soon as I had talked to Mr. Quick. You should have waited there for me."

"Oh!" She rose from her knees with a huff and a whirl of skirts. "You teased me by saying you have found the perfect husband for me and then you go away and I don't see you for a month."

"I never said he was perfect. Only that I think the two of you would suit. I told you this would take time. If you are uneasy about a prearranged marriage tell me now and we can forget about it."

She folded her hands across her chest and stared down at him in disbelief. "Why should I want to choose my own husband when you can do it for me? You know all these men—their families, their habits, their pockets. I don't."

"Most young ladies want to choose their own husbands."

"But most young ladies are not the daughter and the sister of a duke. Why should I go to all that trouble of sorting them out when you can do it for me? Papa always told me he would see to it that I married a young man who would be perfect for me. Now that he's gone it's up to you to do that for me."

"And I will," he answered patiently. "You must allow me the time to do it. I've just returned from trying to see Mr. Quick. He wasn't at home."

"Oh," she said curiously. "Why not?"

"I really have no idea. Miss Quick, his sister, wasn't very forthcoming about his whereabouts."

"You didn't tell me he had a sister." Adele's eyes lit with sparkles, and she knelt beside him again. "What is she like?"

A warmth settled over Hawk. He remembered Miss Quick standing in front of the glowing fireplace, looking like an angel. He remembered her delicate hands as she gently removed the cold, muddy boots from the sick lad.

Hawk looked back to his sister and said, "You. In certain ways, she's like you."

"What are those certain ways?" she asked excitedly. "Tell me now."

"She's gentle and kind but she's also very outspoken just as you are. She wants her way about everything. And I do believe she loves her brother as much you love yours."

Adele laughed. "She sounds positively charming. She and I should get along together grandly. I'm glad the brandy is calming you. I do enjoy being with you when you aren't cross with me."

"I never intend to be cross," he admitted, doing his best to give her a contrite expression.

"I know, but—oh, Hawk, I just had an idea. Since you can't find Mr. Quick, let's invite him to Hawksthorn."

"What?"

"Invite him to come see me. We'd talked about me meeting him before we settle anything."

"But that was going to be after you made your curtsy before the queen and are officially on the marriage mart."

"What a bore that will be. I want to meet Mr. Quick now and I think I should. Besides, what good does it do to be the sister of a duke if I can't break the rules? If you want me engaged by the time the Season starts, I really need to meet him now. And I'd like to be acquainted with his sister as well. I want her to come, too."

Hawk sat up straighter in the chair. "Miss Quick?"

"I'm intrigued by what you said about her. Besides, Miss Wiggins should have her puppies by the time a visit can be arranged. You can judge a lot about a person by how they treat puppies, don't you think?"

Hawk felt a kick in his breathing. He remembered Miss Quick being in his arms. Her soft lips, her warm body, and the whispered satisfied sighs of enjoyment while he kissed her. Suddenly his mind started reeling with the possibilities of Miss Quick visiting his estate. Yes, he very much liked the idea of her coming to Hawksthorn with her brother.

Perhaps Hawk was happy his sister had come to London after all.

"Yes, Adele, you're right." He cupped her chin affectionately. "You can judge a person by how they handle puppies." *And sickly beggar boys, too.*

Chapter 8

A few lines of self-written romantic poetry is the
perfect gift for a gentleman to present to a lady.

∼⟡∼

*A Proper Gentleman's Guide to Wooing
the Perfect Lady*
Sir Vincent Tybalt Valentine

Farley.

Loretta worked the dark-gray yarn with her knitting needles and watched him from a large, comfortable wingback chair she'd moved over by the one window in the small room. His pain-racked cough had started before the apothecary had arrived from Grimsfield a few days ago. It was deep, throaty, and hoarse. A wet cloth that she often dipped in a basin of cool water lay on his hot forehead. His chest rose and fell with loud, long, labored breathing.

The apothecary had assessed what Loretta had already realized. Farley was gravely ill. The man didn't know if the boy's frail, lean body could fight off the fever and weakness that had developed in his lungs. Before leaving the next morning, the apothecary gave them a plethora of tinctures, tonics, poultices, and medical herbs of varying kinds along with instructions on how to use them all.

There was nothing more he could do.

During one of the boy's semi-lucid moments yesterday, he'd answered "Farley" when she'd asked his name. Through most of his wakefulness he mumbled delirious, unintelligible words before slipping back into a fidgety sleep. Occasionally he would groan and thrash about wildly in the bed. From time to time she'd rouse him and force him to swallow a spoonful of broth or an herbal concoction Mrs. Huddleston had mixed for him before he'd succumb to fitful sleep again.

Though she was only seven years of age when her mother had died, Loretta remembered a few things about her mother's care. For one, she was never to be left alone. Loretta didn't intend for Farley to be alone, either. All the servants helped see to that by taking turns sitting with him, including Arnold, who hadn't seemed to mind that he'd had to give up his own room to the stranger.

Loretta tried to remain positive by thinking of the future. If the Duke of Hawksthorn's observation was correct and Farley was indeed a street child, without family and with no place to call home, Mammoth House would be the best place for him.

Once Farley was well enough, she'd ask her uncle if he could stay and be a part of her household. There certainly was plenty of room. He could learn how to help Arnold care for the horses, or plant and tend to the herb and vegetable gardens. The two cows had to be milked each day, and the eggs had to be gathered. There were any number of daily chores and other animals that needed attention. The house and grounds were so extensive that there was always something that needed to be cleaned, repaired, moved, or taken away.

Farley shouldn't require much payment, if any, since he was so young. Perhaps just a place to live and food to eat would be enough to tempt the lad to stay—if he had no place to go. The main thing was that he could start learning how to do something other than beg for a loaf of bread at a stranger's door.

The knitting needles went still in her hands and she rested them on the ball of yarn. Besides, it was easier on her to think about Farley than to think about the duke. When she thought about him, she remembered stimulating conversations, sharing a meal, and tasting a sip of brandy with him from his glass. She remembered being in his arms, being touched, and—and yes, thinking about Farley was much less stressful for her.

But despite her best efforts, she thought often about the duke and wondered what he meant when he'd said they were in a battle for her. Did it mean he wanted to kiss her again? That he intended to seduce her and go even further given the opportunity? Maybe he knew that deep inside, her resolve was weaker than she proclaimed. Her fear was that maybe he could win her over. She was not immune to him as she had been to the viscount.

"Miss Quick?"

Loretta turned to see her maid standing in the doorway. Bitsy was a robust, rawboned young woman with one of the softest voices Loretta had ever heard. At her first interview, Bitsy had told Loretta she knew her size didn't match her name but that her mother never expected her to grow so tall.

Bitsy didn't know much about being a lady's maid, but Loretta hadn't been left with many choices after word spread among the servants about the isolation of Mammoth House. Neither of her first two maids had been able to tolerate the loneliness of not even having a village to walk to once a week and had left her after only a few months of service.

So far, there hadn't been any signs of restlessness or regret from the young woman, and Loretta hadn't heard any complaints from Bitsy since she came to work almost a year ago. Not having a social life outside the other servants hadn't seemed to bother her at all. When there wasn't much for her to do for Loretta, she made herself useful to Mrs. Huddleston, which made her and the housekeeper happy.

"I came to tell you right away just like you asked me to," Bitsy said. "I saw Mr. Quick riding up to the front of the house."

"Oh, wonderful!" Loretta exclaimed excitedly, swinging the knitting over to the table beside her chair and slipping her feet back into her slippers before jumping up. "Yes, thank you for letting me know. And please stay with Farley for me."

Loretta picked up the hem of her skirt and hurried toward the front of the house. She made it to the vestibule just as Paxton was walking through the doorway with a carefree bounce to his steps. He took off his hat when she stopped and smiled.

Her brother was such a handsome man. Tall, and thin as a reed. His thick, wavy blond hair, which had been creased by his hat, swept low across his forehead. His blue eyes sparkled and danced with a happiness that never quite seemed to leave even when he was angry or sad.

She laughed and rushed up to him. Paxton threw his hat onto the table and took hold of her upper arms. He quickly pressed a cold kiss to first one of her cheeks and then the other.

"How is my favorite sister?" he asked in his usual jovial tone.

"Your *only* sister is delighted, now that you're home. You've never been gone so long," she said, trying not to sound as if she were complaining or issuing a reprimand. "I was beginning to worry about you."

"I feared as much," he said, keeping a smile on his lips. "I should have been more considerate of you. Heath and I decided to spend a few days with Morris Hubbard. You remember him, don't you?"

"How could I forget him?" she said, helping Paxton swing his cloak off his shoulders. "He always squeezed my fingers too tightly when he kissed my hand."

"The big brute does forget his gentlemanly manners from time to time. I should speak to him about that."

"Please don't on my account. I doubt I shall ever see him again, but it might save other young ladies' fingers if you do." Paxton allowed her to take his cloak, and she laid it on the table beside his hat.

"I know I was gone far too long, but while we were at the Hubbards' house we had a fierce ice-and-snow storm. And this late in the winter? Did it come this way, too?"

"Yes," she answered, feeling a flush come to her cheeks at remembrance of that night. She would never forget the chill of the icy wind on her face or the consuming warmth of being in the duke's arms.

"Anyway," Paxton continued, "we stayed a few more nights as we were invited to a house party at one of their neighbors'. There was the most beautiful young lady there. Miss Anabelle Pritchard." He laid a hand over his heart and sighed contentedly. "So lovely and such a sweet disposition. I must tell you all about her later. I hope it won't be the last time I see her. And I think she is hoping I will call on her in the spring, which I'm happy to say is not far away now." He stopped and his big blue eyes blinked slowly. "But what am I doing going on about ladies, parties, and such?" He reached down and kissed her cheek again. "I'm sorry I was gone long. I know how lonely it gets here for you."

"No, no," Loretta said, brushing off his concern. She certainly hadn't felt lonely when the duke was with her. And with having Farley to care for now, too, she was busy. For the first time since coming to Mammoth House, she hadn't felt lonely. "I think it's splendid that a young lady has caught your fancy. I was just worried about you."

"I can see that. You look tired."

"Do I? Perhaps I am a little. Come into the drawing room where it's warm. Shall I pour you a drink?"

He rubbed his hands together. "I do believe a spot of brandy will take the chill off my bones."

"Good," she offered, feeling such relief that he was home. "I want to hear all about the house party and Miss Pritchard for sure. And I have some things I need to tell you as well."

Paxton followed her into the drawing room and warmed by the fire while she poured a measure of brandy into a glass. Watching the amber liquid flow, her thoughts returned to the duke. She remembered him standing where her brother stood now. There was the same crackling sound of a fire, though this time no ice hitting the windowpanes. There was remembrance of the duke sometimes glowering at her and at other times looking at her as if he thought she was the most beautiful lady he'd ever seen. She remembered taking sips from the duke's glass, feeling the strength of his tight embrace, and tasting the passion in his eager kisses.

Loretta managed a hard swallow when she realized her brother had been talking to her. Replacing the top on the decanter she asked, "I'm sorry, what did you say?"

"I said what is it that has you looking as if you haven't slept a wink while I've been gone?"

She joined Paxton in front of the fire. "Oh, please tell me I don't look that tired?"

"You don't look that tired." He repeated her words, laughed, and took the glass. "More worried, actually, which is most unusual for you. I can see that something has disturbed you more than my prolonged absence. Now tell me what it is."

What should she divulge to him first? The story about the duke or about the boy? Farley, she decided quickly. It was much simpler and better to get it out of the way.

"Do you want to sit down?" she asked.

Paxton shook his head. "I've been in the saddle for most of the day. I think I want to stand for a while, but you go ahead and make yourself comfortable."

"I've been sitting most of the day, too." And without further delay she said, "The night of the storm, we had a frightened boy come to our kitchen door asking for food. I knew at once by the look of him that he'd been on his own for some time. I had to take him in because it was clear he was quite ill and still is."

Paxton's smile faded. "An ill child. Good Lord. Lost? Have you notified his family?"

"No. I don't know who they are. He's been too ill to say much more than his name. Farley. The fever has stayed with him. I think he must have been on his own for quite some time because of the condition of his clothing and how thin he is."

"That's dreadful. We must try to find out who he is. His parents must be worried sick."

Loretta hoped he had parents or someone looking for him, but each day that passed with no one showing up to ask about him she became more doubtful. He'd seemed very much alone to her that first night when she'd looked into his scared eyes. She'd wondered if he'd run away from someone, or if he'd been thrown away.

"Right now he just needs to get better so we can talk to him."

"So it's that bad?"

Loretta's heart filled anew with compassion for Farley. "I'm afraid it is. I wish there were more I could do for him."

Paxton put his hand on her shoulder. "I'm sorry you've had to cope with this alone."

Loretta suddenly realized she wasn't sorry her brother hadn't been here when Farley arrived because the duke had been with her. He'd taken control and gone after Farley. The duke, a man who didn't have to lift a finger to do anything he didn't want to do, had no qualms about helping remove the dirty, soggy clothing. Those memories would always be with her.

"Don't worry about any of it now," Paxton continued in his cheerful tone. "I'll take over from here and see what I can find out about him. Have you sent Mr. Huddleston to Grimsfield to ask if anyone knows him?"

"I asked the apothecary when he came, and he didn't know of any missing children from the village."

"Where is Farley now?"

"In Arnold's room. Bitsy is with him, but there's more you need to know."

"I can tell by your expression that it's not good news."

"No, that's not true," she answered honestly. Loretta looked at the fire for a moment before turning her attention back to her brother and saying, "Most would not consider it bad news by any standard. The Duke of Hawksthorn came to see you a few days ago."

Paxton blinked. "Hawksthorn? To see me? All the way out here? That's rather odd. Are you sure?"

"Quite sure. How could I not be when he asked specifically for you?"

The smile returned to Paxton's face. "I suppose that was an inane question. I just find it surprising. I have played a game or two of cards with him when an extra player was needed at his table, but I don't think we've spoken more than a greeting or two with each other. Did he happen to say what he wanted?"

"Yes, as a matter of fact, he did. He wants to arrange a betrothal between you and his sister."

Paxton laughed in his usual jovial way and then took a sip of his drink. "You look serious, but I can't believe you are."

"I have never been more serious."

"Truly? The duke wants me to marry his sister?" Paxton brushed his hair away from his forehead but it fell right back. "Are you sure?" he asked again.

Loretta let out an exasperated sigh. "Paxton, please. I'm quite sure about everything I've said. This is not the sort of thing one makes up."

"It's just I don't know what to say." His eyes brightened with good humor again. "I'm flabbergasted."

So was I.

"I would like to think you'd say no," Loretta offered cautiously. "And that would be the end of it."

"Well, of course I will." His exuberance returned. "Yes. I'm only twenty-four. Goodness me! I haven't ever considered the idea of marriage to anyone."

Loretta took an easy breath. "That was my thought as well. You're much too young."

"But did he happen to say why he was thinking of me for a match with his sister?"

"Somewhat. He said you don't gamble more than is in your pockets or drink more than you can hold. You don't gossip about others, and no one has anything unpleasant to say about you."

"All that?" His shoulders lifted and his eyebrows rose with confidence. "Now, that's the sort of description that can give one a high step in a hurry. But you and I both know I don't wager or play cards often because I don't have much blunt to lose. That's the same reason I don't drink too much. If I want my allowance to last from month to month I must be careful. And for that same reason, I couldn't support a wife properly on what the earl provides me." Paxton took another sip of his drink and looked at Loretta thoughtfully for a moment. "Yet I suppose if I were to marry a duke's sister, there would be a generous dowry. If that were the case, I wouldn't have to worry about such things."

Loretta folded her arms across her chest and glared at him. "Paxton?"

"No." He chuckled. "I mean I won't do it, of course. I've said it. But I suppose I will have to think about it. Don't you agree? Or, no. I'll just wait and hear what the duke has to say to me. That will be the best thing to do, right? First thing tomorrow morning I'll ride to London and see what the duke's intentions are."

"No," Loretta said.

Paxton lifted his free hand in the air. "Of course! What was I thinking? Yes, dear sister, you're right. Say no more. I was thinking selfishly. The duke can wait. I've left you alone for far too long as it is. And you've been taking care of this sickly boy, too. I'll stay here and take care of this for you first. Going to see the duke at this time is out of the question."

Loretta shook her head and smiled. Her brother had

always amused her with his sidestepping and overtalking whatever issue was at hand. "That isn't what I meant, Paxton. You don't have to go anywhere to see the duke because he insisted on coming back here to talk to you."

"Here, you say? Really? I wonder why he would do that."

The fire heated her cheeks and she took a step back. "He said he wanted to check on Farley."

Paxton's eyebrows rose and he brushed his hair away from his forehead again. "He knows about the lad?"

"Yes," she said slowly, wanting to choose her words carefully. "The duke was here when Farley came to the door."

"You didn't bother the duke with the story of a lost boy, did you?"

"No, I wouldn't have, but—" Loretta sucked in a long breath and let it out quickly. "I was with the duke when Mrs. Huddleston came and told me about Farley, and the duke was, of course, interested and wanted to help, as we all did. It's still a mystery how Farley managed to get so far from the village. Anyway, the duke insisted he'd be back to check on Farley and to see you."

Paxton looked confused, and Loretta didn't blame him. In trying to keep her brother from knowing the duke had dined with her and stayed the night, she'd made a muddle of that explanation. Still, she didn't want to enlighten him with any more details than was necessary. As her brother, Paxton probably deserved to know the whole story. Most of it anyway, but in some things the less said the better, and this was one of them.

"I can't believe I missed all this. I mean it's quite shocking when I think about it. A duke and a lost boy make their way to Mammoth House on the same day at the same time."

"It was shocking for me, too." She admitted to herself that it was also gratifying to have someone and something to think about other than how she was going to fill another day. "But all that aside, the duke asked that you remain here until he returns and that neither of us breathe a word about his proposal to anyone. I assured him we wouldn't."

"I agree. We won't concern the earl or anyone else with this until I've had a chance to speak to the duke. Did he say when he'd return?"

"It should be the latter part of this week."

Paxton downed the rest of his drink. "I must confess I'm quite flattered by his consideration and a little pleased, too, that he chose me." Paxton eyed her carefully and suddenly asked, "Is he considering others?"

"I don't know for sure, but I don't think so," she said honestly. "He seemed quite adamant about you being the one he wanted." A niggle of worry settled between her shoulder blades. "You wouldn't really consider it, would you?"

"Of course I'll consider it." Joy returned to Paxton's features. "But no, I won't agree to anything. I have not forgotten how wretched the arranged marriage turned out for you."

"Good," Loretta said, but Paxton was so unconcerned about this whole idea she wasn't sure she believed him. Without thinking she quickly added, "Besides, the duke's sister is probably selfish, terribly spoiled and—and . . ."

"And what?" he asked, folding his arms across his chest and giving her a devilish grin. "Go on," he prompted again. "If you're going to say it to anyone it probably should be to me."

"All right," she huffed. "Unattractive in some way."

"She probably is," he answered.

"See, even you think that."

His smile widened and his eyes narrowed just a little. "But what if she isn't?"

"Then she would be choosing her own husband and not allowing her arrogant brother to do it for her."

Loretta thought about her argument as Paxton just stood there smiling, nodding, not the least disturbed or alarmed by her words. He knew her argument about Lady Adele's appearance wasn't very solid. The duke was exceedingly handsome, so there was a good chance that his sister was beautiful, too.

That thought aggravated her all the more.

"Forget about that for now, please," Loretta said. "I'm feeling quite ill at myself for being so unkind about a person I don't even know. But I stand by my conviction that marriage should be about you finding someone to love. Someone your heart yearns for and you can't live without. You came in the door not ten minutes ago talking about how lovely Miss Pritchard was and how you want to see her again." Loretta's heart softened. "Paxton, I want you to marry someone you adore. Someone who makes your heart sing like a verse of beautifully written poetry. Not someone who can give you prestige, wealth, and freedom from our uncle."

"Then I shall be like a flower petal on the wind and simply float about until the duke returns and talks with me about this engagement." Paxton smiled, laughed, and then reached down and kissed her on the cheek for the third time. "You are such a worry berry."

"And you don't worry about anything," she countered, knowing she couldn't be upset with Paxton. There was no fault in either of them. Just the hands that fate had dealt them. She was serious about everything, and he wasn't serious about anything.

"For now," Paxton said, "the offer has not been made

to me. I must respect the duke and listen to what he has to say." He extended his glass to her. "Now, be a good sister to your only brother and pour me another brandy. I have a lot to think about."

So did Loretta.

My Dearest Readers:

It is with great anticipation that we await the first ball and the first dance of the Season to begin. Not only will we have the Duke of Hawksthorn's sister, Lady Adele, making her debut, but I have it on good authority that the Duke of Griffin's sister, Lady Vera, will return for her second Season to continue her foray into the marriage mart. But handsomely garbed gentlemen and fashionably gowned ladies twirling on the dance floor will not be the only thing swirling this year. Rumors still abound that mischief is in the air. And said mischief could be directed against Lady Adele and Lady Vera because of their brothers' past misdeeds as the Rakes of St. James.

MISS HONORA TRUTH'S WEEKLY SCANDAL SHEET

Chapter 9

A gentleman should never discuss his wooing
of the perfect lady with his friends.

—ঙ৩ৎ—

A Proper Gentleman's Guide to Wooing
the Perfect Lady
Sir Vincent Tybalt Valentine

White's.

There were other gentlemen's clubs in London.
Some less important, others more exclusive—such as the
Heirs' Club, which allowed only titled gentlemen—but
there were none more revered or celebrated than the club
that was established over one hundred years ago for the
elite of Society. The stone building in St. James wasn't ex-
cessively grand inside or out, though the address alone
would make it notable. The lighting was dim, the ceilings
low, and the rooms small. Most of the chairs were uncomfortable for a man the size of Hawk, who stood well over
six feet tall. It was the membership and the infamous wager book that made White's the most prestigious and most
talked-about club in all of England.

White's was the first place Hawk always wanted to go

when he returned to London. The taproom, billiard tables, and reading room were always busy with members. No matter the time of day or night he frequented the place, he could always rely on someone being there to catch him up on the latest news if Rath, the Duke of Rathburne, or Griffin, the Duke of Griffin, were out of Town.

However, they were not today.

They were sitting across the table from him in the taproom. Studying him.

And with good reason.

He'd just told them the same thing he'd told Adele yesterday. He had no answer from Mr. Quick about marrying her.

Amid the low hum of masculine chatter, the rattle of glasses knocking together, and the thunk of tankards hitting wood tables, he looked at them, too. The friends he'd known since they were boys. They were tall, broad-shouldered, and British aristocracy through and through—though Rath hardly looked his heritage. His dark eyes and recently trimmed, shorter-than-usual dark hair made him look more European or Greek than true-blood British.

Hawk and Griffin had entered Eton at the same time and quickly formed a bond. Rath had come a year later and was welcomed by them a year after that, when he'd shared a bottle of his father's best port that he'd sneaked into the school hidden in a false bottom in his satchel. Over the next few years, their friendships had withstood rivalries in grades as well as shooting, archery, fencing, and other games of sport. No matter what they were doing, each of them wanted to best the other two.

They weren't all dukes when they met, but they were all exceptionally intelligent and overly reckless. Hellions who grew up to become rakes—of the highest order, most people would say. After Oxford, they turned to sharpening their skills in gambling, horse racing, women, and, most infamously, wagers.

Though Griffin shouldn't bear the status of rake anymore, Hawk and Rath had recently decided. He'd married last year and now spent more time with his beautiful bride than with the two of them at the gentlemen's clubs, gaming hells, and private parties that were havens of pleasure for raucous young men.

"Does Mr. Quick want more incentive?" Griffin asked as the server put three pewter tankards of ale on the table in front of them.

"Blunt or property?" Rath asked, casually leaning his chair back on two legs.

"Neither, right now," Hawk answered as the pungent scent of the dark ale drifted up to him. "I didn't get the opportunity to talk to him. He wasn't there."

"All that way and the man was gone?" Griffin questioned.

Rath blew out a breath. "How did that happen? I thought he knew you were coming. What a waste of time."

No, Hawk thought. It wasn't a waste of time. Meeting Miss Quick, talking with her, holding her in his arms, and kissing her soft lips made the half-day walk in the freezing rain worth every step.

"He'd been gone more than a fortnight and hadn't received the letter that I was coming for a visit."

"I haven't seen him in London while you've been away," Griffin said and turned to Rath. "Have you?"

Rath shook his head. "Where was the fellow?"

"I never found out. His sister didn't seem to know where he'd gone." Or if she did, she wasn't going to tell Hawk. "Not that I would have hunted him down, but it would have been good to know exactly when he was expected to return."

"Sister?" Griffin asked and cut his eyes around to Rath, who then quickly looked at Hawk.

"Yes, that's right," Rath said. "I remember now. The man does have a sister. I thought she went into a convent." He turned to Griffin. "Maybe I'm wrong?"

"No," Griffin replied. "That was the rumor I heard—what was it . . . two or three years ago now. She was to marry Viscount Denningcourt. I believe they were at the church about to say vows when she decided she couldn't go through with the wedding. I don't remember the precise wording, but she told her uncle she'd rather be a nun taking care of the poor than be a wife to the viscount."

It wouldn't surprise Hawk if she'd said exactly that. If she were quite comfortable speaking her mind to a duke, she certainly wouldn't cower before the viscount or the earl.

Rath took a drink of his ale before adding, "I remember someone saying her uncle was so furious, they thought the old man's heart might fail him right there in the church. It's no wonder he agreed she could enter a convent."

She wasn't in one, but she might as well be for all the social life she had at Mammoth House, Hawk thought as he stayed quiet and listened to his friends discuss what they remembered concerning Miss Quick. He wanted to know what they'd heard. It appeared the rumors varied only a little from what Miss Quick had told him, but obviously Society had a different view of her than Hawk had. The lady he'd met was outspoken but not rude. Strong, but not hard. She was soft but not weak. And much to his chagrin, it looked as if Hawk was going to have to set his friends straight concerning where she lived.

"Take my word for it she's not in a convent, nor does she look or talk anything like the nuns I've seen. She lives at Mammoth House with her brother—whenever he is there.

Which obviously isn't often. She's beautiful, forthright, and compassionate."

Rath let his chair down slowly and picked up his drink again. Griffin's brows rose just enough to let Hawk know he'd said all he needed to say to interest them in hearing more.

"You're right," Rath offered. "She is beautiful. I remember meeting her once at a ball."

"Really?" Hawk asked.

"She was already betrothed to the viscount at that time so, naturally, I didn't say much to her. I remember thinking later, when the rumor about her was the talk of the clubs, that it was a shame such a beautiful young lady was going into a convent."

"We know about her past, so tell us something about her now that we don't know," Griffin prodded.

Hawk hadn't intended to mention Miss Quick. He knew his friends well enough to know they'd ask more questions than he wanted to answer.

And he was right.

Hawk looked from one friend to the other. They would not be satisfied until he gave them what they wanted. Choosing his words carefully, he said, "Miss Quick intends to try her best to keep her brother from accepting my offer of a match with Adele."

Rath grabbed the lapels of his dark-blue coat and straightened it on his shoulders as he sat up a little taller in the chair. "So she's not just against marriage for herself, she's against it for her brother, too, and probably everyone else would be my guess. And you say she's not in a convent?"

"And she doesn't believe in marriage," Griffin added as he looked from Hawk to Rath. "Hmm. I believe I hear a challenge in that statement. What do you hear?"

"A challenge," Rath said with a grin. "Even if a lady says she isn't interested in marriage, you can bet she is. Unless she is a nun."

Hawk chuckled under his breath. "Have as much enjoyment at my expense as you wish, my fellow rakes. I won't fall into the trap you are setting." Hawk waited for a couple of gentlemen to walk past them and then added, "It's clear she is against *arranged* marriages. And the reason is because hers didn't turn out well. We all know, they aren't common anymore—not in the strictest sense. I'll know more once I actually talk to Quick. How he handles himself concerning this will have a lot to do with how I proceed from here. Now," Hawk said, eager to change the subject from Miss Quick. "Has there been talk recently about anyone wanting to get even with us for the letters we wrote?"

"The indomitable Miss Honora Truth had another mention of it in her column just today," Griffin complained. "Apparently she's not finished with the story yet. She mentioned that Vera was returning for her second Season and then hinted that both Vera and Lady Adele could be at risk from unscrupulous men wanting to break their hearts, ruin their reputations, or just cause us grief by making us worry about the possibility of it."

"Damnation," Hawk grumbled. "I wish we could find out who she is. Perhaps I should give it another try and stop her drivel."

"It would do no good," Griffin offered dryly. "I don't think the King and the Prince are as well guarded as that person's identity."

"It's my thought," Rath said, "that whoever knows who she is will take it to their grave. I've heard her scandal sheet sells more than all the others combined."

Hawk grunted. "I just hope that whoever it is, they don't

get wind of the fact I'm trying to make a match for Adele before the Season starts."

"You know they won't hear anything about it from us," Griffin said, "but do you know if Miss Quick or her brother will say anything?"

"I can't be sure, but she agreed not to mention our conversation to anyone but her brother." Not wanting to give them time to turn the conversation back to Miss Quick, Hawk faced Griffin and asked, "Have you considered asking Lady Vera if she'd like your help in finding a husband? It would take her off the marriage mart and thwart any possibility of mischief-makers eying her."

Griffin grunted and then laughed. "If only I could. She is not as docile as Lady Adele. Vera is so contrary she would never agree to any help from me. No, I will have to leave all matchmaking to her. I'm just happy Sara is married and that half of my responsibility concerning them is now finished."

"If only Adele were more contrary," Hawk mumbled with a sighing breath. "She was spoiled to the point of madness by our parents and has been pampered far too long by me, our cousin, and the servants. She wants me to handle everything for her. I swear she'd let me decide which dress she is to wear each day if I'd do it for her. She has no desire to make any decisions or to think for herself. All she wants is for someone to take care of her every need and want. So I find myself trying to find her a husband who will do that without taking advantage of her gentle nature and wealth as well."

"I am glad I don't have sister woes," Rath said and then wiped the corner of his mouth with his thumb. "But both of you know I'll do everything I can to help see that Lady Vera and Lady Adele come to no harm from anyone seeking revenge against us. Short of marrying either of them, you understand. Not that they aren't both beautiful, desirable, and all the rest, but they are deserving of someone far better than I am."

"I don't think either of us would wish our sisters on you or you on them," Hawk said with a bit of a grumbling tone to his voice.

"I thought Lady Sara and Lady Vera handled the Season well last year," Griffin commented. "The only problem was the incident with Lord Henry, and we know how that turned out."

Rath snorted a short laugh. "I never heard any rumors about him getting struck with the sharp end of a lady's parasol one day and her brother's strong fist the next."

Hawk and Griffin chuckled, too.

"I suppose he didn't want that rumor making the rounds at the dinner parties, clubs and scandal sheets," Rath continued, humor edging his voice. "He either left London or hid out at his town house until his face healed."

Griffin drummed his fingers on the table a time or two and then said, "But as for whether or not there are other bachelors wanting to get even with us because of the secret admirer letters we sent to the young ladies, only time will tell."

"And speaking of *tell*," Rath said, with an I'm-not-going-to-let-this-subject-drop gleam in his eyes, "I'm wanting you to tell us more about Mr. Quick's sister. I find her story quite intriguing."

Hawk picked up his tankard again. Over all the sounds in the taproom, he heard billiard balls knocking together as the players took their shots. It didn't surprise him that Rath didn't want to leave the subject alone. He had always been too perceptive for his own good. And he didn't mind stirring up trouble—indeed he relished it.

Even among friends.

"There's nothing more to tell. I didn't spend a lot of time with her," he said and didn't consider it a lie. It was the best way to protect her reputation. And he could have easily spent much more time with her than he had. If she'd agreed.

"Will she come to London with Quick when he comes to see you?" Griffin asked.

"I told her I'd be going back to Mammoth House and to have her brother wait there until I returned."

Rath and Griffin gave each other a knowing look.

Hawk knew he wasn't fooling them. They knew that meant Hawk wanted to see her again, and they were right, but it didn't mean he was going to tell them more than he wanted them to know.

It was true that he couldn't remember an evening that he was as comfortable as he had been with Miss Quick. There had been plenty of nights with young ladies and women that he'd enjoyed. Some that he'd detested, and some he'd simply tolerated. But sitting alone with her, eating, talking, drinking, even sharing their pasts, he couldn't remember a time he'd felt so contented—it was a strange feeling, one he hadn't had before to that depth. It was as if the two of them belonged together, arguing their differing points and looking into each other's eyes, trying to understand as much from the other's expressions as their words.

"Back to Mammoth House, you say," Rath teased. "Perhaps we should go with you. What do you say, Griffin?"

"That he doesn't need both of us to hold his hand. I don't think Esmeralda will want me gone for a couple of days."

Rath grinned. "I think it's that you don't want to leave her."

Griffin shrugged good-naturedly and sat back in his chair. "Let me think about this. Two days riding in a cold carriage or staying at home with my beautiful wife?" He gave them a satisfied grin. "No, I don't even need to think about it. I'm quite content to say I'd rather stay with Esmeralda. But I do think you should go, Rath, and help Hawk persuade Mr. Quick to accept his generous proposal."

Hawk grimaced. "I can handle this quite well without help from either of you."

"Always willing to do what I can," Rath said.

"That was never in doubt. And contrary to what you're thinking, I have another reason for wanting to return to Mammoth House."

That caught their attention.

"What?" Griffin asked.

"The night I was there, a winter storm blew in. A young beggar came to her door. He was wet, cold, and quite ill. He fainted before we could find out who he was. Miss Quick had to take him in. There was something about the lad that bothered me. I don't think he was just a poor farmer's boy who had gotten lost. The truth is, he was so sick I don't know whether the lad made it, but if he did, I want to get him, and take him back to wherever he belongs."

A low chuckle rumbled in Rath's chest.

"Damnation, Rath," Hawk muttered. "What about what I just told you is so amusing?"

"You, a beautiful young lady, a storm, and a sick beggar at the young lady's door. It sounds like a book. How long did it take you to come up with that story?"

"And I just have one question," Griffin added with an amused smirk. "Why in the devil were you at Miss Quick's house at night? And her brother not home?"

Griffin and Rath had a good laugh. Hawk took their teasing in stride. He was partly to blame for even mentioning the boy.

"You are both blackguards. I should have never said a word to you about her, the beggar, or anything else."

"But you did," Griffin reminded him in a lighthearted tone. "And now that you have, you can't tell us only half the story. If you do, we will fill in the rest with our own imaginations. I don't think you want that."

Hawk grumbled for a moment and then, having no fear his friends would divulge what happened to anyone, he told them almost everything, starting with the lame horse and how he ended up having dinner with Miss Quick and staying the night in her home.

He conveniently omitted the part about the kisses, but by the expressions on Griffin's and Rath's faces, he didn't have to tell them. They knew.

"So I want to go back and see if the boy is still there. If he is, and he has no home to go to, as I suspect, it's my plan to bring him back to London with me. He may be just a common ragamuffin scrounging for food, or he could be a pickpocket or a footpad. I don't know. And I don't know how he managed to get as far out as Mammoth House, but I don't want him taking advantage of anyone there."

Especially Miss Quick.

Rath and Griffin's laughter died away, and Rath sounded more serious when he asked, "What will you do if you bring him back to London? Put him in an orphanage?"

"I don't know. He's probably be too old for that kind of home. He may have lived on his own too long for that to be something that would work for him anyway. If he turns out to be a decent lad, I'll try to settle him with a family on one of my estates or help him learn a trade here in Town. All I know right now is that when I tried to help him, he had the mouth of a guttersnipe."

Hawk knew there was no way he was leaving him with Miss Quick for any longer than it took for him to get back there. It was easy to see she had a soft heart. She wasn't looking at him as a beggar, a possible thief, or even just a lost boy. She only saw a youngster who was in need.

The lad wasn't the only reason he was eager to return to Mammoth House. And it wasn't Mr. Quick and the matter he had with the man about Adele that was on his mind.

It was Miss Quick.

There was something about her that had him thinking his business with her wasn't yet finished. Since returning to London, Hawk had found it didn't take much to remind him of her. Whenever he thought about her, which was more often than he thought he would, he remembered seeing her standing in front of the fire dressed in the buttery-yellow gown looking so *angelic*. He remembered her soft lips, her warm body, and the whispered satisfied sighs of enjoyment while he kissed her.

Perhaps he'd pick up a box of confections for her from that new bakery that had opened up down the street. He'd have them wrapped with a yellow ribbon. The thought of that made him smile.

And there was one other thing he wanted to do for Miss Quick, but it wasn't anything he wanted to tell his friends, so he picked up his ale and took a drink.

"When is it you plan to return?" Griffin asked.

"Probably Thursday. I wanted to make sure I gave her brother plenty of time to get home before I returned."

"Wait," Griffin said, interrupting Hawk. "Don't look now but I see the Lord Mayor walking in. No doubt he'll want to stop and talk to us if we don't make a hasty retreat to one of the gaming rooms."

Hawk and Rath immediately ignored Griffin's instructions and turned to look at the Lord Mayor, who'd stopped to speak to the gentlemen at another table.

"No doubt he will want to bend our ear concerning the

number of streetlamps that don't work or how many shop signs are in a state of disrepair."

"Something we can't do anything about, nor do we care about," Griffin offered. "So before he makes his way over here, I say we make our way out the other door."

"Let's plan to meet back here next week so we can hear how Hawk's second visit to Mammoth House turns out."

Griffin and Rath looked at Hawk.

"I wouldn't dream of denying you two the salacious details of my next visit there," he said, not meaning a word of it, and feeling comfortable that his friends knew that. Hawk slid his chair back as he rose. "You two go ahead, and I'll catch up with you later. I see Sir Welby walking in. I think I'll have a word with him."

"Is he walking with a cane now?" Rath asked, rising to stand between Griffin and Hawk.

"Looks like it," Hawk answered. "But he doesn't seem to be hobbling as if something is wrong with his foot or leg. See how he's holding it out in front of him. I think he's using it as a guide so he won't stumble into anything."

"I don't suppose his sight is any better," Griffin offered.

Rath ran a hand through his hair and sighed. "From the looks of the poor man, it's worse."

"It can't be easy for him to get around even though his driver helps him out of the carriage and to the door. I have to admire the man for making the effort and not giving up."

"I agree," Hawk added. "And since he's here, it won't hurt to ask him if he's heard any new rumors this year or if he has remembered any more from last year."

"Good luck getting anything out of him," Griffin murmured.

Hawk said good-bye to his friends, picked up his tankard, and headed over to the table by the entrance where

Sir Welby was pulling out a chair. The old gentleman was the person who'd overheard some young bucks talking last spring about the possibility of ruining Griffin's twin sisters' debut Season. The old man never admitted to knowing who they were, and Hawk doubted he'd confess their names this year, but it was worth a try.

"Let me help you with that," Hawk said and took hold of the old man's arm.

"Hawksthorn, is that you?" the white-haired man asked.

"It is."

"Thank you, thank you, most kind of you," he said, easing into the wooden chair with a groan. "I know one of these days I'm going to have to give up coming to this club, but I decided it won't be today. No, not today."

"And looks to me as if it won't be anytime soon, either. I think the cane is helping. You seem to be getting around quite well to me."

"Ah, yes, the cane." The old man huffed a tired laugh and hit the floor with the tip of his walking stick before settling it to rest between his legs. "It keeps me from running into doors and stumbling over chairs. People and guttering lampposts, too."

"You don't mind if I join you for a moment and ask you a couple of questions, do you?"

"I'd be happy for you to, Your Grace. Life can get lonely at times. Mighty lonely. You know I sit by the entrance so everyone will speak to me when they come in and when they leave, too. The club doesn't mind."

"I didn't know," Hawk said, though it wasn't true. Everyone knew. "I thought it was your favorite table."

"That, too, but now you know why it is my favorite. I hated having to give up going to the card room and playing a hand or two. Had to give up billiards and dice, too, but that's what happens when you can't see the cards or the balls and spectacles don't seem to help." His bushy gray eyebrows drew close together. "I heard your tankard hit the table. What are you drinking?"

"Ale," Hawk said, motioning for the server to come over. "Want the same?"

"Are you buying?" the old man asked with a sudden twinkle in his narrow, unfocused eyes.

"Yes."

"In that case I'll have a nip of their best brandy."

Hawk chuckled and told the server to get Sir Welby what he wanted. "I thought I'd ask if you've heard any more from or about the bucks who started the rumor about the Duke of Griffin's twin sisters last year."

"No, no, can't say I have. Never heard the fellows' voices again. Not once. Odd as it seems, it was just that one time when one of them said the Rakes of St. James never had to pay a price for their scandalous behavior for writing those letters years ago and that it was time they did. Then another said it would be fitting if something happened to ruin the Duke of Griffin's sisters' first season."

The hair on the back of Hawk's neck rose every time he heard that story. "Have you heard that, even though nothing happened to Griffin's sisters last year, *Miss Honora Truth's Weekly Scandal Sheet* has renewed the story and is now suggesting my sister, Lady Adele, might be marked for mischief, too?"

A strand of his long gray hair fell across the old man's wrinkled face as he leaned over the table and said, "No, no, Your Grace. I hadn't heard that, but I can't say I'm surprised."

"Neither was I. Not much respect from the younger fellows these days. No, not much. Guess that's why they don't come around White's often. They know this is a respectable club. Did Griffin ever talk with the barkeep? He might remember who was here that night. He sees better than I do."

"The barkeep sees drinks, not people."

"That's probably the best way for him to be. Members respect that."

"You will keep your ears open and let me know if you hear anything else?"

"Yes, yes. Just like I told the Duke of Griffin. He'll be the first to know. I'll make sure you are the second." The server placed the glass of brandy in front of Sir Welby and helped him take hold of the glass before turning it loose.

Sir Welby lowered his head and inhaled the scent of the strong liquor and then took a wee sip. He then looked in Hawk's direction and smiled. "On second thought, I'll let you know first."

Hawk thanked the man and, steering clear of the Lord Mayor, started making his way to the card room to join his friends, but his mind easily drifted back to the business he'd left undone at Mammoth House—not with Quick but with his sister, Miss Quick.

Chapter 10

A gentleman must never be mysterious about his
affection for a young lady.

~•~

*A Proper Gentleman's Guide to Wooing
the Perfect Lady*
Sir Vincent Tybalt Valentine

Loretta gasped with indignation. "Did you just call me
an old hag?"

"That's what ye are. Now leave me be. Go off and be a
bother to someone else."

She looked down at Farley. His long, dark-brown hair
was matted in places and sticking out wildly in others. The
nightcap she'd knitted for him and placed on his head while
he slept had been slung to the foot of the bed. His bor-
rowed, rumpled nightshirt hung loosely on his thin shoulders and chest. His deep-brown, angry eyes seemed too big
for his pale face. Loretta was certain no one had ever called
her anything remotely resembling an old hag.

It surprised her he was being so disrespectful and so
ungrateful, too. Obviously he had no memory of her sooth-

ing his brow and whispering words of comfort when he was so sick he could only twitch and mumble. He didn't seem to remember how he'd clung to her arms when he'd called out for his mama and she'd gone to his bedside and held him. Maybe he didn't know that it was because of her constant care and attention for the past week and a half that his life had been spared?

But Loretta remembered. As much as she might like to, Loretta couldn't blame the discourteous talk on his fever. It had left him yesterday and hadn't returned overnight. There was still no color to his thin lips or gaunt cheeks. His voice wasn't much more than a hoarse, cracked whisper. And the cough that had plagued him almost from the beginning of his sickness seemed to be worse.

Yet one thing was abundantly clear. Farley was a fighter. That she appreciated, admired, and understood. But he had to learn right now she would fight back, and in her house she would win. Illness or no, destitute or not, she wouldn't allow his insolence to continue without taking him to task about it.

"Young man," she said, resting the backs of her hands on her hips. "You are a guest in this house, and I am mistress of it. I am not old, and I am most certainly not a hag. While you are in my home, you will address me properly or I will have you put in the barn until you are well enough to leave. And take my word for it, you will not find a soft bed with warm covers on it in the barn, nor will anyone come in to keep a fire going for you and bring food to your bedside. Now, I am Miss Quick, and don't address me in any other fashion."

His eyebrows twitched. "I don't care if ye the Queen of England. I'm not drinking that gutter water ye trying to feed me."

"It is medicine, and it will help your cough get better."

His expression remained angry as he struck his thumb in the center of his chest and blurted, "I'd rather die, harpy."

Stunned, Loretta blinked rapidly. His language was abhorrent and his temperament spiteful. Was there no gracious bone in this youngster's body? Where was the softness in the child who had whimpered and called her his mama?

Loretta would have known how to deal with fear, the kind she'd seen on his face the night he'd appeared at her door, but not this raw anger. The only thing she knew to do was continue to be strong without being harsh.

"You will die one day," she agreed in a calm voice. "But it won't be today and it won't be in this house. And there are other things we don't do in this house, and you're going to learn them right now." She frowned tightly and bent over him. "Listen to me. We don't call each other unkind names, and we don't usually throw people out just because they are angry, but we will if they remain disrespectful."

To her surprise Farley started laughing, which caused him to start coughing, which caused him to start choking for breath. Loretta grabbed a handkerchief to cover his mouth and rubbed his back, hoping to calm the spasms racking his whole body. When at last he quieted and lay back against the pillow gasping for breath, she plopped down on the side of the bed, almost as spent as Farley.

He wasn't going to be easily won over. She wasn't going to give up. Farley may not care whether he lived or died right now, but Loretta did.

It would have been consoling if she could have called on Paxton to help her from time to time. Even though he'd said he'd take charge of the lad, her brother had been almost useless concerning Farley. There was always a reason Paxton couldn't sit with him or check on him for her.

She knew it wasn't that Paxton didn't care. He encouraged Loretta and the staff to do all they could for Farley, but her brother wasn't good at offering comfort himself. The two or three times he'd been in Farley's room all Paxton had done was look at him, and say he hoped the lad recovered soon. Paxton later admitted he had no idea how to cope with sickness and suggested that Loretta should leave the care of the boy to the servants.

That would have been the proper thing to do, and Mrs. Huddleston tried to insist upon it, but Loretta had so few things to fill her time as it was. Helping with Farley, as worrisome as it had been to tend a sick child, had been a bright spot in her life. She didn't want to stop the attention she was giving him.

After Farley's breathing had calmed, she reached over to the table, picked up the cup, and extended it to him. "Now will you trust me that this will make you feel better and drink it?"

He stared at her. The anger was gone from his watery eyes, and in its place was a pitiful blank stare. He took the medicine and downed it all without stopping to frown, wince, or complain about the foul taste, and then handed the cup back to her without so much as a hint of thanks.

Farley wasn't making it easy for her to like him, but she did. In a way, he reminded her of the Duke of Hawksthorn. When she'd first met the duke, he certainly hadn't made it easy for her to like him, either, but she had.

Very much.

Too much.

Shaking those troubling thoughts from her mind, Loretta turned her attention back to Farley and said, "Now, I'd like for you to answer some questions for me."

Her guest made no comment, and she took that as a good sign. At least he didn't say anything vulgar to her.

"You told me your name is Farley. Is that your surname or your first name?"

He shrugged but said nothing.

She tried again with a different angle. "What is your first name?"

"Farley."

"What is your last name?"

"Farley."

Well, this line of questioning wasn't getting her anywhere. Did he really not know who he was or was he simply being uncooperative in order to frustrate her?

He started laughing again, which led to another spell of deep, choking coughing, but thankfully this time it wasn't as bad or as long as the last.

"Where is your family?" she asked when his breathing settled down again. "Someone must be worried about you and wondering what happened to you."

"I'm all the family I got," he answered in a hoarse whisper, averting his gaze from hers. "I take care of myself."

As she and the duke had suspected but hoped wasn't the case. "That's commendable. Where are you from?"

He shrugged again and looked down at his bony hands. There was dirt under his fingernails that Mrs. Huddleston hadn't been able to wash away.

"Are you from somewhere near this area? Grimsfield? Or London, perhaps?"

His eyes shifted a little when she said "London." Maybe the duke was right and he was a street urchin who had somehow managed to wander from London to Mammoth House. But how did he get all the way out here in the dead of winter with holey boots and threadbare clothing?

"All right, I suppose it doesn't matter where you came from, but I do need to know where you want to go. Like it or not, I will have to know. When you are well enough, I can help you get there."

He remained silent.

"I can't assist you if you aren't willing to talk to me," she said in a determined tone and rose from the side of the bed. "Will you at least tell me how old you are so I don't have to guess if you are about the age of ten, or twelve, or thirteen?"

"I don't know no age. Don't need one. What good would it do me or ye to know that?" All of a sudden, a cocky grin lifted his thin lips. "Since ye want me to have a name and ye name is Miss Quick, ye can call me Mr. Slow."

Loretta smiled, too. "That was very clever." And obnoxious.

She saw by the light that flashed in his eyes that he appreciated her praise. Perhaps she'd try to get more information from him later. The tonic he swallowed would soon put him to sleep.

Facing him again she said, "Very well, if you want to continue to be obstinate, I shall return to what I was doing, and you can return to your world that only you know about."

After making herself comfortable in the chair, Loretta looked at the table beside her. Over the days Farley had been in the room, she'd brought in yarn and knitting needles, embroidery samples to stitch, and two different books of poetry. She looked at them all and decided on the knitting again.

No more than a few minutes later she heard a mumble and looked over at Farley. He looked asleep but restless, his head moving from side to side and his body twitching. He was dreaming. Again.

"Mama."

Loretta's stomach clenched and her hands stilled in her lap.

"Mama, don't go," he whimpered.

A chill shook Loretta. Her throat instantly clogged and her eyes watered with tears. Memories of her own mother flooded her. She'd cried those very words: *Mama, don't go.* But the sickness claimed her mother and she left anyway.

Loretta dropped her knitting and went to sit on the edge of the bed.

"Come back," Farley whimpered again. His head rolled from side to side. His chest heaved and his slight body stirred beneath the covers.

"Shh," she whispered, soothing his brow with one hand and pulling him close to her chest with the other, as she had several times before.

But today she felt unusually weepy, and long-held tears rolled down her cheeks. Instincts she didn't know she had surfaced and she said, "Everything is all right, my child. You're just dreaming."

"Mama," he murmured softly.

"Yes, I'm here." She whispered the words she'd wanted to hear her mother say so long ago. The words that never came for her. "Rest easy, my darling. I'm here and I'm not going to leave you."

Farley's face relaxed. His body stilled and Loretta shed silent tears for the mothers they'd lost, the vow she should have never made, and because of it, the child she'd never have.

Loretta stayed by his side until his breathing was heavy and he was in a deep sleep. Only then did she rise, dry her face, renew her strength, and continue with her knitting.

Sometime later, the distant reverberating sound of the front door knocker startled Loretta, and she realized she must have nodded off. Had someone arrived? They never had visitors at Mammoth House. But the duke was expected tomorrow. Her head felt a little fuzzy, and she shook it to clear her thoughts. She sometimes lost track of the days. Yes, tomorrow was Thursday. The day the duke was to arrive.

But who else could it be at the door? She should go see, she thought, placing the half-finished shawl she was knitting back on the table. Still she didn't rise. She looked down and, to her horror, saw she had on the same plain morning dress that she'd worn the last time the duke had come. Tomorrow, she'd planned to wear one of her more elegant day dresses, take care to put her hair up properly with a pretty ribbon.

Drifting through the wide corridors, she heard the muted sound of male voices. It had to be the duke and her brother. Neither Mr. Huddleston nor Arnold would come to the front door. Loretta remained still. She wouldn't go and greet him. The duke wasn't coming to see her. It was Paxton he wanted to talk to.

Besides, she didn't care if it was the duke. She didn't want to see him anyway.

A soft laugh passed her lips and she shook her head. Of course she wanted to see him. She was eager to see him again! Why would she try to fool herself? But as much as she wanted be a part of their conversation and argue her point on arranged marriages, she had to respect Paxton and allow him to have private time with the duke without her interference.

She must let them talk first.

Then she would speak to Paxton again.

So, as much as it pained her to do it, Loretta stayed in the chair, her chest tight, her stomach quivering, and she did the only thing she could do. She laid her head against the back of the chair, closed her eyes, and remembered the thrill of being caught up in the duke's strong embrace, the taste of his lips on hers, and the feel of his hands on her breasts.

She didn't understand why the feelings she'd had for the duke were so different from the ones she'd had for the viscount. Lord Denningcourt wasn't an old, horrible man. While the duke was kissing her, she kept thinking that it was the way kisses were supposed to make a person feel. It was those exhilarating sensations she'd hoped would happen when the viscount had pressed his lips to hers. She would have joyfully married the man if she'd felt the same deep-in-her-soul passion for him that she'd experienced when the duke had held and kissed her.

"Miss Quick."

Loretta's eyes popped open. Mrs. Huddleston was standing in the doorway.

"Yes?" She cleared her throat and rose. Her housekeeper couldn't have known what she was thinking about; all the same, Loretta didn't like getting caught thinking about kissing the duke.

"His Grace is here."

"I heard him arrive. That is, I assumed it was him when I heard someone at the door."

"He was asking if you might join him and Mr. Quick in the drawing room."

"Oh." Her heart fluttered excitedly. He'd asked for her. So soon? Did that mean he and Paxton had already reached an agreement and he wanted her to know? No, she wouldn't frighten herself by thinking anything like that. Paxton had told her he wouldn't agree to the marriage. So she would wait and hear what he had to say. Inhaling deeply, she tried to calm the rapid thumping of her heart. "Thank you for letting me know."

"Should I get Nollie to stay with Farley?"

"Yes. Thank you."

Mrs. Huddleston turned away, but Loretta called to her and said, "Farley is well enough to be cantankerous now."

"I noticed," Mrs. Huddleston said.

"We'll need to get him up and moving about soon. Will you see what you can do about getting some appropriate clothing for him?"

"I'll be glad to, miss. I can rework something from Arnold's wardrobe until Mr. Huddleston goes back to Grimsfield. There's a lady there who does a real fine stitch with cloth."

"That sounds good. And maybe you could see to it that his hair is trimmed and given a better shape."

"Bitsy is better at that than I would be, but I'll take care of seeing that it's done. He's not very friendly, but I'm glad the little fellow is better."

"So am I. I must admit I had my doubts at times that he would make it to recover."

"I think we all did," Mrs. Huddleston responded.

"Maybe he needs more to occupy his mind. Would you ask Mr. Huddleston to see if he can find a shop in Grimsfield where he can buy Farley some wooden soldiers, horses, a carriage or two, or something to help keep him entertained now that he's better?"

A wide smile crossed her housekeeper's face. "Mr. Huddleston will enjoy finding Farley something to play with. I'm sure he'll know the usual things a boy his age would want to amuse himself with in the evenings."

"And before you go, did Paxton say anything about— the duke staying for dinner or for the night?" she asked cautiously.

"No, miss, but he came in a carriage this time. A big fancy one with a driver all dressed up as if he was a member of the King's Guard. The black doors are as shiny as sun-shine gleaming on water. They have red and gold crests painted on them, too."

Loretta gasped. "Mrs. Huddleston, did you peek inside the duke's carriage?"

"I did. Dark-rose velvet cushions on the inside that look like nobody's ever put a rump on them. Mr. Huddleston was watching to make sure no one caught me. I didn't touch it, though I wanted to. He's got four big gray horses hitched to that carriage." Mrs. Huddleston stopped, shook her head, and smiled broadly. "Can't blame him for having that many with him after what happened the last time he came here. Guess he didn't want to get caught having to stay overnight again in case one of his horses went lame. He has three extra ones now."

The housekeeper turned away chuckling. Loretta laughed, too, and wiped her hands down the skirt of her dress. She then tucked some stray strands of hair into the chignon at the back of her neck while she took in several deep breaths.

If luck was with her, and Paxton was true to his word, this would be the last time she had to see the tempting duke. Paxton would turn him down, and that would be the end of it. The duke would approach a different man for his sister. The thought of that should have made her happy, but all it left her with was a cold, empty feeling inside.

Hoping to show more courage than she was feeling at the moment, Loretta walked into the drawing room with head and shoulders high. The duke was standing near the window. A slice of sunshine beamed on him. Oh, he was such a handsome man. He wore a dark-green coat and brown waistcoat that had large leather buttons. He stood tall, strapping in black knee boots and buff-colored breeches. And Lord help her, he was a feast for her eyes.

"Your Grace." She stopped just inside the entrance and curtsied.

"Miss Quick." He bowed.

She noticed that his gaze never left her face, because hers didn't leave his. She didn't understand why, but it made her feel wonderful to just see him again.

"There you are," Paxton said, walking over to her and kissing her on each cheek as he whispered, "Don't worry. Everything is going to be fine."

That was what she was afraid of.

"I hope I'm not interrupting," she said, as cheerfully as Paxton had greeted her. "Mrs. Huddleston said you asked for me." She walked farther into the room.

"Yes, I wanted you to join us," the duke said. "Your brother and I have finished discussing the particulars of my proposal to him."

Loretta's throat tightened. She looked at Paxton, who stood in front of the fireplace. He seemed happy as a lark singing from a budding tree on the first day of spring. But she couldn't read anything into that. Her brother always appeared happy. She didn't know how he managed to do it, but he was seldom without a smile on his face.

"Oh," she said softly, giving her attention back to the duke.

"It didn't take long. I asked that he not give me an answer today. I want him to think about my proposal."

A measure of hope soared through her. Perhaps that meant he was considering other gentlemen for Lady Adele, after all.

"That's very generous of you, but surprises me," she said.

"I thought it might. However, my reasoning is not whatever it is that just made your eyes light up with hope that this match might never take place."

Loretta felt like stomping her foot in frustration. His perception was too keen to be believed.

"You do like to imagine that you can decipher what I am thinking, don't you?"

"And you like to imagine that I am always wrong." The duke chuckled softly. "I wanted you both here so I could extend an invitation for the two of you to come for a visit to Hawksthorn in the very near future. I talked with Lady Adele a few days ago, and she'd like to meet both of you before we go any further with this arrangement."

"That's a most gracious invitation, Your Grace," Paxton said, his wide smile beaming with joy. "And yes, thank you, I'd like very much to go to Hawksthorn and meet Lady Adele."

"And you, Miss Quick?" the duke asked as much with his eyes as his words.

Loretta's lashes lowered for a second or two before she sought his gaze once again. "Thank you for the invitation, but I must decline."

He studied her a moment. "My sister would feel more comfortable if you accompanied your brother, and I thought you would want to be there to give him wise counsel."

Yes, she would love to go to Hawksthorn. To be there for Paxton and to meet Lady Adele, but she couldn't.

"If you are afraid that you won't be properly chaperoned, I assure you in my house you will be. Our widowed cousin lives with us and she's a force to be reckoned with when it comes to making sure everything is as it should be in our home."

"No, that's not the problem at all, Your Grace," Paxton said, stepping forward. "It's nothing of the kind. We would have no fear for Loretta's reputation while in your care. It's because of our uncle. He prefers that Loretta stay at Mammoth House and not travel."

The duke's eyes darkened, narrowed. His brows and forehead creased into a tight frown. "Ever?"

"For now, that is how it is," Loretta answered.

"I see. I didn't realize that."

Loretta's gaze stayed on the duke's. "It was kind of you to make the offer. Especially considering the fact you know my feelings so well."

"You know I appreciate a fair fight." The duke turned to Paxton. "Mr. Quick, I brought a gift for your sister but forgot and left it in the carriage, or perhaps it's in my satchel. My driver will know where to look for it. Would you mind going out and asking him to get it for you to bring back to me?"

"Not at all. I'll be happy to. I'll go right now."

"Thank you."

As Paxton was walking out with the usual buoyant bounce in his step, the duke was walking closer to Loretta. His concerned expression hadn't changed. "Does the earl forbid you to travel anywhere for any reason?"

"Yes," she admitted with a lift of her chin. "Or maybe to be fair I should say no. It's not that he forbids it. Just that whenever I've asked to go somewhere in the past, he's always said no. He's never granted any of my wishes, so I stopped asking. It's just easier not to plan anything away from Mammoth House. But I don't mind."

"I do." His eyes flashed with displeasure.

"That decision is not up to you. Besides, why would your sister want me to come? I'm sure she has aunts, cousins, or someone who would be willing to come and visit with her while Paxton is there. Someone she could confide in, which I am not. Someone other than you to give her an opinion on my brother's suitability for her."

He stepped closer to her. "Perhaps it is me who wants you there, Miss Quick."

His words brought curls of pleasure swirling low in her stomach. "No matter. I can't go."

"What kind of monster holds a young lady prisoner in her own home?" he continued. "He forces you to live out here in an empty valley like a hermit. Why would he ban you from traveling as well? That's inhumane."

"Don't be ridiculous," she said, defending her uncle, but why she had no idea. In truth, she would love to be able to travel. She'd asked many times to be allowed to visit London until she could no longer stand the disappointment of hearing him refuse her. "Look at this grand home. I have more books than I could ever read, a pianoforte that I know how to play quite well, and kind, sensible, and trustworthy servants to care for my every need." She took hold of the sides of her skirt and held them out. "Though this dress doesn't represent it, I have gorgeous clothing and fine jewels for whenever I choose to wear them. I am not treated inhumanely."

"I will admit you are well cared for in your daily life, so why is it he won't let you leave?"

"You know why," she answered softly. "Not the small details maybe, but you know that I refused to marry Viscount Denningcourt."

The duke's gaze seemed to burn into hers. She watched him swallow. It pleased her he was so interested in her life, but it frightened her as well. He could very easily cause her to do something foolish if she wasn't wary of him every second.

"Give me the small details, Miss Quick."

Loretta turned away from him and walked over to the window, standing where the little slice of sun that beamed through the panes could shine on her face. The warmth that came through was comforting. She looked out on the spacious, barren grounds. It had taken her a long time, but she'd finally made peace with her life and found a measure of contentment. If she wasn't careful, the duke could easily upset that balance and leave her starting all over again with her journey to stay sane.

She knew he could be as determined as a dog after a bone. He would probably stay after her until she told him everything. Besides, it really didn't matter whether or not he knew it all, as long as she didn't let it change the way she felt about her life.

Turning, she walked back to stand before the duke. "Viscount Denningcourt wasn't an unpleasant man." Her gaze swept up and down the duke's face. "His hair is darker than yours. He's shorter, a little pudgy perhaps." She stopped and laughed softly. "I don't know why I'm telling you what he looks like. I'm sure you know him."

He nodded.

"Perhaps I only wanted to convey to you that there really wasn't anything wrong with him, except whenever I thought about spending the rest of my life as his wife, I didn't want to do it. I knew it almost from the time I met him. As horrible as it sounds, I knew I didn't want to marry him—" She paused for a moment then finished. "—or bear his children. And yet I agreed."

"That's not horrible."

"But I didn't tell Uncle. I didn't let him know when the arrangements were being formalized, or the wedding plans were being made. I wanted to be happy with my uncle's choice. I thought I could be. I thought I just needed time to get to know the viscount. In hindsight, I never should have agreed to the wedding. I shouldn't have waited until the guests arrived to tell the earl I would rather live alone the rest of my days than marry Viscount Denningcourt."

"What happened when you told him?"

"He said, either you will marry the viscount this day

or you will take a vow, here and now in this church before the vicar, that you will never marry anyone."

"And you made the vow."

"Yes," she said, remaining resolute. "In the church. But before I did, the earl warned me that I would never be allowed to enter Society again. He said he wouldn't have me prancing about gaily at all the parties and balls, to be a constant reminder to him about how I'd disobeyed him and the embarrassment I caused to both him and the viscount in front of so many guests. And he has kept his word."

"You were not the first person to ever break an engagement in such a manner."

"No, but the first person my uncle had to deal with, and he was quite irate and firm in taking care of the matter. He said if I'd rather be alone than marry, he'd see to it that I would do just that. Live alone. And so I have. Except, of course, for Paxton, who was never forced to live here by Uncle. It was always his choice to stay with me because he's such a devoted brother."

"But he's spending less and less time here," the duke offered.

Regrettably, she had to say, "Yes. But the servants are always here. So you see, Your Grace, I knew exactly what life I would be living when I took that vow."

"The earl is being overly severe concerning this," the duke said with only slightly veiled disdain. "It appears he is living by the old adage, *Out of sight is out of mind*, no matter how unjust his reasons."

"Perhaps. Remember, I could have married. I chose this life. I am not complaining, because there is no need, and I have made peace with my fate and harbor no ill will. I was allowed to make the choice."

His eyes swept up and down her face. "I can see that,

but I don't think coming to that conclusion was as easy as you now make it sound."

He was so perceptive. A chill washed over her. For a while she thought she might lose her mind. "No" was all she said.

"I'm surprised the earl doesn't want you to marry now, so he doesn't have to be responsible for you."

"There is no reason for him to want that. I have no suitors. I cause him no trouble and very little expense."

"I can see that, as well. However, it won't bother me at all to trouble him, and I will. I want you to come with your brother to Hawksthorn. I'll clear it with the earl."

"You obviously don't know my uncle very well."

"No, I don't. But I know men, Miss Quick. And I know peers. He may have denied you time and time again to wield his power over you for the shame he feels you caused him, but he won't deny me this request to have you come with your brother."

"As you said, he is a severe man, Your Grace."

"Do not underestimate me, no matter what it is I'm fighting for. Plan to be ready to travel with your brother. I'll be sending a carriage for you."

Her heart started pounding and her knees trembling. She was attracted to the confidence she heard in his voice and the strength she sensed inside him to win. But no, she wouldn't get her hopes up that she would be allowed to leave Mammoth House. She'd had them dashed far too many times, and she didn't want to go through it again.

"I will wait to hear that from my uncle."

His frown relaxed and he gave her a half smile. "You will challenge me even on this."

"I know my uncle."

"Earls seldom turn down dukes when they request a favor."

"Then I will defer to your power of persuasion, if that happens."

He stepped in close to her and spoke softly. "You know there is another reason I want you to come with your brother, don't you?"

Her breaths turned to choppy silent gasps of anticipation. Did he want to kiss her again? Right now? Should she let him? Her body could almost feel the wanton sensations he'd caused inside her the last time his lips touched hers.

But no. She couldn't let him. His kisses were too overwhelming, too inviting. She could easily give in to anything he asked of her if she allowed him to kiss her again.

She swallowed hard and said, "I know there will be no repeat of what happened between us that night we were alone during the storm—in this room."

"Are you sure about that, Miss Quick?"

No.

"Yes," she answered but wasn't at all sure it was the truth.

"All right, for now I'll save that battle for another day." A teasing light sparkled in his green eyes. "But rest assured, we will return to it and I will prove that you are wrong. For now, I'll take it as a good sign that you remember what happened between us that night and how it felt, even though that's not what I was referring to when I said there was another reason I wanted you to come to Hawksthorn."

Loretta's cheeks flamed hot and she balked at her natural instinct to swirl away from him. Instead she managed to say, "It's not?"

"No, but I'm heartened it was the first thing that came to your mind." He smiled easily, attractively.

"You're a beast," she whispered.

"Yes," he agreed. "I want you, Miss Quick, and you might as well know it now."

Without warning he slid his open hand around to the back of her neck. He cupped it gently but tightly, pulling her up close. Keeping his gaze solidly on hers, he lowered his head and claimed her lips in a sudden, hard, and demanding kiss that stole the air from her lungs.

Chapter 11

A gentleman must never take advantage of a lady
even if she gives him permission to do so.

❧

*A Proper Gentleman's Guide to Wooing
the Perfect Lady*
Sir Vincent Tybalt Valentine

Loretta's surprised gasp dissolved in her throat as the duke's lips moved quickly and hungrily over hers, instantly feeding the longing she'd felt since their last kiss. Her lips parted. His tongue filled her mouth, thoroughly exploring its depths with swiftness. She swallowed his breaths, his moans, and he inhaled hers with an eagerness that thrilled her.

The wait for this moment had been long, and she needed no encouragement to join the kiss. She was as fervent as he. With his lips moving back and forth over hers with such intensity, Loretta felt as if his passion for her were seeping deep into her soul, branding her and forever making her his.

"Yes, I've wanted this," he whispered against her lips as his wide hand slid down her neck and chest to cover her breast and gently massage her. "I've needed this. To feel your lips on mine." He kissed her swiftly and then lifted his head only enough to look into her eyes and whisper, "To touch you like this and know that you want me to even while you deny it," before claiming her lips once again.

Yes, that was true, her mind whispered, but she couldn't say the words aloud. She couldn't admit to him that she wanted this, too. Loretta had no control over the thrilling sensations hurling through her but knew she had no desire to stop them. The duke's lips were possessive, demanding, and thorough.

Just the way she'd remembered them in her dreams.

She slid her arms up and around his shoulders, letting her hands skim across his strong back. His body was firm, warm. Her body ached to feel him closer, for him to touch her with more strength, but she wasn't exactly sure how to accomplish that without asking him to press her closer, tighter, and she was almost to the point of doing that.

The duke's lips captured hers over and over again. Some kisses were light, so soft it was as if his lips were barely touching hers. Others were hard and passionate, and felt as if he were ravishing her. They kissed and kissed until Loretta was so languid with delicious pleasure she only wanted to lie down on the settee, let him cover her body with his, and then kiss her some more. But just as all good and glorious things come to an end, so did the duke's powerful and passionate kisses.

He lifted his lips from hers, kissed his way down to the crook of her neck, letting his tongue moisten her skin there, before lifting his head and looking down into her eyes.

The duke's lips were tempting and she wanted more. It felt as if his gaze were caressing her face, and she was almost persuaded to force him to kiss her again. Loretta's chest heaved with indecision.

"I believe that settles your concern about whether or not there will be more kisses between us, Miss Quick. There will be."

Yes, she believed that, too, now.

He released her neck and stepped a respectable distance from her. "But I do have other reasons for wanting you to come to Hawksthorn. I want to prove to you that my sister is worthy of your brother."

Reminding her of the unkind things she'd said about Lady Adele was almost as embarrassing as her referring to their shared kisses when he indicated they weren't even on his mind at the time, and then kissing her into delirium to prove to her that they were.

"You know I never should have said those things about your sister. I'm deeply ashamed of myself for that, and I'm sure they aren't true. But all that aside, you are no gentleman for reminding me of it."

He hid a smile by wiping the corner of his mouth with his thumb. "It's not easy to get the best of you, Miss Quick, and I must take the opportunity to do so when you present it to me. I didn't mind you expressing your doubts about Adele. And it's quite noble for you to want your brother to marry a *vicar's daughter.* However, I—"

"Here it is," Paxton said, striding into the room as if he were walking only on his toes.

Loretta hoped he would have no inkling she'd just been so thoroughly kissed.

He handed the package to the duke. "He finally found it. Took him a while but there's not a rumple in the pretty yellow ribbon."

"Thank you, Mr. Quick." His Grace looked down at it and asked, "Did he give you just one?"

Paxton blinked rapidly. "Yes, only one. I thought—I mean, were there more?"

"Perhaps my driver misunderstood, but yes. There are two packages. This is the book I brought for Miss Quick, but there is another. A box of confections. Sweets from a new bakery in London." He turned to Loretta. "I thought, perhaps, you might like some. There are plenty to share. I suppose I'll have to go get it."

"No, of course not," Paxton said. "Nonsense. Don't trouble yourself. I'll do it for you."

"Are you sure? Or perhaps you could have a servant to get it for me. I hate to see you take care of an errand for me."

"Happy to, Your Grace. Not a problem at all. I'll dash back out and get them right now." His exuberance was infectious, and Loretta had to smile. "It is just one more box, correct? Small box or large?" Paxton made sizes with his hands.

"Yes, about that size," the duke answered. "My driver will find it, I'm sure. Thank you, Mr. Quick."

As soon as Paxton was out the door for the second time, the duke moved close to Loretta again and spoke in a low voice, saying, "You are looking well. I see you have had no ill effects from the encounter with the icy wind the night of the storm."

"Nor you, and don't try to change the subject."

"I didn't know I was."

"You didn't forget to tell Paxton or your driver about the second package. Did you?"

"Of course not. I didn't forget the first by mistake, either. They were both by my design. I arranged everything with my driver before I came inside. I knew it would be the only way I could have a few minutes alone with you. Twice."

"That was sneaky."

He shrugged. "It was strategy. Something that you will

find I'm very good at. Here." He handed her the package. "This is for you."

"Thank you."

Loretta eagerly untied the yellow ribbon, peeled away the stiff parchment, and read: *"A Proper Gentleman's Guide to Wooing the Perfect Lady* by Sir Vincent Tybalt Valentine."

With delighted surprise, she looked up at him and smiled. "The book that caused you so much grief."

"And is responsible for creating the three Rakes of St. James. You did say you'd like to read it one day, didn't you?"

"Yes, I did. I had asked Mr. Huddleston to see if he could find a copy for me in Grimsfield but there wasn't a shop that had one."

"Perhaps one day there will be no copies for anyone to buy, but for now it sells because there is always a man who wants a few suggestions on how to woo a lady."

"I'll start on it tonight. Thank you. It is a beguiling title." She looked at the cover and then back up to the duke. "I wonder if Paxton would like to read it, too."

"Do him a favor and don't suggest it." The duke gave her one of his very attractive grins and said, "I hope you find it as amusing as I did years ago."

"I will let you know."

He nodded. "Now tell me about the lad who showed up at your door. Is he still here? Did you find out who he is and where he's from?"

"Yes, he's still here, and I'm sorry to say I haven't learned much more about him." She absently hugged the book to her chest as she talked. "His name is Farley. Whether it's his first name or surname, he wouldn't say. He won't tell me his age, where he came from, or where he wants to go."

"How was his attitude when you talked to him?"

"Wary and a bit impish."

"I had thought that might be the case. It sounds as if he's being obstinate or perhaps even secretive on purpose. He doesn't want you to know who he is."

"Maybe, but I think it could very well be that he really doesn't know the answers."

"I would venture to say that, by age five, most people know both their names and their age."

Knowing the duke was right, she remained quiet.

"I had wondered how forthcoming he would be about himself. How is his health?"

"Better, but far from well."

"I'll see what I can find out about him. I brought my carriage this time so I could take him back to London with me."

Loretta smiled. "Yes, I heard about your fancy carriage. Mrs. Huddleston was quite taken with it. And your horses, too."

The duke shifted his shoulders uncomfortably. Apparently he didn't like being teased about the elaborate workmanship of his conveyance. Getting the best of him, no matter if it was in such a small way, made her feel good.

"However, I'm afraid that taking Farley back with you is impossible, Your Grace. His fever only broke just yesterday and his cough is frequent and unmerciful. He hasn't even been out of the bed yet. He is not well enough to travel. I would have you see for yourself, but he just took a tonic to help him sleep."

"All right, if you think it's best for him to stay a little longer. I had asked about him when I stopped in Grimsfield last week to make arrangements to have your horse returned. It's a fairly small village, and I thought perhaps someone there might have heard of a missing boy. No one had. And almost everyone I talked to agreed that it wasn't common to have children living on the streets or in the countryside. There's always someone willing to take in an orphaned child."

She nodded. "I had asked the apothecary about that as well, and received much the same answer as you. He said Grimsfield is filled with goodhearted people and they would never leave a young boy to fend on the streets for himself."

"I see by your expression and hear in your voice that you still have great concern for him."

"It's only natural," she answered, having no reason to deny his observation. "He's still basically helpless."

"I think it may be more than that."

She quirked her head. "What do you mean? He was lost, ill, and uncared for. What could there be other than benevolence from me?"

His eyes searched hers, as they often did. "Kinship. Maybe you feel that because you have both been left alone, you have something in common."

No, she would not let the duke wake all those feelings of being abandoned. She'd had a short cry with Farley earlier and that was all the sympathy she'd allow herself. She'd worked too hard to overcome her pain, rejection, and loneliness. It wasn't easy. It wasn't accomplished overnight, but she had buried them and moved on.

"How can you say that when I have Paxton? And it looks as if he didn't have refreshments brought in for you after your long journey. May I offer you a drink? Tea or brandy before you go?"

"Are you trying to get rid of me again, Miss Quick?"

"If you'll remember our conversation when you were last here, I thought it best that you not return at all."

"Ah, yes. How could I forget? But you're not going to

get rid of me that easily." His gaze swept down her face and then lingered on her eyes. "Perhaps I didn't make that clear earlier when I kissed you. I'm thinking I should do it again."

Hearing her brother approaching, Loretta whirled away from the duke.

"Here we are, Your Grace," Paxton said, entering the room. "The packaging itself on this one looks good enough to eat. Another beautiful yellow ribbon tied around it." He extended it toward the duke and then pulled it back and said, "Or should I just hand it to Loretta for you? I mean, you did say it was for her—but no, you really should. I don't know what I was thinking."

"Yes, Mr. Quick," the duke answered calmly. "It's fine for you to just give the box to her. And I think you'll be happy to know I've talked her into accompanying you to Hawksthorn. Hopefully next week."

Paxton's gaze immediately cut to his sister. "That's wonderful, Your Grace, but I don't know if she will be able to make it."

"I realize I must get your uncle's permission, but I don't foresee a problem with that. The earl and I have met on several occasions. I'll be back in touch with you after I've spoken to him. I trust you'll keep all this to yourself."

"You can be sure of that," Paxton answered.

"And I can count on you to see that Miss Quick is packed and on the carriage with you before it leaves, yes?"

Paxton put his arm around Loretta's shoulder and hugged her close to his side. "Absolutely, Your Grace. I'll see to it that she's with me."

Chapter 12

There may be times when a man is desperate to gain
a lady's attention, but a gentleman would never
resort to desperate measures to obtain it.

❧

*A PROPER GENTLEMAN'S GUIDE TO WOOING
THE PERFECT LADY*
SIR VINCENT TYBALT VALENTINE

Hawk paced in front of the fireplace, before the window, and alongside the settee. And then paced some
more.

Being the son of a duke had afforded him many advantages when he was growing up, and now that he was the
duke, even more. He wasn't used to waiting for people.
They waited for him.

Yet in all fairness, Hawk had tried to temper his impatience as best he could. Whether or not he saw Miss Quick
again anytime soon depended on this meeting, and the longer he went without seeing her, the more he wanted to see
her again. Her kisses had left him with a hunger that he
hadn't been able to satisfy—and he'd tried.

He'd arrived at the Earl of Switchingham's home unannounced and early enough in the afternoon that no one else would dare consider paying a call to an earl. But even if the earl had to change his neckcloth, vest, and all the rest of his clothing thrice before greeting Hawk, it shouldn't have taken over an hour for the earl's valet to put him together. Still, Hawk didn't know the man well. Perhaps he'd studied how to tie a neckcloth under the tutelage of Beau Brummell, who reportedly took hours to dress each day, sometimes tying as many as thirty neckcloths before he concluded he was fit to be seen.

Along with the pacing, Hawk kept himself busy by stirring the dying fire from time to time, studying all the paintings and figurines in the room, and watching the hands on a large ornate clock that was perched atop a slender stone column crowned with a Tuscan capital. He'd never had reason to study a room more.

Hawk huffed, swore, hummed, and had even caught himself whistling once or twice. He'd had time to memorize every item in the entire room except for maybe a miniature of an afternoon in the park that had been painted on an elephant tusk. He hoped the damned thing had been found on a dried-up, long-dead carcass and not one shot just for the precious ivory, but he had his doubts that was true.

Yet the waiting had been beneficial, too, he decided, eyeing the delicate piece of artwork. It had given him time to rethink his approach to the earl. Instead of lambasting the man, as Hawk wanted to do for his disgraceful treatment of Miss Quick, he'd decided to mask his growing outrage, as best he could anyway, and take a different approach.

As objectionable as it was to even think it, he was going to mollycoddle the man. If that didn't work, he'd do whatever he had to do in order to get permission for Miss Quick to come to Hawksthorn.

Memories of their kisses came easily to his thoughts, reminding Hawk why he must see her again, and he silently thanked Adele again for the idea. He wanted to explore further the desire Miss Quick had aroused so quickly in him. He recalled the taste of her lips, her mouth, and her skin. He remembered the feel of her soft yet firm body, pliant, trembling, and willing in his arms. He'd wanted to seduce her, but she'd seduced him and left him wanting more. Anticipation flooded his loins as he thought of sliding his hands beneath her clothing, to feel her warm, bare skin and to pull her breast in his mouth, to—

"Your Grace."

Hawk turned to greet the tall, heavyset man with shoulders as straight as a rod, a head full of thick gray hair, and enough arrogance to fill every ship in the Spanish Armada. The earl stopped just inside the entrance to the room and bowed stiffly, reminding Hawk that while they were acquaintances, they had never been friends.

Hawk returned the respect in the same manner and said, "Forgive me, my lord, for arriving unannounced."

"Nothing to forgive, Hawksthorn," Lord Switchingham said, lumbering into the room with a sway and hobble to his steps that indicated he had a hip or possibly a knee he was favoring. "It's an honor to have a duke visit me, whether he has an appointment or not and whether business or pleasure. I hope you'll forgive me for making you wait."

"As you said, there's nothing to forgive."

"Glad to hear it. Please, have a seat and tell me what's on your mind this early in the day."

The earl motioned to the servant who'd walked in behind him, and the man walked over to a side table and poured two glasses of what looked to be port while Hawk made himself comfortable on the settee. Hawk couldn't help but notice the abundance of lace on the earl's cuffs and the ends of his neckcloth, too.

"Thank you for understanding," Hawk said. "I do have a matter of business to discuss with you that recently came up concerning your niece, Miss Quick."

"Loretta?" the earl asked as the lines around his mouth deepened. His thinning gray eyebrows puckered as he seated himself in a low-back armchair near the settee. He grunted as he stretched a leg out in front of him. The sound reminded Hawk of a pig who was enjoying a fresh patch of mud. "Has she done something wrong that I haven't heard about?"

It perturbed Hawk that her uncle had immediately assumed she'd done something wrong. Hiding his irritation, he answered, "No. Actually, I'm hoping she will be able to do something for me."

"You?" Lord Switchingham squirmed in the chair, as if he hadn't yet made himself content with how he was sitting. "Whatever would you need with her? She's been out of Society for quite some time now."

"I know," Hawk said with as little derision as he was capable of, considering he felt as if the man talked about Miss Quick as if she were the lowest scullery maid in his employ rather than his niece and a lady of the highest quality.

"I'm surprised you even remember her at all."

Hawk felt a prick of guilt. He'd hadn't actually remembered her until he saw her. Even so, the earl was not endearing himself to Hawk. Still, he held his tongue and proceeded calmly. "Let me get right to my reasoning for being here. I'm going to share something with you that only a couple of people know at this time, my lord. But first, I must have your word that you won't discuss it with anyone."

That got the earl's attention, and he leaned forward. "Of course. You have my word."

"Good." Hawk took a glass from the tray the servant held before him, but he wasn't in a mood to share a drink with his host. "I'm in discussions with your nephew, Mr. Paxton Quick, about a possible matrimonial arrangement between him and my sister, Lady Adele."

"I didn't know this," the earl said, sounding somewhat affronted as he reached for his drink. "When did this discussion happen? He never said a word to me."

"He has only been aware of the offer a few days. I have sworn him to secrecy on this matter, as I have you. Don't blame him."

"No, no blame. The fact is, it would please me greatly for our families to be joined by a mutually agreeable marriage."

Hawk wouldn't go so far as to say that. "It's very important to me that this not be made known to anyone in case we can't work out an amicable agreement. I don't want anything to blemish Lady Adele's reputation before the Season starts. If there was talk of an arrangement that didn't work out, it might reflect badly on her."

"Certainly, I understand." He preened and leaned back in the chair. His long, wide face seemed to flatten slightly, thickening his jowls. "Paxton is an affable fellow, but he doesn't seem to always have both feet on the ground. I'm sure you know what I mean. Especially when it comes to business matters. You were quite right to come to me concerning this offer. I'll need to handle it for him. Did you bring contracts for me to look over?"

Hawk shifted in the settee and gritted his teeth. He really didn't want the earl to help finalize the contracts with Quick, if an arrangement was, indeed, made with the man. But since Quick was under the earl's financial protection, Hawk would have to at least hear what the man had to say.

"No, we're not that far along in our talks. But back to your niece and the main reason I'm here. Lady Adele would very much like to be introduced to Mr. Quick before further discussions take place. Though a bit unusual for sure, I've agreed that an informal meeting between them could take place at Hawksthorn, where Lady Adele will be well chaperoned by our widowed cousin. And your niece as well. Lady Adele believes she will feel more comfortable if Mr. Quick's sister accompanies him on the visit. However, Mr. Quick told me she doesn't travel, and if she did, she'd need your permission."

"That's true," he said with no emotion in his words.

Hawk wanted to be careful how he worded his next statement. "I was hoping you could speak to her for me about this and ask if she'd be willing to make an exception, this once, for my sister, and make the journey to Hawksthorn with her brother for a short visit." Hawk hated putting the blame for Loretta not traveling on her, but felt it was best not to antagonize the earl.

"Hmm," Lord Switchingham murmured and drank from his port again. "I'm not sure I can accomplish that. You see, she's very headstrong, that one, and she and I have come to an understanding about her not traveling. It suits both of us well, and I must tell you it's not something I'm inclined to disturb."

Loretta had told him this wouldn't be easy, but Hawk didn't intend to walk away the loser. "It would only be a short visit. Two nights would accomplish allowing Mr. Quick and Lady Adele to meet."

"I will have to put some thought into this."

Time wasn't something Hawk had a lot of. He wanted Adele's future settled before the Season started, and that was only a few weeks away.

"You do know," Hawk said, "that if an arrangement between Lady Adele and Mr. Quick occurs, I will assume all responsibility for him."

The earl's brows rose again. "Oh, well, of course, Your Grace, it's not expected, but it would be most kind of you and greatly appreciated, let me assure you."

Hawk smiled. "But if you don't feel you can persuade your niece to make the visit with her brother, I'll have to disappoint Lady Adele and not allow Mr. Quick to come, either. And without that meeting, I'm not sure how discussions for an arrangement could proceed."

Lord Switchingham sighed and placed his drink on the table by his chair. He then pulled on the lace of first one cuff and then the other, making sure the many layers of it showed like a billow of froth from beneath the sleeve of his coat.

"It's always something to handle with those two. If only my brother were still alive, but no, he had to foolishly challenge a man to a duel shortly after his daughter was born." The earl sniffed and then sighed. "And then got himself killed. So their support is left up to me. Loretta seems to have taken quite well to Mammoth House. I thought for sure she'd come begging for me to let her live at Switchingham again but she hasn't. Not yet, anyway."

Hawk couldn't see Loretta ever begging this man or anyone for anything.

"A more contrary gel I've never had the displeasure of being acquainted with," the earl continued. "But then I suppose she's just like her mother, my dearly departed sister-in-law. She was strongheaded, too. However, I'll see what I can do about allowing Loretta to accompany her brother."

A pang of frustration settled between Hawk's shoulder blades. He wanted this matter settled now. "Would you mind doing that for me at once? I'm hoping to have them visit in the next couple of weeks while I'm there."

The earl grunted as he reached for his port. "That soon?"

"It's important to me."

"And you want them to go all the way to Hawksthorn, you say?" The earl sniffed. "I don't know, Hawksthorn, that's quite a distance from Mammoth House and will require much preparation. And within a couple of weeks? That will be almost impossible for me to arrange. I'll need to see to getting a carriage and driver and—"

"No, my lord," Hawk said, interrupting him. "There will be no details for you to worry about concerning this visit. Since Mr. and Miss Quick would be coming at my invitation, I'll send a carriage for them and one for their staff, too. It will take some planning but all will be taken care of by me. I've already looked into the arrangements. If they leave Mammoth House at sunrise, they can be at Hawksthorn before dark—assuming the weather is not drenching. That way there won't be any overnight stay at an inn to worry about. I'll see to it the horses are changed often and the carriage wheels are checked along the way as well. So you see you won't need to do anything but assure me Miss Quick will be allowed to come."

"I must say that's most generous of you, Your Grace. I suppose I can talk to her right away, though I don't look forward to the long drive out to Mammoth House. I do try to go out every spring, just to make sure everything is proper there, but it's not as easy for me to travel as it used to be. Why my great-grandfather built a house that far out in the wilderness, I'll never understand."

Hawk couldn't find it inside himself to feel sorry for the man about having to make the journey out to the isolated hunting lodge. The earl should have never banished Loretta to the Mammoth House in the middle of nowhere in the first place. And Hawk wanted to get her away from it. If only for a short time.

It was a strange feeling for him, this need to rescue her—or perhaps it was more of a protective feeling. He just kept thinking that she should be with him. And it wasn't simply because he desired her. He had wanted many different women over the years. He'd pursued more than he could count. But he was certain he'd never longed for any of them the way he hungered for Loretta.

Loretta?

Yes, he thought. He liked the idea of thinking of her as Loretta. It was a beautiful and poetic name. Much more intimate sounding than Miss Quick. He would call her by her name. And it was time he told her to address him as Hawk, too.

"I would appreciate you making the effort for me, my lord, and I'll personally consider it a favor that I'll be happy to repay one day, should you ever find yourself in the position of seeking me out in some way that I might be of service to you."

Lord Switchingham's eyebrows rose, signaling his appreciation of Hawk's declaration. "I'll remember that when we are in contract negotiations for the marriage."

Hawk swallowed a silent sigh. Now he was talking the earl's language. As he'd told Loretta, he knew men, peers, and the common man alike. If you wanted something from someone, you had to give something in return, and he would honor his pledge to do a favor for the man when he asked.

Though it would irritate Hawk to do it.

"Of course. I want to have a settlement agreed upon and contracts signed before the Season starts."

The earl sniffed again and picked up his port, drained the glass, and held it up for his servant to take. "I understand, Your Grace, and I'll do it posthaste for you. Perhaps I'll just send a letter to her with instructions about what she is to do," the earl continued. "I don't think she'll dare disobey me again. She did that once, you know. Of course you do, everyone does. And though I'm sure she'd rather drink burning oil than ever admit it, I do believe she regrets her unthinkable disregard for my feelings and wishes she'd married Viscount Denningcourt when she had the chance. But there's nothing to be done about that now. The man seems happy enough with the wife he has."

Hawk looked at the earl and, once again, had to bite his tongue to keep from telling him what he thought about his poor treatment of Loretta. Hawk would have liked to boast to Lord Switchingham that he was certain she didn't regret not marrying the viscount. But that was for Loretta to say to him one day, not Hawk. It's just that he hoped to be around to hear it when she did.

"I am most appreciative that I can rely on you to accomplish getting Miss Quick to Hawksthorn for me."

The earl took the refilled glass from his servant and lifted it in a toast toward Hawk. "Consider it done."

Chapter 13

A gentleman should never try to get the best of a
young lady. You may win the argument, but you
might lose the lady in the process.

❧

*A Proper Gentleman's Guide to Wooing
the Perfect Lady*
Sir Vincent Tybalt Valentine

Loretta smiled.

It was amazing the kind of things one could find in
the attic of an old house. There were the usual things: old
furniture, dusty trunks, and paintings of family members
long departed. Disintegrating mounds of newsprint,
chipped china, and cracked chamber pots were just some
of the items Loretta came across, and couldn't understand
why someone deemed them worthy of keeping. But then
the attic at Mammoth House also had a collection of unusual things: a generous number of trophies from deer to
boar, and stuffed fowl of varying sizes. Some were in
flight, displaying their wing size, while others had been
perched on a short limb. Piled high in one corner of the
huge dark room were more antlers than anyone could
imagine, several dozen pairs of worn riding boots, and, sit-

ting away from the massive collection of discarded family *treasures* near the stairway door, a chair with wheels instead of legs.

Just what she needed.

It helped that Mrs. Huddleston already knew the chair was there, with a broken wheel that her husband had repaired in less than half a day. And now Farley was sitting in it wearing a white shirt buttoned high on his neck, dark-brown trousers that went past his ankles, and thick woolen stockings that he would grow out of before he wore a hole into the sole of them. His damp hair had been trimmed by Bitsy and was neatly parted on the right side. But the thing that had brought a smile to Loretta's face was that, for the first time since coming to Mammoth House, Farley had a little color to his lips.

She walked into the room but before she could utter the first word, Farley started coughing. Long, deep, and hard. He pulled a handkerchief from his pocket and bent double. She hated seeing him in such agony and wanted to go over to him but didn't. Now that he'd gotten better, he'd made it clear he didn't want her help. And really there was nothing she could do but whisper calming words and wait until the spasms ceased.

After the coughing spell was over, he slumped to one side of the big chair. She saw his chest moving slow and heavy with each breath. After the fever left him and he'd started eating better, she thought the bouts of coughing would subside, but she wasn't even sure their frequency had decreased. More and more she was beginning to worry that instead of simply having a lingering cough, Farley might have consumption.

Keeping those disturbing thoughts at bay, and with her voice cheerful, she said, "Bitsy did a wonderful job on your hair, Farley."

He didn't respond, so she added, "It makes you look older."

Still no acknowledgment from him, but she refused to let his attitude discourage her so she went on. "And Mrs. Huddleston did fine work of remaking the clothing for you."

Loretta recognized that Farley was still quite ill, and she knew he didn't feel well, but it didn't take much breath to say thank you. "I hope you managed to let Bitsy and Mrs. Huddleston know how much you appreciate what they've done for you."

His dark-brown eyes glared at her. "I didn't ask 'em to do it for me," he answered in a hoarse whisper and straightened himself in the large chair.

With all the coughing night and day, she had no doubt his throat stayed sore and talking wasn't easy, but it wouldn't help him if she treated him like an infant. He needed to manage a few words every now and again.

"Oh, I see," she said, keeping her tone light while folding her arms across her chest and looking down at him. "You think you have to ask someone to do something before you can say a word of thanks to them. Let me assure you that isn't true. A thank-you is never out of place, and every time someone does something nice for you appreciation is in order. Why don't you try saying it?"

He lowered his head, stared down at his folded hands in his lap, and mumbled, "Thank you."

Loretta smiled. They'd just made progress.

"That's better, and thank you for saying it for me." Loretta turned and tugged a wool blanket from the foot of the bed and laid it on his lap. "I thought you might enjoy getting out of this room for a while since you are sitting up."

The look in his eyes was wary. "And go where?"

She bent down in front of him and started tucking the

wrap around his legs. He must have been treated very badly at some time because he was very watchful. "Only to the other end of the house—which in this old place can be quite a stroll. I thought I'd take you to the music room with me. There's a big window there that overlooks a garden and a fountain."

"What do I want to look at flowers for?"

"Well, I hope you don't want to today. You'd be disappointed if you did."

"What'd ye mean? Ye said a garden."

It pleased Loretta that she'd actually gotten him talking. "There aren't any flowers to see right now. Just barren trees, bushes stripped of all their leaves, and a few dead vines that are still clinging to the trellises as they flap and fly in the wind. It's too early in the year for flowers to bloom, and the freezing storm that brought you to our door killed almost all the budding that had already started. So I expect it will be a while before we have any color in the garden this year. And it's also too early for Mr. Huddleston to put the fountain into working order."

"What ye want me to look at that for?"

"Oh, I don't," she said, lifting his feet and folding the blanket under them. "This time of year you can clearly see the stone-and-tile pathway that was laid in the garden when the house was built. It's a beautiful, intricate circle pattern. There are paths leading off the circle that are mosaics of some of the constellations, most of them having to do with hunting because this used to be a hunting lodge. There's Orion, which is the hunter. Sagittarius is the archer. Taurus is a bull and—" She looked up and saw that Farley's mouth hung open and his eyes were glazed. He had no idea what she was talking about. Not knowing about the constellations meant he hadn't had much schooling— and she wondered if he'd had any at all.

"But never mind about all that right now," she said. "We'll just leave it as the pathway is interesting to look at when there are no colorful flowers or overgrown bushes to distract from it."

Satisfied the blanket was tightly tucked, she rose. "If you want to continue to stare at these four walls and wish you were tall enough to look out the one small window over there, I'll leave you be and go play the pianoforte alone."

"I'll go with ye," he mumbled.

More progress.

"Good." Loretta moved behind the chair and gave it a push.

She soon realized it was not as easy to roll the big chair as she'd expected it to be. It was definitely easier to move on the wooden floor than on the rugs. With a lot of effort she managed to get it out the door and start it down the long corridor toward the music room. She hadn't played the piano since Farley had arrived because she hadn't wanted to disturb his rest. Sounds carried very easily from one room to the next in the mostly empty house. Now that Farley was better, perhaps a little music might lift his spirits.

It would hers.

Loretta finally stopped the chair in front of the double window in the music room. She should probably just call it the pianoforte room. There was no harp, lyre, violin, or any other type of instrument, and by the size of the room there must have been at one time.

She drew the draperies back as far as they would go. It would have been lovely to see sunshine streaming in and feel its warmth on her face, but it was not to be. The sky was a vast expanse of smoldering gray clouds that promised rain before the day was at an end.

"There," she said, turning back to face Farley as she took a resting breath from the exertion of getting the heavy wooden chair in place. "Can you see the pathway? I know it's not as good as being outside, but it's better than not even being able to look outside."

He leaned forward, shook his head, then lifted his eyes to her and said, "I can't see a 'unter or the archer."

"That's because you are looking at the constellations of them—the pattern of the stars in the night sky. We'll take a walk outside as soon as the weather gets better and I'll explain more about it. I have a book with some drawings in it that will help you understand." She hesitated and then asked, "Can you read?"

"Don't need to," he said defiantly. "Don't want to. Don't 'ave nothing to read."

Loretta knew many people couldn't read so that wasn't unusual, and suddenly she wondered if Arnold could. She would ask Mr. Huddleston if he knew whether his helper could read. If not, maybe she could teach them both to read and write their names, too. Liking that idea, she smiled to herself. It would certainly give her more to occupy her time, especially when the days were either too cold or too rainy to take a stroll around the grounds and through the garden.

"Well, we don't need to talk about reading today," she answered, feeling heartened by his honest response and her thoughts to rectify that situation. Loretta walked over to the pianoforte and sat down. She immediately started playing a slow, melodic score she knew from memory. It felt good to hear music again. She'd missed it. But she could only concentrate on the tune for so long. While her fingers pressed and moved across the keys, her thoughts drifted to the duke and her conversations with him.

It wasn't that she hadn't thought about their discussions,

their kisses. She had. Many times. She couldn't seem to
stop herself from thinking about him and the time he made
the bold statement that he was in a battle with her for *her*.

He had stunned her with those words, more so maybe
than even by his ardent kisses. Was it because she'd let him
be so intimate with her that he now wanted more from her?
And God help her, she'd wanted more from him, too. But
she couldn't, wouldn't allow it. The risks were too great.

It was no wonder the Duke of Hawksthorn was called
a rake. An apt name for such an alluring man.

At night, it was becoming common for her to lie in her
bed, long after she should have been asleep, and think
about the duke. About his kisses. About his most recent
proclamation: There would be more kisses. Sometimes
it soothed her to remember his presence in her home, to
think about how wonderful it had felt being in his arms.
And more times than she could count, she'd had to chas-
tise herself when she'd found herself wondering if she
wanted him to win the battle they were waging.

Still, at other times she'd wonder if the duke had talked
to her uncle about her going to Hawksthorn or if the duke
had completely forgotten about her once he'd left. It had
been well over a week since he'd been at Mammoth House,
and still there was no word. And he was an admitted rake.
Perhaps he'd only hoped to seduce her into his bed and
when that hadn't happened, he'd simply brushed her from
his mind.

One thing was sure: She didn't doubt the duke's persuasive powers if he had spoken to the earl. They had been
used on her and they were strong. But neither did she doubt
her uncle's harshness. She knew his strength as well. And
would it be best for her if the duke won or the earl?

She believed Paxton needed her to keep him strong in
his conviction that he wouldn't accept the duke's offer if

he didn't desire with all his heart a match with Lady Adele. And while it would be like making a trip to heaven to get away from Mammoth House for a time, would it also be her downfall? She desired the duke and wondered if she could resist him if he chose to pursue her again.

Lost in her thoughts, it took Loretta a moment or two to realize she was hearing a pounding knock at the back door. For an instant her stomach jumped. She thought it might be her uncle and that he'd come to talk to her about a visit to Hawksthorn, but then she smiled at that foolish notion and kept playing.

Her uncle would never arrive at the back door of any home and most assuredly not his own. It must be one of Mr. Huddleston's relatives. They would occasionally hunt pheasant or some type of fowl in the area and offer to share some of whatever they'd shot for the evening meal. The rumble of voices didn't last long and Loretta soon went back to thinking about the duke until she noticed Paxton standing in the doorway. Smiling as usual.

He motioned for her to come join him.

She looked over her shoulder at Farley. His eyes were closed and his chin had fallen to his chest. The piano music had put him to sleep. She played another chord or two and then quietly rose and walked over to greet Paxton.

"How's Farley doing?" her brother asked in a whispered tone as they walked down the corridor.

"The cough is still with him. It worries me that it's still so deep in his chest."

"Perhaps in another few days it will be gone, because it looks as if he's making progress. He's out of bed."

"Yes, he's eating well and regaining strength."

"I'm glad to hear it." Paxton pulled a hand from behind his back and held up two notes. "Look what I have from our uncle. Letters. One for you and one for me."

Loretta's stomach felt as if it fell to her feet. "Did the duke speak to him? Did he give in to the duke's wishes? Will I be going to Hawksthorn with you? What did he say?"

Paxton chuckled. "So many questions, and I don't know the answer to any of them."

"Why not?" she queried.

"I haven't opened my note and you haven't opened yours. They just arrived." He threw his hands out wide and laughed. "I thought it would be better if we did it together. Ladies first." He handed her one of the letters.

Now her stomach felt as if it were tumbling over and over inside her. How like Paxton to be so carefree and make a game of this when she was full of apprehension. Would she be allowed to go or wouldn't she? Did she want to go or didn't she?

"No, you go first," she said anxiously, utterly dithering about her feelings on this.

"All right, my dear sister. To please you, I will. Though it is not a gentlemanly thing to do."

Loretta held herself stiffly while Paxton opened the letter and read it. Silently. Oh, heaven's gate! All her earlier muddled thoughts be damned. Yes, she wanted to go to Hawksthorn. Of course she wanted to see the duke again and to know if her heart would still feel like it was skipping a beat every time she looked at him. But would she be allowed?

Paxton continued to look at the sheet and was quiet for so long she finally blurted, "Oh, for the sake of the jitters in my stomach, Paxton, what does he say?"

"Nothing much, as usual. He has instructed me to not agree to anything the duke says, nor to sign anything that the duke might give me. Uncle said that once I have made it known to him that I find Lady Adele acceptable to make a match, which he has all confidence I will do, he will then take over and handle everything with the duke for me so that he can ensure all will be settled for my best benefit."

Loretta could see the parchment he was holding. It had a lot of writing on it. "Is that all he says?" she asked.

"Yes."

Her insides calmed. Her shoulders relaxed. Her breathing eased. The decision had been made. "So I wasn't mentioned."

"No, but I'm sure you were in the letter you are holding."

A lump formed in her throat. Yes, she was sure of that, too. But if the earl didn't mention her going in Paxton's letter, that probably meant she wouldn't be going.

"Then it is as I expected," she said softly. "Uncle is encouraging you to go to Hawksthorn and make the match with Lady Adele."

"Yes and he says the quicker the better. To quote him"— Paxton looked down at the letter and read—" 'Before another, more worthy gentleman snatches her from beneath your nose while you dally about life doing nothing of importance.' " He lifted his head and smiled at Loretta.

How he could smile after such a callous remark, Loretta didn't know. "That was unkind of Uncle."

"But expected. Our father wasn't his favorite brother so we never had a chance at being favored, either. Now read yours."

She didn't want to but knew she must. She turned the parchment over, broke the earl's seal, and read. He was allowing her to go. Her legs turned weak. The duke had won. He had convinced her uncle to allow her to travel.

Loretta looked up at Paxton. "Uncle is giving me permission to go to Hawksthorn. But says the only reason he is allowing it is because he wants me to make friends with Lady Adele and do all within my power to see to it you and the duke's sister marry with all haste."

Paxton laughed heartily and, grabbing Loretta's fore-arms, kissed first one cheek and then the other. "I hope you are happy, my dear, because I am delighted you'll be with me!"

"Yes, I do want to go," she said knowing in her heart it was the truth, despite her troubling thoughts about what might happen between Paxton and Lady Adele or with her and the duke while she was there.

"See, I told you it is difficult to refuse a duke," Paxton said.

Oh, she knew how hard it was.

"But if *you* don't refuse him," Loretta said, "will you always wonder about Miss Pritchard and what could have developed between you two? You seemed quite taken with her when you returned home and said you wanted to pay her a visit in the spring."

"So I do. Just now I was referring to it being difficult for our uncle to refuse the duke. Not me."

"Oh." Loretta smiled. "I was thinking you were talking about yourself. I'm happy you are taking your time about this and not rushing into saying you will marry Lady Adele."

"If your experience with Lord Denningcourt taught me anything, it was that one doesn't rush into making a match."

"I wonder what the duke said to make the earl soften his heart and agree to let me travel this time. It's been so long since I've asked to go anywhere."

"I can't know for sure, but he probably had to promise to give the earl something in return. That is the way people usually do things. Even children. Remember when I used to say to you that I would play with you and your teacups if you would play hide-and-seek with me?"

"I do remember that."

Happy memories of their early childhood came flooding back to her: When they lived in their own home. When they chased each other up and down the stairs. When the governess taught them their lessons together and when they threw stones into the pond behind their house. When their mother brushed their hair and patted their cheeks affectionately. A warm feeling washed over her, and she smiled.

All that was before their mother died. Before Paxton went to boarding school and she to Switchingham to learn how to be a lady.

"I don't know for sure how it came about," Paxton said, his earlier statement obviously not jogging memories as it had for her. "I don't care, Loretta, and neither should you. Not only am I pleased you're going to get away from this monstrosity for a while, but I also want to know what you think of Lady Adele."

"I want to meet her, too."

"To make sure she doesn't have a wart on her nose or a missing front tooth."

They both laughed.

Paxton then reached into his pocket and said, "There's another letter that has come. It was given to Mr. Huddleston by a messenger earlier this morning. He stuffed it in his pocket and forgot to bring it inside until the other messenger arrived."

"From Uncle?" she asked, suddenly wary that he might have changed his mind and sent another letter rescinding his earlier one.

"No. The duke."

Loretta's heartbeat raced. "Really? What does he say?"

"I don't know. I haven't read it."

She huffed and felt like stomping her foot, as well, but was able to refrain from doing so. "Merciful heavens! Have you no curiosity in any of your bones! Do so at once and tell me what he says."

"I would be happy to, but I can't."

"Why?"

Paxton laughed. "I've already read my letter from the duke, dearest sister. This one is addressed to you."

Chapter 14

A gentleman must never bring up an objectionable subject such as politics or money in front of a lady's delicate hearing.

❧

A Proper Gentleman's Guide to Wooing the Perfect Lady
Sir Vincent Tybalt Valentine

Oh, you are a wretched brother!" Loretta exclaimed. "Why didn't you say I had a letter from the duke?"

He laughed. "I was trying not to overwhelm you with news."

"I'm not that easily overwhelmed and you know it." She took the note, hoping Paxton wouldn't see that her hands were trembling—from excitement and a little fear, too. "But I do wonder why the duke wrote to me."

"I suppose you will have to read it and discover for yourself. My thoughts are that he simply wants to make sure you are coming with me. He seemed quite determined."

"Yes, I'm sure you're right."

Carefully, she lifted the seal so she wouldn't break the wax and cause it to crumble away. She didn't know why, but wanted to keep everything about the letter perfect so she could look at it again and again. She unfolded the paper and read:

> *Miss Quick,*
> *The battle has begun and I am well armed. I am working on my strategy for our next meeting, and I have no doubt you are working on yours. Until we meet at Hawksthorn.*
>
>   *Hawk*

Loretta's heartbeat pounded. He hadn't forgotten about her. He was preparing for her. Oh, dear, what was she going to do? What defenses could she muster that would win against his alluring offenses? How could she resist him when he'd already showed her the pleasures she could experience in his arms?

"What did he say?" Paxton asked.

She folded the letter over and kept it firmly clutched in her hand. "Nothing really, other than he's preparing for our visit."

"That was kind of him to remember to send you a personal note as well. He's a very busy man, you know."

"Yes, it was," she answered cautiously. "And I'm sure he is busy. What did he have to say to you?"

"He explained the details of our visit. He's very thorough. He'll send two coaches for us. We'll leave promptly at first light and stop only to change the horses, which he's already arranged. Baskets with food and drink will be in each carriage. He said we should arrive at Hawksthorn late in the afternoon but before dark. We should be ready to leave a week from Friday. That will give us several days to get ready. Can you do that?"

That was almost laughable. She could be ready to leave before the afternoon was over. "Yes, plenty of time for me," she said, excited at the thought of leaving Mammoth House for a few days and seeing the duke.

Loretta talked a minute or two longer with Paxton before walking back toward the music room. She would rather go to her room and think about what the duke had written about planning his strategy but she couldn't leave Farley sleeping in the chair. Instead, she was surprised to see Farley standing at the window with his hands and forehead flattened against the pane, looking out and seeming in deep thought. He looked taller than she'd remembered from the night he'd arrived, but no less thin or lonely.

"I'm glad to see you are feeling strong enough to stand up," she said in a cheerful voice as she entered the room and stopped beside him.

He turned to her and quietly asked, "Where is this place?"

"You mean this house?"

He nodded.

So it was as she'd thought, he wasn't familiar with the area. It was no wonder he was asking. There was nothing but barren tree lines or empty flat lands as far as the eye could see in any direction. "You're in Mammoth House, which is about a half day's ride from Grimsfield. Do you know where that is?"

He shook his head.

"Do you remember how you got here?"

"Walked," he said, turning his attention back out the window.

"From where?"

He shrugged. "The road mostly."

She couldn't say he wasn't answering her questions,

though they weren't telling her much. "How did you get onto the road?"

"A man left me standing on it."

That didn't sound good. "Can you tell me more about how that came about or tell me about the man?"

"I was minding my ownself, wasn't stealing anything or causing trouble to anyone. Just looking at the meat pies cooling in the window of a bread shop. A man grabbed me from behind, put 'is hand over me mouth, and tossed me inside a wagon as if I were a sack of coal. And 'e locked the door so we couldn't get out."

"That's terrifying," Loretta said and shivered. She didn't want to alarm Farley and show how horrified she was about what had happened to him. "What man? Do you know who he was?"

Farley turned toward her again. His big brown eyes had narrowed with anger. "No. But 'e was big and strong. Lifted me right off me feet, he did."

"Did anyone try to help you?"

"Won't nobody 'elp a kid like me. I 'elped my ownself. I bit 'is 'and 'ard as I could. Tried to box his ears. I wasn't going with 'im without a fight."

Loretta understood his fury. She was angry, too. Anyone would be under the circumstances. "That's dreadful. But you didn't get away?"

"'E was too strong."

"You said *we* couldn't get out. Was someone with you? Your parents? Your mama?" she asked cautiously, hoping to trigger that softness in him that she'd only seen when he was dreaming of his mother.

Farley shook his head and his expression relaxed a little. His tone evened out as he said, "Got no parents. Got no one but me. Other boys were in the wagon—just like me." He struck a thin, limber thumb to his chest. "The big oaf that took me stole them all right off the street and locked us inside. People watched, but no one cared."

Still trying to comprehend his story of being abducted, she asked, "You didn't know the man or the other boys?"

Farley coughed into his handkerchief a few times before saying, "Didn't know him from any other devil or cur that walks the streets."

Loretta blinked at his language but held the reprimand that wanted to spring forth. Since this was the first time Farley had opened up and was talking about himself, she wanted to be careful and not say anything that would cause him to go quiet.

She remained very still with her hands folded in front of her and kept her voice even as she asked, "Where was the shop you were standing in front of when the man grabbed you?"

"Near St. James Park."

"So you were in London when you were taken?"

He nodded again. His eyes had softened and watered when he looked up at her and said, "'Ow am I going to get back?"

At present, she didn't know. She hadn't given much thought to him leaving, only staying at Mammoth House.

She inhaled a deep breath and let it out slowly. "I don't know the answer to that at the moment. And for now it's not important. You aren't well enough to go anywhere yet. There's still time to consider that. Did the man say where he was taking you?"

Farley's face relaxed. He shrugged and turned back to the window. "'E didn't tell me anything. One of the boys said 'e was taking us to a place where we would work, get paid, and 'ave something to eat every day. But another one said we'd never get paid a halfpence and we'd be beaten if we didn't work."

Loretta's heart constricted and another shiver shook her. She'd heard a little about workhouses where the very poor were given a place to live and food in exchange for labor, but had never seen one and certainly had never met anyone who was destined for such a place.

"So what happened?" she asked. "Did you escape from the workhouse?"

"No," he said, to her surprise.

"How did you get away?"

"'E threw me out on the road and left me, 'e did."

She covered her mouth with her hand to silence her gasp as she heard his words. Old feelings of abandonment flooded her. She'd felt them years ago when her mother had died even after promising Loretta she wouldn't leave her. And more recently when her uncle had banished her to the loneliness of Mammoth House.

"What a vile soul that man must have to throw a young boy along the side of the road," she said with a shaky voice. "And out here in the middle of nowhere."

"Said it wasn't 'is fault. 'E had to do it. I was sick with fever and I'd give it to the other boys. Said we'd all die if I stayed in the wagon with them. Then 'e wouldn't get any money for us."

Anger grew inside Loretta. She wanted to find the man and have him punished.

"So he just left you beside the road in the freezing rain! That was a wicked thing for him to do to you."

"I didn't care. 'E was a cur. I didn't want to go wherever 'e was taking me anyway."

She blinked at his swearing again but only asked, "How did you find Mammoth House? There's no distinct road leading here anymore."

"I followed the road for a while, until I saw the man

walking 'is 'orse and followed 'im. I figured 'e knew where 'e was going."

"So you followed the Duke of Hawksthorn here?"

When she said the duke's name, Farley looked over his shoulder at her with distrust in his eyes. "'E don't like me."

"Who?" she asked cautiously. "The duke? I know it may have seemed that way when you first arrived. I didn't think he liked me the first time we met, either. He can be rather strong and commanding. But he's a fair person."

"'Is kind got no use for someone like me," Farley said as a determined expression settled onto his face. "I seen it in 'is eyes, I did."

"That may be true for some gentlemen but not the duke," she defended.

"'E's like all the gents, 'e is. They just soon give ye the backs of their hand as a penny. They brush you away like dust off their fancy cuffs."

She gasped. "The duke never struck you, did he?"

"'E grabbed me and wouldn't let me go."

"That's because he knew you were in peril. He saved your life that night. If the duke hadn't gone out into the storm and brought you back, you probably would have—well, there is no telling what may have happened to you. As it is, you were saved from the storm and the fever and you're getting stronger each day. And you don't have to go to a workhouse, either. But if you have no parents, where do you live?"

He looked back out the window and defiantly said, "Got my ownself a place under the steps of an old building near St. James Park. Dug it out my ownself. Even found enough wood for a floor and a blanket, too."

"That's good," she said softly, her heart feeling heavy and thinking that she couldn't imagine anything more horrible than not having a home to live in, nor a bed to sleep in. And not even a fire to warm her during the freezing winter nights. Just a cold wooden floor and a blanket.

"Where do you get food?"

He looked at her with his big brown eyes and calmly said, "Wherever I can find it. Got no one to bring it to me like you do."

Loretta felt the sting of what he said, though she knew he didn't mean it as a rebuke—only an observation. Knowing he had so little, she wondered if she'd ever truly feel hungry again. She was overly blessed compared with Farley and so many children who'd been abandoned by the good side of life.

"Ye don't need to look sad for me. I don't mind." Farley started coughing. He turned away from her and bent double as he struggled to recover his breath.

Loretta wished again she could keep the bouts from returning. She would ask Mr. Huddleston to talk to the apothecary again the next time he went to Grimsfield and see if there was something else they could try that might help Farley.

They'd probably talked enough for one day anyway. When the coughing had subsided she said, "I think we should get you back to your room, and in order to do that you have to get back into the chair. I don't want you up too long."

"I can walk," he muttered.

"Yes, you can, but you're not going to this time," she said, pointing to the chair. "We'll try that tomorrow."

Farley hesitated, as if he might challenge her, but instead he crawled back into the big chair and allowed her to tuck the blanket around his legs again.

When she rose and started around to the back of the chair she heard him say, "Thank you."

Loretta lifted her chin and smiled.

The two of them were silent as they started the trek back to his room. This time her step was much lighter. She had learned so much more about Farley. The next time they talked she was confident she would learn even more.

Loretta knew there were plenty of uncared for and mistreated children like Farley. She couldn't help them all, but she would find a way to help this one. If it were in her power to do so, he wouldn't go to a workhouse or back to the streets of London.

He would find a home here at Mammoth House.

Chapter 15

A gentleman would never be bored and fall asleep
in a lady's presence.

❧

*A Proper Gentleman's Guide to Wooing
the Perfect Lady*
Sir Vincent Tybalt Valentine

It was late in the day, and it had been a long and bumpy
one. Loretta had not cared. She'd taken every jostle,
rumble, snatch, and rock of the coach with immense pleasure. Even the occasional slurring shouts the driver directed at the horses couldn't put a damper on her day.

The sun had just broken on the horizon with shades of
pink, blue, and gray when she'd boarded the coach that
morning. The view from the back window of the carriage
had been blocked with all the luggage that had been piled
high, but she'd still waved good-bye to the big stone house
in the beautiful light of dawn. She had no idea when or if
she'd ever be allowed to leave again, and she was determined to enjoy every moment of her journey, her freedom,
and her short stay at Hawksthorn.

The last time their small caravan of two coaches made

a stop, the driver had informed Loretta the next one would be when they arrived at the front door of the Hawksthorn Estate. That was welcome news. Her joyful attitude hadn't waned, but she was tired of the constant sitting and was eager to see the duke, his home, and of course his sister—the main reason she was allowed to accompany Paxton.

It had been a cloudy and windy day. Light rain had fallen from time to time, but not enough to drench the roads and make wheels bog into the soggy earth. The temperature had stayed well above freezing, making the journey bearable for everyone, including the drivers and their helpers.

Loretta and Paxton rode in the lead carriage, which when they started was pulled by six magnificent-looking bays. The horses had already been changed several times since then, because their pace had been brisk. Their coach wasn't as elaborate as the one Mrs. Huddleston had described to her with such relish when the duke had last visited Mammoth House, but it was far fancier than Loretta was used to. Tastefully handsome on the outside and divinely plush on the inside.

The luxurious cushions were a deep shade of blue velvet and stuffed with the softest of feathers. The extra filling beneath her bottom made all the jostling from side to side, and the shallow holes, deep ruts, and large pebbles the wheels ran over, easier to bear. Fine wood framing around the windows and side panels had been polished to a high gleam. A basket filled with cheese, bread, and dried fruits rested on the seat beside Loretta, along with a generous supply of chocolate, wine for Paxton, and enough water to keep them all well satisfied.

Bitsy, Paxton's valet, Farley, and Mrs. Huddleston rode in the carriage following them. It was only a little less ornate, and it pleased Loretta's housekeeper greatly that she had the opportunity to ride in such elegant style.

Farley hadn't been invited to Hawksthorn, but at the last moment, and against her brother's wishes, Loretta decided she couldn't leave him at Mammoth House. That decision meant she had to bring Mrs. Huddleston along to take care of him. With all the changing of clothing Loretta would have to do at the duke's house, Bitsy wouldn't have time to take care of the lad.

Besides, he was feeling better, staying out of bed for most of the day, and eating well. They'd even spent time walking outside together on three afternoons. Much to her delight, he had been patient and attentive when they'd strolled through the back garden and she'd explained more to him about the constellations in the night sky. He'd laughed at her suggestion of him learning to read, but she reminded him that he would be able to read the street and shop window signs when he returned to London and that intrigued him. Later, Bitsy had told her she saw him looking through the pages in one of the books Loretta had left on the night chest by his bed. That gave her hope he would change his mind. She would mention reading again when he was feeling stronger.

Loretta's main concern about Farley's health was his lingering cough. It wasn't improving. The debilitating spells were frequent and long, and seemed to drain his energy quickly. She worried about the thought there might be permanent damage to his lungs from the fever. Getting him away from Mammoth House for a few days so he could see and do some different things might do him more good than harm.

But all those noble reasons aside, Loretta had to be completely truthful, at least with herself. Not a one of them was the real reason she wanted Farley with her. Even though his body was still weak, she didn't doubt his mental fortitude. If he decided he was ready to leave, she believed he'd simply start walking with no real knowledge of just how long a walk it would be back to London, or how to get there. In the end, that is what made her decide to bring him along. If she didn't, she was afraid he'd be gone by the time she returned. Loretta was making such progress with him, she couldn't bear the thought of him leaving.

Perhaps it was only natural, but she'd felt a greater concern for him since he'd opened up about his past. Being grabbed off the street and thrown into a locked wagon would be frightening for anyone. She knew something of how he felt. Mammoth House was gigantic compared with a wagon, but she had, in effect, been locked away, too. And the thought of being sold to a workhouse must have been even more horrific for him. It was no wonder there was no trust in Farley's eyes or his attitude for anyone. Loretta hoped that in time her kindness to him would show him that not everyone was cruel.

She hadn't mentioned the lad to her uncle yet and knew she must do that as soon as she returned. It would take some time to write the letter in a way that would lead the earl to decide it would be to his benefit to keep Farley at Mammoth House. She would talk to Mr. Huddleston first about things that Farley could do. Each day her hope grew stronger that if she offered Farley a permanent home and a place to work, he would agree to stay and not want to go back to living under the steps of an abandoned building.

Loretta looked over at Paxton, seated opposite her with his back facing the horses. His long, lean legs stretched out as far as he could get them and were crossed at the ankles. He'd fallen asleep, again, snuggled deep into his cloak, with his hat covering his face. She smiled. Paxton had chatted for most of the trip—jumping from one subject to the other and then on to another. She assumed to avoid talking about the real reason for their visit to Hawksthorn.

Along with the excitement of making this trip, leaving Mammoth House for the first time in almost three years, she also had a fair amount of apprehension that kept wanting to tamp down the good feelings. Paxton was a happy, carefree soul and could be easily led. She didn't want him only to become enamored of the change in his lifestyle that marriage to a duke's sister would bring him; she wanted him to fall deeply in love with Lady Adele or refuse the duke's offer to make a match with her.

The duke.

Thinking about him had become a much-desired pastime. She liked that she could say whatever she wanted to him without fear of reprisal in any way. Courtship and marriage were not available to her so she was free to enjoy being with him, answer his banter, and relish the kisses he had all but promised. But she had to be wary, too. She must guard herself and not let their kisses go too far. She knew the dangers. Her goal had to be that she would not let the duke seduce her into his bed no matter how much she would like to fall victim to all the duke's charms.

Noticing that the light of day was waning, Loretta was beginning to wonder if they would, indeed, make Hawksthorn before nightfall. She thought about laying her head back to nap, but her mind was too busy with thoughts of the duke. Instead, she quietly reached into her satchel and pulled out her copy of *A Proper Gentleman's Guide to Wooing the Perfect Lady*. It brought a smile to her face every time she held the small leather-bound book in her hands. It wasn't a long book, but it had brought her such joy.

She lightly rubbed her fingertips over the title and the author's name, feeling the smoothness of the cold leather. Silly as it was, she treasured the volume. Not because of the contents, but because it was an unexpected gift from the duke.

He was right in that for the most part it was filled with useless advice most men learned from the time they left the cradle. One such rule was: *It is never permissible for a gentleman to remove his coat in the presence of a lady.*

That one baffled her. What gentleman would do that anyway? Men were taught that lesson from the time they slid their arms into their first coat.

And then there was: *A gentleman must always watch his language in front of a lady.* This, too, was another rule of manners that gentlemen were taught almost from their birth.

There were a few of the guidelines and rules that she felt were good and something a gentleman might need to be reminded of. Her favorite was: *It is never permissible for a gentleman to suggest to a lady that she is wrong.* That one made her smile every time she read it.

Loretta fully agreed with that rule, though she couldn't see the duke or the earl ever following it. Not as far as Loretta was concerned anyway. The duke and her uncle considered it their duty to tell her when they thought she was wrong. But then, neither of them was trying to woo her, so maybe this would only apply if they were trying to win a certain lady's favor.

There were some instructions that were so unbelievably odd it was easy to see humor in them: *There is only one time a gentleman should tell a lady how beautiful she is and that is from the time she arrives in his presence until the time she leaves.*

Some of the rules she absolutely agreed with: *A proper lady appreciates a gentleman who is always cheerful.* And: *It is best for a gentleman to always let a young lady have the last word.*

And then there were some guides she wished were true, though she had her doubts: *A gentleman should always let a lady know that her heart would be safe if she gave it to him.* Now that was a truly romantic notion she and all ladies could agree with.

Loretta heard a whooping holler from the driver. She closed the book and gently stowed it back in her satchel. Paxton roused from his slumber and rubbed his nose with the back of his hand while he stretched and yawned.

She leaned over and looked out the window. They were traveling on a curve and turning onto a tree-lined lane. Although it wasn't quite dusk yet, lampposts had been lit as far down as she could see.

"What are you looking at?" Paxton asked.

Her breathing increased sharply. Anticipation at seeing the duke flooded her. "Hawksthorn," she whispered almost reverently. "We've arrived onto the estate."

"Splendid," he said, sitting up straight in the cushion and combing through his hair with his hands. "And about time. I've not slept so much in years."

In the far distance, she saw the roofline of a large, L-shaped building. It had to be the manor at Hawksthorn. The main building was so long and wide, it looked as if Mammoth House would have fit inside a small section of it. She should have known it would be. It was the center of the dukedom. She could see the tops of smaller buildings that were probably cottages for the workers, servants, and tenants, or possibly even the paddocks, barns, and carriage houses.

Within a couple of moments the main house came into full view. Loretta was awed at the magnificence of its stately grandeur. To the left, near the horizon, the clouds had separated; the sun hung low in the sky, giving off a spectacular golden glow of light in the heavens, making the stone structure seem majestic.

The colors in the sky were a good sign the weather was going to take a turn for the better. It was the beginning of spring after all, and winter had finally passed.

Loretta picked up the dark-brown bonnet that matched her cape and the trim on her pale-brown traveling dress and placed it back on her head. With cold, eager fingers she tied the satin ribbon under her chin. "Did I get it straight?" she asked her brother.

He studied her a second and said, "It looks perfect."

"How about my hair?" he asked, smoothing it down the sides with an open hand. "Is it sticking up anywhere?"

"The front and sides look nice. Turn around and let me see the back."

Paxton twisted around.

"Oh, my," Loretta said in a worried voice. "I do believe it looks as if two squirrels have been nesting in the back of your hair."

"What?" Paxton licked the pads of his three middle fingers and started frantically pressing down his hair.

"No, stop, please!" She laughed. "I was only teasing you. I didn't think you would take me seriously. Your hair is in good order and you don't need to do a thing to it."

"A fine sister you are," he grumbled lightheartedly and fiddled with the ends of his neckcloth to make sure they were laying properly. "If we were at home, I'd hold you down and tickle your sides for that prank."

"You would have to catch me first."

"Though I haven't tried in a few years, I still have no doubt I could."

They laughed together as the carriage rolled to a stop. Through the window Loretta caught a glimpse of the duke.

Her heart skipped a couple of beats at the sight of him. He stood with a young lady who had to be his sister and an older woman whom Loretta assumed was Lady Adele's cousin. The three were waiting to greet Loretta and Paxton in front of two giant, beautifully carved doors that looked as if they belonged on a castle.

Loretta was surprised how much at ease she felt about this visit. Coming to the duke's home should have made her a ball of jitters, but she felt calm and wonderful. The amusing exchange with Paxton must have been exactly what she'd needed to make her feel content about seeing the duke again and eager to meet Lady Adele.

The steps were put in place and the door opened. Paxton stepped down first and reached back to help Loretta. When she entered the carriage doorway, she looked up and immediately saw the duke. Tingles of wonderful sensations washed over her. Heaven help her, when she looked at him, she felt as if a feast of all her desires had been spread before her to enjoy. Somehow, even with his elegantly tied neckcloth, light-blue quilted waistcoat, and impeccably tailored dark-blue coat, he managed to look casual, commanding, and yet approachable, all at the same time.

He smiled, and so did she. When both feet were on the ground, she turned to Lady Adele and knew she would have to apologize to the duke again for disparaging his sister. Lady Adele was lovely and wouldn't have any problems attracting a husband during the Season if she chose to attend.

Not quite as tall as Loretta, Lady Adele had thick, golden-brown hair that waved beautifully about her head with small wispy curls framing her delicate face. Her complexion looked pure, with just the right amount of healthy color to her lips and cheeks. Sparkling eyes, as green as her brother's, looked directly at Loretta. Lady Adele nodded graciously before shifting her focus to Paxton.

Loretta knew the second Paxton's gaze met Lady Adele's that he was drawn to her. Loretta's vivacious brother, who was never at a loss for words, seemed momentarily shy and speechless. It was as if he were in awe of the duke's sister and didn't know what to say. And from the smile on Lady Adele's pretty face, she was quite pleased with the way Paxton looked as well.

"Miss Quick. Mr. Quick," the duke said. "Welcome to Hawksthorn."

Loretta curtsied. Paxton bowed and they both said "Your Grace" at the same time.

The proper introductions, greetings, and platitudes were said among everyone, including Mrs. Minerva Philbert, Lady Adele's cousin, chaperone, and companion. She was a little shorter than Lady Adele, thin, and what Loretta would call a severely prim-looking lady. Strands of gray streaked her brown upswept hair. Her almond-shaped, greenish-blue gaze seemed to glance quickly by Loretta but held long and steadfast on Paxton. She was looking him over from hair to boot.

If the duke had told Lady Adele about the misgivings Loretta had concerning her and the possibility of a match with Paxton, she'd decided not to take offense. There wasn't a hint of animosity in her expression when they were introduced.

"Miss Quick," Lady Adele said, "Hawk has told me how devoted you and your brother are to each other. That's something I respect and admire." She glanced over at the duke. "I'm very fond of my brother, too."

From the corner of her eye, Loretta could see the duke giving his sister an indulgent smile. To Lady Adele she said, "It's wonderful we both have such fine brothers to take care of us."

"I think Hawk will consider it a blessing when he no longer has to be responsible for me. I do believe he sees me only as trouble on his hands."

The duke remained silent and continued to smile.

"See," Lady Adele said, and playfully hit him on the arm with her lace-trimmed handkerchief. "He isn't even going to bother denying it's true. He's always been a brute whenever my feelings are concerned. I suppose I will have to offer my attention and my affections elsewhere, dear brother."

"Please, feel free to do so at any time," the duke answered in the same lighthearted tone. "You will have my blessing."

Loretta enjoyed the teasing banter between the duke and his sister. It was so much like the relationship she had with Paxton. Loving, but each getting their points across.

Lady Adele then turned her attention to Paxton and said, "Tell me, Mr. Quick, was your journey a pleasant one?"

The duke let his gaze settle on Loretta's face after Lady Adele's concentration was centered on Paxton. "And how about you, Miss Quick?" the duke said. "Did everything go smoothly for you today?"

She loved the way she felt when he looked at her. "Yes," she answered, feeling as if her gaze was melting into his. "You had every detail attended to so there was nothing to do but enjoy the countryside."

"I must admit to having a bit of help with getting all the particulars accomplished."

Her gaze drifted to the massive, carved doors behind him. "Your home is so grand." She then glanced toward the huge front lawn, still brown with winter. It was outlined with a short hedge of yew and tall topiary trees. "I can imagine the grounds are spectacular with color in the late spring and summer."

"The gardeners are good at what they do."

"I do believe Hawksthorn is almost as large as Mammoth House," she added with a teasing smile, and hoped a sparkle of humor danced in her eyes as well.

The duke chuckled softly. "I have always found your wit charming, Miss Quick. I'm glad you're here," he added quietly.

So was she.

"And I trust you left Farley feeling better, and in the good care of Mrs. Huddleston?"

"No, actually—" She turned her head and stared down the drive to where the second coach had stopped at the servants' entrance. Mrs. Huddleston was stepping off the carriage. Farley stepped down behind her. "I brought him with me, along with Mrs. Huddleston to care for him."

"You brought Farley here?"

Loretta knew the duke wasn't happy by the tightness around his mouth and fine crinkles around his eyes as they narrowed. She'd suspected that he might not approve of her decision not to leave the boy behind, but as far as she was concerned, there was no other choice.

"Yes," she answered as if nothing were unusual about what she'd done. She might be guilty, but she didn't have to act as if she were.

"Minerva, would you show Adele and Mr. Quick inside? His sister would like a few more minutes to stretch her legs. We are going to take a walk."

"I'm sure that will be fine, Your Grace. You won't be long, will you?"

"No, Minerva, we'll be in shortly."

"Shortly?" Mrs. Philbert asked, frowning at the duke.

"If that's the case, we can wait here for you. It won't be a problem."

"That's not necessary, Minerva. You have no cause to worry. I think Miss Quick's reputation will be safe with me on the front lawn since the servants are still milling about with the luggage."

She sniffed. "Yes, of course. I didn't mean to imply otherwise. Please, follow me, my lady, Mr. Quick."

Loretta watched Paxton and Lady Adele exchange a glance, and then—completely ignoring the conversation between the duke and their cousin—Lady Adele said, "Do you enjoy playing cards in the evenings after dinner, Mr. Quick?"

"Of course," he answered as they started toward the door. "It's one of our favorite pastimes. Loretta and I will often play a game or two, and chess, too. Though I admit if the game takes too long to finish I become restless."

"I feel the same about chess. It can become a bore. You do like dogs, don't you, Mr. Quick?"

"Absolutely. Though I don't have one at this time."

Loretta slowly shook her head as the three disappeared through the massive doorway. Here it had been less than five minutes and Paxton was already smitten by Lady Adele and the duke was upset with her. Her first visit to Hawksthorn wasn't getting off to a very good start. And the devil take it, she had no one to blame but herself.

Chapter 16

A gentleman should always fill a lady's heart and
mind with sweet words of romantic notions. That's
all she really wants to hear.

～✦～

*A Proper Gentleman's Guide to Wooing
the Perfect Lady*
Sir Vincent Tybalt Valentine

After the trio had cleared the doorway, the duke said,
"Let's take a stroll, Miss Quick."

The merriment the exchange with his sister had left in
his face was gone. A serious expression had replaced it.
"Thank you," she said, "I'd like that." If he were going to
take her to task for bringing Farley she had just as soon no
one else heard him.

They started down the middle of the spacious lawn in
front of the house at a leisurely pace. Dusk was falling
around them and the chill of night wind stirred the air, but
she was warm enough in her traveling cape.

"He should have been left at Mammoth House," the
duke said.

That was straightforward enough. It might have been
the right thing to do, but Loretta didn't want to do it. She

looked down the way at Farley again. He seemed so small, lost even, standing with his hands in the pockets of his coat looking around while the luggage was being unloaded.

She hadn't wanted to argue with the duke the minute she stepped off the coach. Yet her happiness at seeing him was rapidly dissipating. When he'd smiled at her, she felt wonderful, with not a care in the world, and now she suddenly felt miserable. She didn't like disappointing him any more than he did. He didn't have to tell her it wasn't polite to bring anyone uninvited to his house.

"I'm sorry you're upset about my decision. I know it was forward of me and I should have written to ask if it would be all right," she said, though she remained firm on her conviction she'd had to bring him with her.

"That's not what I meant."

She felt him looking at her but she kept her eyes cast down to the dormant grass beneath her feet and let out a deep breath. Perhaps she could smooth things over if she deliberately misread the duke's comment. It was worth a try.

Lifting her gaze to his, she said, "I agree that Farley still isn't well. There's a chance the traveling will have been too much for him, and he'll have a relapse, but I felt I couldn't leave him alone. Too, I knew that if he did get worse from the strain of traveling, he would receive excellent care here in your house."

A gleam in his eyes let her know that he knew exactly what she was doing. It didn't surprise her she couldn't fool him, and she was also sure he wasn't surprised she'd tried.

"First, he wouldn't have been alone; Mrs. Huddleston would have been there with him. Second, he was getting excellent care in your house. Never mind those things, I wasn't speaking of his health."

"Then perhaps there isn't enough room for a child and Mrs. Huddleston in your servants' wing here at Hawksthorn. If that's the case, Mrs. Huddleston can stay in my room with me and Farley with Paxton."

The duke blew out an aggravated laugh and ran a hand through his hair. Loretta could have watched him do that fifty more times. There was something especially soothing and sensual about watching his fingers thread through his thick hair even though he wasn't happy with her at the moment. That didn't seem to stunt his appeal.

"You know that's not the reason I'm speaking to you about bringing him here."

Yes, she knew but still felt justified in continuing her present interpretation. "No, but you are being most unkind to a child who is an orphan."

"You are deliberately misunderstanding everything I say."

"Then what is your reason for not wanting him here? Is it that you simply don't like him because he has no surname, no family, and no home?"

A grimace narrowed the duke's eyes. "What I don't like is that you've welcomed him into your home and your life when you don't know anything about him."

"That's not the point. No matter who he is, he is part of my household at this time and should be treated with the same respect given to all our servants when visiting your home. I am not asking for special treatment for him."

Loretta stopped walking and stared at the duke intensely. "But I do say this. If Farley isn't welcome in your home, then I shan't be, either. I'll have to ask you to make arrangements and we'll leave immediately."

"Will you?" he asked, stepping closer to her.

"Yes," she answered standing her ground, knowing the last thing she wanted to do was get back in the coach.

"Now that I have you here, Loretta, do you really think I am going to let you go?"

Her chest heaved with deep, heavy breaths. His words and tone sounded possessive and— "Do you realize you just called me Loretta?"

"That's your name."

"But you can't use it."

"By now you should know that I don't always follow the rules of polite Society."

Oh, yes. She knew. "And you should know by now that I don't always follow them, either."

She was pretty sure he gritted his teeth for a moment or two before he nodded. An attractive grin lifted the corners of his lips when he said, "You are a worthy opponent, Loretta."

Oh, he knew just what to say to settle her anger, to calm her spirit, and to thrill her heart.

"But I am being rational and you are not," he continued.

"Ah! That is not a valid argument and you know it."

"We don't know who he is. You don't know where he came from, where he was going, or what he'd planned to do."

"That's not entirely true anymore. I don't know his full name or where he lives, but I now know a little more about him than when you last saw him. I'll be happy to tell you what I've learned."

The duke's expression softened. He stared at her for a long moment as if he were taking stock of what she'd said. "All right, if it would please you to do so, I'll listen."

"I won't go into all the details, but briefly, he has no family that he knows about. He lives under the steps of an old, abandoned building in London. Near St. James Park. He was abducted from a street near there and locked in a wagon with other boys who'd suffered the same fate. He was told they were being taken to a workhouse, where they were to be sold. The man would get money for delivering the children he'd stolen from the streets," she said with disdain. "They were traveling somewhere near Mammoth House when the abductor realized Farley was sick. He didn't want the others boys to catch the fever and die, too. That would keep him from getting any money. So he threw Farley out of the wagon and left him beside the road. Alone!" Loretta choked on the last word and had to suck in a deep breath.

"I'm sure it's all true," the duke said in a soft understanding voice. "And that it happens far too often in London."

"Yes. I only wish I could save them all."

He gave her a kind smile. "You know that's impossible, don't you?"

She nodded and realized she'd clasped her hands together so tightly they were aching. "But I can save Farley."

"You know, I believe I've changed my mind. I'm actually glad that you brought him."

"Are you?" she asked hopefully. "Truly?"

"Yes. Now that he is here, I'll take over caring for him and ease that burden from you."

Loretta's back stiffened and her chin lifted a little higher. "He is no burden to me," she challenged. "You may feel some sense of responsibility to him, as do I, because you ventured out into the storm to find and save him, but he is quite safe with me."

"You mistake my motives, Loretta."

"How?"

"I only want to see that he gets back to London, to his home."

"He's not well enough to go back. His cough is no better. Just yesterday Mr. Huddleston picked up a new tonic from the apothecary in Grimsfield, and we have hope this one will help him. There is simply no way he can return to London now."

"He can stay here with me until he's ready."

Loretta's stomach tightened. "I appreciate you wanting to do that, Your Grace, but it wouldn't be best for him. He already believes you don't like him, and I think he is afraid of you. Perhaps he's afraid of all tall"—her gaze swept down his shoulders, across his wide chest, and then back up to his green eyes—"strong men since his abduction."

"I won't hurt him, Loretta."

"No, of course you won't. I know that but he doesn't. He's not used to people being kind to him."

"All the more reason I should keep him here."

She couldn't let the duke take Farley away from her. He needed her. She needed him. They were just beginning to get to know each other.

Loretta took a step closer to the duke. "You will not take responsibility for him," she insisted. "He doesn't know how to trust anyone yet, but I believe he is beginning to trust me because he's responding to my questions and instructions. I will continue to take care of him until his future is settled. Besides, when we return, I plan to talk to my uncle about allowing Farley to stay and work at Mammoth House."

The duke's eyes narrowed again. "I don't think that's wise. He's not a farmer's boy or a village lad who will easily fit into a normal household."

"You don't know that."

"All right, it's my guess that he's grown up unsupervised on the streets of London for several years now and would find it very difficult to change his ways."

"And I'm sure he wouldn't have lived the life he has if he'd had any choice in the matter," she said with all the conviction she felt. "He wouldn't have chosen the life he's been forced to live simply because fate has dealt harshly with him. All he needs is a chance for a better life. I believe he wants that, and I am in a position to give him that if my uncle is willing."

"My greatest fear is that you are allowing yourself to start to care for him, and I don't think that's best for either of you."

"What is wrong with caring for someone? Being nice. Helping them. I plead guilty to that."

The duke's gaze held steady on hers for a long time before he nodded. "All right. Perhaps I'm wrong about him. We will leave it as you wish—for now. I didn't want you to come here so we could have disagreeable words about Farley. Truce?"

Loretta let out a deep breath and looked back at the imposing manor house. She hadn't wanted to argue, either. She didn't fully understand her obsession with Farley. Perhaps it was that she knew she'd never have a child of her own to worry about and to care for. Her brother would be marrying soon—if not to Lady Adele then to Miss Pritchard, or someone else—and leaving her on her own, at Mammoth House. She would have no one who needed her. Right now she did, and she wouldn't willingly give him up.

She faced the duke again and said, "I would welcome a truce, Your Grace, for both our battles."

He quirked his head and said, "Both?"

"The battle for Farley and for me. You haven't forgotten, have you?"

He smiled at her and she felt as if sundown had suddenly become sunrise. She wanted to throw herself into the duke's arms, feel his strength, bury her nose in the warmth of his neck, and give herself over to the desire she felt for him. But all she could do was look at him and wish.

"No, Loretta," he said with a slight shake of his head. "I just surrendered Farley to you. That is all I am willing to relinquish. Even if you are battle-weary there will be no truce in my campaign for you. I will show no mercy. I won't give up the fight and concede in my struggle for you."

"Then the battle will continue, Your Grace."

"It will," he echoed. "And my name is Hawk. I want you to know the name of the man you are fighting and not be afraid to say it. When we're alone, you are Loretta, and I am Hawk."

She leaned back. "I couldn't do that, Your Grace."

"Hawk," he corrected. "You're one who is accustomed to ignoring the rules, remember. Now, let me hear you say my name."

Looking at him now, the breeze blowing his hair, the serious thought of combat in his expression and the hope of victory sparkling in his eyes, Loretta wondered who she wanted to win.

"Very well, Hawk." She moistened her lips and added, "I suppose we should head back. We've probably left Paxton and Lady Adele alone together long enough."

"They're not alone. Minerva is Adele's shadow. She's been taking care of Adele since we lost our parents. She's been her mother, her sister, and her friend, depending on what Adele wanted or needed at the time. And she's a saint for putting up with Adele without complaint."

"I could see that she was looking Paxton over very carefully, but I can't say that I blame her. It's her duty."

"It's more than that. She's not happy about my arranging someone for Adele to marry."

"How nice. Another lady who thinks as I do." Loretta smiled pleasingly. "That's refreshing and I'm so glad to hear it."

"No, no, Loretta, you misunderstand. She is unhappy because she wanted to choose the man for Adele herself."

Loretta laughed. "You are teasing me."

He chuckled, too, and then said, "It's true. And you know, seeing you laugh makes me want to take you in my arms right now and kiss you."

She glanced toward the house, and then over to the servants' coach. All of them had gone in but one. "But you wouldn't do that here, out in the open, would you?"

"No, Minerva is probably watching us out the window. She didn't want me to allow this meeting between Adele and Paxton in first place. Highly irregular and most improper of me to have him here with Adele before the Season starts, as she has reminded me often. And as you will soon find out, she believes herself your chaperone as well."

"Mine?"

"You are an innocent young lady and you have no chaperone other than your brother. She considers herself responsible for your reputation as well as Adele's while you are in my home and without what she considers a proper chaperone of your own. She aims to see that I don't tarnish your reputation while you're here."

A smile twitched the corners of her mouth. "That's most comforting, Hawk."

He chuckled huskily. "Do not be fooled by her hovering, Loretta. I have a strategy planned. There will be a time and a place that I can be alone with you."

His words sounded like a promise. A sizzle of desire raced across her breasts, plunged down into her abdomen, and then spread between her legs. It was madness all the things Hawk could make her feel with just a few whispered words.

"So you haven't changed your mind about anything since we last spoke."

"I am more adamant than ever, more eager than ever. Not one thing has changed for me. And you?"

Had her decision to be with him changed? She didn't know. She wanted what his words and glances promised, but the price was so high.

She cleared her throat, hoping it would also clear the fluttering of indecision and anticipation running rampant in her chest and her stomach. "Well, perhaps Paxton and Lady Adele are staring at each other and in need of something to say."

"I can see you don't know my sister at all," he said as they started walking. "She seldom stops talking. I do hope Paxton can live with that."

"I fear he will lap up every word like a kitten after sweet cream, and he will talk just as much if not more."

Hawk chuckled and they walked in silence the few steps back to the lane in front of the house, where he stopped again and said, "Is there anything you want to say to me before you go inside? Does it feel like there is something you're forgetting?"

"I don't think so."

She studied his handsome face. Was she? She must be. He wouldn't have mentioned it if she hadn't. But what was it? Something else about Farley? About her brother or their journey? For heaven's sake, nothing would come to her mind and she was forced to say to him, "I'm not sure what you're referring—oh, yes, of course. I remember now. I thought about it the moment I saw Lady Adele. I must apologize to you again for my remarks about her. She is truly lovely, with an engaging sense of humor as well."

"Accepted, but that's not what I was thinking about. You must try again to figure it out."

Loretta held her breath, hating to bring up the subject again. "Thank you for allowing Farley and Mrs. Huddleston to stay when they weren't invited."

Hawk stared into her eyes for a long time before saying, "I'm not referring to that, Loretta."

She couldn't think of anything but kisses and sighs and wonderful feelings when he looked at her like he wanted to take her into his arms. "You will have to remind me."

"It's about the small matter that I talked your uncle into letting you come to Hawksthorn when you were quite clear it would be impossible for me to do."

"Oh, yes, of course." She placed a gloved hand over her mouth for a moment. "Uncle denied my requests to travel for so long. How could I have forgotten that? Thank you for reminding me of that, as well. You'd think I had no manners at all." Her gaze caressed his face, willing him to know how much she appreciated his efforts. "I was very pleased to be allowed to come with Paxton. I admit I didn't know who would win because both of you are such strong men."

His gaze held tightly on hers. "The earl is a hard man. That is not strength, Loretta."

No, it wasn't. "If you don't mind me asking, what did you say to get him to acquiesce to your wishes?"

"I don't mind you asking at all." A roguish grin lifted one corner of his mouth. "But I'm not going to tell you. What was said between us was private."

"But I know him well. He will, no doubt, seek a favor from you in the future."

The duke nodded. "He will."

"And what will you do if it's something you don't want to do?"

"I will do it. Whatever it is he asks of me—it will have been worth it to have had your brother"—he paused for a moment before adding—"and you here at Hawksthorn with me."

Chapter 17

A gentleman should always look at the lady
he is wooing as if she were the most beautiful
lady in the world.

～⚬～

*A Proper Gentleman's Guide to Wooing
the Perfect Lady*
Sir Vincent Tybalt Valentine

Dinner was a lavish affair.

There was no other way to describe it. The table
had been covered in a gleaming white cloth. More sparkling silver and crystal than Loretta had ever seen on her
uncle's Christmastide dinner table had been placed in perfect order at each chair. The room glowed richly with
candlelight and leaping flames from the roaring fireplace.
The duke was seated at the head of the table with Loretta
and then Paxton to his right and Lady Adele and Mrs. Philbert to his left. A dark red wine filled the crystal glasses,
and small courses of soup, fish, fowl, potatoes, and meat
had been consumed. Now a sweet confection of stewed
apples and cinnamon folded into a delicate pastry bowl,
and served on gold-etched plates, had been placed in front
of everyone.

Loretta wore a pale-lavender gown with a sheer, cream-colored overskirt. It flowed with scalloped flounces that fluttered and swished like butterfly wings every time she took a step. Delicate beading trimmed the scooped neckline, the hem of her capped sleeves, and the high waist. The diamond-and-amethyst necklace she wore was fashioned in an elaborate starlike design. According to her uncle, it had been her mother's favorite. Therefore, it was Loretta's favorite, too, and it made her happy to have the opportunity to wear it again.

Just as the wineglasses were never empty, the conversation had never lagged. Paxton and Lady Adele had chatted like magpies enjoying an early summer morning while perched in their favorite tree. They exchanged stories about their childhood, books they had read, and their shared interest in all of nature's beauty. They moved from one subject to the other with hardly a break to take a breath in between.

Hawk and Loretta had discussions, too, but theirs were softer, less hurried and excited. And they'd included Mrs. Philbert from time to time, who seemed to welcome the chance to speak. She was a good distraction so that Loretta wasn't constantly looking at the duke as she wanted to do. Their talks weren't as open and freely spoken as Paxton's and Lady Adele's. They all knew how to manipulate the dialogue along, and yet be wary, evasive, or persuasive with their words and expressions when they needed or wanted to be.

One bite of the scrumptious fruit was all Loretta could manage after feeling obligated to taste each of the five previous courses. Gingerly she laid her spoon aside and picked up her wine. She watched, amused and amazed, as Hawk finished off his dessert with vigor, as if he hadn't eaten another mouthful all evening.

When he noticed she was watching him, he set his spoon on the empty plate and said, "I don't believe you've told me what you thought of the book I gave you. *A Proper Gentleman's Guide to Wooing the Perfect Lady*. Did you read it?"

It was more like she'd memorized it, but not wanting him to know how precious it was to her, she only answered, "I read it straightaway as I promised I would."

"What did you think of the man's ramblings? A bit high-handed, priggish, and rather an egotist, wasn't he?"

"Egotist? In what way?" she asked.

"That he felt qualified to lecture other gentlemen on the proper rules of wooing a lady."

Her lips twitched in a smile. "Well, he did do quite a good job of it."

"You truly think so?" Hawk grunted ruefully, smiled, and then said, "It might be nice to know just how many successful courtships the man had in order to deem himself an expert in the art of wooing a lady."

"Perhaps not any."

His eyes concentrated on hers as if he were trying to figure out her meaning before he said, "Why do you say that?"

"He was so insightful, my first thought was that the author must have been a woman writing under a man's name."

Hawk laughed softly, huskily. "Your humor pleases me, Miss Quick. So does your imagination."

She sipped her wine. "I wasn't trying to amuse you," she pointed out to him. "I was being honest. I thought: How does this man know so well what it is a lady appreciates, what she wants, how she desires to be treated, and what pleases her most?" She could tell by the look in his eyes and expression on his face that she had captivated him, and it thrilled her immensely. She smiled and added,

"And then I said to myself, it must be because he is really a woman."

His expression of awe settled into a look of disbelief as his eyes narrowed. "You really believe that?"

"I think it's possible," she said evasively. "Have you ever met the man?"

He shifted in his chair, shrugged, and finally said, "No, and I have never wanted to."

Loretta really had no idea whether or not a woman wrote the book, but there was something infinitely delightful about dueling with the duke in a tit-for-tat way. She believed she could do it all night and not grow tired. "Do you know anyone who has ever met him?"

"I can't say I do. I didn't have a fondness for the man's book so I didn't go around asking about the fellow. Especially considering the uproar going on in Society at the time I was reading it. The person who actually wrote the book was of no importance."

"I'm sure that was true."

"To say the least. I had all but forgotten about the book until *Miss Honora Truth's Weekly Scandal Sheet* brought it to everyone's attention again last year, when the Duke of Griffin's sisters made their debut. But you have given me cause for thought on this. I may have to ask about him when I return to London. You've now made me curious about Sir Vincent Tybalt Valentine and"—he paused—"other things."

From the corner of her eye, Loretta saw that Mrs. Philbert had started listening to them again, so she wasn't about to ask what other things he was talking about, but she would have if they'd been alone.

Instead, she abruptly changed the conversation. "Tell me, Your Grace, do you dine with such elegance every night?"

"Never when I dine alone in London, but always when we have guests at Hawksthorn."

"But," Mrs. Philbert added as she looked at the duke, "if you don't mind me joining your conversation again, Your Grace?"

He acknowledged her question with a nod.

"I wanted to tell Miss Quick there are times when we are less formal here as well. When it's just the three of us. We dress for dinner, of course, but the food is not as elaborately prepared with so many courses and the table not quite so majestic. When the duke is away, which is often"— she gave Hawk a passing glance—"Lady Adele will, on a rare occasion, say she doesn't want to dress for dinner, and she has the freedom to have something delivered to her room for her."

Hawk kept his attention on Loretta, but said, "Thank you for clarifying that for Miss Quick, Minerva. Now, if everyone is finished, I think it's time for a brandy."

He rose and stepped over to help Loretta with her chair while Paxton hurried to the other side of the table to help Lady Adele and Mrs. Philbert. Hawk deliberately let the backs of his fingers press against her shoulders as she stood. A delicious shiver of pleasure rippled through her at his brief touch. It intensified as he bent close to her ear and whispered, "I'll see you in the drawing room later."

"You won't be too long, will you?" Lady Adele asked her brother.

"I promise we won't be," he said indulgently.

"See that you aren't." She gave him a smile and then a kiss on his cheek. "It always seems to take you longer to have a brandy than for ladies to have a cup of tea."

"That is because you drink your tea fast because you don't want it to get cold. We don't have that problem with brandy."

"Come along, Miss Quick," Lady Adele said and marched from the room.

Loretta, Lady Adele, and Mrs. Philbert started making their way back to the drawing room. Lady Adele talked while Loretta once again looked at all the beautiful things she'd seen when she'd first entered earlier that evening. Life-sized portraits, mirrors, and paintings of flowers, horses, and dogs hung on the plaster-covered walls. Large urns had been placed in all the corners, and on both sides of the fireplace stood regal-looking suits of armor that included swords and pikes. Clocks, music boxes, and figurines of varying styles, sizes, and shapes had been arranged on handsome pieces of furniture.

The drawing room was extravagantly furnished with gilt-washed wood chairs and dark-wood settees upholstered in elegant-looking fabrics dyed in rich colors and soft hues. Some were floral, others striped, and two matching armchairs near a window were covered in a material that looked as if it could have been made from gold thread. Baroque-styled woodwork trimmed the ceilings and frames, and fancy-topped lamps burned brightly to show it all.

Loretta had always thought the Earl of Switchingham's home was the most impressive manor house she'd ever seen. That was of course, before she'd walked into the Duke of Hawksthorn's home. This was just the kind of house she'd imagined the duke growing up in. She could see a little boy running from room to room, darting around the side table and away from his tutor, laughing as he hid behind the heavy velvet draperies. And the duke's children would grow up here one day, too, she thought with a sigh of longing.

"Would you mind playing something for us, Minerva?" Lady Adele asked. "I'd like to visit with Miss Quick."

"Not at all," Mrs. Philbert said, and headed for the

pianoforte at the far end of the large room. "Did you have something special in mind that you wanted to hear tonight?"

"Thank you, Minerva, and no, you decide. Come sit by me on the settee, Miss Quick. Right here." She patted the cushion. "I want you to tell me more about your brother."

"All right," Loretta said, making herself comfortable on the small sofa beside her hostess. She would have thought that by now Lady Adele had asked Paxton everything possible under the sun. Loretta couldn't believe there was more she wanted to know about him.

"He never stops smiling," Lady Adele said and then turned to her cousin. "Not that one, Minerva. It's simply too slow and makes me feel sad. I'd rather you play a lively tune. Do you mind?" Mrs. Philbert immediately changed the tempo of the score without saying a word or even looking up from the pianoforte. "Thank you," Lady Adele said to her cousin and turned back to Loretta again. "So I want to know, is happy his true disposition or is he putting on an act for me?"

"It's not an act, I assure you. I've never known him to be given to bouts of melancholy, and it's just not in his nature to be disagreeable. I think your brother will attest to that, as well."

"Hawk did make mention of that. Mr. Quick is quite handsome, too. That's something else our brothers have in common, don't you think so?"

"Yes," Loretta agreed. Hawk was most pleasing to look at.

"Does Mr. Quick ever get angry and raise his voice to you?"

"Certainly not," Loretta said, appalled Lady Adele

would ask such a question and as casually as if she were talking about the weather on a sunny day.

"You would tell me the truth about him, wouldn't you?"

"Yes, of course," Loretta argued, not appreciating the way the conversation was going. If there was one person who didn't need defending for any presumed wrongs, it was Paxton. "I would tell you or anyone for that matter the truth about anything asked. If Paxton has a fault, it's that he finds it difficult to take his time and be serious-minded. Even when there is a concern of great importance that should be treated with critical attention, he sometimes handles the matter too carelessly."

"Good," she said, seeming satisfied with Loretta's answer. "I don't see that as a problem, Miss Quick. There is always someone around here who can handle a serious situation for us."

"Then you are well cared for," Loretta said, thinking she'd prefer to handle her own difficulties and settle them herself.

Wanting to change the subject, Loretta asked, "I'm wondering why you're considering an arranged marriage and not attending the Season when it's hardly more than a month away."

"I've heard it can be quite alarming."

"The Season?" Loretta frowned. "In what way?"

"Minerva says that all the young ladies are on constant display for all the gentlemen to look at and talk about, and if they so wish, they can dally with our tender affections at no cost to their reputations at all and possible dire consequences to our own."

Loretta had never heard the Season described in such an unflattering light. "I would never want to contradict your cousin," Loretta said, glancing over to the woman who sat straight and stiff on the pianoforte stool, and played with excellent skill. "But while some gentlemen might be so boorish and crass, not all are, I'm sure."

"Too," Lady Adele continued as if Loretta hadn't spoken, "it's the gentlemen who have to ask for our hands. All we have to do is look beautiful, flutter around like a butterfly, and wait for them to do it! And what if no gentleman does?" she asked, a horrified expression on her face. "Minerva said many young ladies who haven't been asked to make a match by the end of their first Season are completely devastated and never get over the rejection. Why go through that if you have a brother such as mine who knows all the gentlemen so well and can pick the best one for me?"

Loretta wondered if Mrs. Philbert's opinion had been formed from personal experience about how her own first Season had been, or if perhaps she'd had an arranged marriage, too, and was only spouting rumors she'd heard years ago concerning the famed marriage mart. In any case, as far as Loretta was concerned, Lady Adele's cousin had a jaded view of the Season that needed a counter. Most young ladies she knew looked forward to it.

"But you are lovely, intelligent, and the daughter of a duke," Loretta said, speaking softly, not wanting her words overheard by Lady Adele's cousin. "There would be many fine and worthy gentlemen who would seek your hand. What Mrs. Philbert spoke of simply wouldn't happen to you—unless you wanted it to. I'd venture to say that most young ladies wouldn't be bothered at all to be left on the shelf a year or two if it meant the right match was made in the end."

"Do you truly believe that?" she asked emphatically.

"I told you I would always tell you the truth. I believe the number of devastated ladies would be very few. I attended some of the Season before my—well, I talked with ladies who couldn't wait for the parties and balls to begin so they could be courted by the handsome gentlemen. They were eager for each new Season to begin, because they enjoyed the company, the attention, the dancing, the rides in the park, and the tea and card parties in the afternoons."

Lady Adele's expression turned quizzical. "But you had an arranged marriage, did you not?"

"At my uncle's wishes, yes. An engagement, though, I'm sure you've heard it didn't end in a marriage."

"Yes, of course." She placed one hand over Loretta's briefly as concern suddenly etched her face. "I hope it's not too difficult for you to talk about?"

"Not at all. It's well past, and I seldom think about it."

Lady Adele turned toward her cousin. "Please change to a different melody now, Minerva, that one has become tiresome." She waited until Mrs. Philbert changed to another score and said, "Yes, that's a lovely one. I remember it well. And you play it so gracefully."

Facing Loretta again, she continued, "But it is easier, an arranged marriage, isn't it? To let someone you trust pick the best person for you? Then you don't have to go through meeting all the gentlemen who want nothing more than to measure you against all the other young ladies. Is she prettier, is her dowry as plump, does she have all her teeth?"

Loretta and Lady Adele laughed at her last comment.

"It's true, is it not?" Lady Adele asked when their laughter subsided. "They look us over as if we were an expensive race horse they wanted to purchase."

Loretta blinked a couple of times over that statement. "That's an interesting way of thinking about it, I guess. Keep in mind, if you attended the Season you would be looking them over, too, and making your own judgments about each one of the gentlemen. Some you will enjoy more than others. Some will make you laugh, some may bore you to tears. One or two may even make you angry. But then, there might be one who will make you breathless just to look at him. Make you feel as if a stallion is racing in your chest every time he looks at you. You'll lie awake at night thinking about him, wondering when you will see him again, if you'll see him again."

Abruptly, Loretta stopped. She realized she was telling Lady Adele the way she felt about Hawk.

"Oh, my." Lady Adele seemed to study on what Loretta said as she pulled at a ribbon on the neckline of her gown. "What a dreadful thing to happen. I mean, who would want to stay awake all night thinking about anything? Do you really think it's possible for someone to make you feel that way?"

For some reason Lady Adele didn't seem to comprehend what Loretta was trying to say about how a man could make a young lady feel. Loretta hadn't understood, either, until she met the duke.

"I do," she said and knew that if Lady Adele had to ask, it meant she hadn't felt that way about Paxton, and Loretta didn't know yet how Paxton felt about Lady Adele.

"I've had a little opportunity to be in the company of gentlemen," Lady Adele commented. "We usually have a Christmas ball each year here at Hawksthorn, and I've been allowed to attend. Not for the entire evening, of course, just briefly, because I've not curtsied before the queen, but I will when we go to London next month. I've seen a few gentlemen whom I think would make fine husbands. Some handsome, some not, and some Hawk said absolutely not." Lady Adele laughed again, clasped her hands under her chin thoughtfully, and said, "I think I would absolutely adore marrying the Duke of Rathburne, but Hawk won't let me consider him. He's such a rake. And of course Hawk would know all about them because he is a rake himself."

"You know about your brother's reputation as—"

"One of the Rakes of St. James?" Lady Adele finished for Loretta. "Everyone does. That's one of the reasons I trust him to pick a husband for me. He knows all about men. The good ones and the bad ones. Speaking of gentlemen," Lady Adele continued, "I wonder where Hawk and Mr. Quick are. They certainly are taking their time over their drinks and talks, aren't they?"

Loretta stared at Lady Adele's green eyes. It had not been more than five or six minutes since they left the gentlemen. So not long at all.

"It's Hawk's wish, as well as mine," Lady Adele continued, "that I be happy in my marriage, and I trust him to pick the very best gentleman for me. And if that person turns out to be your brother, I will trust Hawk made the right choice."

Loretta had thought her uncle would be the best person to pick a husband for her, too, until she attended the Season and realized there were gentlemen she enjoyed being with much more than Viscount Denningcourt. That had been a shocking realization for her and one of the reasons in the end that she didn't marry the viscount.

"If you were to ask me, I would suggest you wait and meet all the gentlemen who attend the Season. To find the man who makes your heart beat faster and your breath grow short every time you look at him. And if Paxton doesn't do that for you, keep looking. I do believe you will find one who does."

"But what if I don't? I am not foolish, Miss Quick. And I do like what I see in your brother. He suits me very well. Enough talk of gentlemen," she said suddenly. "It's making my head hurt and it's really quite boring, is it not? To waste so much time talking about men. Would you like to see my dog's new puppies?" Lady Adele asked, completely changing the subject. "Miss Wiggins had a litter. Mr. Quick saw them this afternoon while you took a walk with Hawk."

It was difficult for Loretta to understand Lady Adele's simple way of looking at life, but she must have been the same way when she was eighteen. She had allowed her uncle to choose a husband for her. She couldn't fault Lady Adele, only try to help her. Maybe it was that now Loretta knew more about life, feelings, and men and she didn't want to see either Lady Adele or her brother be unhappy with their decisions.

"Yes, I'd like that very much. I haven't seen a puppy in years. What kind of dogs are they?"

Lady Adele rose from the settee. "Spaniels. A small breed and they are all so adorable, but of course I have a favorite already. Minerva, we're going to see the puppies. Do you want to go with us?"

Minerva stopped playing and stood. "If you don't mind, I'll take this time to go upstairs for a few minutes. I'll meet you back down here by the time the gentlemen come in."

"Of course. I know you don't really care to look at the puppies again." Lady Adele looked at Loretta and smiled. "She must see them at least five or six times a day. I hate to stay away from them."

"Have you ladies finished your tea?" Mrs. Philbert asked. "I can have the tray removed."

"Yes," Lady Adele said. "And take your time. We are quite able to care for ourselves for a few minutes."

Loretta saw the untouched tray sitting on the table in front of them, and smiled as she rose from the settee. Lady

Adele had been so busy talking, she'd never even thought to offer the tea.

The duke's sister took Loretta to a small storage room at the back of the house. There were chairs, tables, sofas, and other pieces of furniture stacked in the room. Near a window, fenced in by wooden crates, she saw three little fur balls in the makeshift pen. One was trying to sleep and the other two kept running over him.

"Miss Wiggins isn't here," Lady Adele offered. "I guess she has been let outside for a few minutes, which means we have come at the right time. She's a bit jealous and doesn't like for me to hold them."

They knelt and Lady Adele reached down, picked up one of the puppies, and held it up for Loretta to see. "This one is my favorite. See how she has no white patches on her anywhere. Her coat is so many shades of brown and tan that she reminds me of dried chocolate mixture before the milk is added to it. Isn't she the most beautiful creature you have ever seen?"

Loretta smiled at the squirming puppy. One side of her face was blond, tan, and light golden-brown tufts of fur, and the other side was more chocolate and chestnut coloring. "She absolutely is."

"Here, you hold her."

Loretta looked at her white gloves and wished she didn't have them on so she could feel the softness of the fur. Lady Adele hadn't bothered removing her gloves, so Loretta took her lead and took the puppy in both her hands. She lifted it up to her face and smiled. The pup tried to bark but hadn't yet found her voice and sounded more like a goose. She squirmed a little but didn't fight to be put down.

"Oh, you must have just eaten!" Loretta laughed, as she smelled the distinct puppy breath. "Your stomach is so round and firm."

She put the puppy's head up to the bare skin of her neck and cuddled it. The fur was silky soft, and its body so warm. With her hind paws, she tried to climb up higher on Loretta, and she laughed when the puppy started to nibble on her chin with sharp teeth and licked her neck.

"I can't decide what to name her," Lady Adele said. "I was thinking maybe I'd call her Cocoa. Not only because of the beautiful coloring, but she reminds me of a delicious dessert that we sometimes have that's creamy chocolate and divinely sweet. What would you name her if she were yours, Miss Quick?"

"Cocoa is a very clever name and certainly seems to fit."

Loretta continued to rub silky fur against her bare skin and delight in the warm, squirming body next to her. "She's so lovable. I wish I could take her home with me."

"I'm sorry, Miss Quick, I would give you one of the other two, but they're already promised out to others."

"Oh, of course. I only meant how loving she is," Loretta said, looking at Lady Adele and shaking her head to dismiss the idea. "I wasn't asking for one of these. No. I only meant that it would be wonderful to have a dog. Someday."

"I can save you one from Miss Wiggins's next litter."

"In that case, that would be lovely if it works out that you can. Thank you for offering."

Loretta realized the puppy was chewing on the trim at the neckline of her dress and said, "No, no, little one. We can't have you swallowing a bead and getting choked." She pulled the puppy away from her chest. One of Cocoa's front paws hung in the trim and the other grabbed for Loretta's neck and a nail scratched her. "Ouch," she said, feeling the sting as it slashed into her tender flesh.

"Cocoa, what a bad puppy you are," Lady Adele said. "Are you hurt, Miss Quick?"

"No, I'm fine." She couldn't see the scratch, but she didn't see any blood running down her skin so knew she was all right.

"What ye looking at?"

Startled, Loretta and Lady Adele turned. Farley stood in the doorway.

"Who are you?" Lady Adele asked.

"He's Farley," Loretta said softly. "He's with my staff. Or he is supposed to be. What are you doing here?"

He coughed into his hand a couple of times, and shrugged before saying, "Looking around."

Loretta handed the puppy back to Lady Adele. "That's not allowed, Farley. It should have been made clear to you that you aren't supposed to be in this part of the house. Where is Mrs. Huddleston?"

He shrugged again.

"Let him come see the puppies before he goes," Lady Adele said. "I don't mind."

"No, really. That's not necessary."

"Nonsense," Lady Adele said, brushing aside Loretta's opinion. "All boys love puppies."

Farley walked farther into the room and looked down at them. Loretta was surprised the expression on his face didn't change. Who didn't smile at the sight of a puppy?

"Aren't they adorable?" Lady Adele asked him.

Farley didn't bother to look at her, but without any passion in his voice, said, "They're dogs. I see dogs in London all the time. 'E looks like the runt of the litter to me."

Loretta was horrified that Farley had been so disrespectful to Lady Adele, but she hadn't seemed the least offended by his comment.

"Well, it's a she not a he and she's not a runt. She just doesn't eat as much as the other two. And I'm sure you haven't ever seen any puppies as charming and playful as these in London or anywhere else you may have been," Lady Adele said. She then looked up at Farley and with a pleasant tone said, "Would you like to hold her?"

At that, Farley's eyes lit up like a candlewick that had caught fire. He glanced at Loretta. "Can I 'old 'er?"

At that moment Loretta knew she liked Lady Adele and wouldn't mind at all if Paxton had fallen in love with her and wanted to marry her. Even after Farley had been rude to her and disparaged her favorite puppy, she brushed it off and was still kind to him.

"Yes, you may hold her."

Lady Adele lifted Cocoa to him. "Don't squeeze her too hard," she prompted as she turned loose.

Loretta watched a look of awe spread over Farley's face and light seemed to spread into his eyes. He gently cradled the squirming puppy to his chest as if she were a baby. He slowly swung his arms and with one hand stroked Cocoa's head and back. The dog wiggled and tried again to bark while burying her head in the crook of Farley's arm.

"Shh," he whispered as if talking to a baby. "Shh. I won't hurt you."

Loretta's heart melted. It was rewarding to see the softer side of Farley again. She knew she was making a difference in his life. His eyes were bright with wonder, and there was a small, beautiful smile on his face. Loretta decided she would get a dog from somewhere, if Farley stayed at Mammoth House.

"Have you ever held a puppy?" Lady Adele asked him.

Farley shook his head. "But she's nice."

Loretta let him rub the puppy a few more times and then said, "We must give him back now."

She took the puppy and handed her back to Lady Adele. "Thank you for showing them to us. It was lovely to get to hold her."

Farley looked up at her, and then over to Lady Adele, and said, "Thank ye for letting me 'old 'er."

Lady Adele smiled, and Loretta was pleased that Farley had remembered to be kind without her urging him to do so. "Please excuse us, Lady Adele," she said and rose. "I need to get him back to where he belongs."

"Which way do we go?" she asked Farley when they stepped into the hallway.

"This way," he said and took the lead. Hawksthorn was huge, and Loretta had already discovered it wasn't easy finding her way around the monstrous house. She wondered if Farley could lead them back. If not, she hoped they could find a servant somewhere along the way to show them the right section of the house to go to.

After they were well away from the puppy room, Loretta said, "Thank you for being kind to Lady Adele and remembering your manners." He kept walking down the corridor and didn't respond to her. "I appreciate you handling yourself so well, but you are not to come to this section of the house again. Mrs. Huddleston should have made that clear to you."

He stopped walking and looked up at her with big brown eyes. "Ye angry with me?"

She stopped, too. "No, it's not anger as much as it's that I'm upset. It's one thing to do something wrong when you don't know any better. But you know you were told to stay where you were and not be wandering around this house."

"What am I to do in that room all the time?"

"Didn't you bring the toys Mr. Huddleston brought you back from Grimsfield?"

"What do I want with soldiers and 'orses and a wooden dog? Don't mean nothing to me. Toys are for little boys."

Loretta asked, "How old are you, Farley?"

He shrugged again. "I don't know."

"Do you know how old you were when you lost your mother?"

He stared at her unblinking for several seconds before saying, "Eight."

"And do you know how many years have passed since she's been gone?"

He blinked slowly as his face remained expression-less. "Four winters," he said, then stuffed his hands in the pockets of his trousers, turned, and started down the cor-ridor again.

So Farley was twelve or possibly thirteen, but small for his age. Probably because he hadn't had proper food or care. Loretta watched him. He had a shuffle to his feet and a swing to his slight shoulders. He was still young enough for her to help him grow into a fine young man. Already he was nicer than when he'd first come to Mammoth House. She took pleasure in that accomplishment. And there was so much more she could do for him if she was given the time.

The only thing she had to do was find a way to make Farley want to stay and make his home with her. Then she had to get her uncle to grant her wish. That might be the hardest thing to do.

Chapter 18

A gentleman should never press a lady for an
answer—no matter what the question is.

⊷⊷

*A Proper Gentleman's Guide to Wooing
the Perfect Lady*
Sir Vincent Tybalt Valentine

He had a plan to be alone with Loretta.

It wasn't especially clever or inventive, but it had
the best chance of working of all the ideas he'd come up
with, including his outrageous thought of just waking her
in the middle of the night and kidnapping her. He never
knew he had such an imagination until he was trying to
think of ways to find some time alone with Loretta. None
of them were easy, because none of them were proper. According
to Society's rules, there were no acceptable ways
for a gentleman to be alone with an innocent young lady.

So he had to invent some possibilities and settle on the
one he thought had the best chance of being successful.

He was going to spend a short time in the drawing room,
and then excuse himself for the evening. The plan was to go
up to the empty room beside Loretta's bedchamber and

wait until he heard her maid leave. He would then go immediately and knock on her door. Hopefully, Loretta would assume it was her maid returning and open it without questioning who was on the other side.

When he'd returned to London after seeing Loretta for the first time, it hadn't taken him long to decide he no longer had any desire for a woman or a lady who didn't speak her own mind truthfully to him without fear. Hawk knew he preferred a lady who was constantly challenging him, not agreeing with him.

Like Loretta. The challenge she presented to him each time he saw her was irresistible, invigorating, and consistent.

Somehow, he'd made it through dinner without resorting to some of the awkward tricks of his youth. He hadn't tried to rub his leg against hers under the table, nor had he placed his wine on the wrong side of his plate hoping to make an accidental brush of her hand as she reached for her glass. But now the evening had gone long and he was ready to be alone with her. He wanted to talk to her with no one else around. The way they had at Mammoth House. He wanted to touch her, feel her in his arms, and taste her lips beneath his.

Hawk had finished his brandy in short order and had hurried Quick along, too. They were now on their way to the drawing room to join the ladies. He was right in his assessment of Quick. The man was perfect for Adele. And she certainly seemed happy with him. Neither of them had stopped smiling or talking since they'd met. Adele had wanted Hawk to find her a husband, and he'd wanted her to avoid the Season and the possible risk of mischief against her. From the way the two of them had taken to each other, he didn't think he could have found anyone better suited for Adele than Loretta's brother.

Quick was a natural pleaser, and that's what Adele was used to. It was what she expected, wanted, and loved. If she was waited on, listened to, and pacified, all was right with her world.

In the few minutes it'd taken them to drink their brandy, Hawk decided the man's constant good nature and his penchant not to let more than thirty seconds pass without uttering a word would wear thin in a hurry. Quick had told him it was fine if the earl wanted to handle all the particulars should they go ahead with a contract of marriage. Though Hawk didn't want to deal with Lord Switchingham, he might not have a choice. He had to remind himself that it was Adele who needed to be happy with Quick, not him.

Hawk walked into the drawing room, immediately noticing that Loretta wasn't there. Had she gone up upstairs for just a few minutes or had she already retired for the night?

"There you two are," Adele said, rising from the settee to greet them. "I was beginning to think you had decided not to join us tonight, and that would have been a dour ending to the evening."

"It has hardly been fifteen minutes since you left the dining room," Hawk countered.

"That's a long time."

"You have no patience, Adele," Hawk mumbled more to himself than to her.

But she answered, "You've told me so countless times."

"We wouldn't have left you on your own for the rest of the evening, Lady Adele," Quick offered. "It was all my fault we kept you waiting so long. I'm afraid I'm the one who had the duke talking so much."

"Shame on you, Mr. Quick," she said with a smile of

delight on her face. "Didn't you say you wanted to show me a clever move on the chessboard that would make a match go faster?"

"I'd planned to. If you still want me to."

"Indeed, I do. I've had a board set up for us over here." She pointed to the far corner.

"Adele," Hawk said, when his sister turned away. "Where are Minerva and Miss Quick?

"I would assume Miss Quick needed a few moments to herself after dinner, as I did," Minerva said, coming up behind him.

"Oh, yes," Adele said. "I didn't think to tell you she went up to the servants' wing."

To check on Farley, Hawk thought, with a mild tinge of aggravation.

"But," Adele continued, "I suppose she could have decided to go to her room after that. I really don't know, and she didn't say. It shouldn't have taken her this long. Perhaps she got lost." She turned to Quick. "Our guests often do before they become familiar with the house."

"Did she say why she was going to the servants' wing?" Hawk asked, though he was certain he knew the answer.

"To return a boy who had gotten lost. She said he was part of her staff. He found us when we were looking at Miss Wiggins's puppies. Miss Quick decided to go with him to make sure he made it back to his room without losing his way again." Adele stopped and frowned. "Now that I think about it, I suppose I should have gone with them, but then I've seldom been to that section of the house, either. I might have never found my way back myself."

"Neither of you should have gone. You should have pulled the bell cord and had one of the servants take him back," Hawk said, his irritation growing increasingly difficult to control. Though Loretta was perfectly safe in the house, he didn't like the thought of her wandering through corridor after corridor, trying to get back to the drawing room.

"Should I go look for her, Your Grace?" Minerva asked.

"No, no," Quick said, striding over to Hawk. "I don't want to bother either of you with this. She's my sister; I'll go find her."

"I'll handle this, Quick," Hawk said in a tone that let the man know arguing would be futile. "It would be my luck you'd get lost, too, and then I'd have to find both of you. Minerva, you need to stay with Adele and Mr. Quick."

Hawk grabbed a candle off a side table, dipped it into the flame of one of the lamps to light it, and then strode out of the drawing room without further comment. It was best to begin where Loretta had started, at the back of the house where the puppies were kept.

It didn't surprise him that Farley had wandered off to have a look around the house. Hawk was fairly certain that roaming the streets of London was what Farley was used to doing every day. He also had doubts the lad was lost when he stumbled upon Loretta and Adele. More likely than not, he heard Miss Wiggins or the puppies barking and went to investigate. If Farley had been on his own as long as Hawk suspected, he'd probably learned how to go wherever he wanted with no trouble finding his way back.

The door where the dogs were kept was closed. Hawk opened it, and held the candle up to look inside. Miss Wiggins got to her feet, walked over to a crate, and peered over the top at him. She wagged her tail and licked her chops. "Go back to sleep," he whispered. "I have nothing for you." No doubt the dog was used to Adele bringing her a treat from the dinner table about this time every night.

After closing the door quietly, he started down the corridor. At the end of it, he had two choices. Either route would take him to the back stairway, which led up to the third-floor wing where the staff resided. If he turned left, a long corridor and one turn would take him to the stairs. If he went right, he'd have to make two opposite turns and then cut through the staff's kitchen and dining area before making it to the stairs.

Hawk thought for a moment. He remembered how Farley had skillfully dodged him when he was running from him during the storm. Instinct told Hawk the boy was fairly good at taking turns, cutting through parks, squares, and corners. Hawk turned right and then took an immediate left. He'd gone about twenty-five steps when he saw a shape, and the swishing of a cream-colored skirt coming toward him.

His stomach clinched.

Loretta.

A tremor of arousal gripped him.

He stopped, leaned against the wall, and blew out a huffed laugh of relief. It wasn't his strategy that had Loretta walking out of the darkness toward him, in a part of the house where they would likely be seen only by servants. It was fate smiling on him, and damned if he wouldn't take it with a smile.

And use it to his advantage.

Halting in front of him, she casually folded her arms across her chest and with a measured smile, said, "Don't tell me you just happened to be in this secluded section of the house."

He stared at her for a long time, drinking in the contentment he felt at finally having her to himself. Candlelight made her eyes sparkle. Her complexion looked as pale as shaved ivory and softer than finest silk. She was the most enticing lady he'd ever met. He was certain no other lady had ever made his heart thump so hard in his chest, and he wanted her to know just how much he wanted her. He had a sudden feeling that she belonged to him and no other. Though he didn't want to explore the implications of that thought right now.

"As a matter of fact, I was"—he paused—"looking for you. Adele thought, perhaps, you'd gotten lost when you went to take Farley back to his room."

"I admit the return would have been easier if I'd had a candle to guide and help me, as you do. The corridors are long and not well lit; however, I made it after taking a wrong turn or two."

He made an overt effort of looking behind her. "So Farley is safely back where he belongs?"

"Yes," she said defensively, and hugged her arms tighter to her chest. "I had a few words with him about not leaving his room to explore his surroundings again, and then with Mrs. Huddleston for failing to keep a proper eye on him. I don't think he'll venture out on his own again. Please, don't be too angry with him."

"I'm not angry with him at all, Loretta. In fact, I thank him."

Her blue eyes widened suspiciously. Her arms relaxed a little. "You do? Why?"

"Farley managed to accomplish for me what I was going to have a devil of a time doing."

"What's that?"

"Be alone with you. And since this is the servants' route, we are not completely alone yet." He took hold of Loretta's wrist and said, "Come with me."

He guided her along the corridor with him, then around a corner where he stopped, opened a door, and ushered her into a small, dark room where he closed them inside. Now they were alone.

He walked over to a square worktable and placed the

candle on top of it. The light wasn't harsh or glaring. It gave enough of a glow so they could make out each other's features.

Hawk turned, fully intending to rush her, crush her to him, and have his way with her for as long as he wanted. He was aching to fill the deep unsatisfied longing for her that grew more intensely inside him every day. He was a man, after all, and he wanted her. Now. Fast. Hard.

Looking at her, knowing she was innocent and trusting, he couldn't go where his mind and body wanted to take him. That was only a fantasy, and it couldn't be played out anywhere but in his mind. Loretta had to come to him willingly. For her to do that, he had to take his time, make her comfortable, and slowly seduce her.

"What is this room?" she asked. "There's an odd smell in here."

His gaze followed hers. A tall wall of shelving stacked with fat jars, round tins, and bundles of dried leaves and roots covered the space behind the table.

"The medicinal room," he said, walking back over to her, feeling calmer than when he'd entered. "Hawksthorn is large, with several hundred people in and around the estate. It helps to have herbs, spices, and various items available to readily make potions, tinctures, tonics, or whatever might be needed for fevers, broken bones, or cuts."

"That explains the woodsy scent in the room."

"Is it too overpowering for you?"

"No." She breathed in deeply. "It's pungent, but not unpleasant, and I detect a little mint and lavender, too."

He smiled. "Good. I think the really vile-smelling plants are sealed in the tins and jars."

"A blessing for anyone who has to be in here a long time, I'm sure."

Hawk reached out and fingered the neckline of her dress. "The beading on your gown has been torn loose, and you have a scratch on your chest near the tear." His heartbeat increased. His gaze searched hers. "That wasn't there at dinner. Did something happen to you?"

"Yes." She smiled. "But there is no cause for you to be alarmed. Your sister's puppy decided she wanted to chew on the trim of my gown. When I tried to pull her away, she resisted and her nails accidently caught me." Loretta reached up to her neckline, but her fingers tangled with his and she dropped her hand to her side.

"Ah—Adele and her puppies. She might be obsessed with them."

"No one could blame her. They are warm, soft, and loving."

Just like you, he thought and nodded. "Your necklace lies so beautifully on your skin. You're lucky the puppy didn't decide to chew on one of the diamonds in it rather than the glass bead on your dress."

"I wouldn't have liked that," she said, shaking her head. "This was my mother's favorite."

"Then it's precious to you."

"It's my favorite, too."

"As it should be. And you wore it tonight for me, didn't you?" he asked, not knowing if she'd admit it.

"Yes."

His lower body tightened, reminding him it didn't want to go this slow. "Does the scratch hurt?" he asked.

"There was a little burn at first. It's fine now. I forgot it was there until you mentioned it."

Silence fell between them while he contemplated doing what felt natural. "You know what I'm thinking?" he asked.

She shook her head.

"If there's going to be any nibbling on you or your clothing," he said, running his forefinger ever so lightly along her jawline, "it will be by me." He dipped his head and lightly kissed the red line.

She gasped softly.

"And it will be gentle." He kissed the same place a second time and smiled to himself. Her skin had pebbled with tiny goose bumps, just as he'd hoped.

"And wherever I touch you, it will leave no marks on you," he murmured against her skin, letting his lips touch the scratch thrice.

Hawk heard her breaths change from even and slow to fast. Her chest softly heaved. It was gratifying to know he disturbed the rhythm of her heart and breathing as much as she disturbed his. He moved away from the scrape, but he wasn't moving away from her. Taking his time, he kissed the soft pillow of her breasts that swelled gently along the neckline of her gown. Moving from one side to the other and back again, he couldn't resist tasting her skin along the way.

She stood quietly, but not stiffly, and allowed him to gently caress her with his lips while tension and passion started a low rumble of anticipation in both of them. He didn't want to frighten her. Now that he had her alone, he wanted to enjoy her, savor her for as long as possible.

Hawk lifted his head and looked down into her beautiful, trusting eyes as he slid his hands up to her arms, to that small area of exposed skin between her short sleeves and the top of her gloves. It soothed him to touch her. Somehow, it helped ease his eagerness, and yet stimulated his hunger for her at the same time.

"Your arms are cold," he murmured softly.

"That's surprising since I feel unusually warm."

Her honest answer made him move closer to her. "So do I."

Slowly, he placed his hands on each side of her face, bent his head, and briefly brushed his lips lightly across hers. His thumbs lightly caressed her earlobes, his fingers the back of her neck and the tops of her bare shoulders. He then kissed her eyelids, her nose, across first one cheek and then the other. There wasn't a place on her beautiful face he wanted to miss touching or tasting.

"Oh, yes," he whispered on a moan of pleasure. "So sweet. I needed to touch you. Kiss you."

Not waiting any longer, he took her lips beneath his. The contact was warm, inviting, and instantly arousing. A rush of need bolted through him. Pleasure and impatience tightened his thighs and lower body. He kissed her softly, lingeringly. He took his time pressing, nibbling, and seeking the silent response she finally gave him when she lifted her arms then slid them inside his coat and around his waist, to pull him closer to the warmth of her body. Now he was certain. She'd been waiting for this, too. They had no soft bed, no sheets to tangle in, but those things weren't needed. They had all they needed growing and bursting between them.

Hawk was going to make their coming together for the first time glorious for both of them.

Fighting with himself to keep his manner slow and unhurried, he plundered her mouth, her lips, her cheeks, and her neck over and over again, making her familiar with his touch. Wanting her to enjoy every sensation he created inside her.

With eager but tender movements, he eased his hands down to her breasts and caressed them reverently, loving the feel of them even though they were hidden from him beneath the fabrics of her clothing. She accepted his caresses and explored his back and shoulders, past his waist to his hips. Her hands roved over the contours of his body. Her gentle caresses soothed yet tortured him, making him want to beg for more of her touch. He wanted her to slip her hands past his waist to the center of his desire for her.

He lifted his lips from hers, looked into her eyes, and with a smile said, "Don't be afraid to give your hands the freedom to go wherever they wish."

"I don't have much control left, and I'd best keep what I have," she answered with a shy lowering of her lashes.

Hawk chuckled softly as his hands molded her breasts ever so softly. "I thought you were bolder than that, my beautiful Loretta."

"I am brave but wary to go where I've not been before."

"You are not one to back away from a challenge."

"But I always like to know I would have a chance to win."

He laughed again and caught her up in his arms and hugged her tightly to his chest. Their lips met again and again, open mouths with tongues darting, playing, and teasing and closed with gasps, moans, and swallowing long deep breaths of pleasure. He had no idea how long they kissed. It didn't matter. He didn't want it to end.

Yet all the endless kisses and touches made Hawk desperate for more of her. His body kept telling him to rush to end this aching, craving need that possessed him, but his heart and mind reminded him to take it slow and relish every sensation.

Carefully, he pushed her sleeves off her shoulders, down her gloved arms, and then worked her gown and chemise past the top of her corset, exposing her breasts, arousing him even more. He slowly moved his hand over one breast and then the other, taking his time to feel her firm soft-ness before taking their full weight in his hands.

Loretta sucked in a deep, loud breath and he savored it. His body throbbed and ached. He kissed her all the harder, thrusting his tongue deeper into her mouth time and time again before moving to kiss her shoulders, her neck, and her chest until he could no longer deny himself. Hawk bent his head lower and pulled her nipple into his mouth. She sighed contentedly, letting him know she'd wanted this in-timacy with him as much as he'd wanted it with her. His tongue circled her nipple, bathed it, and then gently drew it more fully into his mouth.

He groaned as if being tortured, for surely he was when she threw her head back and lifted her chest to him. She cupped his head to her bosom with her arms, surrender-ing to him. It was all glory for him—and for her, too, he knew when he felt her body tremble.

"Yes, yes," she whispered on a soft moan of passion that thrilled him to his very soul.

"Does that please you?" he asked when he took the time to move to her other breast, wanting to moisten it, pull the taut bud into his mouth and feel it swell and harden as tight as the other.

"Immensely. More than I could have ever imagined."

A flood of bundled new and exciting feelings that he'd never felt swept through him and burned as hot as oil on fire. Hawk skimmed his hand down her waist and then down the plane of her hip over to her stomach and to the firm roundness of her buttocks; he cupped them and lifted her against his hardness. With a gentle shove, he pinned her to the wall and pressed his lower body against her.

When she arched her hips toward him, Hawk threw his head back in pleasure. The tempo of her breathing turned choppy. His muscles contracted in the sweet pain of loving her so thoroughly. He gulped in a ragged breath. Her body teased him and offered no mercy for his desperate need to take her.

Over and over he pressed against her. With his desire for her at a fevered pitch he kissed her passionately, feeling like a thirsty man in need of fresh, cool water. He shuddered a moan of satisfying pleasure as her hips joined his gentle thrusts against her.

She moaned softly in pleasure, too, and trembled beneath his touch. Hawk smiled against her lips. Loretta wanted this union between them as much as he did. She was eager and receptive to his desire for her, and that aroused him all the more. He hadn't planned they'd go this far this soon but knew from her response to him they both wanted this coming together of their bodies and souls.

With impatience to make her his, he gathered her long, flowing skirts and found her thigh. It was delicious as hell to touch her warm skin. His fingers and hands explored her soft flesh before he lifted her leg and rested it around his hip. His hands moved to the center of her womanhood, cupping the warmth of her there.

She gasped softly.

He groaned as his body pulsed rapidly. A spiraling heat of desire swirled and seared deep in his loins.

"I know I shouldn't want to seduce you like this, Loretta. You deserve better but God help me, I want you right now. I don't want to wait."

Suddenly, after breathing out those few untimely words, he felt Loretta's instant withdrawal. Her hands stilled. Her body relaxed. Her labored breathing slowed.

Damnation.

Of all the things he'd said, could have said, why was it those few words that penetrated her senses and stopped the flow of unbridled passion in her?

He wasn't satisfied.

She wasn't.

He still wanted her and knew she wanted him, too. He waited a moment to be sure, but there was no going back for her. And though it was the hardest thing he'd ever done, he respected her wish. He lowered her leg, dropped her skirts, turned her loose, and stepped back.

Her chest still heaved as she pulled her gown up to her shoulders and over her breasts. His body still burned stiff, hard, and tight.

She swallowed before saying, "Aren't there enough women in London for you to pursue?"

If she'd hoped to give him a verbal slap, she'd accomplished it with great strength. The words stung, for surely he'd never felt for any other woman what he felt for Loretta right now. Yet Hawk shook it off and said, "Plenty."

But none that he wanted.

"Then, perhaps, it's that you've already been through all of them."

"Most, I'd say."

"So you will be all right with not adding me to that number tonight."

"I'm sure I'll survive," he answered on a frustrated sigh.

Hawk ran his hand through his hair and silently swore the vilest word he knew before saying, "Now that we have the insults out of the way, Loretta, can we talk?"

"There's really nothing I have to say."

"Well, I do. I know you're angry with me for wanting you, for helping you to want me, but you can't deny the passion you were feeling in my arms. It was as real as what I was feeling for you. It is there, whether we are kissing, or just looking at each other, or if you are at Mammoth House and I'm in London. My desire for you never diminishes.

And if you are truthful, I think you will admit that you feel the same about me."

"It would be useless to deny it. I agree you saw and felt my yearning for you."

He needed to know. "Then why stop us?"

"You must know why I can't give in to the madness that I feel for you," she pleaded.

"The vow?" He pushed the word past his teeth as if it were a foul taste in his mouth.

"I thought so the first time we kissed, and maybe the second time, too. I told you I considered chastity a part of my vow. I'm sure it was implied. Though if it was just my purity that troubled me, I believe I could live with that because I never said the words about chastity aloud in the church. I never even thought about purity or innocence when I vowed not to marry. But that's not all that keeps me from—continuing."

He didn't like seeing her uncomfortable, struggling for the right words to say, but he had to know.

"What else could there be? You don't mean—" He really didn't know how to say it, either. Men didn't talk about a woman being in the family way.

"Yes," she finally said. "I'm not wise to a lot of the things that go on between a man and a woman, but I do know if we go further I could be left with child."

He stepped closer to her again. "Loretta, I would never—"

"Abandon me?" she interrupted, and raised her hand to keep him from coming closer. "Since you wanted to know, let me talk first. Please."

His throat was tight, full of what he wanted to say, but he gave in to her wishes and nodded.

"It's more than just knowing that my uncle would disown me if I was in the family way. Though he's been very harsh and unforgiving to me, I don't want to disrespect his house again. I did that once, and it took me a long time to forgive myself for doing it, and even longer to forgive him for his reaction."

"Banishing you. You forgave him for that?"

"Yes," she said softly. "I did. Probably only because it made my life easier to bear and to accept."

"But you—"

"Let me say it all while I can, Hawk," she asked of him again. "And then I'll hear you out."

Uncertainty flickered in her eyes and he nodded again, though he could tell she struggled to gather and control her emotions as she put into words what she wanted to say.

"I know you're going to insist that you would take care of me and the child, should there be one, and we would want for nothing. I believe that. You're an honorable man."

Her features softened, her body relaxed more, and all he could think was that he wanted to hold her. "I would love to have a child."

He watched her eyes glow with expectancy and love at the thought.

"You see, I think I would be fine if that happened between us. But what wouldn't be all right with me is that my child would grow up without a father who acknowledged him with his name. Bearing the shame of never being recognized in Society as anyone's son, or daughter. I won't do that to a child of mine."

"There are things that can prevent a babe."

"I know."

Hawk's eyebrows rose.

She blew out a little laugh. "There are many books in Mammoth House. Some that I'm sure my uncle doesn't even know about, that have been left there over the years by heaven only knows who. I have read about what you speak of, but all precautions are still risky at best. I won't be fooled by any of those devices or methods."

He shook his head slightly. "I wasn't trying to fool you."

"Then accept that this is something I can't do and, thankfully, I came to my senses before it was too late. I'm not as strong as you are, Hawk. The next time I might give in. I ask that you be a gentleman and don't ask this of me again."

"Then marry me," he said quickly, not really knowing where the thought, the words had come from, but knowing that he meant them. He wanted to marry her. For the first time in his life he stood before a woman he didn't want to lose.

After a long intake of breath that ended on a shaky sigh, she whispered, "What?" She stepped back, hitting the wall. "You can't just say something like that to me."

"I can. I know in my heart you belong to me and no one else, Loretta. Marry me."

"I belong to no one. I can't. And you know I can't marry, either. I took a vow to never marry!"

"Break it." He grabbed hold of her shoulders and demanded it hotly.

Her beautiful gaze searched his just long enough to give him hope, but suddenly she tore away from his grip and whispered earnestly, "No. I can't. You're being cruel even to suggest I do such a thing."

"I'm being honest," he said, his anger flaring because she wasn't being reasonable. Did she think he took it lightly when he asked her to be his wife? "You were eighteen, and you were forced by your uncle to take that vow."

"There's truth to what you say, but I was also of a sound mind when I said it and I had a choice not to. I could have married Lord Denningcourt. So no matter what my heart tells me now, it doesn't absolve me from the commitment of the words I said."

"Vows are broken all the time," he answered, not expecting this to be a battle he'd lose.

"But I took the oath in the church, standing in front of the vicar," she exclaimed emphatically. "It was no less binding because of circumstances. And I never looked at them as just some words I flung into the air to try to appease my uncle. Please don't ever ask me to break the vow again. I can't."

Loretta turned, opened the door, and rushed away.

Chapter 19

A gentleman is always prepared with an answer,
no matter what the lady may ask.

꧁꧂

*A Proper Gentleman's Guide to Wooing
the Perfect Lady*
Sir Vincent Tybalt Valentine

The rattle of harnesses and neighing of restless horses
was a welcome sound. It was time to leave Hawksthorn.
Loretta had never thought she would welcome going back
to Mammoth House, but she wanted to be alone with her
heartache. Whether Hawk had been sincere when he'd
asked her to marry him or just caught up in the heat of their
passion and wanting to win the battle he said was between
them, she didn't know.

It was best that she never know.

Her eyes adjusted to the faint gray light of the early
dawn morning. She stood with her back to the manor,
watching the hustle and bustle of servants tying the bag-
gage onto the coaches while she waited for Paxton to come
down so they could leave. Her dark-brown cape and gloves
were on and her bonnet was tied under her chin, but the

outer clothing didn't keep the damp chill from nipping at her cheeks and nose.

She'd managed to get through the whole of yesterday without any uncomfortable words passing between her and the duke. The sunshine had allowed them to ride around the estate in an open landau with Paxton, Lady Adele, and Mrs. Philbert. The wind was still and the temperature warm enough the ladies didn't need blankets for their laps. They'd stopped and enjoyed refreshments on a bluff overlooking the mansion. Paxton and Lady Adele had seemed as happy together as two frogs croaking to each other across the moors.

Dinner had been a repeat of the night before with a glamorously set table, more food served than it was possible for her to eat, and Mrs. Philbert to help keep the conversation level and on casual issues. However, plenty of sudden glances, long stares, and thoughtful expressions had passed between Loretta and the duke.

At the sound of male voices, she turned to see Paxton and Hawk walking out of the house side by side. Her heart started beating faster. It didn't help that Hawk's gaze was fixed on her face. Perhaps it was womanly intuition or maybe just a great desire for it to be so, but she felt he was looking at her as if he were hoping she would ask to stay.

He stopped in front of her. "Miss Quick."

She caught the calming, clean scent of his shaving soap that she enjoyed every time she was near him. She breathed it in deeply, hoping to memorize it.

"Your Grace, I didn't expect you to rise and see us off this morning. I thought we said our good-byes last night."

"Did we?" he asked, as much with his expression as his words.

"I thought we did, too," Paxton added. "But it was kind of you to come down."

"No matter," Hawk answered. "You're my guests, and under my protection, until you arrive safely back at Mammoth House."

"Thank you for making this visit happen for me. I am glad I met Lady Adele. She's—"

"Not a vicar's daughter?" Hawk cut in and asked before Loretta could finish her sentence, and then he smiled.

Loretta felt as if the sun had suddenly popped above the horizon and lit the entire sky with a bright light. He wanted them to part on a friendly note and not with strained tensions between them. She felt as if a weight had been lifted off her shoulders. It made her so happy she wanted to reach up and hug him, and might have done it, if Paxton hadn't been standing right beside her.

"No," she answered with a smile that she hoped wasn't as sad as she suddenly felt at leaving this man and his home. "But she could be. She's one of the kindest young ladies I've ever met."

His eyes caressed her face and he nodded, then turned to Paxton. "So now that you and Lady Adele have met, I'll talk with her and then see you in London later in the week to confirm whether or not we'll go forward?"

"Yes. I'll send you word when I've arrived," her brother answered.

"Pardon the interruption, miss."

Loretta turned to see Mrs. Huddleston hurrying up beside her. She looked almost frightened with her eyes wide and clutching her hands together tightly in front of her.

"It's not a problem. What can I do for you?"

"I need you to come with me to see about something. I think you'll want to take care of this yourself."

Loretta looked down the lane to where the servants' coach was being packed. Bitsy and her brother's valet were standing by the carriage, and Farley stood off to the side and away from the house. "All right," she told her housekeeper. "I'll be right there."

The woman hurried away and Loretta looked at Hawk, not knowing when she might see him again. "Thank you. For everything."

She turned away before he could respond and before she jumped into his arms. She walked fast and hard following Mrs. Huddleston. As her travel boots crunched on the gravel lane, she wished Hawk would follow her, catch her up in his strong embrace, and kiss her one more time before they parted.

Loretta sucked in a cold breath and shook away those foolish notions as she walked up to Farley and Mrs. Huddleston. "Now tell me, what's the problem here?"

"Show her what you have in your satchel," Mrs. Huddleston said in a rattled tone that surprised Loretta. She was never in a quarrelsome mood.

Farley gave the woman a fierce, angry stare and didn't move an inch.

"Go on," she said, harshly. "You heard me. Show her right now, or I'll take it away from you and show her myself."

Farley took a step toward Loretta, held up his satchel, and jerked it open. She peered inside and gasped. For a moment she felt so light-headed she thought she might faint. And she had never fainted! Lady Adele's puppy, Cocoa, was squirming around on top of Farley's clothing.

"That's Lady Adele's puppy! You were hiding it—in your clothing to take home with you? You sto—" She bit off the word before she completed it, then gasped again. "By all the stars in the heavens, Farley! What were you thinking?"

"It's not for me," he said, cutting his big brown eyes around to Mrs. Huddleston again before locking his glaring gaze on Loretta. "I don't want it. I did it for ye. I 'eard ye tell her ye wanted one of 'em. I thought ye'd be 'appy I got it for ye."

Loretta's heart was beating so fast she didn't know if she could speak. "What? For me?" She splayed her hand on her chest. "I'm touched you wanted to do something for me, but I can't be happy you took something that didn't belong to you! That's not right."

"She didn't need it," he said without a hint of regret in his tone. "She's got two more of 'em just like this one. I wanted to be nice to ye 'cause nobody's been as good to me as ye are since my mama died."

What could she say to make him see how wrong this action was no matter the reason? She knew he had nothing to call his own to give her, and she understood his wanting to repay her in some way, but . . . "Farley, this is stealing, and it's wrong. You can't be nice to me by being unkind to someone else. By taking something that's not yours to take. Do you understand that?"

His expression hadn't changed, so she added, "I'm touched here in my heart that you wanted to do something for me, but what you did is not acceptable behavior. All I needed was a thank-you, a hug, a flower from the garden when it blooms."

Loretta needed a moment to catch her breath, to calm the disappointment that was so great she felt she might drown in it. Had she ever said or done anything that made him think she wanted him to give her something in return for taking care of him? Was she somehow at fault for this behavior? She looked down at the puppy. She would have to figure out all those feelings later. There was no time now.

She reached down into the satchel and took Cocoa. "Thank you, Mrs. Huddleston. I'm so glad you saw her before we left. I'll take her back inside the house before anyone knows she's missing. No one will be the wiser." She turned to look at Farley, who finally seemed as if he was sad rather than angry. "We'll talk more about this when we get back to Mammoth House."

"What's going on? Do you need some help?"

By the heavens and all the saints who lived there! It was the duke behind her. She looked down at the warm, squirming little dog in her hands and wanted to cry. What was she going to do? What could she say? The evidence of what Farley did was in her hands and no chance to hide it now.

She whirled and thrust the puppy at the duke's chest and said, "Here, Your Grace."

Startled, he grabbed hold of it.

"Thank Lady Adele for letting us say good-bye to her." Loretta spun back to an astonished Mrs. Huddleston and to Farley. "Both of you get in the carriage," she ordered. "We're ready to leave. Don't tarry. Go now."

Mrs. Huddleston took hold of Farley's shoulder and tried to direct him toward the coach but he shrugged away from her and turned back to Loretta. He threw his arms around her waist, laid his head on her midriff, and hugged her tightly for a second or two. He let go of her without saying a word and ran toward the coach, coughing as he went. Mrs. Huddleston was right behind him. It happened so quickly and Loretta was so surprised she didn't have time to react.

Speechless, Loretta turned and tramped off without another glance toward Hawk, but as she feared would happen, within seconds he came walking up beside her.

"He was going to steal the dog, wasn't he?"

She couldn't lie to him, so she remained silent.

"Talk to me, Loretta."

"Leave me alone, Your Grace."

All she had to do was keep looking straight ahead and make it to the carriage and shut herself inside. She needed to think about the duke and about Farley's hug and how she felt about both. But before she could get halfway there, Hawk grabbed hold of her arm and forced her to stop.

"Look at me," he said earnestly.

"No," she whispered, keeping her head down. "I don't want to look at you." She wanted to cry so badly her throat ached and her chest heaved, but somehow she managed to control her emotions and not let them spill over into weeping.

"Listen to me, Loretta. I won't leave you alone." His hand tightened on her arm. "Hear me well. I will never leave you alone, so look at me."

She lifted her head, and then her lashes, and what she saw made her want to forget who she was, what she had vowed. Cocoa lay on her stomach on the duke's up-turned forearm. Her neck stretched over his wrist, her little head was cradled in his palm, and she was licking his thumb. Loretta's heart melted. At that moment, she knew why she'd been on the verge of giving her innocence to him. She was deeply, madly in love with the duke.

"Farley was trying to steal the puppy, wasn't he?"

Hawk's eyes were gleaming. A breathy sigh of despair pushed forth from her aching lungs. Only with the will of an inner strength she'd developed since being banished to Mammoth House, did she manage to say, "You are doing a pitiful job of trying to console me."

"I'm not trying to console you. I'm trying to help you to see that Farley isn't the boy you want him to be, and he never will be. I can understand a boy like Farley wanting a dog, a friend, someone to love."

Loretta bit back the tears that collected in her throat but was unable to keep them from pooling in her eyes as she remembered the spindly arms wrapped around her, giving her a hug for being kind. "He didn't want it for himself. He'd overheard me telling your sister I wanted a puppy." She choked down a sob. "He said he was stealing the puppy as a gift for me, because I had been so kind to him."

"Loretta," Hawk whispered as his hand squeezed even tighter on her arm.

"No, don't say it. He didn't know it was wrong."

"He did."

"But it shows he has goodness in his heart. He just doesn't know the right way to express it."

"You're making excuses for him," Hawk insisted.

His not allowing her to lie to herself, his expression of compassion, the soothing sound of his voice was more than she could accept at the moment. She knew all he said was true, but what the duke didn't seem to know was that Farley's actions, though meant to please her, had broken her heart, too.

She cleared her tight throat and swallowed another lump of sorrow.

Unwanted tears continued to pool in her eyes, blurring her vision, but somehow, once again, she kept them from spilling. Didn't Hawk know she just needed to get away from him?

"Let go of me," she managed to whisper earnestly.

"Farley's reasons for taking the puppy are purely his own. He cannot put the blame for this act on you."

"Perhaps you didn't notice, Your Grace, but I am very close to tears, and I would rather you not see me cry," she said as she felt a tear trickle from the corner of one of her eyes. "So if over the course of these few weeks I have known you, if you have developed any warm feelings for me, I would appreciate it if you would let go of me at once and allow me to get on that coach without saying another word to me."

"Loretta." He whispered her name almost desperately and looked at her for so long she thought she was going to break down into prolonged weeping right in front of him before he turned her loose. But then, after another gentle squeeze on her arm, he stepped back.

She would have liked nothing more than to rush into his arms, bury her face in his warm chest, and cry until her eyes hurt. That wouldn't do. She kept her chin up, her shoulders straight, and looked straight ahead as she walked past him. Somehow she managed make it to the carriage and climb inside before a heaving sob of heartache left her mouth. A second and third came rushing out before she was able to stop the flow and hold the rest of her anguish inside her aching throat. Those tears of anguish would be saved until she was alone at Mammoth. She would have plenty of time to cry there.

What Farley had done upset her greatly. Later, she would explain in detail to him why he must never do anything like that again. But what could she do about the duke? There was nothing to compare to the hurt of realizing she was in love with him and could never be with him. She would have never come to Hawksthorn if she'd known that she would be leaving her heart when she left.

Paxton entered the coach and sat quietly opposite her. There could have been no doubt that he knew she was upset. Tears continued to roll down her cheeks as fast as she could wipe them away, and her sniffing was impossible to hide. She stared out the window at the sun peeking above the horizon and lighting the sky. The coach took off with a rumble, rattle, and jerk.

Thankfully, the estate was well behind them and her emotions under control when Paxton, obviously, couldn't take the silence of not knowing any longer and asked, "Were you and the duke having an argument?"

"Yes," she said quietly, and wiped her eyes again with her damp handkerchief.

"About me and Lady Adele?"

"No. Farley."

"Oh. The duke doesn't trust him."

"Farley doesn't trust the duke, either."

"What about you? Do you trust the duke?"

"Yes." The answer wasn't quite as simple as the softly spoken word, but she didn't want to say more.

They were silent once more for a few minutes when Paxton suddenly said, "She really does talk too much."

Loretta looked at Paxton. Was that a serious expression on his face? Did he not realize that he talked as much as Lady Adele? That, when the two of them were together, there was no room for anyone else in the conversation and it seemed as if they could talk each other into oblivion?

Suddenly Loretta started laughing. She laughed so hard, and for so long, her side was beginning to hurt. It felt good to release the tension that Farley and Hawk had caused to knot inside her.

"Thank you, Paxton. I needed a reason to laugh so badly."

"That's good for you, but what am I to think when I poured my heart out to you and you start laughing?"

She stared more closely at Paxton. He *was* being serious. "Oh, I'm sorry, I didn't realize. I'm afraid I was being selfish and thinking only about what I needed. What do you mean by pouring your heart out?"

"Nothing really." He shook his head as if to dismiss his comment.

"No, you meant something. Tell me so that I don't feel

totally wretched for ignoring your feelings in favor of my own."

He pushed his cloak away from his shoulders, propped one foot on his other knee, and answered, "I got on very well with Lady Adele. To be the daughter and sister of a duke, she really wants nothing more than a simple life."

"I realized that, too," she said cautiously.

"She's quite fetching, vivacious, and clever as the day is long. And terribly spoiled. Her cousin does her every bidding, as does everyone else in the house, except for her brother, of course. Yet Lady Adele wasn't snappish, demanding, or rude. She was polite in every way. Always saying please and thank you to everyone, even though she's treated like a princess."

"I found all that to be true about her as well."

"So you liked her, too?" he asked.

"I did." Loretta paused. "But what do you feel for her?"

"I feel that I'd be perfect for her." There was no guile, nor even a hint of arrogance in his tone. He then added, "But—"

"But what?" she asked, realizing Paxton was unusually somber.

"There is an important matter the duke and I must settle before discussions of marriage can go forward."

"I'm glad you're taking your time to think this through and I assume Lady Adele is, too. I'm sorry I haven't been a very good sister to you on this trip. Is there any way I can help with this important matter?"

"No, no." He shook his head. "I know what needs to be done and how to settle it. I think I'll rest, if you don't mind."

"Not at all. I'll probably lay my head back for a few minutes as well."

Loretta watched Paxton snuggle into his cloak and fit

his hat over his face, and a fierce sadness gripped her. She would not back down from wanting Paxton to marry Lady Adele only if he loved her, but the sad truth was that if Paxton didn't marry Adele, Loretta would never have a reason to see the duke again. And that thought filled her with grief.

Dear Readers:

The Duke of Hawksthorn has been in London most of the winter, and I have it on good authority that his sister, Lady Adele, has arrived to join him. She was sighted coming out of a well-known modiste shop with her cousin and chaperone, Mrs. Philbert. No doubt they were making sure the last bead has been sewn, the last bow has been tied, and the last feather has been glued in their final preparations of her gowns for the Season. And one can't help but wonder if the duke is making final preparations, as well, to ensure that Lady Adele isn't beset by a mischief-maker in her quest to find the perfect gentleman and make a match.

MISS HONORA TRUTH'S WEEKLY SCANDAL SHEET

Chapter 20

A gentleman must always show a lady the proper
respect in any situation that may arise.

~∞~

*A PROPER GENTLEMAN'S GUIDE TO WOOING
THE PERFECT LADY*
SIR VINCENT TYBALT VALENTINE

Hawk was in a hell of a mood.

And had been for the better part of a week. He
didn't like to lose whether he was boxing, fencing, betting
on a horse race, or trying to win the hand of the lady he
wanted to marry.

He sat before the fire in his book room, legs stretched
out toward it, hoping the licking flames of heat would dry
out the soles of his favorite boots while he drank his coffee and tried to clear his head of all the brandy he'd consumed while playing cards for most of the night. It had
rained for three days straight, and every time he went out
his boots soaked up more water from the drenched board-
walks and pavement. He'd come in so late last night they
hadn't had time to dry before he dressed again.

And he wasn't of a mind to go upstairs and change.

A person's honor was a tough thing to challenge. Be it man or woman. Hawk certainly didn't want anyone meddling with his. He understood and respected the dedication it took to remain true to a code of principle and a vow.

He didn't have to like that Loretta had made her vow. But he wasn't in a position to do a lot of arguing with her about it. After the secret admirer letters became public knowledge and scandalized almost everyone in London, Hawk made a vow that he'd stay away from innocent young ladies.

That didn't mean he didn't enjoy them. Over the years, he'd paid attention to the new belles of the ball each Season. He did his part as an eligible duke and danced with them, enjoying their beauty and charms at dinner parties, afternoons of cards, and even an occasional ride in Hyde Park. He'd never touched one of them.

Until he met Loretta.

Hawk's respect and admiration for Loretta, for her conviction to her vow, and for what she'd asked of him the last time he saw her were the only things that had kept him in London for the past week, and not where he wanted to be: sitting at Mammoth House trying to talk her into marrying him.

Looking down into the tepid pool of black liquid in his cup, Hawk wondered if the coffee was helping his mood or deteriorating it. Either way he intended to finish the damned stuff before going over the account books his solicitor dropped off yesterday. As long as he had coffee in the cup, he could put off work and continue to think about Loretta.

He hadn't given up on making her his wife. He just hadn't decided what the best course of action was to take. She was more than simply a lady of high principle. Her convictions ran deep, and she'd shown that she wouldn't be easily swayed from what she believed she was honor bound to hold to.

Yet.

It had stung that she'd turned him down when he'd asked her to marry him. Didn't she know that he'd never asked a lady to marry him? He'd never wanted to.

Until he'd met Loretta.

And he'd had all confidence that whenever he finally asked a lady to marry him, she wouldn't say no. But Loretta had without blinking an eye. She had a keen sense of what was right. And marrying wasn't right for her.

He might not have put any thought into it before he asked her, and it might not have been the most eloquent proposal, but that hadn't made his question any less sincere.

The sexual tension between them at the time had been overwhelmingly pure, eager, and sublimely passionate. Just thinking about her now sent a heady warmth spinning through him, igniting a masculine response of desire. He wanted her.

It wasn't the heat of the moment that had him professing he wanted to marry her. It was that he'd suddenly realized he loved her. He'd loved everything about her from the first day they met. From sitting down to dinner with her at Mammoth House and Hawksthorn, to arguing with her about the merits of an arranged marriage.

His primal attraction wasn't all that drew him to her. He respected her strength to defend, to cope, and then to adjust when necessary. She wasn't afraid to fight for what she believed was right. She was forgiving even when it wasn't deserved, and was kind and loving to a street child. She was the kind of woman Hawk wanted to be the mother of his children.

Hawk wasn't an ogre. He'd understood her concerns about a babe. Those fears were real and troubling. She was right to be cautious because of it. Nothing was foolproof except abstinence. That was another reason to admire her. It showed how strong she was.

There were many men in London who had bastard sons they could never legally call their own. Hawk had to admit he didn't want that stigma for a son of his, either. It had to be a hard burden for a man to bear that shame when he did nothing to bring it upon himself. Hawk even understood her not wanting to cause her uncle more pain and disrespect his house again.

That was damned admirable of her, too. Especially considering the earl's severe stance with her. What Hawk didn't understand was her refusing to marry him because of the vow. He hadn't realized how seriously she took it. He should have. She'd lived with the ramifications of it for almost three years now, and he knew they weren't easy years. Somehow, he wanted to make her see that vows were broken all the time—whether or not they were said in the presence of a vicar in the church. Why did that matter to her?

Oh, hell, he thought and took another drink from the coffee that had gone from tepid to cold. He could sit here all morning thinking about how much he admired Loretta. About how much he wanted her in his life and in his home. Nothing changed the fact that he wanted to talk with her about whatever came to his mind. He wanted to laugh with her, and he even wanted to argue with her. It was invigorating to match wits with her bold assertions. He remembered her warm soft body pressed close to his. His lower body stirred.

A disgruntled laugh escaped past his lips. He wanted her in his bed, too. Snuggled close, loving her all night, and then waking with her by his side in the morning.

So no, he thought. He didn't like to lose. He didn't intend to lose. Whether she knew it or not, the battle for her wasn't over. It was only just beginning. He was coming for her again, and again, and still again if he had to.

Denying him her hand only meant he would have to work harder to make her say yes. He didn't mind. He'd always welcomed a challenge.

Hawk crossed his feet at the ankles and slipped lower into the armchair. There was Farley to consider, too. Of much less importance as far as Hawk was concerned, but a factor nonetheless.

"Your Grace."

Hawk looked up to see his butler standing in the doorway. "What is it, Price?"

"There's a gentleman here to see you. I told him it was too early in the day for you to accept callers but he insisted you'd see him if I told you his name was Mr. Paxton Quick."

Hawk placed his cup on the table beside him and rose from the chair. "He's right, I will. Show him in."

A few moments later Quick walked in and stopped, bowed, and then said, "Your Grace, thank you for seeing me."

Hawk knew immediately something was wrong. The man wasn't smiling and there was no bounce to his step. In fact, he looked nervous. Almost fearful. "It's not a problem, but I thought we agreed you'd let me know when you made it to Town and we'd make arrangements to meet at a set time."

"Oh, no, you're right about that. We did." His head bobbled. "But, well, it's because of the nature of this visit I felt it couldn't wait until you made time for me."

Hawk eyed him closer. Was that a quiver he heard in Quick's voice? The man who was always so jovial it got on Hawk's nerves. That worried him. "What's wrong?"

After a loud intake and even louder exhale of a deep breath, Quick rushed to say, "You made my sister cry."

Hawk couldn't have been more surprised if Quick had

sucker-punched him in the gut. No, Farley had made her cry. Hawk frowned. "Did she tell you that?"

"No. She didn't have to." The tremble in his voice continued. He clutched his hands together in front of him and then fretfully moved them to his back. "I saw how the two of you looked at each other throughout our time at Hawksthorn. I noticed even earlier at Mammoth House how the two of you—were around each other. Then I saw you arguing the morning we left your estate. In the coach she was crying."

Hawk's chest tightened. He knew she was on the verge of tears. She'd told him. He'd seen the tears pooling in her eyes as she fought to keep them under control. He'd wanted to hold her and comfort her but she didn't want it. Hawk's gut wrenched. He'd wanted to shake Farley for trying to steal the puppy. She wasn't upset because of Hawk, she was devastated because she had thought Farley was changing. She thought she was making a difference in his life and the little imp had proved to her she wasn't by taking the puppy.

"I think you are pursuing her," Quick added.

Now that, he was guilty of. Perhaps Loretta's brother was keener than he thought. "My relationship with your sister is our concern. Not yours."

"No, Your Grace, it's mine." His voice seemed steadier and stronger, though his eyes blinked rapidly. He slowly walked closer to Hawk. "I will vigorously confront anyone who hurts her."

"I'm glad to hear that."

"And that includes you."

So the gentle soul had a breaking point, and it was his sister's tears. "As it should." Hawk had to admit that Quick was impressing him with his assertiveness. Hawk hadn't known the man had it in him to be so courageous. "Though I don't have any obligation to tell you, I will let you know that what made Loretta cry was our argument about Farley and something he did."

"She said the same."

"Yet you remain unconvinced?"

"Your reputation as a rake gives me cause for concern about her innocence if you are pursuing her." He stopped and swallowed hard. "I know my sister. I watched the many times she asked to go to London to visit a friend, to attend a wedding, or for the christening of a babe, or even to Grimsfield for a day of shopping, and Uncle always denied her because he was so angry with her he didn't want her to have any source of pleasure. Through all the pain he caused I never saw her cry." He took another step closer. His gaze was intent and his voice solid when he said, "If you hurt her again, I will call you out."

"I would expect you to," Hawk answered calmly, knowing he would find a way to get Loretta for his own.

"So you are warned."

Hawk nodded, giving Quick stare for stare. Hawk had made all his answers as short as he could. He didn't like what Quick was saying but he understood the man had the right to defend his sister. Hawk respected him for the courage it took. That didn't mean it wasn't damned hard to take.

Quick took a step back and continued. "I know I will no longer be considered to win the hand of Lady Adele and be her husband, but I do want you to know if I had married her and you had made her cry I would have been saying these same things to you. I expect to cherish my wife, honor her, and protect her from those who would make her cry."

"I believe you."

Quick nodded, pulled on the tail of his coat, and said, "Then it's settled."

"All but the contracts."

"What?" Quick faltered on the word.

"After you left Hawksthorn, Adele and I had a long talk. She wants to marry you. I think you just told me you want to marry her."

Hawk was sure he heard the man gulp. His lids fluttered, and for a moment Hawk worried the man might need to sit down.

"You mean she—you want me to marry her? After all I just said?"

"I'm not sure it's reason to be happy, Quick. You will have your hands full taking care of Adele. However, since you both want it, my solicitors should have the contracts written and ready for you and your solicitors to read in a couple of weeks."

"I don't know what to say other than all right. I'll let my uncle know and we'll make plans to return to London in a fortnight."

"I know the earl preferred that he handle the contracts for you, but I'd rather negotiate with just you and your solicitors and leave him out of this."

"Like you, Uncle is more versed than I am in contracts of any nature, their meanings, and what a proper dowry should be. Though he's been a stern guardian most of the time, he has taken care of Loretta and me for a long time. I must respect his wishes in this."

Hawk nodded again, knowing it would take great restraint to remain civil while talking to the earl. Quick and Loretta might respect the man, but Hawk didn't.

"Then I'll comply with your wishes."

Quick nodded, turned, and started walking out.

"Paxton," Hawk said, calling him by his Christian name for the first time.

Looking back, he said, "Yes, Your Grace?"

Hawk's gaze penetrated Paxton's. "Don't ever threaten me again."

"I don't expect that you'll give me a reason to."

Paxton left the room and Hawk picked up the cup and downed the last of the stone-cold coffee.

He had to come up with a way to make Loretta forget about that damned vow. He turned to throw the cup into the fireplce when from the corner of his eye he saw Adele rushing toward him. She flew into his arms, making him drop the cup to the floor. By some miracle it didn't break.

"Oh, Hawk, you are the most wonderful brother in the whole world."

"By the devil, Adele, what's wrong with you? If I'm so wonderful why do I see tears streaming down your face?"

"Because I'm so happy. I heard what Mr. Quick said and it made my heart melt. He is not only the happiest man I know, he is a knight in shining, gleaming armor. Did you hear how he defended his sister?"

"Of course I heard. He was talking to me. Not you." Hawk frowned and set Adele away from him. "You eaves-dropped on my conversation?"

"No," she said, wiping her cheeks with the back of her hands. "I mean, yes, I overheard it. Most of it, maybe. Except when you talked very low. But no, I didn't eavesdrop, I just listened."

"Adele, you are supposed to be in London for dress fittings, not to be listening to my private conversations."

"Oh, I know." She huffed. "It was rude of me and I'm sorry, but I was coming to see you when I heard Mr. Quick's voice say you had made Miss Quick cry. How could I leave after that? I had to know what you'd done to her."

The devil take it! "I didn't make her cry," he said from between clenched teeth.

"Even so, as I told you at Hawksthorn, I liked Miss Quick and I stand with her brother. If you make her cry again, you'll have me to answer to me, too."

Hawk was in no mood to pacify his sister. The conversation with Paxton had been more than enough to put him in an ill humor.

"Fine. He will be your husband. You may do so. Now I have things to do."

"Wait." She reached up and kissed his cheek and hugged him tightly. "I am happy with Mr. Quick, Hawk." She turned him loose and smiled again. "I think he'll make a wonderful husband and Miss Quick a true sister. You did hear him say he would feel the same way if you made me cry, didn't you?"

"I heard every word he said, Adele," he said indulgently.

She gave him a satisfied sigh. "Thank you for choosing him for me."

Hawk's thoughts strayed to Loretta and how she'd stood up to her uncle and had refused to marry Viscount Denningcourt. What she'd endured because of her uncle's unforgiving nature. Hawk shook his head. "I didn't choose him. I introduced you to him. It was always your choice. Even if contracts are signed, and you are standing at the altar in the church, you can change your mind about him and I will accept your decision."

"I know that," she answered innocently. "You have always wanted me to be happy."

"And you are free to attend the Season even if you are betrothed. If someone else catches your fancy, I will understand. I'll cancel the contracts and pay the forfeiture."

"Thank you, Hawk. See, you are the most wonderful brother in the world. And I've decided I will attend the Season and dance at every ball as Miss Quick suggested. I will look the gentlemen over as carefully as they will study me." She paused for a moment. "I think I have already given my heart to Mr. Quick."

Chapter 21

A gentleman should always know when to offer
a lady his handkerchief.

❧

*A PROPER GENTLEMAN'S GUIDE TO WOOING
THE PERFECT LADY*
SIR VINCENT TYBALT VALENTINE

As was so often the case in early spring, light-gray
thunderclouds blended and swirled with darker ones
as the winds swept them along. Loretta was sure there
would be a shower before dark. Yet for now, she stood on
the front lawn of Mammoth House watching Arnold give
Farley lessons in handling two horses and a wagon. It was
their second day of working together, and Farley was doing
a little better today. She was pleased he'd asked her if Arnold could show him the proper care of horses. The animals didn't seem to be as agitated with the new driver
today as they clopped up and down the winding lane that
led from the main road to the house.

She hadn't yet written to her uncle to ask if Farley could
stay. She hadn't even asked Farley if he wanted to. Since
the incident with the puppy, he'd been trying hard to be

nice and have a more accommodating and thankful attitude toward everyone. After they returned to Mammoth House she'd explained why trying to take the puppy was wrong no matter his reasons for wanting to do it. She believed he understood. She didn't expect anything like that to happen again.

While she watched for the wagon to come back into view, two riders appeared on the lane. Loretta smiled. Paxton was back. She was always so much happier when he was around. She wrapped her woolen shawl tighter about her arms and waited, eager to hear what he had to say about his meeting with the duke and the earl.

Paxton dismounted and handed the reins to his valet, who walked away leading the two horses to the barn. In his usual style Paxton grabbed both Loretta's upper arms and kissed each cheek, greeting her with a joyous smile that seemed to reach from ear to ear.

"I'm glad you're back," she said, smiling up at him.

"Me, too. I have good news. It's settled. Lady Adele and I are going to be married. The duke is drawing up the contracts, and Uncle and I will return to London in two weeks to go over them."

Now she knew why Paxton's smile was so big. "Did you see Lady Adele while you were in London?" Loretta asked.

"No, just the duke. I told you we had a matter of great importance to discuss. After it was resolved to both our satisfaction, he told me that he'd talked with Lady Adele after we left Hawksthorn and she wanted to proceed with the betrothal."

Paxton seemed happy, but as she looked at him, she thought about the duke and how she longed to look at him just one more time. Without hesitation she asked, "Did it make you sad when you didn't see her? Did you have an ache in your heart when you left her at Hawksthorn?"

"What?" he asked, looking confused by her words.

"When you looked at Lady Adele for the last time before you left, did you have a burning desire to take her in your arms and sweep her away somewhere privately where you could kiss her until you were both breathless?"

Paxton folded his arms across his chest and said, "I think I might need to take a look at what kind of romantic poetry books you're reading."

Perhaps she'd said too much, but she had started this conversation and had to finish it. "It's not poetry that has me asking you that."

His eyes and expression gentled. "I didn't think that it was, but I had hope."

With that Loretta knew she hadn't been able to hide her feelings about the duke from her brother. "Never mind about that. I've told you before that I want you to love and adore whomever you marry. I want you to have that excited, I-don't-know-how-I-can-live-without-this-person feeling."

Paxton looked around at the sprawling countryside before them and then settled his gaze on the wagon and horses heading up the lane at a jaunty clop. He then said, "Not everyone needs that turbulent wind-in-your-hair-during-a-storm feeling for the one they marry. I guess I'm one of them."

"No, Paxton. Don't cheat yourself. I want you to know what it's like to feel so desperate for someone, you know your life won't ever be complete without them."

He turned to her again and leaned forward. "I'm sure it's thrilling, but I have to want it, too, Loretta. It's not enough that you want it for me."

His words took her by surprise. How could Paxton not want to experience all the passionate sensations for the person he married? The kind of tempestuous yearnings that the duke had stirred within her?

"What about Miss Pritchard?" she asked. "You were excited about her when you came back from being with her. You wanted to see her again. There must have been some desirous feelings for her."

Paxton remained calm. "For a time. She was a pretty miss who smiled at me, and I danced with her."

Was that all it was for him, or was it just all he was willing to admit to Loretta?

"Don't you think you'll regret it someday if you don't go back and see her at least once again? To see if what you felt for her when you left is still there."

"No," he said earnestly. "I think I'll regret it if I let this chance with Lady Adele slip through my hands."

Was it the clouds in the sky that darkened or Loretta's spirit? "You know why the duke wants you to marry her, don't you?"

"Yes. He made it clear he doesn't want her to be subjected to any kind of payback against him for the secret admirer prank he pulled on some young ladies years ago. If she's betrothed, there will be no reason for anyone to pursue her."

"And you're all right with that?"

Paxton's smile returned. "Why wouldn't I be? He wants to protect his sister. I don't blame him. I agree with him. I understand a man wanting to protect his sister from someone who wants to hurt her."

"Is that why you're going to say you'll marry her? You think it will be good for me?"

"Yes. That's part of it. I should be the one taking care of you, not Uncle. But you know I can't because our father had nothing to leave us. We are both totally dependent on the earl. I've no doubt he would cut off my allowance if I tried to take you away from Mammoth House."

Loretta stiffened indignantly. "I don't need you to support me. I'm fine at Mammoth House. I don't even think about the fact that I live here anymore." She fibbed without guilt.

"I'm not fine with you being trapped here like a nun in a cloister. You're strong, and you are coping, but you deserve better. I thought, with time, Uncle would soften and let you go back to Switchingham or give you a place in London, but he hasn't forgiven you for embarrassing him. If I had more income, I would no longer be under Uncle's thumb and could take care of you myself. And yes, Lady Adele's dowry will do that."

"This isn't about me," she argued earnestly. "And shouldn't be about me."

"It's about both of us, Loretta."

"You know that living here now doesn't bother me. I have never lied to you. You know it took me a long time to adjust to Mammoth House, to forgive Uncle for being so hard and unforgiving himself, but I have learned how to be at peace with myself."

"No. You simply hide it well. I saw how happy you were to get away and go to Hawksthorn even for such a short time. So yes, I told the duke I want to marry Lady Adele. This is best for you, for me, and for Lady Adele. Loretta, it's not that difficult. Surely you see that she's lovely. She's kind. We get along together so easily."

"You could be describing me."

"What's wrong with adoring my wife as much as I adore my sister? Dash it all, Loretta, I could do a lot worse, but I don't think I could do any better than Lady Adele."

"Did you kiss her?" Loretta asked as soon as the words popped into her head.

"That's rather personal."

"Did you?"

"Yes," he said folding his arms across his chest in a

relaxed manner. "Not that I should admit that to you or anyone else, but since I have, I'll add that it was really quite a nice experience for both of us."

Nice?

When the duke had kissed Loretta, nice hadn't even entered her mind. It was thrilling, exalting, beyond reasonable or comprehensible explanation. Hawk's kiss had completely changed her.

"This burning desire and yearning ache for breathless kisses you talk about is really rather rare anyway, don't you think?" Paxton asked.

"Is it?" Loretta asked, coming to terms with the fact she'd lost the battle. Paxton didn't want to help her fight it, and neither did Lady Adele. Maybe Paxton was right. He—they had to want that all-consuming desire to be with the other person and it didn't appear either of them did. "I didn't think it was, but I guess I really don't know."

She just knew that's how she felt about the Duke of Hawksthorn.

"It doesn't matter. I know I will be good to Lady Adele. I don't know about other men. It would be easy for someone to take advantage of her and I know I never will. She has a sweet nature, and she's innocent and trusting in a lot of ways."

"Her brother knows that, too," Loretta admitted.

"That's why I told the duke I will marry her. I meant it when I said I'd be perfect for her. Uncle and I will go to London in two weeks, finalize the contracts, and I'll be prepared to marry as soon as the duke and Lady Adele want it to happen." His eyes brightened. "And there's something I'm going to tell Uncle. Do you want to know what it is?"

"Yes, of course," she answered without any real enthusiasm. "You know I want to know everything."

"I'm going to tell him that you are coming to London with us when we go."

Loretta's stomach jumped at the thought she might see the duke again so soon. That wonderful feeling of butterflies fluttering in her chest started again. "I don't know that the earl will be as generous with you as he was with the duke about my traveling. The duke could offer him a favor in return. You cannot."

"Oh, but I can and he knows what it is. As soon as Lady Adele and I are married, I am accepting responsibility for you. The dowry from Lady Adele will ensure you will no longer be under his guardianship or a resident of Mammoth House. You will be with me."

Just the thought of not being under her uncle's command filled her with such relief. "I never dared to hope that might be possible for either of us."

The wagon stopped at the top of the lane. Though it was a fair distance away, Loretta could hear Farley coughing. She turned to Paxton. "I will go to London with you on one condition."

He quirked his head and laughed. "You amaze me, Loretta. You haven't been to London in almost three years and you're going to put conditions on going with me?"

"Yes. I want to take Farley with me. I want to find the best physician, apothecary, or whomever. I just want him to see the best London has. I want to know if Farley has a lingering cough from being so ill, or if he has developed consumption."

"Dear sister." Paxton shook his head slightly. "I believe I can talk the earl into allowing you to go to London for the reasons I just stated, but you have to know getting the boy there will not be as easy. There is simply no reason for him to go. The town house is small. I'm not sure there would room for him. As much as I'd like to do this for you, I don't think I can help you with this."

"You must do it for me," she argued. Hawk was already lost to her. She was losing Paxton to Lady Adele. If she lost Farley, too, she'd have no one to offer her love, her help. "He can stay with your valet and you can say that he is being trained."

"He's so young, I really don't see Uncle agreeing to that."

Loretta reached over and placed her hand on Paxton's cheek. "You know I've seldom asked anything of you." She didn't like pleading but in this she had no choice. "Please try to do this for me. I need to know if there's a reasonable chance Farley can completely recover, or if it's too late for that."

Paxton gave her a sympathetic smile. "I'll see that it's done."

Chapter 22

A gentleman who wants to woo a lady should never
call on her without a bouquet of flowers in his hand.

∽✧∾

*A Proper Gentleman's Guide to Wooing
the Perfect Lady*
Sir Vincent Tybalt Valentine

Loretta had gotten up early after little sleep. She'd forgotten how busy and noisy London streets were even
in the middle of quiet Mayfair where her uncle's town
house was located. Throughout the night she'd heard the
sounds of carriage wheels squeaking, horses' hooves on
packed ground, shouts from the drivers, and even the bay-
ing of hounds. None of those things were ever heard during the night at Mammoth House, and seldom were any
of them heard during the day, either.

Thankfully she wouldn't have many more days to spend
in the old hunting lodge. To her surprise, the earl had welcomed the idea of Paxton taking over responsibility for her
welfare. A young lady's guardianship usually fell the closest male in the family anyway. Paxton had been far too
young for that when their mother died, and then when he

came of age the problem was that his allowance came from the earl. He didn't give Paxton enough money to care for the both of them. And besides, Loretta was supposed to marry and have a husband to care for her. Now, after Paxton married Lady Adele, there would be more than enough for her to leave her uncle's care.

There were other reasons she hadn't slept well, she thought, as she looked out the drawing room window at the rainy street before her. She saw her reflection in the pane. Her brow was furrowed, and her lips firmly set. She appeared and felt anxious. Loretta wondered if there would be an opportunity for her to see Hawk. Would he bring the contracts to her uncle's house? Would the earl and Paxton go to the duke's home? They might even go to the solicitor's office to handle them. She hadn't wanted to ask. She'd rather have hope than disappointment.

She wanted to see Hawk, of course, even though she knew it would be best if she didn't. Nothing could change between them, but seeing him always made her feel good. It warmed her, and though just seeing him would never satisfy her longing to be in his arms again, it might ease a little of the heartbreak and longing.

But now she had Farley to contend with and help fill her time. She was relieved his cough had improved and that Paxton had convinced her uncle he could come with them to assist his valet. In fact, ever since the earl had heard that the duke wanted Paxton to marry Lady Adele, her uncle had been amiable to everything Paxton had asked. No doubt, he was eager to have them both be someone else's responsibility, but mostly Loretta knew it was because of the clout having a duke in the family would give him with other peers.

Paxton had gone out some time ago to see if he could find the name of a person in town that she could take Farley to. She'd brought all of her pin money with her, which wasn't much, but she hoped would be enough to pay for the man's services. Paxton had added what he could to help her with the expense, too.

Loretta leaned in a little closer to the window when a carriage stopped in front of her uncle's house. Her stomach quickened. She wiped the foggy pane with her hand. Was that the duke's crest on the shiny black door? Her breath caught in her throat and held until she saw him alight from the coach and head for the house.

"He's come to see me," she whispered aloud to herself. But immediately she shook her head. What was she thinking? He'd come to see Paxton and her uncle. She had rebuffed him and he'd accepted that.

Paxton had said he was going to send a message to Hawk that they'd arrived in London. But her brother had gone out and hadn't returned. Her uncle was still in his chambers. Hawk would be sent away. She rushed from the drawing room to the front of the house, where the maid was standing in the open doorway.

She saw Hawk across the threshold. He saw her, too. Her heart started pounding so hard she heard it in her ears.

"I'll just come in and wait for him," Hawk said, not waiting for the maid to respond. He took off his hat, cloak, and gloves and handed them to the woman.

"Good morning, Miss Quick."

"Your Grace," she said and curtsied.

"You don't think the earl will mind if I wait for him in the drawing room, do you?" he asked.

"Knowing how much my uncle wants Paxton to marry Lady Adele, I'd say he'd be upset if you didn't."

"I'll show you," the maid said. "And then let his lordship know you are here."

"Let me do that for you while you alert the earl," Loretta

offered. "I'm sure my uncle wouldn't want to be delayed in knowing the duke is here to see him."

"Yes, miss," the servant said without question.

Loretta heard every step Hawk took behind her as they made their way down the corridor and into the drawing room, where she turned in front of the fireplace to face him. She felt flushed and out of breath. Just looking at him filled her with such longing feelings.

"I can see you wasted no time coming over," she said. "I'm surprised my brother's note has even had time to reach your house."

His gaze caressed her face. "It didn't."

"Oh, then how did you know we were here?"

"Gossip passes around fast in London, Loretta. I heard that your brother was in the clubs first thing this morning asking who might be the best physicians in Town."

"Oh, yes, I see. I suppose that would be the place to go to get information."

"For Farley?" the duke asked.

"Yes."

"So he's no better."

"Actually, he is a little better," she answered. "The frequency of coughing spasms has slowed, but when he has them, they are still quite severe. I would feel better if a physician looked at him and confirmed to me whether or not he has consumption."

Hawk nodded, then reached in his pocket and extended a folded piece of vellum to her. "Here's the name and address of one for you. I've sent him word that you will be around to see him this afternoon and for him to send the amount of his fee to me."

"Thank you, Your Grace," she said, taking the paper from his hand, though her gaze never left his face. "I'm grateful for this, but I have money to pay him."

"I want to do it, Loretta. I would do anything to help you. You must know that."

"Very well," she said, knowing that would give her more to pay a hackney, so they wouldn't have to walk, and for any tonics or elixirs Farley might need to aid his healing. "My uncle will be going to White's later this afternoon to catch up on all the latest news. That's when I'd planned to take Farley. My uncle doesn't know about this and I would rather keep it that way."

Hawk smiled. "I can help you with that, too. I'll make sure to see the earl while he's at White's and detain him as long as possible."

The rate of her heartbeat kept increasing. "That's very kind of you, considering—"

"Considering what? That I'm not usually such a nice man?" Hawk said as the corners of his mouth lifted just enough to let her know he was teasing her.

Loretta smiled, too. "That's not true, and it's not what I was going to say. Considering you aren't that fond of Farley."

"It's never been that. It's that I don't trust him. It's been that way from the beginning."

"I know. And he doesn't trust you."

He nodded once. "I think he and I came to an understanding of each other that night of the storm."

"You never told me what you two said to each other."

"Nothing of any importance," he offered. "How have you been?"

"I'm well. And you look"—*magnificent*—"well, too."

His gaze swept down her face again and then back to her eyes. A tingle ran from her breasts down to the core of her womanhood. There was no denying she loved the way he looked at her and the way it made her feel when he did.

"I am. It's good to see you."

She didn't want to get into a personal conversation with

him. It made her want him to reach over and touch her cheek, slip his arms around her waist, and hug her close to his strong, wide chest and wrap her in his arms.

Denying her desires, and returning to a safe subject, she asked, "Are the contracts for Paxton ready? If you don't mind me asking?"

"You can ask me anything, Loretta. They're ready. My solicitor will be sending them over to the earl's. I expect his lordship will want some adjustments. That will be fine. I'll do them to make him happy."

She nodded. "And that will make you happy."

"I know you don't want to believe it but pleasing Adele has always been important to me. She's in London with me," he added.

"I didn't know. Perhaps I'll get to see her."

"I'll make sure you do. She'd like that, too. She and I had a long talk after Paxton's last visit."

"He told me."

"But perhaps you don't know that she's agreed to attend the Season before they marry."

"No, I didn't know, of course. I'm glad, but—perhaps a little confused, too. I mean, will you still go ahead with plans for the betrothal contracts?"

"Yes. I want everyone to know she's engaged. This has been my goal since we met, as you know." He moved closer to her.

"How could I forget that?" she stated ruefully.

He walked closer still. "I also told her she's free to revoke the engagement at any time for any reason. If she falls madly in love with someone during the Season or even if she's standing in front of the altar, with the church filled with people and she's about to say *I do*, she is still free to change her mind and there will be no unfavorably repercussions. Your brother is free to change his mind, too.

Though, I won't look as favorably on him as I will Adele, if he decides to do so."

Loretta's heart swelled with gratitude. "You told her that?"

He nodded.

"I don't know what to say other than that's most uncommon and very generous and understanding of you."

"Though I detest having to admit it, there is one thing your uncle has taught me. I learned from him that people should be allowed to change their minds without being punished for the decision for the rest of their lives."

Loretta suddenly wanted to hug Hawk tightly, but knowing the folly of doing so in her uncle's home, she simply said, "He taught me something as well."

Hawk questioned her with his expression.

"How much easier it is to live with forgiveness in your heart than with bitterness."

"That shows how strong you are," Hawk said.

She wasn't feeling very strong at the moment. In fact, she was feeling extremely weak against her loving feelings for the duke. She was very near to the point of rushing him and burying her face in his neck and the consequences be damned.

Hawk moved close enough he could have touched her cheek. "You've always known if Paxton married Adele he would have enough income to provide for you. That you could leave Mammoth House and your uncle's control, yet you have always talked against this marriage and tried to keep the betrothal from going forward. Why, when it would have made your life so much easier to bear?"

She inhaled softly and enjoyed being so close to Hawk. "My fate was set long ago, and as lonely as it has been at that large stone house, I knew that if I couldn't be happy, I wanted to do my best to see that Paxton would be."

"I want you happy, too, Loretta."

Hawk reached to touch her cheek just as she heard her uncle lumbering down the corridor. She stepped away from Hawk just as the earl walked into the room with a grunt, a limp, and a surprised look in Loretta's direction.

"Your Grace," the earl said and bowed.

"Earl," Hawk answered. "Miss Quick just walked in and offered refreshment. I told her I couldn't stay. I only stopped in because I was out. I wanted to let you know that the contracts of marriage were delivered to your solicitor this morning."

"Ah. That's good to hear. Thank you for letting me know," her uncle said, stretching his leg out straight as he eased into an upholstered armchair with a fair amount of huffing and puffing. "Loretta, get me that stool to prop my foot on."

"Yes, of course, Uncle." She reached for the stool but Hawk grabbed it first and positioned it to where her uncle could use it.

"Most kind of you, Your Grace," he said, continuing to adjust his body in the chair. "It's a nuisance that I can't get around as I want to anymore."

"Do you need anything else?" Loretta asked. "Perhaps a pillow would help?"

"That might work. Let's try it." The earl then looked at Hawk and said, "We just arrived last evening, but I'm not surprised you heard so quickly we're in Town."

"Mr. Quick sent a note around early this morning. Now I must take my leave. Perhaps I'll see you at White's this afternoon?"

"Ah, yes," the earl said. "If I can get my knee to cooperate with my leg and allow me to get in and out of the carriage again, I do plan to be there."

"Good. I'll see you later."

Hawk glanced over at Loretta and nodded.

She gave him a grateful smile.

Chapter 23

A gentleman should never discuss the wooing of a
lady. Not even with his closest friends.

❦

*A PROPER GENTLEMAN'S GUIDE TO WOOING
THE PERFECT LADY*
SIR VINCENT TYBALT VALENTINE

The card room at White's was active. Not a table was
empty. Perhaps it was the steady drizzle outside that
kept the gentlemen playing and not wanting to venture out
into the cold rain to make their way home. Some conversations were loud, cheerful, and long, while the gentlemen
at other tables talked low, determined and serious as their
cards were laid down, hands were won or lost, and money
was swept from the tables.

Thoughts of Loretta had consumed Hawk since he'd left
her at her uncle's house, though he'd done a fairly good job
of hiding it from Rath and Griffin as they played. He con-
versed, laughed, and carried on in the normal way with
them, drinking his brandy and winning enough hands to
keep up with his losses.

Occasionally he'd think about Farley and Loretta's

attachment to him. But Hawk tried to keep his mind off the lad. Even though the boy had been very ill, and still might be, every time Hawk remembered that the footpad had made Loretta cry he wanted to wring the boy's neck with his bare hands—but only for a second or two. Just long enough to scare the devil out of him.

Loretta cared too much for Farley. One reason could be that he was the first person she'd ever nursed back to health. Hawk could understand how something that momentous could form a kinship between two people. Too, it could have something to do with her stubborn will to hold fast to her vow. Maybe she saw Farley as the child she'd never have because she'd never marry, or perhaps she even thought he'd replace the brother she would be losing when Paxton married and had family of his own. Or, hell. He didn't know. It could be a combination of all of it and then more.

Hawk only knew he didn't trust Farley because the lad hadn't given him any reason to think he was changing. In fact, trying to steal the puppy from Adele had only convinced Hawk he wanted Farley out of Loretta's life. But he had to do it in a way she'd accept. And the only way he could think to do it was to find Farley another home. A good home. The lad going back to the streets and his old way of life would not satisfy her. And Hawk supposed he wasn't keen on that idea either.

Loretta had strength in spades and a kind heart, too. Why else would she have forgiven her uncle for being so incredibly punitive? Why did she care if she disrespected his house again? Hawk sure as hell didn't care if she did. But because of her, Hawk would be civil to the man when they discussed the marriage contracts, when what Hawk really wanted to do was call him out for the stern, black-hearted man he was.

"If you don't want your winnings, I'll happily take them off the table for you," Rath said.

Instinctively Hawk looked down and started to rake the pile of coins toward him. Rath took hold of his wrist and stopped him.

"Look at the cards, Hawk."

He glanced at all three hands. He hadn't won. Griffin had. Damnation. Hawk pulled his wrist from Rath's hold. So he hadn't been fooling his friends about his participation in the evening after all.

"Your mind's not on the game tonight," Rath said, and leaned his chair back on its hind legs.

"It hasn't been for some time," Griffin added, dragging all the cards back into the deck. "I'm beginning to wonder if you're even in the room with us."

Hawk harrumphed. "You both should know when it's best not to take me to task." Hawk picked up his brandy and took a sip.

"We've been friends too long to stay silent," Rath said.

Griffin thumped the cards on the table a couple of times. "It's because we've known you so long we have to ask what has your attention."

"Because we don't," Rath added.

"Mr. Quick's in town to finalize the marriage contracts between him and Adele," Hawk answered, hoping to avoid further questions.

"This is what you wanted," Griffin said as he started shuffling the cards. "That's not bothering you. It's something else."

"Is Mr. Quick's sister here with him?" Rath asked.

Hawk let Rath's question hang between them unanswered. He heard chatter from the other tables, billiard balls smacking together in the other room, and the rasp of drinks hitting wood. Rath had always been too damned perceptive. "Yes," Hawk finally said.

"She's on your mind." Rath's dark-brown gaze stayed on Hawk's. "Not the contracts."

Knowing he had few secrets from his friends, and knowing they would keep picking at him until they were sure they had the right answers, he took another sip of his brandy and said, "She turned me down when I asked her to marry me."

"The devil she did!" Rath's chair legs hit the floor with a thud. "No wonder your mind's not on the cards."

"Did she really tell you no?" Griffin asked.

"What I want to know is did you really ask her to marry you?"

"Yes," Hawk said emphatically.

"What did you do to her?"

Hawk frowned at Griffin's last question. "What do you mean?"

Griffin pushed the deck aside and leaned forward. "Did you do something to her brother she didn't like? Did you pursue her too heavily? Remember, she contemplated going into a convent rather than marry Denningcourt."

Hawk blew out an exasperated sigh. "She never wanted to enter a convent. That was just a rumor. I might as well tell you as I will find no peace from you until I do. When she refused to marry Lord Denningcourt, her uncle forced her to take a vow never to marry. She plans to honor that vow, and I haven't been able to persuade her differently."

Both Rath and Griffin looked at him as if he'd lost all his senses. And maybe he had. If he couldn't understand Loretta's reasoning for holding fast to her oath, he certainly couldn't explain it to them.

"If she won't cooperate, perhaps you could abduct her in the middle of the night and rush off to Scotland with her. Swear to her you won't bring her back to civilization until she marries you."

"Don't think I haven't thought about it," Hawk mumbled. "She's stubborn. It wouldn't work."

"You could compromise her?" Rath offered.

Hawk grimaced. "That is not an option either."

"I didn't think it was," Rath said seriously.

"What's this about anyway?" Griffin asked, leaning back in his chair. "It's not uncommon for people to break vows. It's done all the time."

Rath placed his hands on the table in front of him in a frustrated gesture. "Every morning that I wake with a pounding head I vow I'll never dip that far into the brandy bottle again." He picked up his glass. "But I always do."

"So do I and everyone else I know, but not Loretta. She took her vow seriously and refuses to let go of it."

"Don't take offense, my friend," Griffin said, "but maybe she doesn't fancy you and this is—"

"No," Hawk said, a little rougher than he intended. "I know it's not that."

Both Rath and Griffin were silent for a few moments. Griffin let his thumb flutter the cards again before saying, "So you're telling us she takes this as seriously as one would wedding vows, or a priest or monk who takes his vows of celibacy in the church?"

"Yes," Hawk answered, thinking again that she'd always noted that she swore her oath in the church. Then a prickle of an idea struck him. He thought on it deeper. Suddenly it was clear to him what needed to be done. "Thank you, my friends." He laughed, reached over and clapped each of them on their shoulders.

They looked at him, baffled by his sudden good humor.

Hawk raked his coins from the table into the palm of his hand and then dropped them into his pocket. "I should have talked to the two of you long ago. I now know exactly what I need to do."

It was obviously too late in the evening now to pay a call at the earl's house but tomorrow would find him there.

Chapter 24

A gentleman should always know when a lady
desires his attentions.

~◆~

A Proper Gentleman's Guide to Wooing
the Perfect Lady
Sir Vincent Tybalt Valentine

Loretta sat in a large chair in front of the fire, her feet curled under her. Late afternoon had turned to early evening and she hadn't moved. A lamp burned brightly beside her. She would read a few words, then stare at the flames and think about Hawk. Seeing him for those few minutes during the morning had been like a sweet balm to her heart and soul. She knew she shouldn't even think about him, but already she was desperate to see him again.

The physician had put her fears about Farley's health to rest. The man said that because Farley's cough was getting better, not worse, and he wasn't spitting up blood or anything else, he didn't believe Farley had consumption. His only remedy going forward for the boy was sunshine whenever possible and warmer weather to put an end to the bouts of coughing.

That relieved her mind immensely and left her free to think about the duke. Her destiny had been sealed long ago. She couldn't be with him, but no one could stop her from daydreaming about him. It was easy to lay her head back, close her eyes, and give her thoughts all the freedom they wanted.

"Miss?"

Loretta looked up from the flames to see Bitsy standing near the doorway worrying her hands together and visibly trembling. Loretta had never seen her strong, robust maid even slightly troubled. Knowing immediately something was wrong, Loretta closed her book, lowered her legs, and stood up. "What's wrong?"

"Will you come with me, miss? I need to show you something right now."

"Yes, of course."

Bitsy turned and headed toward the door.

More than a little concerned about what the matter could be, Loretta laid her book in the chair and followed her maid up the stairs. Bitsy opened the door to Loretta's bedchamber, entered, and walked over to her dressing table. Loretta followed her again.

At first, she didn't know what Bitsy wanted her to see. But then Loretta saw the open chest sitting on the stool. It was empty. Her mother's jewelry chest.

Refusing to let her mind or emotions take a leap about what might have happened, she looked at Bitsy and asked, "Where's the jewelry?"

"I don't know, miss." Bitsy sniffed. "I came in here to lay out your nightclothes and saw the box sitting there just as it is now. Empty. I—I thought, I was hoping you'd tell me you'd taken all of it and put it in a safe somewhere in the house."

At the implication of what was before her, denial shot through her mind and a lump tightened Loretta's throat. *This can't have happened* was all she could think. "I haven't been upstairs since I returned with Farley late this afternoon."

"I swear I didn't take it, miss." Bitsy's pale lips trembled. "I have no need for all those fancy jewels and such."

"No, no. I'm sure of that, too," Loretta reassured her maid, begging her mind not to take her where her thoughts wanted to go. "Have you looked everywhere for the jewelry? I mean, did you check my satchel, the trunks, and the drawers?"

"Everywhere, miss," she whispered, barely controlling her voice. "I checked every pocket, shawl, shoe, and bonnet. It's not anywhere in this room."

Mrs. Huddleston wasn't with them in London. The only people who'd been in the house during the afternoon were Bitsy, her brother's valet, the couple who lived at the town house and took care of it for her uncle, and Farley.

Denial raced through Loretta's mind again and she shivered. Perhaps her uncle had the jewelry removed to a safe place by one of his staff.

"I'd never take anything that didn't belong to me. I swear I didn't touch it."

"Bitsy, please. I know that."

Loretta also knew her uncle wouldn't pilfer her belongings or ask any of his staff to do it, either. She squeezed her eyes shut and her hands curled into tight fists. It broke her heart to admit it to herself but she knew who would take something that didn't belong to him.

Struggling to remain calm, she opened her eyes and

asked, "Have you talked with anyone else in the house about this?

"No, miss. I came straightaway to tell you."

"Good. I don't want you to mention this to anyone. Now, show me to Farley's room."

Feeling as if iron weights had been shackled around her ankles, Loretta climbed the stairs to the servants' floor. They hurried down the corridor to a small room that had nothing more than a bed, a chair, and a short chest in it. Loretta shook the covers, pounded the pillow, looked under the bed, and pulled out the drawers in the chest. There was nothing in the room to even suggest Farley had ever been in it. No clothing, hairbrush, or satchel. Not even the nightcaps she'd knitted for him when he was so ill she didn't know if he'd make it through the night.

Disbelief, anger, and heartache crawled like little black ants scurrying inside her. "Are you sure this is his room?"

"Yes, miss."

"But none of his things are in here."

"I see that, miss."

"Maybe there's a reason for this. Farley must be staying with Paxton's valet."

"He wouldn't allow that."

"We'll ask," she said, still fighting to stay calm and keep her inner turmoil from spilling out. "Farley's here. Somewhere. He must be. We'll find him. We'll check every room until we do."

Yet the only thing the search of the rest of the town house revealed was that there was no sign of Farley.

Loretta returned to the chair before the fire in the drawing room, refusing dinner, refusing to believe that the wayward lad wasn't coming back with her jewelry to explain what had happened.

The night wore on. The earl came home and went to

bed, but there was no word from Farley. Paxton came home and went to bed, but there was no sign of the youngster she'd tried so hard to help. She'd put on a brave face and had spoken briefly to both her uncle and brother, promising them she'd be up to her room soon. She didn't mention the missing jewelry or the missing boy. She couldn't make herself tell them. The burden was too great to share.

Loretta kept thinking that Hawk was right from the very first night he saw Farley. Hawk had tried to warn her, and she wouldn't listen. Now she was devastated. She'd not only lost precious remembrances from her mother but also lost her faith in Farley. The two were equally painful, just in different ways.

When the last ember of fire went out, Loretta rose and went to her bedchamber. But not to go to bed. She dismissed Bitsy, who had fallen asleep waiting for her to come up and change. Loretta then donned her hooded cloak, grabbed her reticule with her pin money in it, and quietly slipped out of the house.

Loretta knew the duke lived in St. James, but not exactly where. That didn't matter. She was fairly certain every hackney driver in London would know where the Duke of Hawksthorn's town house was located. She hurried along the streets until she came to one that still had a small amount of traffic for the late hour. Several carriages passed her, but none stopped. Frustrated, she tried to wave one down by standing in the street. All that accomplished was having the driver curse at her, call her an unspeakable name, and yell that he didn't carry the likes of her kind in his carriage after he'd almost run her down.

A cold, misting rain fell and she pulled her cloak and hood tighter about her neck. Not thinking clearly about what she was wearing, Loretta had left on her satin house slippers instead of putting on walking boots. Soon her shoes and feet were soaked from puddles. Her toes were freezing, but she refused to give up and walk back to her uncle's house. Her determination paid off when a hackney approached, slowed, and stopped. An old man with a gray beard looked down at her from his high perch.

Rain dripped from the brim of his hat. "Where ye going?" he asked.

Too cold to care that she might once again be mistaken for the type of person she wasn't, she swallowed and said, "To the Duke of Hawksthorn's house. Can you take me there?"

Loretta held her breath while he ran a hand down his long beard and looked at her.

"Do ye have enough pence to pay?"

"I'll double the fare, if you can get me there," she said, loosening the drawstrings on her knitted reticule.

"Then I know where he lives." The man jumped down, opened the door, and said, "Climb aboard."

The ride wasn't long. Loretta watched out the window and looked for landmarks to remember in case she had to find her way back to Mayfair on her own. She hadn't even begun to stop shivering, let alone to get warm, when the carriage stopped in front of an imposing, stately home. She hadn't expected a tall iron fence enclosing it. Some of the homes in Mayfair were bordered by tall yew hedges or short wooden fences, but few had tall iron gates.

Loretta wouldn't let the unfriendly entrance stop her. She paid her fare, thanked the man, and hurried up to the gates. After a couple of deep breaths, she grabbed hold of the gates and pushed. Relief flooded through her. They weren't locked, and a lamp was lit above the door.

Keeping her hood low to cover her face, she walked up

to the house and rapped the knocker. It sounded so loud in the still of the darkness, she was afraid it could be heard all over London.

She waited and was about to knock again when the door opened. A slim man with narrow eyes and a long nose frowned at her.

Before she could open her mouth, he said, "Beggars go to the back door, and they wait until morning."

"Oh, wait," she said, sticking out her hand to stop him from closing the door. "I'm not a beggar. I'm here to see the duke."

"No, madame, you are not. The duke doesn't allow solicitations"—his eyes looked her up and down—"of any kind."

"I am a miss, not a madame," she said indignantly. "And I am most assuredly not whatever it is that you're thinking," she continued. "I am a proper lady."

His expression didn't change. She realized too late that it was her own fault. He knew that proper young ladies wouldn't knock on a gentleman's door in the middle of the night or at any other time, either. Loretta knew that, too, but sometimes she simply couldn't follow the accepted rules of Society.

"It doesn't matter to me who you are, miss, madame, or madam. If you want food, come back in the morning. To the back of the house." And with that, the door shut.

This was ridiculous! "By the saints!" she whispered out loud to herself. It shouldn't be so hard to see the duke. She didn't appreciate the assumption she was an unrespectable lady, or having a door shut in her face, or the fact her toes were slowly going numb from thin wet slippers. She hit the knocker again and again, determined not to go back to her uncle's until she saw Hawk.

The man opened the door with such a forceful jerk it rattled the door knocker. A snarl wrinkled his nose and curled his lip.

"Tell the duke there is a *lady* here to see him. I know he will come to the door."

"He's not here," the man said. "I don't know when or if he'll return this evening, and if you knock on this door one more time, I will have you forcibly removed from this property."

The door slammed shut again. Loretta's shoulders slumped. Oh, why hadn't she just sent the duke a note to come see her? He would have come. Why had she fled into the night without really thinking things through?

Loretta knew the answer. She'd wanted to see the duke now. She needed to see him. If she was honest with herself, she had to admit she wanted to cry on his shoulder, feel his strength, and hear his calming voice—even if it was to tell her he was right and she was wrong.

Sighing softly, she looked around. A light mist continued to fall. The chill had settled in and her feet were still freezing. What should she do? Go or stay in the hope the duke would be home soon? There was no doubt she wanted to stay, but what if Hawk didn't return tonight? What would she do?

For the first time since finding Farley and her mother's jewelry missing, she wanted to cry. That thought forced her to inhale deeply. She wouldn't shed any more tears. She was strong. Capable. If she could withstand the isolation of Mammoth House for near three years, she could live through a cold night at the duke's door. If he didn't return by first light, she would be forced to start making her way back to her uncle's house.

She sucked in another deep, cold breath. The wind kicked up and blew misting rain in on her. Shaking, she looked around again. There was no place to go. Nowhere to sit and wait for Hawk, so she moved in as close to the corner of the door as possible, lowered herself to the ground, and covered herself with her cloak.

Some time later, the squeal of carriage wheels stopping and someone shouting "Whoa" disturbed her slumber. Was that the duke who had come home? She tried to turn and look but realized how miserably stiff her body was from the cold and from having curled into such a tight ball for so long. It took a moment to brush her cloak aside and unwind her legs so she could stand up. When she did, Hawk was coming up the walkway toward her.

His steps halted for a moment when he noticed someone standing in front of him. Then, recognizing her, he rushed up the steps and pushed the hood off her head as if to prove to himself it was Loretta standing by his door.

He grabbed her upper arms. "Hell's teeth, Loretta! What are you doing out here? Your cloak is soggy and you're shivering. What's happened?"

Under the pale-yellow glow of the porch light, she could see his lips formed a grim line. His brow creased. Was he concerned or angry? She didn't know, but she couldn't be sorry she'd stayed. Just to see him—if only for a few seconds, a few minutes—was worth what she'd gone through to get to his house.

"I had to come tell you about Farley."

Hawk's eyes and expression instantly gentled. He immediately circled her into his embrace and hugged her close. Laying his cheek against her hair, he ran his hand soothingly up and down her back, over her shoulder, seeming to have no concern that her cape was drenched with rain and getting him wet, too.

Loretta burrowed into his solid warmth.

"I'm sorry," he whispered and kissed the side of her

damp forehead. "I was hoping the physician would have better news for you about Farley. I've never wished him any harm. You know that."

His comforting words and tenderness caused her throat to tighten. She raised her head, gazed into his eyes, and whispered, "He's not dying of consumption."

Hawk brushed his gloved fingers along the side of her face, his expression questioning her. "Then what does the physician think it is? Damage from the fever?"

Loretta moistened her lips and swallowed hard, before saying, "He thinks Farley's health will be fine if given a little more time to heal and warmer weather. That's not the reason I came over. What you said about his nature and how he would go back to his old way of life was true. This afternoon he stole my mother's jewelry and left. The kindness he's been shown by everyone didn't change him."

Hawk hissed and pulled her to his chest again, holding her tightly around her shoulders. Loretta rested her cheek against his coat and hid her face in the warmth of his clothing, drawing strength from his arms and the steady beat of his racing heart against her ear.

"I will strangle him until he coughs up every piece that he stole from you," Hawk whispered harshly.

"I kept waiting for him to come back," she said, not knowing if Hawk could understand her words muffled into his chest. "To realize what he'd done was wrong."

"You know, I don't think it was that Farley wanted to hurt you. I don't think it mattered to him who the jewelry belonged to. He was only doing what came natural to him. He stole because it's what he does. It's the only way he knows how to live."

Hawk's words didn't make her feel any better about what Farley had done or the fact she hadn't been able to make him see there was a better life for him if he was only willing to accept it. "I wanted to help him. I should have listened to you when you told me he probably wouldn't change."

"I wish he'd appreciated your goodness and made more of an effort to accept help from you."

Hawk's words soothed her disappointment in what Farley had done. "I don't know which hurts worse: that he stole from me after all I did to help him, or that it was my mother's jewelry he took. I don't remember her that well, so everything I have from her is precious to me."

Hawk's arms tightened around her again. "I'll find him and get it back."

She shook her head. "Where would you begin?"

"That's not something you need to worry about. I will take care of it. I will start looking for him as soon as the sun rises. I'm glad you wanted to let me know, but you should have just sent me a note. It was dangerous for you to be out alone. Especially at this late hour."

"I might have been hasty in my decision to slip out of the house."

"Might?" He smiled.

Her throat tightened. "I knew you would understand how I feel."

"I do," he said earnestly. "I know how hard you tried. How much you wanted to make a difference in his life." His expression softened again. "It's all right if you want to cry. It would give me an excuse to hold you a little longer."

"No," she answered, feeling stronger just talking to him. "I don't want to weep for him again. I'm only sad I couldn't help him and, maybe, I even have a little hope that he'll come back and return what he took."

"And you will forgive him if he does."

"I'll have to."

The sound of a carriage rumbling down the street

caused Hawk to move her from underneath the light and into the shadows. "You can't be seen here."

Hawk swung his cloak off his shoulders and wrapped it around her. Its warmth flooded her. He pulled the hood low over her face again and hooked the silver clasp at the throat.

"Does anyone know you're here? Your maid?"

"I slipped out of the house after everyone went to bed. I kept my hood low. Only a hackney driver and your butler saw me. He thought I was—I was—anyway, he wouldn't let me in."

"Price was only following my orders. There are many people who come to my door seeking my attention. He has to be firm."

"I understand."

He looked down into her eyes and asked huskily, "Do you? Do you know now that you have come to me, I will never let you go?"

Loretta stiffened. "No. That's not why I came to you. We have been over this, Hawk. I'm not free. You know that. I probably shouldn't have come at all, but I had to let you know you were right all along about Farley."

"I had an idea earlier tonight, Loretta. I was talking to Griffin and Rath and it came to me what needs to be done."

She took a step back. "You were talking with the other two Rakes of St. James about this? Us? My oath?"

"Yes," he said as innocently as if he'd just told her it was raining. Suddenly Hawk whipped his head around and looked down the street. "I know what we need to do," he whispered, and then quickly turned back to her. "And because of my discussion with them, I know what to do."

"Are you serious? Don't you know by now that whatever you three rakes come up with is not going to end well?"

Hawk smiled and then blew out a soft laugh as he shook his head.

"I admit we've had our failures in the past, but not this time. I was going to wait until tomorrow to come see you, but it just so happens the perfect place is just down the street and around the corner. I don't know why it wasn't clear to me before, but for whatever reason, I now know the answer."

"To what?"

"I'll explain later. I've already sent my carriage to be put away for the night. I'll have to send someone for it later and take you home. But there's something we must do first." He took hold of her hand and said, "Can you run?"

"Yes, of course," she answered, confused by his question.

"Good. Hold the hood over your head."

"Where are we going?"

"You'll see. Just keep up with me. We need to hurry so no one will see us."

Hawk started pulling her along with him down the steps, into the misting rain. He rushed her along the walkway, and through the gates. At the pavement, he turned right and suddenly they were running in the rain, down the street past the dark houses, the tall hedges, and the flickering streetlamps.

Chapter 25

A gentleman should always understand what a lady needs, even when she doesn't know what it is she wants.

A PROPER GENTLEMAN'S GUIDE TO WOOING THE PERFECT LADY
SIR VINCENT TYBALT VALENTINE

Loretta's feet were freezing as they splashed in puddles. A steady light rain beat down on them. Hawk held one of her hands securely in his, and with her other hand she held the hood of his heavy cloak on her head. She had no problem keeping up with Hawk's longer stride in her low-heeled satin slippers. She had no idea where they were going or why they were going so fast to get there. She only knew it was exciting and invigorating to run in the rain with Hawk.

At the end of the street, they turned another corner, ran a few seconds more, and then climbed four steps and stopped in front of tall double doors with large iron handles. Hawk pulled on one of them. It didn't open. He yanked on the other door. It didn't budge, either.

"Damnation," he muttered softly, and hit the door with the heel of his palm.

"What is it?" she asked, her chest heaving hard from the running, and her whole body shivering from the wet and cold.

"It's locked," he answered on a heavy breath.

Loretta pushed the hood farther up her head so she could see. She still hadn't caught her breath, but managed to ask "Where are we?"

"At a church."

"Church?" She choked out the word. She hadn't been to a church since she left Viscount Denningcourt standing at the altar waiting for her to join him to say their nuptials. A nervous jerk shook her. "Why are we here?"

"You'll see," he said, looking from one side of the building to the other. "Keep your hood on and stay here." He turned away.

She caught his arm. "No, wait. You can't leave me here."

Hawk put his hand over hers that held on to his arm. "I'll be right back."

Fighting to control her wildly beating heart, calm her breath, and make sense of this, she tightened her hold on Hawk's arm and stayed him. "Where are you going?"

"To find a window at the back to break and crawl inside. I'll come around to the door, unlock it, and let you inside."

"Hawk!" she exclaimed in a hushed whisper, shivering all the more. "You can't do that."

"I can. When the hell did they start locking the doors of a church?" He glanced at her. "Sorry about the disrespectful language, but just how are people to get in when they need to?"

Startled by his intense exasperation, she offered, "They wait until morning when the doors are open to all."

"I'm not waiting."

"You can't break into a church," she said in horror at what he'd planned. "Have you gone mad?"

"No," he said as calmly as if he'd been talking about the weather as he again looked down one side of the building and then the other. "I've finally figured out what you need to do and I intend to see that it's done now."

"I do not *need* to break into a church!" she said as loudly and earnestly as she dared.

"You're not. I am. Now stay right here in front of the door."

Loretta watched, stunned, as Hawk ran down the side of the building and disappeared around the corner. Was he actually going to shatter a window in a church? Moments later, she heard glass crack and fall to the ground.

She gasped.

He really meant it.

She heard a carriage in the distance and quickly turned and put her face to the door, hoping that with the misting rain, the driver wouldn't notice anyone was standing in front of the church—that had just been broken into! The wind howled and rattled signs, streetlamps, and rooftops. Loretta's toes started going numb again. She felt as cold as ice that collected on the outside of windowpanes during the deepest onset of winter.

It seemed like hours that Hawk had been gone and longer still before the carriage passed without anyone calling out to her. She kept her body still and faced toward the massive door until finally she heard the latch thrown from inside. Her body trembled with relief. The door creaked open, and Hawk gently pulled her inside.

It was dark. Cold. All she heard were their loud breaths.

At first she saw nothing, but then down toward the front, a single small, lamp burned low on a table.

"Don't be afraid. I've checked. There's no one here." He took her hand and they walked down the aisle toward the light.

She couldn't say she wasn't wary. She was. A church wasn't a place she'd planned to ever go again. Her last experience in one had not turned out well. She didn't know what Hawk was planning to do; but in her heart of hearts, she knew she wasn't afraid. Whatever he had in mind, if he was by her side, she had no fear.

They stopped in front of the lamp and Hawk lowered the hood from her hair. He smiled and said, "You're wet."

She smiled, too. "So are you. You didn't even have a cloak. And what happened to your hat?"

"You needed the cloak more than I did. My hat blew off while we were running." He raked his dripping hair away from his forehead with his hands and laughed softly. "Have you figured out why we're here?"

"No," she answered truthfully. "I can't say I expected ever to step a foot in a church again."

Hawk took off his gloves, stuffed them in the pocket of his coat, and then took both her hands in his. "We're here because you've been adamant that your vow was made in the church. That meant something to you when you said it. I admire you for honoring that. But now it's time to let it go, and this is the place for you to do it. You took your oath in a church and this is where you need to recant it."

Loretta's breaths halted in her throat, but somehow she managed to whisper, "What?"

"Recant it. Here and now."

Her shivering returned. "I—I can't."

"You can." He squeezed her hands tighter. "If it's wrong, this is also the place for forgiveness, too. Just ask for it."

Loretta couldn't speak. She didn't know what to say. She'd never thought about coming to a church, the place where she'd made the vow, and recanting it.

"Did you forgive your uncle for banishing you to Mammoth House?" Hawk asked.

"Yes. You know I did. I told you."

"And you will forgive Farley for stealing from you. Maybe not yet, but in time, even though what he took was precious to you."

"Yes. I will. In time." She shook her head. "No, I probably already have. He's only a wayward boy. It's not his fault he's had no one to help him know right from wrong and how to behave."

"And you, Loretta, can be forgiven for recanting a vow you were forced to make when you were an eighteen-year-old girl. Forgiveness should be given to everyone who asks for it." He pulled her closer to him. "You can't change the number of seconds in a minute, the length of an hour, or the days in a week. But you can change your future. Recant and save yourself from a life you were never destined to live."

Hope grew inside her. Could she do it? Was Hawk right? Was it up to her to save herself? All he said sounded rational. She looked around the small church. Stone walls held few adornments. There were several sconces, three tapestries, and a small stained-glass window. It was cold and deeply shadowed, but suddenly a warm, peaceful feeling settled over her. Her body relaxed with an almost liquid quality to it.

"You deserve to do it for yourself, but if you won't, Loretta, then do it for me."

She looked into Hawk's eyes and without further thought whispered, "I recant the vow I made to never marry." She smiled and then added, "To the duke, with love."

An almost painful sigh of relief passed Hawk's lips as he whispered, "Yes." He laid his forehead against the top of her head. "I didn't know if I could convince you to do it."

"You were right," she answered, swallowing a small lump of emotion that had formed in her throat. "I needed to do it here. It feels right. Gone. Over. I know I'm free from it."

Hawk lifted his head and touched his lips to hers in a brief, gentle kiss. He then straightened. "Your lips are cold."

"My feet are freezing, too," she said, her teeth beginning to chatter.

"I should have realized that after all the pools of water we ran through. Let's get back to my house."

Hawk once again lifted the hood over Loretta's head and they turned and ran up the aisle, out the church doors, down the steps, and away into the rainy darkness. Fate was with them once again. No carriages passed them along the street. They rushed through the iron gates and up the steps.

At his door, Hawk stopped and guided her to the far side of the portico, away from the light. "I know you're cold, but you must stand here in the shadows for a little longer. I don't want a blemish on your reputation. I'm going inside to send someone to ready my carriage and bring it around front so I can take you home. If Price or anyone else is up, I'll send them to bed so they won't see you when we go inside."

"There's no need for that," she offered. "I can wait out here until the carriage comes."

"No. You've been in the cold long enough. It will take time to get someone dressed and off to the stable, and then to get the horses harnessed and hitched to the carriage. I won't leave you out here that long." He cupped her cheek lovingly. "Remain here. I'll be right back for you."

Loretta nodded and Hawk disappeared into the house.

The wait wasn't long. Within minutes, Hawk opened the door again and ushered her into his house, down the corridor, and into his book room, where he shut the door and locked it. He led her over to the fireplace. Looking around, he grabbed a woolen blanket off a chair and placed it on the floor. Taking the damp cloaks from around her shoulders, he threw them aside and helped her sit down. He then bent to his knees and went to work building a small fire.

When the flame caught the wood, Loretta extended her legs toward the heat. Hawk sat down, and then with some effort stretched and wiggled his foot until he tugged off first one damp boot and then the other, placing them before the fire.

He turned to her. "Your hair and clothing are damp. Just like the first night we met."

"I was remembering that night, too," she answered, softly. "But tonight my toes are so cold they're feeling quite numb."

"I know just how to take care of that."

He then moved closer to Loretta and slowly reached for her. He lifted one foot by her ankle onto his lap and slipped off the soggy, satin slipper. Laying it close to the fire to dry, he rubbed her cold foot in his warm hands before he put it down and treated the other the same way. He then grasped her ankles again and positioned her feet up tight at the junction of his legs and gently closed his thighs around them. From the bottom of her feet, Loretta felt the hardness beneath his trousers grow firmer. Her breasts tightened and a quiver started low in her stomach.

The warmth from his body permeated all through her, instantly bringing her comfort. She was certain that his heat was hotter than the now leaping flames of the fire he'd built.

His gaze caressed her face. "How does that feel?"

"Heavenly."

He smiled. "For me, too," he said, slowly rubbing his hands up and down her ankles and lower legs.

"Do you have any regrets about what you did in the church?"

"No." She shook her head emphatically, inhaled deeply, and let her breath out slowly. "It's not that I hadn't thought about being free of the oath. I wanted to be free of it. I just didn't know how to do it and be able to live with myself after. I have no regrets about what I did, and though I still have some unsettling feelings swirling inside me to sort out, I know I'm free of the vow."

"What troubles you now?" His hands slid farther up her legs. "Is it me, Loretta?" he asked huskily. "Are you conflicted in your emotions for me?"

Without the slightest hesitation, she answered, "No. I know exactly how I feel about you. I meant it when I said to you, with love."

"Good. Because I know exactly how I feel about you, too."

Though it was so enticingly warm where her feet rested, she pulled them out of Hawk's grasp and scooted between his knees. Looking into his glorious blue eyes, she said, "I have no doubts about what I want right now."

"Neither do I." He pulled a pin from her hair. "It will dry faster if it's down."

She smiled. "Then let me help you."

"You do understand this means you belong to me, don't you?"

Loretta nodded, enjoying the soft stroke of his hands in her hair and the warmth of the fire to her back.

"Not as a lover or a mistress, but as my wife, my duchess. Forever."

"Yes," she whispered as the last pin and lock of hair fell around her shoulders. She just didn't know if her uncle would. But that thought was for another time. Tomorrow. Not tonight.

Hawk's strong, masculine arms slid around her back. He caught her up tightly to his chest, and tenderly covered her mouth with his.

Loretta leaned into him and wound her arms around his neck. His lips moved smoothly, tenderly, and effortlessly over hers, slanting first one way and then the other as their bodies strained to get closer. Their tongues swirled and plundered deftly in each other's mouths. He tasted of brandy, smelled of shaving soap. They kissed over and over again before his lips made a trail of light, delicious nibbles down her neck to the base of her throat and back up to her lips once more.

When she felt him trying to shrug out of his coat, she grabbed the lapels, shoved it off his shoulders, down his arms, and helped him fling it away. He then pulled on the bow of his neckcloth and started unwinding it from around his neck. Though she wasn't sure why, it seemed natural for her to unbutton his quilted waistcoat, tug the tail of his shirt from the waistband of his trousers, and slip her hands underneath the front his shirt. His skin was warm, taut; rippled muscles covered his ribs and upper chest.

His loud intake of breath pleased her and he murmured a husky, "Yes, that feels good."

His tongue continued to explore inside her mouth while his hands pulled and loosened the laces at the back of her bodice. Desire settled low in Loretta's abdomen, between her legs, and she moaned softly against his lips as their kisses and caresses became more frantic.

The bodice of her dress slipped off her shoulders. Hawk kissed his way down her neck, across each bare shoulder, and along the swells of her breasts. He pulled the top lower. Eagerly, she helped him slide the long sleeves down her arms and off her hands, leaving the fabric to fall around her waist. Working together they did the same with her shift, all the while kissing passionately, desperately, as if they might never have opportunity to be so intimate again.

Hawk's hands moved up her rib cage to fondle her breasts, lift them free of her stays, and cover them with his mouth. Loretta moaned softly and gave herself up to all the glorious sensations his gentle touch spread throughout her. She savored every tingle that rushed through her body and every sigh and endearment she heard whispered past his lip. The impatient but tender gliding movements of his hands and mouth thrilled her. Over and over again he favored her breasts. She delighted in every touch, every taste, and every moan that came from him while she enjoyed exploring the expanse of his muscular back. She felt power in his firm, broad shoulders.

Even though she was still delirious with pleasure, Hawk stopped kissing her. With one easy movement, he rose to his knees and gazed down into her eyes. "Are you warm now?"

"Oh, yes," she whispered.

"So am I."

He shrugged out of his waistcoat and threw it aside. He pulled his shirt over his head and dropped it to the floor, too.

The fire was the only light in the room, but it was enough. Loretta's breaths quickened at the sight of his bare, masculine chest so close to her. It amazed her at how firmly his muscles filled out his skin from the top of his shoulders to his flat stomach.

She smiled at him.

He chuckled softly. "Are you enjoying looking at me?"

"And touching you, too," she said and ran the palm of her hand over his chest. "You're beautiful."

"I am not beautiful, Loretta."

"You are. To me."

"You know that night, so long ago now, that we had dinner at Mammoth House? You were dressed in pale yellow. Almost the color of candlelight."

"I will never forget that night."

"When I walked in and saw you standing before the fireplace you looked like an angel to me. You still do."

"I am not an angel," she whispered.

"You are to me," he said huskily, echoing her words, letting his fingertips glide easily from one side of her chest to the other, from the swell of one breast to the other, and down to her very sensitive nipples where he caressed her gently.

A tremor shook her body. Shivers ran along her spine, down her abdomen, to gather and settle between her legs again. She watched while he unbuttoned first one side and then the other of his trousers, letting the flap fall, revealing the bulge beneath his underclothes.

"Are you frightened?"

"I'm eager," she answered.

"Then let me love you."

He gently laid her on the blanket and stretched his long, lean body beside her. He rose on his elbow, letting his gaze drift down her face, and lingered over her breasts, drinking in the sight of her. A tremor of expectancy shivered through her as he looked at her with appreciation in his gaze.

"I've wanted this since the first night I met you."

"So have I."

He reached over and kissed her softly. His lips were warm, moist, and she knew she could kiss him forever. She wound her arms around his back, hugging him to her. Hawk rose over her, propping himself up with one hand, while with the other he grabbed her skirts and shift and bundled them around her waist. He found the waistband of her drawers, slid his hand around, and untied the sash. She lifted her hips and helped him slide the garment down her legs and off her feet, and kicked it away.

While he kissed her tenderly, passionately, his hand moved between them to the warm, womanly spot between her legs. He softly touched her most intimate part, tenderly caressing her. Loretta was powerless to do anything but enjoy the feelings he created inside her. He rubbed the center of her desire while he lovingly kissed her lips.

Her hands roved over his back, his shoulders, down his firm buttocks, and back up again over his slim hips and flat waist. She eased her hands around to his chest, down to his waist, and down to the band of his trousers, the hardness beneath them evident as she helped slip the garments past his lean hips. Hawk rewarded her with an eager moan and deepened their kiss.

Chills of sensations skipped along her spine. Desire as strong as waves crashing to shore tumbled through her, filled her, and fed pleasure all over her body. With his knees, he opened her legs, and then slowly, gently, yet firmly pressed his weight upon her and carefully, skillfully joined his body to hers.

His invasion was welcomed, tender, yet commanding. And only slightly painful.

He made love to her with a tenderness that calmed her. His movements were slow and sensual. He kissed her, stroked her body from her shoulder to the plane of her hip. She joined the steady rhythm of his hips meeting hers, and he moved so gently on top of her that she gave herself over to an indescribable pleasure that seem to shatter every sensation in her body.

She buried her face into his shoulder as an inexplicable explosion gripped her, speeding through her body before slowly fading into pleasant, languid ripples that wafted from head to toe. Whispering his name softly, she relaxed onto the woolen blanket, feeling as if all the breath had left her lungs.

Oblivious for a few seconds, she then heard Hawk's breath quicken, felt him tremble. She raised her hips up to meet his demand until he shuddered with passion and a soft moan of pleasure passed his lips. His arms slid under her back and cupped her to him as he rested his weight upon her. Loretta smoothed her hands over his back, down to his buttocks, and up to his shoulders again.

For how long, she didn't know, but they rested quietly until Hawk rolled to his side. He bent his head and kissed that warm, soft spot behind her ear and buried his nose in the length of her long, damp hair. With a gentle hand, he raked his fingers down her breast, to the curve of her waist and then over her slim hip and thigh.

"I love you," she whispered.

Hawk slowly raised his head and smiled down at her. "I was wondering if you were ever going to get around to admitting that to me."

She frowned. "For your information, and according to Sir Vincent, gentlemen are supposed to say the words first to the lady they are wooing."

"I did."

Her frown deepened. "When?"

"At Hawksthorn. When I asked you to marry me—which you declined by the way."

Her gaze searched his face with intensity. "I don't think you said the words *I love you*."

"Maybe not those exact words but—"

She placed a finger to his lips and gave him an amused smile. "No buts. You didn't say it."

He kissed the pad of her finger and said, "Then let me make this clear to you right now, Loretta. I love you. Deeply. Why do you think I worked so hard to free you from your oath?"

She smiled. "So we could do what we just did."

"That, too." Hawk chuckled. "Which I was beginning to think might never happen." He rose over her again and kissed her passionately. His hand lovingly caressed her shoulder. "I haven't heard you say yes, Hawk, I'll marry you."

"I will," she whispered earnestly. "You know I want to, but I don't know what my uncle will say about what I've done."

"He will never know about what happened between us just now, Loretta. No one will ever know about this, but us."

"I meant recanting my vow."

"What can he say? *No, you can't do it*?" Hawk kissed the tip of her nose. "You already have. It is done. And dare I say the earl has probably broken more than a few vows himself."

"He is an unforgiving man. I'm not sure how he will react when I tell him I have recanted my vow and want to marry you."

Hawk brushed his hand through her long, golden tresses. "I understand why you are concerned, but this is not something you need to worry about. He will be delighted to learn you have done this and that his niece will be married to a duke. But no matter his reaction, you are mine. I will tell him."

Loretta moistened her lips. "No, thank you for offering, but I must tell him. I can't let you do that for me."

"All right, but I want to be there so I can then ask for your hand. I don't want to wait to tell him or to marry you. We'll settle this tomorrow evening at my house. I'll send over an invitation for all of you to come for dinner. Trust me, he won't deny us."

Loretta softly cupped Hawk's cheek and stared into his loving eyes. "I didn't think he'd leave me at Mammoth House for almost three years, but he did. With my uncle, I can never be sure of anything."

"I am." Hawk grinned. "Because I am a duke, and he is but a lowly earl."

Chapter 26

A gentleman must never make a promise to a lady
that he doesn't know he can keep.

~◆~

A Proper Gentleman's Guide to Wooing
the Perfect Lady
Sir Vincent Tybalt Valentine

It was already late afternoon. Dusk was near. Still Hawk
waited at the entrance to an alcove that led to several
shops. People came and went all afternoon, but Hawk
didn't take his eyes off the steps. Farley had to return at
some time, and when he did, Hawk was ready.

When Loretta had visited Hawksthorn, she'd told him
Farley said he lived under the steps of an old building near
St. James Park. That wasn't much to go on, but enough in-
formation for Hawk to get started looking for the boy.

At dawn, when Hawk had seen that Loretta was safely
inside her uncle's house, he went straight to Bow Street.
Knowing he couldn't cover such a large area around the
park by himself, he hired three runners to help him. They
scoured the area for buildings tall enough that a boy could
build a room underneath the steps to sleep in. It had taken

most of the day, but damnation, if one of the men hadn't found Farley's little hole of a room that had been dug out of the dirt.

Hawk was certain it was Farley's. There was no sign of the jewelry, but Hawk recognized some of the lad's clothing. The little thief had been quite skillful in making the space dry and fairly safe, where he could come and go from each side of the steps. Hawk didn't intend to lose the bugger now that he'd found him. He'd stationed runners near the building to help if he had to give chase.

But time wasn't on his side as the afternoon grew late. He'd hoped to be done with this by now and be home, dressed and ready for Loretta, Paxton, and their uncle. He couldn't wait to inform the earl that Loretta was going to be his bride as soon as Hawk could arrange it. Loretta didn't trust the man's reaction and for good reason. But Hawk knew the Earl of Switchingham would be pleased and enjoy all the clout the new position of having a niece married to a duke would afford him.

Just as dusk was giving way to darkness, Hawk saw the lad approaching. He was walking slowly and holding his side. Protecting the jewelry, Hawk assumed. He motioned to the runners, giving them all the upturn of his thumb. Each man nodded. He had no doubt that Farley was quick and adept at slipping in and out of his makeshift home with ease.

Hawk waited a couple of minutes, wanting to give Farley time to get settled inside. The runners moved in closer, too, as Hawk approached. But then one of the runners' boots skidded on a rock. The canvas covering was slung aside and Farley shot out of the hole and right past Hawk. He grabbed the back of Farley's coat and locked his arms around the boy's thin chest.

Farley cried out in pain, stunning Hawk. The boy continued to squirm, kick, and groan. Hawk loosed his grip, not wanting to hurt him, but determined he wouldn't get away.

"You might as well stop fighting me, you little thief," Hawk muttered as the three runners circled them. "You're surrounded and not going anywhere."

Farley stilled, and Hawk let go of him. When the boy turned and faced him, Hawk blinked. Both his eyes were bruised and swollen. One almost shut. His bottom lip was thick and cut in two places. His chin had a big bruise, too. He held his left side and winced with each deep intake of breath.

Clearly the lad was in pain.

"Damnation, what happened to you?" Hawk asked, as he motioned for the runners to step away.

"Nothing, you big oaf!" Farley yelled. "Leave me be."

"Something did," Hawk said just as angrily, but his anger wasn't directed at the boy, but whoever had beat him. "You didn't get that face from falling down or running into a streetlamp. Who did this to you?"

"What d'ye care? Ye never liked me anyway."

"I never liked the way you behaved," he challenged. "And I sure as hell don't like you stealing Loretta's jewelry and breaking her heart. How I feel about you isn't what we're talking about right now. I want to know who laid their fist to you and why."

"None of ye concern," Farley answered in a lower voice and without an ounce of fear in his defiant expression.

"All right," Hawk answered, knowing he couldn't make the lad tell him anything. "You probably got what you deserved anyway. I guess you're lucky you don't look worse. You stole from someone who hadn't done anything but be good to you. Loretta wiped your brow when you were sick. Kept you alive when you were dying. She was kind to you, and this is how you repay her? By stealing from her," he said with disgust clearly in his tone. "I want her jewelry now. Where is it?"

Farley stared at Hawk with stark white fury. He jerked his arms out to his side and yelled, "Ye see me 'olding anything? I don't 'ave it."

"But you know where it is, you little imp. I've checked your—bed," he said, nodding toward the steps. "It's not there. That jewelry belonged to Loretta's mother. I will get it back for her, or I'll see to it that you are thrown into the darkest dungeon London has. You won't see sunshine on your face for years to come. Now, where did you stash it?"

"I told ye I don't 'ave it," he said, holding his side and grimacing loudly again as he sucked in another deep breath.

"And I don't believe you. You stole it!"

"I did!" he said, spittle flinging from one side of his swollen mouth. "I took it, but do ye think I beat my ownself? 'E stole it from me and then tried to punch my eyes out."

"Who stole it from you?" Hawk demanded.

"I don't know who 'e was. 'E was a man on the street. Never seen 'im before. 'E seen me carrying the velvet purse. Asked what's a little feller like me doing carrying such a fancy bag." Farley stopped and sucked in another gasp of pain. "I tried to outrun him. Thought I 'ad but 'e fooled me and caught me 'round a corner. I tried to keep it from 'im, but 'e was a big man like you, so now I don't 'ave it anymore."

"Where were you going with it?"

Farley sucked in another breath of pain past his misshapen lips. "Where ye think? To sell it, but I don't 'ave it now. I don't know who does."

Hawk huffed out a grunt of anger at Farley, at whoever had attacked him, and at himself for not finding the boy before someone else did. And Hawk didn't know why, but he believed Farley was telling the truth about the jewelry being stolen from him.

"Why did you do it?" Hawk asked as it was beginning to sink in that he wasn't going to get the jewelry back today. Maybe not at all. "She tried to help you."

"I didn't ask 'er for 'elp," he said with big brown eyes that refused to show any sign of regret for what he'd done. "Didn't ask ye to take me out of the storm, but ye did, so I figured ye owed me."

"Owed you?" Hawk's anger grew hot again. The lad didn't know when it was best to just stay quiet. "You ungrateful little—" He reached for Farley, but the boy jerked back in fear, yelped, and grabbed his side again.

Hawk swore under his breath and then said out loud, "Damnation." He couldn't believe he was feeling sorry for the boy who'd hurt Loretta so deeply. "I should turn you over to the authorities right now."

"She didn't need it. Never saw her wear it often, anyway."

"Whether or not she wore it was of no concern to you," Hawk insisted. "It was hers, and you took it from her."

Farley's fat lips twitched, and for the first time his battered eyes watered. But whether that was from the pain he was experiencing or a tinge of shame for what'd done, Hawk didn't know.

"What did the man look like?"

"'Ow do I know? 'E was big like you, but 'e didn't look as much like a dandy as you do."

A dandy? The lad just wouldn't quit. Hawk wouldn't be caught dead dressed like a dandy, and he had a feeling Farley knew that.

"What color was his hair, his eyes?"

"'E wore a fancy hat. That's all I know."

"You better be telling me the truth," Hawk said in a warning tone.

"I shouldn't 'ave taken it from 'er," Farley mumbled and winced again. "I didn't want to do it, but I couldn't stop myself."

"No, you shouldn't have," Hawk said, and found himself feeling sorry for the lad again. "Have you spit up blood?"

Farley shook his head.

That was a good sign that his ribs were only bruised and not broken. Hawk reached into his coat and grabbed the loose coins in his pocket. It wasn't much, but he said, "Take this and buy some salve for your face and strips of cloth. Bind your chest tight. It'll help your ribs heal and make breathing a little easier."

Farley didn't move.

"Go on, take it. I'm not doing this out of the goodness of my heart. I'm doing it for Loretta. I don't want to have to tell her I didn't help you. It's my thoughts you got what you deserved."

It took a few moments longer, but Farley finally reached up and gathered the coins from Hawk's outstretched hand and quickly stepped back.

"If you see the man again, follow him." Hawk stopped and pointed his finger at Farley. "I don't want you to approach him. Just watch him, see where he goes, and then come get me. And just so we are clear, it's you who owes me. Twice now. You understand?"

Farley nodded once.

"Now go get yourself some help."

Hawk turned away.

Going back to Loretta empty-handed was the last thing he wanted to do. He wanted to find her jewelry so bad his hands made fists. He also wanted to get his hands on the man who'd beat up a skinny, ungrateful lad. And when he did, he'd see to it he never touched another one.

Hawk would have the runners keep a watch over Farley. He believed the lad's story, but there wasn't anything wrong with making sure all he said was true. Too, there was always the chance Farley might lead them to the jewelry.

Hawk wasn't attached to the kid, but Loretta was. And what Loretta wanted was important to him. He'd already decided he needed to find someone who could take Farley into their home and teach him a trade. Maybe the boy had a propensity for something. Though Hawk had no idea what.

Right now the only thing he knew how to do was be a thief, but he had common sense and could learn something else, be it tanner, blacksmith, or shopkeeper. And for Loretta, Hawk would do his best to see that happened.

Chapter 27

A gentleman should always go to a lady's rescue
if he feels she is at a loss for what to say.

~~~

*A PROPER GENTLEMAN'S GUIDE TO WOOING
THE PERFECT LADY*
SIR VINCENT TYBALT VALENTINE

Loretta was nervous but not fearful as she entered the duke's home with her brother and uncle. She immediately recognized Price, the butler who'd refused her admittance into the house when she was at the duke's door last night. However, if he remembered her face, he made no show of it whatsoever. She couldn't help but wonder if he really had no idea she was the same person, or if he felt it in his best interest to pretend he had never seen her. Either way, she was grateful.

They were ushered into the drawing room where Loretta's gaze caught Hawk's the moment she walked in. He smiled at her, and all her apprehension melted away.

"There you are," Lady Adele said, rushing up to them. "I thought you'd never get here."

Loretta slightly shook her head in wonderment. Lady

Adele was such an impatient young lady. They weren't even a minute late.

While greetings were offered by everyone, Loretta found it impossible to keep her gaze from straying to Hawk. Much to her pleasure, he continued to stare at her, too.

"My lord," Adele said to the earl. "I was hoping we'd get to meet while I was in London. Mr. Quick has told me you are a man of your word, that you have a strong will, and that you won't be swayed once you reach a decision about something."

Loretta stiffened, horrified that Lady Adele had divulged what Paxton had said about his uncle. Paxton and Hawk were equally surprised by her words.

"So he did," the earl said rather slowly while he looked determinedly at the other four people in the room.

"I hope you don't mind I mentioned you, Uncle," Paxton said, recovering quickly and seeming to have no trouble keeping a smile on his face and managing his usual jovial tone.

"Of course he doesn't," Lady Adele continued, paying no mind to the startled expressions she was receiving. "My brother has qualities like those as well, my lord. I consider them quiet admirable."

That statement from his sister raised Hawk's eyebrows even higher. Loretta was wondering how being so strong-willed you couldn't show mercy to an eighteen-year-old young lady was an admirable trait. But then she had to remember that Lady Adele didn't know the entire story of Loretta's banishment to Mammoth House.

"And though I haven't known Mr. Quick that long," Lady Adele continued, "I do believe he has the same commendable attributes as the two of you. I should be quite pleased to call such a man my husband."

"I'm glad to hear my nephew spoke so highly of me,"

the earl said with a nod of arrogance. "And that he pleases you."

Loretta knew that Lady Adele had taken the things Paxton had said about his uncle as compliments. Though Loretta would bet her pin money Paxton hadn't meant them that way.

"Yes, Lady Adele, I too believe we are all good, strong men," her uncle said. "Now, I hate to trouble you, but if you don't mind, I'd like to sit down. These days I find it difficult to stand for long at the time."

"Paxton and I will help you," Lady Adele answered, her happy attitude continuing.

"Please let me attend to that," Mrs. Philbert said, hurrying over to the earl.

Hawk looked at Loretta, nodded toward the back of the room, and said, "I think I hear a storm brewing. I'll have a look outside while Price gets everyone a drink."

"A storm you say?" Loretta asked, following Hawk to the window. She stopped as close to Hawk as she dared and whispered, "I thought I was going to faint when Lady Adele mentioned what Paxton had said about Uncle."

"I was thinking I was going to have to stuff her handkerchief in her mouth if she uttered one more word."

Loretta laughed softly. "You wouldn't dare."

"No." A natural, easy smile came to his lips. "But I can't say I haven't been tempted at times."

"She is so innocent. It does seem difficult for her to find fault in anyone. I suppose what Paxton said about Uncle really isn't bad or even unkind given the right circumstances."

"Unless you know the meaning behind his words. Obviously, Adele didn't. Everyone should be willing to bend when the occasion merits it. But I don't want to talk about him." Hawk's gaze caressed her face. "I want to talk about you. How did you feel today? Any ill effects from last night?"

"Actually there was one."

Concern narrowed his eyes. "What?"

She moistened her lips and said, "My feet were cold all day. I had no one to warm them for me."

He chuckled softly. "Soon, my love. I hope you are ready to tell his lordship you recanted your vow because I don't know how much longer I can wait to let him know that you are now mine and under my protection and not his."

She glanced behind her. Paxton, Lady Adele, and Mrs. Philbert were helping the earl settle into a chair. "I'm ready," she answered confidently. "But quickly, before we have to go back over to them, I must ask about Farley. Did you find any trace of him?"

Hawk hesitated.

She knew he was trying to decide what to tell her. "The truth," she whispered.

"I found him. He admitted to taking the jewelry but he no longer has it."

"Oh," she said, and looked out the window as her heart constricted with disappointment. Her pain was more than just that the jewelry was gone. Hawk's words confirmed that Farley had taken it from her. She'd hoped that maybe, somehow it would be proven Farley hadn't been the culprit. A light rain had started to fall against the windowpane. She turned to Hawk. Swallowing her disillusionment, she said, "If he's already sold it, did he tell you who he sold it to? Maybe we can buy it back?"

"No, that would be easy to do. He said someone stole it from him. There are reasons why I believe him. There's no time to go into details right now. I promise I will tell you everything later. The earl is looking at us and it's too involved to go into at the moment. I'm not giving up though. I will get it back for you. It's just that it may take longer than I was hoping."

Loretta swallowed past a lump in her throat. "How is Farley?"

Hawk inhaled deeply. "He's a fighter. You don't have to worry about him. He's going to be all right. Now, are you sure you don't want me to tell the earl what you did last night? It would give me great pleasure to let him know that his reign over you has passed."

"It will give me more."

They walked back to where the earl had made himself comfortable in a chair with Lady Adele and Paxton standing beside him. Mrs. Philbert had gone to ask Price to get a footstool for the earl.

Lady Adele suddenly clasped her arms around Hawk's elbow, beamed a mischievous smile at him, and said, "Hawk, I just had the most wonderful idea."

"I'm not surprised," he said with a hint of a grin. "You have at least one a day."

"Oh, you can be such a cruel brother," she said, her blue eyes sparkling with merriment. "Mr. Quick, I do hope you don't tease your sister so unmercifully."

"Indeed I do not," he assured her with a happy grin on his face. "Nor will I."

"Good. Because one in the family is enough." She turned her attention back to Hawk. "This is truly an exceptional idea. I was looking at all of us here in the room together and thought, wouldn't it be wonderful if you and Miss Quick married, too?"

A prolonged hush washed around the room. There wasn't even a breath of sound to be heard. Loretta felt lightheaded so quickly she thought she might faint. How had Lady Adele managed to take over the reason for evening?

"Why is everyone looking at me as if I opened Pandora's box?" Lady Adele asked. "Surely you've thought about it, Hawk. You've never told me but I know you are terribly interested in her. I've seen the divine way you two look at each other." Adele's gaze darted from Hawk, to Loretta, to Paxton, and then to the earl. "Someone say something."

Hawk pulled out of his sister's grasp, picked up Loretta's hand, and kissed it. He looked down at her and said, "Miss Quick, will you marry me?"

The duke's seductive gaze filled her with pleasure so deeply she felt it bury in her soul.

"By the stars, Loretta," the earl said, struggling to stand. "If the man wants to marry you don't let this opportunity pass you by as you did the last gentleman because you were too young to know what you were doing. Forget that silly, childish oath you made never to marry. This is a *duke* asking you to be his bride! Say yes and this time mean it!"

"Say yes, Miss Quick," Lady Adele pleaded.

"Say yes, dear sister," Paxton encouraged.

Hawk put his lips to the back of Loretta's hand again and whispered softly so only she could hear, "They don't know that you have already pledged your love to me and agreed to marry me. Say yes again and make them happy."

Loretta smiled at Hawk, squeezed his hand with her fingers, and said, "Yes, my love. Yes."

Dear Readers:

If there is one thing Polite Society adores more than the most salacious scandalbroth, it is to be surprised. And the Duke of Hawksthorn gave us two such newsworthy bits! While London was buzzing about the duke preparing for his sister, Lady Adele, to dodge the mischief-makers during the Season, he was busy making a suitable match for her before the Season even began. Lady Adele is betrothed to Mr. Paxton Quick. And while the wily duke was planning a match for his sister, he astounded and fooled everyone in the ton *by making a match for himself, too! There is no date set for Lady Adele's nuptials yet, but I'm told a special license has been granted and the tittle-tattle is flying about like blossoms on a windy spring day for the duke and his bride-to-be. He and Miss Loretta Quick will marry in a private ceremony later this week.*

Apparently, rumors that Miss Quick had entered a convent three years ago were untrue. She's been living a solitary life in the country, waiting for her Prince Charming to come along and make her his bride. Now the prince has arrived. And much to the disappointment of the new belles of the Season, the second Rake of St. James has been taken off the marriage mart.

MISS HONORA TRUTH'S WEEKLY SOCIETY SHEET

Epilogue

Always leave a lady's presence with a compliment,
a bow, and a smile on your face.

~•~

A Proper Gentleman's Guide to Wooing
the Perfect Lady
Sir Vincent Tybalt Valentine

Loretta looked over at Hawk and smiled.

Taking an afternoon ride in Hyde Park was one of Loretta's favorite things to do since marrying the duke a few weeks ago. Though there was a slight chill in the air, spring had finally arrived. Some days were gray, many filled with rain, but a few of them were as gloriously beautiful as this day. Sunny, warm, and blue skies as far as the eye could see.

She couldn't help but think that one of the reasons she enjoyed the park so much was because of all the activity from crowds watching a puppet show, vendors hawking their wares, and couples strolling the grounds oblivious to it all. There had been so few people to see at Mammoth House that the busy streets and parks of London were a delight for her senses.

Loretta enjoyed hearing the noise from carriages, wagons, and milk carts. The clopping of horses' hooves and wheels on hard-packed ground, or milk cans rattling in the backs of wagons, were not an annoyance to her. She welcomed the sounds. She watched everyone who passed by, be they Polite Society, shopkeeper, servant, tradesman, beggar, or peer. She relished the smells, the sounds, and the sights of people going about their daily lives.

"I hope that smile on your face is for me." Hawk said, guiding the horses into the park behind a stream of other carriages.

"It is, my dear husband. I'm happy to be back in London, to be planning our first dinner party for next week, to be attending the Season with Lady Adele and Paxton." She looked back at Hawk. "I'm very happy being back in Society, and I do believe I am the happiest person in all of London, or England—no, make that the whole world."

Hawk chuckled and clicked the ribbons against the horses' rumps to move them along as they left the path and headed toward the grassy area near the Serpentine. "I think Adele might take issue with you on who is happiest," he said. "I didn't think she was going to stop hugging me when she told me that she and Paxton have decided they will marry on the day before Christmas."

"Yes. She was very happy about that, wasn't she?" Loretta answered.

"Just in case she failed to tell you, she still thinks I picked the perfect husband for her, and so do I."

"Oh, no. She told me. More than once. What's even better, now that she is happily engaged, there have been no instances of anyone trying to disrupt her Season. And she seems to be enjoying all the parties, balls, and festivities immensely. She hardly misses a dance."

"You are still trying to keep them apart, aren't you?" Hawk asked with an amused grin.

"No. No. I am not," Loretta insisted. "I know that Paxton adores her and really wants to marry Lady Adele. I will admit that, at one point, before he met her, I think he contemplated accepting your offer in order to help me be free of our uncle, but that was only for a short time."

"Hmm," Hawk said. "He told me just the opposite."

"Really?"

"Yes." Hawk grinned again. "He said to me, 'If my sister is going to marry one of the Rakes of St. James, I'd better be a part of this family in case she ever needs me.'"

Hawk turned his attention back to the horses.

"Did he really say that?"

"Not in those exact words, and in my own way I assured him I'd given up my wicked ways for you and he had no cause to worry about you."

Loretta's heart melted and she placed her hand on his knee. "Thank you," she said sweetly, and then after another thought, added, "You're making up that conversation with Paxton, aren't you?"

"I wouldn't do that. I might not have told it exactly as it was said, but rest assured that your brother said he'd call me out if I should ever hurt you."

Loretta was stunned. "Paxton said that to you? I can't believe it. He's such a docile man."

"I was amazed he had it in him, too."

"What did you say back to him?"

Hawk ignored her, but he didn't stop smiling.

"Well, perhaps it's better I not know. But no matter what you said to him about it," she added playfully, "he assured me that he is marrying Lady Adele because he adores her. Not for me, not for you, or just to help her avoid trouble during the Season, but because he wants to be her husband. But—"

"But what?" He glanced at her.

"I'm glad they're waiting until December to marry. It gives them time to be sure this is what they want."

"Might I remind you," Hawk said while slowing the horses, "that you didn't need almost a year to make up your mind about me?"

Loretta pursed her lips and then laughed. "Oh."

"Yes. Oh."

Hawk was right, but then Lady Adele and Paxton weren't professing undying, passionate love for each other as she and Hawk had. However, she truly believed Lady Adele and Paxton enjoyed being together, and maybe that was enough.

"All I could keep thinking about was all the Christmastide dinners I'd have to sit through listening to the two of them trying to outtalk each other."

Loretta laughed again. "Do you suppose they will ever run out of things to say?"

"No. I'm convinced when they do, they will just come visit us and find more subjects to talk about."

Hawk stopped the curricle at their favorite spot. He jumped down and reached back for her. She smiled as he swung her off the carriage and set her feet on the ground.

Loretta spread the blanket, and then sat down and opened the food basket while Hawk made sure the carriage was secure. She opened a napkin to cheese, bread, preserved currants, and cold chicken. When she was finished, she looked up to tell Hawk she had everything ready and froze.

She blinked and shook her head. He was still there. She wasn't imagining Farley.

He was standing no more than twenty feet from her. He

still wore the same clothes she'd given him, but now they were dirty, worn. His hair was longer and shaggy-looking again, but he looked fuller, healthier than when she'd last seen him. Maybe even taller.

Loretta slowly rose and stared at him. Hawk came from around the curricle saying, "You know I was about to tell—"

He stopped talking but eased up beside Loretta. He slipped his arm around her waist. Farley slowly came closer, his gaze warily darting from Loretta to Hawk.

"I been following ye since ye left the 'ouse."

"Why?" Hawk asked and started toward him.

Farley backed up.

Loretta grabbed Hawk's arm and held him back. "Don't," she whispered. "You'll scare him away."

Loretta saw faint bruising around the bottom of Farley's eyes and a fading scar running from his bottom lip. It was good to know he was healing from the beating Hawk had told her about.

Not wanting to mention that incident to him, she asked, "How's your cough?"

"Gone."

"That's good. You're looking stronger."

With watchful eyes, Farley slowly lowered a small, dirty brown bag to the ground and let go of it. Loretta hadn't even noticed that he held it in his hand until he started moving.

"I wanted to give ye this."

Loretta's intake of breath skipped, and her chest tightened with hope. "My mother's jewelry?" she asked, taking a step herself and feeling Hawk hold her back. "You found it?"

He nodded.

She wanted to immediately run to get the bag and look

in it, but knew Hawk was right to stop her as she had him. They couldn't either one do anything to cause Farley to run away, so she forced herself to stay still.

"Not all of it. 'E already sold some of it."

"You little—" Hawk bit off what he was going to say and finished with, "You told me you didn't know who he was. You were to let me know if you ever saw the man again."

"Didn't need ye."

"How did you get it back?" Loretta asked.

"Same way I got it the first time. I took it."

"The man will come looking for you, Farley," Hawk said.

"'E won't bother me again. I 'ad 'elp this time. Besides, I won't 'ave it to give back to 'im. You have it now."

"I didn't want that for you. That's why I told you to come to me and let me handle this."

Farley shrugged as he did so often.

"Stay here with us, Farley," Loretta said before she could think about the implications of her words. "You'll be safe with us. I know Hawk will help me take care of you. Don't go back to living on the streets. It's too dangerous for you."

"'Ere is my 'ome. Not with ye."

Farley cut his eyes over to Hawk. "'E never liked me anyway."

"I don't suppose I ever will," Hawk said tightly.

"It's who I am."

"You can change if you want to," Hawk argued. "If Loretta wants you to stay I'll find a place for you, but you'll have to work and earn your way."

"Don't need to. I take care of my ownself. Got me a new friend and a new place to live. 'E's a nice man and teaching me 'ow to take care of 'is 'orses. Like Arnold did."

Hope for the lad soared inside Loretta. "Can we know more about your new friend?" she asked.

"Don't need to tell ye."

It saddened her that Farley told her so little, but she'd learned she couldn't help him until he wanted it. "All right." Swallowing past a tight throat, she said, "Thank you for returning my jewelry. I'm very happy to have it back."

Farley looked down at the ground for a few seconds and then back to Loretta and said, "I'm sorry I took it."

Loretta smiled sadly. He'd learned some things from her after all. She'd told him to say he was sorry when he'd done something that was wrong.

"Thank you for letting me know that."

Farley glanced at Hawk again and then started backing up.

"Wait," Loretta said. "Before you go."

Loretta reached down and gathered the cheese, bread, and all the food together and hurriedly wrapped it in a napkin. She slowly walked toward him, holding it out. He waited, took it from her, and then looked up at her and nodded. That was as good as him saying thank you.

"Come winter," she said, "if you've outgrown your coat, will you let me know?"

He shrugged, hugged the napkin to his chest, and continued to back up as if he didn't trust her not to chase him down and take the food. When there was a safe distance between them, he stopped, glanced at Hawk again, and then suddenly turned and ran away.

Loretta didn't know why but she felt a sense of peace as she watched him disappear. And it pleased her that in the end, Farley had done the right thing.

It was the same feeling she'd had when she'd recanted her vow. When someone had done all they could to rectify a wrong, there needed to be a peace about it so that one could move on.

Hawk strode over, picked up the small bag that lay not far from her, and handed it to her. "I hope your favorite necklace is in there."

She opened it, looked inside, and with a smile nodded. "It is. It looks as if most of it is probably in here. I'm surprised whoever had it didn't sell it all."

"Most footpads can't just walk into a shop and hand over a bag of jewelry and sell it all at one time. That would raise too many suspicions. They usually get rid of it a little at a time by saying they found it in the park or on the street. They usually go to different shops, and they don't go often."

There was no reason Loretta should suddenly feel like crying, but she did. She wished Hawk could take her in his arms so she could lay her head on his chest, feel his comfort, but there were too many people in the park to be so bold. She could wait until they returned home and were alone to feel the strength of his embrace.

With the back of her hand, she wiped at the corners of her eyes and said, "He's probably not coming back, is he?"

"I don't know."

"I only wanted to help him have a better life."

Hawk touched her cheek with the backs of his fingers. "I know that. He knows that. I can't say for sure what will become of him, Loretta. But he's young, and he knows his way around. He took the food," Hawk added. "And he didn't reject the offer of a new coat for the winter."

Loretta looked into Hawk's eyes and suddenly knew why she'd felt a peace about Farley. "Since the day you found him, you've been having someone keep an eye on him, haven't you?" she asked.

Hawk remained silent but his expression pled guilty.

"Though he may not know it, you somehow helped him get the jewelry back, too, didn't you? I bet you even know who his new friend is." Loretta laughed. "I should have known immediately you were behind all this."

"I will do anything for you, Loretta. I love you. And I love you for wanting to help him whether or not he accepts it. I know you wanted him to have a true family and not go back to the streets. But he had to want that, too. You wanting it for him wasn't enough."

She tightly squeezed the bag in her hand. "Paxton said something very similar to me recently."

"He was right. Farley now has a safe place to live with an older man who lost his family. He'll be good to him. And because of you, I think Farley now knows how to be good in return."

"How did you find him?" she asked. "How did you work it out so Farley would want to live with him?"

"The man takes care of my stables and several others here in London. He has a good life. With the help of some runners from Bow Street, I made sure the kindly old man was there to help Farley when he approached the thief who had your jewelry. Together they got the best of him and I don't think he'll be bothering anyone anytime soon."

"And Farley wasn't hurt?"

"No. Though he denied it, I was convinced he knew who had your jewelry. It was only a matter of time until he tried to get it back. The owner of the stables will see to it Farley makes a good life for himself. Farley wasn't going to accept help from us. He had to believe he'd found this opportunity all by himself."

"And he does believe that. I love you, Hawk," she whispered earnestly. "So much it swells my heart. Did I ever thank you for being so patient with me about Farley, my stubbornness, my vow, and then loving me anyway?"

"You know"—he touched her cheek again and seemed to think about what she said as merriment danced in his eyes—"perhaps you told me more than once, but I'm not certain you've shown me adequate appreciation for all that I've done."

"Then I promise I will. As soon as we return home."

"I'll eagerly await that, my beautiful bride," he responded. "In fact, I'm thinking that since we no longer have food to eat, we'd best be getting back home. What do you think?"

"I was thinking about something you once said. Do you remember telling me that you are not known for following the rules of Society?"

"I do," he answered. "And you reminded me that you are not known for following them either."

"That's right," she answered. "So why don't we break one of them right now and give London another scandal, because I'm not sure I can wait until we get home for a kiss."

Hawk smiled. "I've been waiting to give the gossipmongers something else to talk about."

With that, Hawk lowered his head and intended to kiss her, but their lips never touched.

"Hawk! Loretta!" came Adele's voice. "We thought we'd never find you!"

Loretta and Hawk looked up to see Adele and Paxton hurrying toward them.

"I was afraid it would be difficult to hide from those two," Hawk said with an exasperated breath. "We've hardly had a moment to ourselves."

Loretta sighed. "I fear our bedchamber might be our only haven from them until they marry and have a home of their own."

"Did she say we had to wait until Christmastide for that happy occasion to arrive?"

"Unfortunately," Loretta whispered as the beaming couple stopped in front of them.

Greetings were ignored as Adele rushed to say, "Why didn't you invite us to join you in the park on this lovely day? You knew we'd want to join you."

"We do like to be alone once in a while, Adele," Hawk informed her.

"Oh, nonsense," she argued. "No one wants to be alone. That's why Minerva has agreed to continue to live with me after Paxton and I marry."

"Yes," Paxton added. "We're delighted she accepted. However, I came over to your house for a special reason today only to find the two of you had left without telling Adele. Luckily Price knew where you were."

Hawk bent to Loretta's ear and whispered, "I must have a talk with Price."

"Oh, it doesn't matter now," Adele said. "We forgive you for not asking us. Your wedding gift arrived today. I had it delivered to Paxton's house so I could surprise you, and when he brought it over, I knew we had to find you."

Loretta looked at them and saw no gift. Adele held only her parasol and a satin drawstring reticule swinging from her wrist. Paxton held only a picnic basket, which he promptly thrust toward Adele and opened the lid for her. She reached inside, and pulled out Cocoa. The puppy wiggled and made the sweetest little bark Loretta had ever heard.

"Here," Adele said, extending the dog to Loretta. "She's yours and Hawk's."

Shivers of delight peppered Loretta's arms and she gasped. "No, no." She looked at Hawk, who was smiling, too. "Adele, she's your favorite puppy. We can't take her from you."

"Of course you can!" Adele exclaimed happily. "She's a gift. I want you to have her."

"Take her, Loretta," Hawk said.

Loretta then joyously scooped Cocoa out of Adele's hands and carried the squirming little pup to her neck and nuzzled her warm fur as she laughed. "Oh, Adele, I don't know what to say." She glanced at Hawk, her expression letting him know she was too overcome with gratefulness and happiness to speak.

"Thank you, Adele," he said for her.

"Yes, you couldn't have given us anything we would love more." Loretta held the warm puppy close to her breast, looked up at Hawk, and whispered, "I love you."

Hawk looked down into her eyes and whispered, "You are my heart, my sunshine, and my soul, Loretta." Hawk then surprised them all by placing a very loving kiss on Loretta's lips.

Loretta thrilled to her husband's touch.

Dear Reader:

I hope you have enjoyed the second book in my Rakes of St. James trilogy. Hawk and Loretta's story is somewhat of a departure from my usual light-hearted romances. Most of the time, I write only about the glamorous side of the Regency and stay away from the harsh realities of life for the less fortunate members of London's society at that time. It's easy to write about a tall, handsome gentleman wearing shiny black knee boots and beautiful young ladies wearing gorgeously beaded gowns and carrying white lace handkerchiefs. I love to describe the serene countryside, stately homes, candlelit ballrooms, and fabulous grounds and gardens. I enjoy the challenge of weaving in and bringing to life London's streets and parks with their secrets, mysteries, and stories.

But in this book I've also written about a young boy who was left an orphan to grow up alone on the dirty, lonely, and often dangerous streets of old London. The lives of these street urchins were often sad and at times disturbing. I'm sure there were kind and generous people, like my heroine in *To the Duke, with Love,* who tried to help these unfortunate, forgotten children, who through no fault of their own had been either lost or abandoned by all in society who could have helped them.

I feel most readers yearn for orphans to be taken in by a true family and not just by a servant or employee. No romance reader wants to see the hero and heroine walk off happily into the sunset if the street child doesn't find happiness, too.

If you missed the first book in the Rakes of St. James series, *Last Night with the Duke*, I hope you'll look for a copy at your favorite bookstore or e-retailer. And don't forget to be watching for the third book in the series, *It's All About the Duke*, which will be published in June 2018.

Until then, I am sending you all good wishes.

Happy reading,
Amelia Grey